The Grave of Arthur

Peter Corbyn

First published in 2016 by
Rob Cooper Limited,
57 Manor Way, Beckenham, Kent BR3 3LN, England

Printed by CreateSpace, An Amazon.com Company

Copyright © Rob Cooper Limited

All rights reserved

ISBN: 13:978-1523950799

This novel is a work of fiction.
Any resemblance to actual events, companies, sects or persons living or dead, is entirely coincidental

To my children and grandchildren:
Amanda, Victoria, Sarah, James,
Isabelle, Samuel, Hannah, Alice, Liam, Chloe and Oliver

(with apologies for some of the scenes and language!)

Acknowledgements

We're confident that Peter would have liked to thank Katrina Henwood, Amanda Rudnick, Bill Burchell & Rob Cooper for transforming a dusty typewritten manuscript into a best seller!

Front cover photographed by Rachel Louise Brown, concept by Ben Cooper

Also by Peter Corbyn

Plucking the Crow

MILLENNIUM THREE

Millennium Three is envisaged as a trilogy. However, each novel is complete, stands on its own and can be read in isolation. Key characters appear in all the novels which are set against an evolving background of the complex and inter-related factors affecting the human condition as the Third Millennium approaches. The first novel, The Grave of Arthur, is set against the upsurge of religious fundamentalism around the world and its potential effects. The others will have environmental, political and military backgrounds. If all this sounds rather pretentious and high flown they are basically thrillers with very human heroes, heroines and villains, both male and female. All subject to human weaknesses, operating in a wide range of conditions and circumstances.

MILLENNIUM THREE

PART ONE

THE GRAVE OF ARTHUR

A grave there is for Mark, a grave for Gwythyr, a grave for Gwgawn of the red sword; but a mystery till the Day of Judgement the grave of Arthur.

From the Welsh Poem

CHAPTER ONE

The headlights of Laura's car were visible three miles down the valley, haloed fireflies dancing on the mist. Lounging easily in the doorway of the cottage, arms folded across his chest, Hawkhurst watched as they traced their way lazily towards him, seeming to drift through the soft spring rain up the crag flanked road. The vivid red body of the approaching Porsche was the only dash of real colour in an afternoon that, after a morning bright and clear, had been reduced to a soft-edged monotint. A freshening breeze tugged at the dark hedgerows, leading them into a pagan dance, as rain and cloud now hid the surrounding peaks. A fine mist swirled menacingly about the sagging, lichen-crusted slates of the ramshackle roof.

Closing the door on the muddy courtyard he checked out the low ceilinged cottage again. Following her unexpected phone call of the previous day he had attempted to restore some semblance of order to the customary chaos in preparation for her visit. Despite all his efforts, however, he had the uncomfortable feeling that, unless she had changed radically, it would inevitably fall short of her uncompromisingly high standards. He shrugged. What the hell? Apart from on TV he hadn't seen Laura Woods in three years – not since they came back from Armenia. She was nothing to him anymore.

Pausing by the bookcase he ran a tentative finger along the dusty spines of a set of Gibbons' *Decline and Fall of the Roman Empire*, his eyes going to the half empty bottle of Scotch that nestled comfortably among the leather bound volumes. Hawkhurst was not by nature a heavy drinker but somehow, on the brink of facing up to the past, he thought it might help. At the window he stared thoughtfully out at the approaching headlights, assessing how long he had before her arrival. Feeling at once both grateful and guilty, he tossed back half a tumbler of the fiery spirit and then slid the bottle out of sight. As the first soothing waves hit him the mud spattered car slewed, with considerable panache, into the quagmire of the yard outside. Exhaling forcefully in the forlorn hope of purging his breath he went outside to greet her.

As she picked her way carefully between the broad puddles Hawkhurst thought how she remained exactly as he always remembered her – strikingly beautiful. Her looks, the pale oval features, the emerald eyes and copper hair, would have guaranteed Laura Woods a successful career on the catwalk. But she was, at twenty eight, probably the best known archaeologist in the western world, possibly the entire world. She wore a long, tan leather coat draped about her shoulders and high boots whose wicked heels pecked disdainfully at the mire. Everything about her spoke of class and money. With a broad confident smile she planted a perfunctory peck on his cheek as she swept past into the cottage. It was a gesture, he guessed, that was meant to lay down the ground rules for their renewed relationship.

To Hawkhurst it said, 'Yes, we are still friends and I am pleased to see you after all this time.' It also said: 'But don't expect to get into my pants the way you used to – I'm a big girl now.'

'I enjoyed your series on the Etruscans,' he said, when she had settled herself into one of the big leather armchairs, slim legs elegantly crossed and a drink in her hand. 'A bit simplistic here and there, I thought, but I guess that's the secret of making successful television.'

She appeared not to hear, her eyes flicking around the room, taking in the rather gloomy ambiance. Ranged on either side of the wide stone fireplace ceiling height bookshelves held phalanxes of dusty, broken spined reference books. Against the farther wall a long refectory table bore an impressive array of flints, potsherds and other artefacts, presumably collected locally. The cottage was not really dirty she decided, just spartan and uncared for. Hawkhurst himself looked better than she had expected too. Still the same tall, broad shouldered frame and tousled black hair that curled about his ears and collar. The check shirt and blue cotton trousers he wore were faded and frayed at the cuffs but clean. Perhaps the hermit life suited him.

'I had a hell of a job finding this place, Tom. How long have you lived out here?'

'Three years – ever since the museum threw me out.'

He expected this mention of her current employer to draw some comment. It did not.

'What on earth do you find to do here? I mean, North Wales is very picturesque – OK for a holiday – but you were always such a gregarious bastard. I'd have thought a couple of weeks in a place like this would have driven you up the wall.'

He refilled her glass and then busied himself, poking at the guttering charcoal fire, sending a vortex of glowing sparks spiralling upwards. He would have liked to tell her that living where he did was first and foremost cheap, that life was a struggle for some. He doubted she would even begin to understand.

'When the academic establishment turned its sanctimonious back on me and overnight I became Thomas Hawkhurst the notorious grave robber, I decided that in future I would work on my own. I was, of course, making a virtue of necessity since no one in the business would have touched me with a barge pole after the Armenian fiasco anyway. So, to cut the cost of living I sold the flat in Islington and bought this place. I've lived up here ever since – after Dad died there was nothing to keep me in London.'

She nodded.

'I heard. I'm sorry'

Hawkhurst and his career had been his bus driver father's pride and joy and the scandal had finished him. He shrugged, ignoring her belated condolences.

'Thanks to the few friends I retained after Armenia I still get to write occasional articles for historical and antiquarian magazines, under a *nom-de-plume* naturally, and there are plenty of interesting sites up here in the mountains. Only last week I found previously unrecorded evidence of Roman lead mines over by Plas Cyfyng'

She was not overly impressed.

'Hardly your level is it? Roman lead workings? Three years ago you could pick your projects and name your price. You were good, Tom – the best.'

'That was before I was discovered smuggling artefacts out of Armenia, grave goods that were rightly the property of the citizens of that noble republic. Gold to the value of five million US dollars according to that lying bastard Kazahk.' He smiled bitterly. 'Although you and I know it was nearer ten million. I'd like to know where the missing five million went. I guess that while we were being given the order of the boot and escorted from the workers' paradise under armed guard, he was melting the rest of the stuff down and moving it over the border to his kinfolk in Iran. Either to them or up north to the Moscow Mafia. What does it matter now? In the end we saved the best pieces, though how long it will be before somebody has the guts to put them on display is anyone's guess. I heard on the grapevine that the British Museum had decided they were too much of a political hot potato and sold them on to some institute in the States. I suppose having the Elgin Marbles is problem enough.'

Outside it was growing dark and he went to the window, pulling the heavy curtains across against the night. Several small spiders fell from the rarely disturbed folds, scurrying for the safety of shadowy corners.

'Everybody on the team was fully aware of what was going on, Tom. What's more we all thoroughly approved of what you did. Kazahk was the grave robber, not you. If you hadn't got the stuff out of the country when you did the finest collection of Bronze Age grave ornaments ever discovered would have vanished forever.'

'That wasn't the way the Armenian authorities saw it.'

Brushing a strand of russet hair from her brow, she ran a moist tongue across her lips, eyes thoughtful. She seemed untypically reticent, he thought, as though in two minds as to whether to confide in him. They had been lovers for two years, back in the good old days when they shared the Islington flat. Then he had been the museum's youngest and most successful field officer and she a promising and ambitious student fresh down from Cambridge. With a First in Classics and a ruthless determination to make her mark she had been a fast learner and they had made an excellent partnership both physically and professionally. Looking up she saw his eyes on her, the same old sardonic smile on his dark features.

'What exactly is it that you want, Laura?' he asked, mildly enough, although from the tightening of her features and the briskness in her voice when she responded, his question might have carried a hidden barb.

'I think I'm onto something big, Tom. If it pans out, maybe the biggest thing to hit British archaeology since Sutton Hoo. I'd like you to help me. You're probably the only one who can.'

He resisted the compliment - he saw domestic complications.

'Won't Michael be miffed if he finds out you're associating with former lovers?' he needled. His opinion of the man who had so easily and rapidly replaced him in Laura's affections was not high. 'I'd hate to be found up some dark alley battered to death by a sequined handbag.'

It was her turn to smile.

'Michael is no longer on the scene, I'm afraid. He reverted to type.'

Hawkhurst frowned.

'Reverted to type? In what way?'

'He ran off with a chorus boy from the Royal Ballet. They were shacked up in a San Francisco love nest last thing I heard. You weren't far wrong when you mentioned sequined handbags. Everyone told me he was AC/DC when we first met, I guess the hassle of living with me finally pushed him off the fence once and for all. I know I can be a difficult bitch at times.'

She stared at him boldly, inviting a riposte. Surprised at her candour and not a little uneasy to find himself on personal matters Hawkhurst moved on.

'OK. If this thing is so big, why come to me? There's nothing I'd like better than to get involved in a major project but with my reputation I could prove more of a liability than an asset.'

She continued to look directly at him.

'I'm here because I owe you. All of us on the Armenian job owe you. You took the rap. You accepted full responsibility – told the world that you alone were involved in getting the stuff out of the country. While none of us would ever care to admit it publicly there are a number of people, respected figures in archaeology these days, who have good reason to be grateful for the way you distanced yourself from us when the manure was flying. We could have all just as easily gone to the wall with you but the fact is, thanks to television and publishing, we are out there making big money these days while you're wasting your time way back here in the sticks. You deserve better, Tom. I'd like to make things right between us if I can.'

He poured himself another inch of Scotch and held the bottle towards her, an offer she declined with a shake of her head, placing a pale hand over her glass. Outside the rain had become heavier, slashing at windows which rattled uneasily in their sashes under the assault. Hawkhurst wished he could believe her unexpected appearance could be put down to personal relationships. He wished he could believe that, even if love had long since died, she still cared about him. Somehow he couldn't.

'Just that, Laura? Just gratitude?' Although the smile remained there was an edge to his words as he sat down opposite her.

The Armenian episode was a major diplomatic incident that had threatened to undermine cultural links between British archaeology and many countries in which it operated. It was during this frenzied interlude when the academic world had been running around like a headless chicken that she had dropped him like a hot brick. Coming as it did a few days after his father's unexpected death, at a time when he needed all the support he could get, her rejection had completely knocked the wind out of his sails. In retrospect he assumed that her reasoning would have been that, even if only by association, the scandal posed a potential threat to her career. Whatever, it had been enough for her to transfer her affections within the space of a few short weeks to Michael Sujic. Sujic, a colourful character who numbered royalty and pop stars among his acquaintances, was a highly competent television producer and, at fifty three, more than twice her age. It was he who had introduced her into television, the medium in which she had, in the space of less than three years, achieved fame and fortune. A spin off from the TV work had been a series of bestselling books, glossy and lavishly illustrated productions without which no fashionable coffee table was considered complete.

With her sharp intelligence, stunning looks, and voracious appetite for hard work she had been a natural. These days it wasn't only antiquarians and history buffs who watched her programmes. Usually dressed in the briefest of shorts and distinctly bra-less beneath the flimsiest of coverings, she could be confident of drawing record viewing figures when she appeared to explain the burial practices of the Beaker Folk or the chronological development of Stonehenge. Laura Woods was undoubtedly a star. She sold a heady mixture of science, legend and sex that held an almost universal appeal. From nine to ninety, she was every schoolboy's fantasy history mistress.

'No, it's not simply gratitude,' she said shortly. 'I wouldn't expect an old cynic like you to believe that. The fact is, if what I've got is what I think it is, then you're the acknowledged expert. It's your specialist period more than mine, Tom. Whatever may have happened in the past, whatever you may think of me, look at it like this. What I'm offering is a chance to re-establish yourself.' Her gaze became combative. 'Don't give me that bull about doing serious work up here. Unless you get back into the mainstream pretty damn quick you're going to remain a forgotten man for the rest of your natural. Leave it too long, Tom, and you'll be a dead duck in the circles where it matters.

How old are you? Thirty one? Thirty two? Forget what happened in Armenia. If we get lucky with this thing you could be back at the top by this time next year. It's up to you.'

As she spoke the wide green eyes blazed, just as they had in the old days when some clumsy digger had damaged a find or failed to submit a sufficiently detailed report. He held up a pacifying hand. Cold, calculating little bitch she might be but Hawkhurst had to admit she was as gorgeous as ever. With Sujic no longer on the scene he wondered who was sharing her bed now. Doubtless it would be someone with money and influence. He moved on.

'OK, OK,' he smiled. 'I'm interested. So tell me about it.'

'Did you ever hear of Whitenditch Down?' Her features softened as, sensing he had taken the bait, she held out her glass for a refill. The way she had posed the question was an undisguised challenge. She wanted to see if he had retained his encyclopaedic store of archaeological minutiae.

Tom frowned, trawling his brain for long stored information.

'You mean the place in Wiltshire? Yes, I think so. A mixed group of round and long barrows – typical Neolithic and bronze age burial mounds as I recall. Didn't Henry Simmonds produce a paper on the excavations? I didn't read it but I thought they were all considered pretty run of the mill – even the ones that hadn't been robbed didn't produce anything exciting as I remember.'

She nodded approvingly. Not many, least of all someone who was in junior school at the time, would recall the Simmonds report; a report which, as he had said, contained nothing in the least newsworthy.

'There was one long barrow about half a mile from the main group that wasn't touched in the original dig because it was on private land. Apparently permission to open it up wasn't forthcoming at the time. Anyway, last year I was approached by the BBC with a view to excavating this last remaining mound. The farm on which it stands had changed hands and the new owner was intending to plough it up. Unlike a lot of farmers in that position he had the decency to give us some warning and an opportunity to excavate it first.' Outside the wind groaned mournfully about the eaves as she took a delaying sip of her drink, deliberately whetting his appetite for more. Setting her glass down she continued.

'Since, on the evidence of the Simmonds report the barrow was unlikely to yield anything earth shattering I put up a proposal to the museum and the television people that we use the opportunity to its best advantage. I suggested that while doing a serious excavation we should at the same time treat it as a public relations exercise.' Her eyes came up, challenging Hawkhurst to make some glib observation about her concern with her public image. He remained silent. 'Well, the proposal was to make a short series of programmes for children's television. A group of children from a wide variety of backgrounds would carry out the excavation under the supervision of a team from the museum with me acting as dig director and narrator. We would use it to demonstrate all the basic surveying and excavating techniques and the intention was that it should be educational and entertaining. It had two things going for it, first it would show the caring face of archaeology. Second, and more importantly, the BBC would put up most of the money. Anyway they went for the idea and, to cut a long story short, we began work last June and finished in October. The weather was kind, the kids had a great time and we had the whole thing in the can by November, ready for showing later this year.'

'And,' Hawkhurst raised a slightly too casual eyebrow, 'what did you find?'

She smiled. For all his show of indifference she knew he was hooked. Keep him dangling a little longer, she decided.

'Nothing. Not even a burial in the chamber – it was a gallery grave by the way – a single gallery about two metres by three and about two and half high. Whatever it may have originally held had been completely cleared out. Of course, so far as screen time was concerned this gave us real problems. You can understand how difficult it is to make six half-hour programmes out of what amounted to very little material. Thank God for computer reconstructions because we had to pad out like mad. We dug horizontally into the sides of the mound in the hope of finding secondary burials and we opened up the spoil ditches on either side. In the end we wound up with a handful of pottery shards, the usual bland digging implements and a handful of coins. Whoever had been there first had done a very thorough job. Even for a dig that wasn't expected to yield very much in the first place it was still pretty disappointing.'

He nodded, his eyes serious, almost sad.

'It's not unusual to find graves robbed. Practically every burial mound I've come across has had some associated legend of buried treasure. Did you get a carbon dating on any of the organic finds?'

'Yes. The laboratories placed it at 3,450BC with a plus or minus factor of 150 years.'

'Five and a half thousand years, give or take a century of two. That's a long time to be exposed to human greed, Laura. Barrow robbing is an ancient profession and one not confined to the criminal classes either. Most of the ruling houses were guilty of ransacking burial mounds for the sake of any treasure they might contain.' He stared into the fire. 'God knows how much gold they found and melted down simply to satisfy royal avarice. It's worse to think of all the other finds they would have thrown away as being of no monetary value and therefore of no consequence. Things that would have provided so much knowledge in the hands of people like us – people with the skills to interpret them.'

'My, my, Tom. Despite everything I do believe you are still an idealist at heart. How sweet.' Although her words were low and mocking Laura realised that, despite everything he had been subjected to over the Armenian affair, the man had retained his integrity.

His head came up sharply, eyes like flints, and she fell silent. His temper was legendary. She had seen him, single handed, harangue and kick a band of opportunist Egyptian labourers back to work when they thought they could hold him to ransom for higher wages. Seeing she was taunting him he shrugged indifferently.

'Cut the crap, Laura. Tell me about the barrow.'

A couple of weeks ago, at the end of March, I went back to Whitenditch. I just happened to be in Salisbury for a book-signing and I thought I'd look in and thank Joss Mallon, the farmer on whose land the barrow lies, for all his help. Anyway when I got there it turned out he was away on holiday so I walked up to the barrow. The chamber was wide open, just as we had left it, and I went inside. At first nothing seemed any different and it was only as I was about to leave that I realised there was a clearly defined rectangle on the floor of the chamber. The place had been open to the elements ever since we quit digging back in October so I can only assume that rain and wind had eroded a few inches of topsoil from the floor. I didn't have any tools with me so the best I could do was to scrape back the earth with my bare hands. About a foot down I struck what, at first, I thought was a large nodule of flint. When I cleared it, however, it turned out to be a sizeable slab of roughly dressed granite.

'You can imagine my feelings. Although we had sieved through the first couple of inches of topsoil the one direction we hadn't dug down into, and who would, was the floor of the chamber. I'll be perfectly honest, my first thought was that if something important was beneath the chamber, something we had totally missed, it wouldn't do the museum's or my reputation any good at all. I was sorely tempted to replace the earth and forget about the whole thing. Then I remembered that Mallon intended at some time to plough the area out. At that depth the ploughshare would be sure to strike the rock and Mallon, who is something of an armchair archaeologist himself, would certainly be astute enough to investigate. If he found something that we supposed experts had missed after three months excavations we would all end up looking pretty stupid.'

'Well, I returned the next day with a few tools and cleared the whole slab. It was about two metres long by just under a metre wide. Initially I assumed it covered the original Neolithic burial and had been a ploy to keep it safe from the attentions of grave robbers. It wasn't something I'd come across before but it seemed the only logical explanation.'

Hawkhurst nodded.

'I agree, any typical internment from that period would normally have been placed inside the chamber not buried under it. But tell me, if you did a proper survey of the site how come the magnometer readings didn't reveal the presence of a slab that size? Surely the geophysics team would have picked up on it?'

Laura sensed a professional criticism here – not something she was accustomed, or amenable to.

'Bloody economies,' she snorted. 'The museum has only one set of equipment and that was in Denmark at the time. Remember, this was supposed to be a kids' programme and as such came pretty low on the list of priorities. Anyway, the slab was too big for me to shift on my own so I intended to cover the damn thing up and return with a proper team at the earliest opportunity. The way I saw it, providing I could make the discovery look like the result of inspired scientific deduction on my part, it would make a magnificent final episode to go with the six we had already put together. More importantly, yours truly would have the satisfaction of saying she discovered it all on her own.'

The fire was dying and, tiring of her seemingly insatiable appetite for fame, Hawkhurst thrust the iron poker into the blackness of the great charred log, prying open its glowing heart in a whirl of incandescence. Thus far he saw little to get excited about in her story and wished she would get to the point.

'So, you may or may not have found an undisturbed Neolithic burial. It's nice of course but hardly unique.'

She stared into the fire, silent for several seconds, then looked to him. 'It's not that simple – there was an inscription on the stone. It had been infilled with soil and clay so I almost missed it at first. I cleared it up with a nail file.'

He had to admit this was definitely interesting yet his manner remained studiedly unimpressed.

'An inscription on a Neolithic tomb? That would be interesting of course. So far as I know nothing that even hints at a written language of that period has ever been found in Britain. Even so, how can I help? I'm not a philologist and it's never been a period I specialised in. Hope-Rogers or Haswell are the best men for…'

'The inscription wasn't Neolithic. It was in Latin.'

She fumbled in the small hand bag by her feet, producing a sheaf of Polaroid photographs which she passed to him. They were not good quality shots and Hawkhurst held them close to the flickering firelight trying to make out the detail. As he passed the photos back to her his eyes, narrowed and questioning, locked on hers.

'I see what you mean.' He stood up and went to the window, drawing the curtain aside and staring out into the darkness beyond the rain beaded pane.

'What do you think?' she asked softly.

'I think we should get down there first thing in the morning and have a closer look.'

'But the inscription?'

'You know as well as I do what it says. Hic lacet Artorius – Here lies Arthur.'

'But do you think …?'

'I'm not allowing myself to think at the moment,' he said shortly. 'I'll believe it when I see it. In the meantime we'd better get some sleep.' He pointed to the door. 'I'm afraid the sleeping accommodation is a bit limited – the only bedroom is through there.' Pulling her skirt down over her knees she raised a haughty questioning eyebrow and he laughed gently, pleased to see her customary cool self-assurance waver momentarily. 'Don't worry about your virtue. Laura, I'll sleep here by the fire. Breakfast at seven, OK? Then we'll drive down to Whitenditch.'

After she had gone to bed Hawkhurst went to the phone. It was nearly twelve and predictably several minutes passed before Angahrad came drowsily on the other end of the line.

'Angie? Sorry to ring at this time of night, darling, but something's come up and I have to go away for a couple of days. I'll look you up at the farm as soon as I get back. No, there's nothing wrong. It's just a job. I'm going down to Wiltshire to have a look at a recent excavation. I'll be back as quickly as I can. Take care, my love.'

Putting down the handset he turned to find Laura, a threadbare towel wrapped tightly about her, watching him from the bedroom door.

'So it's not an entirely celibate life up here in the hills,' she mocked.

His gaze briefly took in the gleaming tan of the silken thighs and shoulders before turning away. He proceeded to push the two armchairs together to form a makeshift bed. Taking the hint she let the banter drop.

'What are the chances,' she whispered, 'of this being what we both hope it is?'

Kicking off his shoes and pulling a blanket up to his chin he eyed her dispassionately.

'The grave of Arthur Pendragon, the Once and Future King of Britain? A thousand to one against.' He quoted the ancient Welsh poem: 'A grave there is for Mark, a grave for Gwythyr, a grave for Gwgawn of the red sword, but a mystery to the Day of Judgement the grave of Arthur.'

CHAPTER TWO

'Before we go any further you should be aware there's not a scrap of concrete evidence to suggest that Arthur ever existed. Nothing to show him as anything but a character of western Celtic mythology who, thanks to medieval literature, became transmuted into a quasi-historical figure. All that nonsense about the Round Table and Camelot. Forget it.'

Laura nodded dutifully as she neatly trepanned her boiled egg. She stoically resisted remarking upon the slightly bloody feather that stubbornly adhered to her breakfast, suggesting that it had but recently been in the possession of one of the scrawny hens that scratched about the open door.

'OK. You've read me the health warning. Now give me the good news.'

The low early sun shone directly into the cramped kitchen, silhouetting spiders hanging in their webs across the windows, as Hawkhurst, his face covered in shaving cream, persisted with his cautionary tale.

'If you look at the evidence dispassionately there isn't any good news. To start with Gildas, the only writer who is both contemporary and relevant to the Arthurian period – say the late fifth to middle sixth centuries – makes no mention of Arthur whatsoever. Apart from one or two vague allusions in Welsh poetry, which might well have been added later, the earliest references appear in manuscripts that were written in the early ninth century.' He rinsed his razor under the tap and shook it dry, running a testing hand across his chin. Turning, he studied her features to see if his deliberately pessimistic message was getting through. 'Hardly encouraging is it?'

She appeared unconcerned as, collecting up the breakfast things, she elbowed him aside without a word and proceeded to wash up in the deep stone sink.

'Nennius,' he persisted grimly, 'who like Gildas was a Welsh monk, gives us quite a lot of information in the *Historia Brittonum*. He is specific on the location of Arthur's famous twelve battles for instance, the majority of which can be identified with some certainty. But he was writing three hundred years after the events he describes and a lot of it simply doesn't add up in the light of our most recent research. Of course, it's just possible that he had access to manuscripts that were subsequently lost but what it amounts to seems to be no more than a garbled mishmash of legend and hearsay laid over an only partially factual background.'

As he spoke he glared at her, defying her to express anything that smacked in the least of wishful thinking. Laura lay the last of the dishes aside and wiped her hands down the thighs of her stylish jeans. She knew of old his insistence on hard evidence and was not the least downcast by any of this. She had, however, had enough of his pessimism for one day.

'So who's this Angie woman then?' she demanded, diving for shelter behind the table as, laughing, he advanced on her, his hands curled into strangling mode.

*****

Two hours later they were over the English border, growling southward down the M6 at a steady ninety. Laura, as with everything else she undertook, drove extremely well. She was fast yet maintained absolute control and Tom felt not the least nervous. Vivaldi was coming loud and clear over the sound system, her slim fingers beating time on the wheel. She had been silent for some time, maybe concentrating on the road, maybe marshalling her thoughts. Now she leant forward and turned the volume down.

'You said that if there ever was a real Arthur he'd have been alive around the beginning of the sixth century. What do you base that assumption on?'

'Typically dodgy late material I'm afraid. *The Annals of Wales*, mainly. The Annals are basically no more than a chronological list of important historical events from the middle of the fifth century onwards. Most of the events listed can be verified and we believe *The Annals of Wales* to be, by and large, a genuine record of the period. However, even here we know that the document we are looking at is only a tenth or eleventh century copy of an eighth or ninth century copy of a possibly genuine Arthurian period original. And It's not a photocopy we're talking about remember. Whoever made it could add, delete and change anything they felt like.'

'Get over, you prat,' Laura grated through clenched teeth, leaning hard on the strident horn as a labouring Volvo estate proved unpardonably slow in giving way. As they swept majestically past the object of her displeasure she made a loose fisted masturbatory gesture to the discomfited driver. Satisfied, she returned to her subject. 'So, what do *The Annals of Wales* tell us?'

'There are two entries relating specifically to Arthur. The first mentions the Battle of Badon, a three-day battle in which with typical heroic excess Arthur is credited with killing close on a thousand of the enemy Anglo-Saxons. The date given is 516, although this, like just about anything else to do with Arthur, has been questioned. Since Gildas, who was born only a few years later, also mentions Badon there seems little doubt it was a real battle and one which put a stop to Anglo-Saxon expansion westwards for the next fifty years. A body count of a thousand on one side is very high for a period when entire armies seldom numbered more than a few thousand fighting men so it must have been quite a ruckus. Unfortunately, Gildas omits to mention the name of the British leader at Badon and archaeological evidence, mainly data on Anglo-Saxon grave distribution, suggests an earlier date for such a battle, possibly as early as 490.'

'You said there were two relevant entries in the Annals. What was the other one?'

'It simply records Arthur's death at the Battle of Camlann twenty one years after the Battle of Badon. Depending on whether you favour an early or late date for Badon that means Arthur would have died sometime between 511 and 537.

For all his desire to bring a coldly analytical eye to matters, she was not to be discouraged.

'You said the locations of Arthur's battles had been identified. Where were Badon and Camlann?' Hawkhurst smiled ruefully.

'Ah, I was afraid you'd ask that. If you remember, what I actually said was that most of them could be identified. Those two, unfortunately for us, are a bit problematic. Badon, although we can be fairly certain that the battle took place in southern England somewhere, could have been fought at what is now the modern City of Bath; Solsbury Hill near Batheaston or, a very strong contender in recent years, Liddington Castle in Wiltshire. Camlann has been variously identified as being Camboglanna, a Roman fort up on Hadrian's Wall which according to those who know about such things has a strong case on philological grounds, the River Cam in Somerset, or the River Camel in Cornwall. You pays your money and you takes your choice.'

Laura exhaled forcibly at this masterly display of prevarication.

'For God's sake, Hawkhurst, what am I paying you for? I thought you were supposed to be a Dark Age specialist. Is there anything you can be certain of?'

He considered the question briefly then nodded.

'Yes. If I don't get a couple of pints and a pork pie down my neck pretty quick you're going to have an advanced case of malnutrition on your hands.'

*****

Laura's idea of what constituted suitable sustenance proving to be considerably more sophisticated than his own meant they spent the next half hour drawing up at various pubs, hotels and restaurants. A cursory scanning of the menu would produce a wrinkled nose from Laura and a rapid departure. Eventually, just as the possibility of cannibalism was creeping into his thoughts, she found a small hotel just south of Cirencester. As they settled themselves in the rather genteel atmosphere of the walnut panelled restaurant, Tom eyed the extensive and outrageously priced menu with some alarm.

'Shit, we'll need a second mortgage unless we stick to the soup.'

Laura smiled, the general condition of the cottage had told its own tale about the state of his finances.

'Don't worry about the prices,' she said. 'The television people will be more than happy to pick up the tab for this. From today, while you're working for me you'll be on £300 a day plus any expenses you incur. Is that OK?'

It certainly was and he made a mental note that at those rates a day's pay would meet a month's outgoings and few weeks' work would get the bank off his back for good. It would be no bad thing, he decided, if he tried to be a little more positive.

'Sounds fine to me but don't expect too much. This could be anything from an elaborate hoax to a genuine grave. Even if it is genuine, Arthur or Artorius was not an uncommon name in the late Romano-British period. More important from our point of view, what's it doing under a burial mound that was already four thousand years old when who or whatever is under the slab was put there?'

'You're the expert, you tell me.' Her tone was sharp, perhaps well aware there might be pitfalls involved and preferring him to test the ground ahead. He knew she placed too high a value on her own status and image as a national celebrity to risk losing credibility. That, he guessed, would be his allotted function in the scheme of things. If anyone was going to end up looking stupid it would be him – Hawkhurst the grave robber. Spearing a gobbet of the fillet steak set before him, he ground the bloody flesh to pulp in his mouth, luxuriating in her barely concealed impatience. To twist the knife he took a thoughtful, delaying sip of the dark claret before continuing.

'I've given that some thought and, if we accept what most authorities on Arthur have said in the past, there seem to be only two credible possibilities. If Camlann was fought up on Hadrian's Wall at Camboglanna then Arthur would have been fighting on territory still held by Celtic tribes. He'd be fighting against his fellow Britons rather than the Anglo-Saxons he'd duffed-up at Badon. That can only mean the Celtic alliance he'd lead to victory down south had begun to break up. Anyway, let's assume that Arthur is killed in some second division skirmish and his war band decide to bring his body back home for burial'.

'To Camelot?' Her eyes glowed and Hawkhurst sighed wearily.

'Forget Camelot. Camelot was the invention of a hyper-imaginative French writer, Chretien de Troyes, who lived 500 years after the Battle of Badon. No, it could have been any of a dozen hilltop forts down in the south west. Best bet is South Cadbury. Alcock carried out a series of digs there in the 60s and 70s which confirmed it was heavily refortified around the period we are looking at suggesting those were exciting times. What's more there has always been a strong tradition associating the place with Arthur.'

'You shouldn't think of Arthur as a king either, not in the sense of a dynastic inheritor of power. That was another later embellishment. He is, in the earliest tales, which we must assume to be nearest the truth, merely a war chief. He would probably be a cavalryman in the tradition of the Roman auxiliaries who had garrisoned Britain at the beginning of the fifth century as part of the crumbling Roman Empire. His title may well have been Dux Bellorum – war leader. Forget Camelot, forget chivalry, the man you are seeking is a soldier, possibly a mercenary. He'd be the head of a professional war band of Celtic tradition. By welding together an alliance of the petty Celtic kingdoms of the west and north he succeeded in temporarily halting the advance of the pagan Anglo-Saxons and their allies who were flooding into the south and east of the country from Germany and Denmark.'

Fascinated by the subject yet impatient to be moving on, Laura held her hand aloft and with a sharp snap of her fingers indicated the bill was required, her eyes never leaving his.

'OK, so we have a scenario where Arthur gets totaled by his erstwhile buddies and his men are bringing the body back down south for burial. What happens next?'

'Look, I'm just guessing at this stage, that's all. Who knows? Maybe the Saxons hear of Arthur's death and were keen to get his scalp. Scalping wasn't invented by American Indians you know. Perhaps things got too hot and Arthur's men, under pressure, had to get rid of the body in a hurry. Maybe they intended to return and collect the body when the heat was off. So, where would they put it? Somewhere the enemy wouldn't be too keen to investigate presumably. An ancient burial mound or barrow, where the fairies lived. We're not talking about your Tinkerbelle-type fairies here, Disneyland creations poncing about with tinsel wands. These fairies are akin to demons, the darkest creations of the superstitious mind, creatures who stole men's souls and kept them prisoner in the bowels of the earth. Right up to the beginning of this century country folk regarded the barrows as entrance ways to the underworld. Those medieval coins you found may well have been the robber paying a tithe to the spirit world for their violation of such a place. Laying Arthur to rest there would certainly discourage the Saxons from poking around. It's only a guess, of course. Equally, the body may have been buried there as a magic charm against the Saxons. Whitenditch lies roughly on the eastern limit of Anglo-Saxon expansion at this time. The body of a national hero of Arthur's standing would be seen as a potent talisman to deter the enemy from crossing that limit. Remember, the dead body of El Cid borne into battle at the head of the Christian armies was sufficient to scatter his Moorish enemies. And compared to the superstitious Anglo-Saxons the Arabs were positively sophisticated.'

'So, you do think there's a chance it is Arthur?' Hope flickered in her eyes as she airily tapped in her credit card details for what, to him, seemed a small fortune. The waitress departing she repeated the question. 'Well? Do you?'

He shook his head; he wasn't going to be steamrollered into wishful thinking.

'No. Not really. I only wish I could. But I want to see for myself.' He wiped his mouth on the napkin and stood up. 'Thanks for the meal. Let's get on the road shall we?'

As he led the way towards the door he found his way barred by the pretty young waitress. Her interest lay not in him, however. Holding out a pen and the menu she asked shyly if Laura would be so kind as to autograph it, just so she could show her mother, a fan, that her heroine had honoured the place with her presence. All eyes in the restaurant upon them, Laura scrawled off a signature with a beaming *noblesse oblige* that made Hawkhurst squirm.

*****

The footpath leading up to the barrow was a sunken gulley of flint-studded chalk, a meandering white ribbon, half a metre deep, carved out by the feet of generations of Wessexmen. It wound up through a thick grove of ancient, gnarled-boughed ash, before emerging onto the green sunlit breast of the down. Laura pointed ahead to where the main group of barrows stretched away along the ridge.

'That's where Simmonds dug back in the sixties. Our barrow is over there to the left and a little way down, among that clump of tress.'

For all his studied display of professional scepticism, Hawkhurst could not deny that old anticipatory thrill as he followed her down the grassy slope towards the mound which materialised from the surrounding screen of silver birch like a sleeping dragon. For him, archaeology had always been like that. In the silent clearing he stopped, his eyes taking in the scene about him while Laura, one thought in mind, hurried towards the dark maw of the open chamber. The mound itself was remarkably well preserved, still standing to a height of some five metres and stretching away for maybe thirty amid a perfumed carpet of scarlet poppies and cow parsley. It was hot now and he tossed his jacket onto the grass, scattering crickets and damsel flies in all directions, before following her inside.

The chamber was a simple affair, three huge slabs of roughly hewn rock supporting an equally massive capstone. In one corner cigarette butts and a used condom suggested the locals had been quick to take advantage of its shelter. Once inside, the warmth of the sun quickly dissipated to be replaced by a coolness that made him shiver.

While Hawkhurst looked about him, trying to get a feel for the place, Laura was already down on her knees, eager fingers in the earth searching for the outline of the buried stone. Indifferent to possible damage to expensive clothing and carefully manicured nails she brushed aside the concealing layer of soil with a grim determination. She twisted towards him and pointed triumphantly, her eyes bright.

'Look Tom, there. There's the inscription.' She whispered.

He hunkered down beside her and stared. The inscription was exactly as she had said; exactly like the photographs. "Hic Lacet Artorius". The words were clearly carved yet it was certainly not the work of a professional mason for the letters were more than a little askew and lacked sharp edged definition. Hardly a fitting epitaph for a leader of Arthur's renown yet understandable if interpreted as the work of some loyal retainer, a battle-weary British warrior, heartsick at his leader's death and heedful of murderous English warriors now ranging the downs above. He took a small trowel from the canvas backpack he had brought and began to carefully scrape away the earth around the edge of the slab, each sweep of the blade ringing hollowly in the silence of the tomb. After half an hour they were looking down at the cleared slab. To Laura it looked immovable.

'We'll need lifting equipment,' she said softly. 'It must weigh a ton.'

He didn't answer but, bending his knees, curled strong fingers under one of the longer sides of the stone, tentatively testing its weight. Watching intently Laura recalled the strength of his body from the old days.

'Let me give it a go first,' he said. 'You're probably right but it'll be best if we can avoid bringing in heavy equipment. We don't want to attract too much attention to our activities. Once the locals get to know about it we'll be up to our ears in sightseers.' He looked at her over his shoulder. 'You'd better stand well back. If it gets away from me it could fall anywhere. She briefly contemplated trying to stop him, fearful that if things went wrong the massive slab might well come crashing down on whatever treasure lay beneath, perhaps damaging it irretrievably. However, since at that moment he appeared unaware of her presence, she stepped back a safe distance and watched. Grunting with the effort, he lifted one edge of the slab and turned it onto its side to rest against the chamber wall. Relieved that no damage had occurred she returned to his side, peering down into the shadowy pit at their feet. Tom moved aside to maximise such natural light as was available.

'Right,' he said, brushing the dirt from his hands. 'Let's see what we've got.'

In seconds Laura had produced a camera and was taking photographs as he stretched a tentative hand into the open earth. Even at this stage she was working from all the angles.

'We may have to fake the actual opening later,' she said, skirting around his crouched form. 'It's always nice to make the viewers think they are witnessing the actual event. What's in there, Tom?'

Little was left of the actual skeleton. Only a few of the larger bones, the femurs and a helmeted skull, remained entire. The ribs concealed beneath the weight of the long chain mail shirt crumbling to dust as he reached down and ran his fingers lightly over the knitted metal links. However, the man's trappings were well preserved. The fluted steel of the long double-edged sword that lay down his left side was still as burnished bright as the day it was laid away. The simple steel cap above the hollow caverns of the skeletal eye sockets still flashed a sharp blue sheen in the dim light. Sealed by clay, little moisture or air would have penetrated this deep beneath the mound Hawkhurst guessed. He lifted the sword carefully into the light, testing its weight, taking in its dimensions. About the bronze banded hardwood hilt fantastic creatures; snakes and dragons, coiled and writhed. The pommel was in the form of a tusked boar's head.

'Well?' she demanded triumphantly. 'What do you think now?'

'First thoughts?' Hawkhurst ran his thumb along the flat of the blade. 'Well, it has all the signs of being a typical late Romano-British burial, possibly from the period ascribed to Arthur. The inscription, the sword and the helmet certainly all point to that. What amazes me is the quality of the grave contents. I mean, look at that chain mail. I've never seen metal so perfectly preserved as that – it's incredible. We'd better get a team up here as quickly as possible. You get back to the car and phone the museum. We need to get a temporary protection order slapped on this place as quickly as possible, too.

She stared at the sword in his hand and then down into the grave. Normally, to move anything before a proper photographic record had been made and careful measurements carried out would have been unthinkable. However, both sensing this was something very out of the ordinary, they put the niceties aside.

'What else is in there,' she whispered, her voice husky with excitement. 'What's that by his feet?'

In his fascination with the sword Hawkhurst had not noticed the bowl. It was a wide, shallow vessel, about fifty centimetres across. It looked to be made of beaten silver. Like the other finds it was in an extraordinarily good state of preservation. Before he could lay the sword aside to investigate this new revelation Laura had pre-empted him and was now examining the bowl at arm's length outside in the warmth of the sunlight.

'It's beautiful,' she whispered, 'look how it sparkles.'

He came closer, the sword in his hand forgotten.

'We could have a problem with that,' he murmured. 'I've never seen anything quite like it before, least of all in a Dark Age context. Look at those figures around the rim. The only thing I've ever seen that looked remotely like that came from late Bronze Age in Bulgaria. It's not my specialist period and I'm only going on stylistic parameters but I'd say this would already have been regarded as an ancient relic by Arthur's time. It's a real mystery.'

The grove about them grew suddenly silent as they stared in wonder at the sword and the bowl. It was Laura who voiced his own first thoughts, thoughts he had already dismissed as too fantastic for words.

'My God, Tom. Just think of it. What we have here could be Excalibur and the Holy Grail.'

They gazed spellbound. Until, overhead, skulking among the boughs, a solitary magpie clacked malevolently as Hawkhurst shook his head definitely. The spell was broken.

'Not a chance. Excalibur and the Grail are both medieval embellishments to the Arthurian legends. There's no factual basis for them whatsoever.'

But Laura wasn't listening anymore. She was already in a world of her own. A world of viewing figures, royalties and international copyrights. She gripped his arm.

'Think of it Tom. The return of Arthur, the Once and Future King. It could warrant an entire series. Properly handled this could be the biggest thing to hit TV screens for years. We'd get prime viewing time – guaranteed – world-wide. The Americans would be falling over themselves to put up the money – remember, the whole of the English speaking world knows about Arthur.'

'Arthur didn't speak English,' he pointed out rather pedantically, trying to retain a grip on reality and annoyed to find that even in the presence of such treasures her prime concern remained her own self-promotion. Nevertheless, there was no denying this was an extremely important find and he was not a little disconcerted to find himself assessing the possible ramifications of his own part in the discovery. 'Arthur was a Briton – he would have spoken a language that was several removes from modern Welsh.'

The pearl of wisdom fell on stony ground.

'Oh yes,' she said absently, the intended rebuke in his comment clearly lost on her. 'A nice point that, must remember to bring it out in the narrative.' She bit her lower lip thoughtfully. 'Put the slab back will you, Tom, I think we should take the Sword and the Grail to London.'

'For Christ's sake, Laura, let's not get carried away. What we have here are, or appear to be, exceptionally well preserved examples of a Romano-British cavalry sword and – less certainly – a central European dish of indeterminate origin that at first glance is in the proto-Celtic style. That's all they are and nothing else. We should be more concerned about protecting the burial in there. We'll get so much information from that. 'He pointed to a scattering of silver coins that lay in one corner of the grave among a few strands of dried cloth that had once been a purse. 'These will be much more useful, they may even give us a precise date for the burial. '

However, she had already tucked the dish firmly under her arm like a hard-won prize in the New Year sales and, if unable to fault his professional concern, was nevertheless not prepared to brook any dissent on his part. She was running this show and no one else.

'Quite right too, Tom. Now put the slab back in position – there's a dear. I'll wait for you back at the car. I must phone the museum to get a protection order drawn up.' She giggled like a schoolgirl. 'It'll be fun to let the Board of Directors know what a surprise I've got for them.'

CHAPTER THREE

Angahrad had been sleeping soundly when, at three in the morning, Hawkhurst arrived back at the farm. Dog tired after two days of frenetic activity in London he had not woken her, grateful to fall into a deep and dreamless slumber between fresh sheets with the regular kiss of her breath on his shoulder. Now, her head resting on one hand, she smiled as she watched him struggle unwillingly to consciousness.

'Thomas,' she whispered, her Welsh lilt bringing the suggestion of a smile to his lips although the eyes remained closed. 'Thomas, wake up. I must go soon to feed the animals.'

He did not stir and suspecting he was feigning she leant forward, smiling, and kissed his mouth, her tongue probing. For a moment longer he lay unmoving, the hint of a languorous smile forming as her hand slid beneath the sheets, finding his organ and coaxing it quickly to life. His eyes opened and in one swift move that made her gasp he rolled her onto her back, pinning her beneath his bulk, laughing triumphantly as he did so. She stared up at him, China blue eyes wide, moist lips parted in exquisite anticipation as with one powerful and practised thrust he entered her. Her eyes fluttered shut and she gave the customary low moan of delight, locking her long slim legs about his, clamping the hardness of him to her very core.

They had met six months before in the Griffin Arms, the dreary little pub in the village. With the debatable exception of the chapel it was the only establishment that could be regarded as a social centre within ten miles of his cottage. Although Hawkhurst – an outsider and, far worse, an English outsider at that – had no access to or interest in local gossip, he already knew a little about her. She was a woman with a reputation.

Despite being locally born and bred she was, like him, regarded as something of a renegade. A young woman of twenty three, living alone and managing to run an efficient sheep farm was anathema to the fiercely chauvinistic hill farmers of Ffoel Goch. Her proficiency and healthy flock shamed and gave the lie to their endless whining about the weather, about lamb prices and about the bureaucrats in Brussels. But though they may have resented her independence and success, for all their narrow chapel-bred disapproval, their shifty eyes would linger on her tall, full breasted figure whenever she came into the village for provisions. A few of the local young men had made tentative attempts at courtship although with little success. She had always told herself she would know when the right man came along and was prepared to trust her own judgement. Now, because of her uncompromising self-sufficiency they treated her with distrust and this she countered with a measured, distant, contempt.

Hawkhurst had seen her on a number of occasions, high in the hills with her dogs, tending her flocks. Once, at a distance, she had waved to him as he trudged to investigate a remote cairn that according to local legend, wrongly as usual, covered a medieval burial. However, until that day in the Griffin Arms they had never spoken.

She had come into the dingy public bar in quest of a bottle of Scotch. It had been a period when Hawkhurst, worryingly overdrawn and under pressure from the bank, had been drinking more heavily than was normal. He had watched from his solitary seat in the alcove window as amid a cold and disapproving silence she strode bravely up to the bar. Any woman who touched hard liquor in this straight-laced community was as good as guaranteed eternal damnation – she was a Jezebel. While the landlord went in search of the whisky, Tom, the book in his hand forgotten, took in the pale profile beneath the piled tangle of golden hair. Defiant yet uneasy in the instantly resentful atmosphere, she had looked tentatively around the bar, her eyes avoiding anything or anyone specific until for one brief moment they had settled on his. In that moment each recognised a kindred loneliness.

Then Glynn Powell, who ran the hardware shop and had once tilted an unsuccessful lance, had grunted something in Welsh that Hawkhurst had not understood yet which had the unmistakable ring of crudity about it. Confirming his suspicions, the group at Powell's table laughed aloud. Whatever had been said the girl smiled at them easily enough, although there was a tightness at the corners of her generous mouth that confirmed the comment had not been entirely pleasant. Then Powell, clearly somewhat the worse for drink, was on his feet. Approaching her, he lounged easily against the bar from where he continued his guttural monologue. Understanding not a word of it yet in no doubt it now verged on the obscene, Hawkhurst, three pints of ale under his belt and at odds with the world in general, lay down his book and strode purposefully to the bar, placing himself between the girl and her tormentor. As the cramped bar fell silent he smiled down reassuringly into her surprised eyes.

'I've no idea what this dickhead is saying I'm afraid, but do I take it he's trying to embarrass you?'

For a moment she hesitated, sensing trouble brewing. Then her chin came up defiantly.

'He is.'

Furious to find himself staring in the back of Tom's head the Welshman launched himself into a fresh verbal torrent.

'What's he saying now?' he enquired innocently. It was her turn to smile.

'I won't bother with an exact translation but in general terms it revolves around your nationality and your parents' marital status.'

Tom gave a sad sigh.

'Funny. I thought it might.'

Folding his arms across his chest, Hawkhurst turned and faced the bulky storekeeper, his eyes hard, his head to one side questioningly. They were both big men but, although he was probably a couple of years younger and for all his scowling menace, Powell had gone soft in the belly. The chapped neck fat that hung over his collar told its own tale.

'Would you care to step outside and repeat that, Boyo?' Hawkhurst asked softly.

The other man, visibly taken aback to find his bluff called, was, nevertheless, in no mood to back down in front of his friends. These now watched spellbound, certainly unwilling to become involved in anything so unseemly as this sort of thing themselves yet fascinated by the prospect of a little vicarious violence. Finding little in the way of support or encouragement from that quarter, and seeing no opportunity for withdrawal short of an abject apology, Powell bit the bullet. His mouth set in a crooked humourless grin.

'OK. Outside it is – Boyo!'

It was a vigorous yet brief encounter. Hawkhurst, who had won his blue for boxing at light-heavyweight for Oxford, was in control from the outset, jabbing his left hand solidly into the bull-necked Welshman's face until eventually he stopped coming forward and his breathing became laboured. Seeing the man falter Tom unleashed a savage combination of punches, hooks and uppercuts that was to prove decisive. However, Powell was no coward and gave of his best before finishing face down in the muddy paddock at the side of the pub. Although defeated, he at least had the satisfaction of raising an angry bruise under Tom's right eye and bringing a smear of blood to his bottom lip. Dabbing tentatively at his throbbing mouth, he watched as Powell's cronies half-dragged the unconscious man away before returning inside. To his disappointment the woman had gone, slipping away during the unseemly fracas. St George may well have slain the dragon but the maiden, or so it appeared, had not been overly impressed.

Half an hour later he was making his way homewards up the steep boulder-strewn flanks of Cwmdower, half regretting his misguided sense of chivalry. He was well aware that it would win him few friends in the village. From the beetling cliffs that hung about the pathway, the yelping jackdaws seemed to mock his quixotic gesture and the scant thanks it had won him as he ruefully massaged his bruised cheekbone. It was as, head thrown back, he laughed aloud at his own stupid, schoolboy sense of honour that the sound of a car horn stopped him in his tracks. He turned to see a bemired Land Rover careering up the hill towards him, bouncing wildly over boulders and rutted grass.

Unable to identify the driver through the smeared windscreen and wondering if Powell might have recovered sufficiently to contemplate launching a counter attack, perhaps with reinforcements this time, he faced the approaching vehicle with some concern. When the truck drew to a halt within a few metres of him, however, he smiled for it wasn't Powell but Angahrad who climbed out. Hands on hips she stood by the wagon taking in his battered features with a slow, slightly disapproving, shake of her head.

'My goodness but you look a mess.' She pointed to the car and in a tone that brooked no argument said: 'Get in. I've got a first aid kit back at the farm.' Seeing him hesitate she held out her hand in introduction. 'Sorry. I'm Angahrad Jenkins. I own Sarnafon Farm.'

He took the offered hand, a hand that was he noticed, surprisingly soft and well cared for in a sheep farmer.

'How do you do,' he said climbing in beside her. 'I'm…'

She pre-empted him.

'You are Thomas Hawkhurst, the English grave robber.' Her tone was gently teasing and with the words came a smile that took his breath away. 'Everyone in the valley knows you, Mr Hawkhurst. They say you are a wicked man.'

That night, after she had cooked him dinner and two bottles of good red wine had been drunk, they had become lovers. Within the span of a week their affair was a scandal that totally preoccupied, outraged and infuriated the locals. It was a situation in which they both took a deep and perverse delight. Both isolated and starved of love for so long, they exalted in the physical release they found in each other and the increasingly supportive bonds of friendship that had grown between them.

'So, Tom, what did you do down in London? It must have been important for you rush off like that.' There was no rebuke in her words; their relationship was now based on trust. He glanced at his watch. It was seven thirty. Reaching for the remote control he switched on the small portable television that stood on the dressing table at the foot of the bed. The picture crystallised into Laura's flawless, perfectly made up features.

This morning she was dressed in a green roll neck sweater that clung to every contour of her magnificent figure and a short leather skirt that revealed a seductive expanse of silk-sheathed thigh. Sitting there, casually brushing back her long copper tresses with a careless hand, she contrived to make her interviewer, considered no slouch in the looks department herself, appear positively dowdy.

'What was I doing in London?' Tom pointed to the screen. 'Gallivanting with her – that's what.' He ducked as Angahrad launched a disbelieving pillow in his direction. Laughing, he held up his hands in surrender. 'I'll explain in a minute,' he said. 'I want to listen to this first.'

'Well, Sue,' Laura was saying. 'There's a lot of work to be done yet but it really is one of the most exciting discoveries I've ever been involved with. I see the papers have got hold of the story somehow but a lot of what they are saying is rather premature. 'She held up a copy of *The Guardian* that bore the headline 'King Arthur Returns' in 20 point bold typeface to lend emphasis to her words. 'It really is far too early to be saying things like that,' she cautioned.

'But it is possible?'

'Yes, it's possible, but these things have to be researched thoroughly and scientifically. There's an awful lot of work to be done before we will be able to state categorically that what we have found is

Arthur's grave.' She looked directly at the camera, professional probity and restraint much in evidence. 'And it's wrong to call him King Arthur incidentally, Sue. He was, so far as we can tell from the few written sources we have available to us, more likely to have been a war lord rather than a king.'

Hawkhurst smiled as he heard her paraphrase his own words. It was the same old Laura; never one to miss an opportunity to sound authoritative on a subject – even when she wasn't. She had also said the press had 'somehow' got hold of the story. Twelve hours ago only half a dozen of the museum's directors had known about the finds and none of them would have welcomed the attention they were now receiving. He suspected Laura, with her insatiable need for publicity, was being less than honest. Certainly her hostess had read the early editions with great interest.

'I see the papers are referring to your finding Excalibur and the Holy Grail in the tomb as well,' she said hopefully. 'What do you say to that?'

Laura pursed her lips and gave an enigmatic smile that confirmed nothing but suggested everything.

'The fact is, Sue, both Excalibur and the Grail are medieval embellishments of the original Arthurian legends and have no basis in history. For the time being we are treating them simply as extremely interesting artefacts that will undoubtedly expand our knowledge of the period tremendously.'

'I understand your reticence, Laura,' the interviewer persisted, 'but nevertheless, you must admit it's a remarkable coincidence to find the inscription referring to Arthur, the body and these two fabulous items all in the same tomb. Did you find anything else that might give you and your colleagues some definite clue as to the identity of the skeleton?'

Laura shifted her long legs and reached forward to the low coffee table before her, taking up a handful of full plate black and white photographs which she held up for the viewers to see.

'Yes. There was a steel helmet and a chain mail shirt which we believe belonged to a cavalryman of the Arthurian period.'

'Here,' Laura pointed a pearl nail at the lower edge of the mail shirt, 'where the chain mail would have covered a mounted man's thighs, we found that many of the links were broken. They were probably sheared through by the blade of a seax, the single edged sword which gave Saxons their name. You have to remember that cavalry gave the British tribes a crucial advantage over the Anglo-Saxons. Right up until the Battle of Hastings the English armies almost invariably fought as infantry.' She laid the picture of the shirt aside and now produced an enlarged print of the coin hoard, maybe a hundred coins in all, lying as they were first discovered, scattered in the dry dust of the grave. 'These will, we hope, allow us to fix a very accurate date for the burial. We have an expert on the Dark Ages examining them at the moment. The only problem we have is that after the Romans withdrew from Britain the country slipped back into a barter economy and the minting of coins became a very haphazard business. The Anglo-Saxon kings didn't mint coinage at all until well into the seventh century. In fact the ones we have here weren't intended to be used as money at all. If you look closely you'll see there's a small hole drilled through each one. They were probably threaded on a leather thong and worn as a bracelet or necklace. A preliminary examination of the coins from the grave shows they came from all over Europe and the near East. Some we already know to date back to before the Romans departed. What we are hoping is that some of the more exotic ones can be precisely dated and allow us to pinpoint to within a few years exactly when the burial was carried out.'

'Who's carrying out the dating of the coins, Laura?'

The question was put innocently enough yet Hawkhurst smiled as, almost imperceptibly, Laura hesitated for the first time. 'Come on,' he willed her. 'Tell them now. They probably know anyway. If they find out you're covering up for me they'll crucify you later.' He sighed in relief as she responded.

'We've been lucky enough to retain the services of Tom Hawkhurst, an old friend and an acknowledged specialist in the period we're talking about. If all goes to plan we should have a definitive analysis of the coins and a likely date for the tomb by the end of the month.' Tom waited for some reaction from the interviewer but his name clearly rang no bells as with time running out she began winding up the interview.

'Well, our thanks to archaeologist Laura Woods for coming in and telling us about her discovery of what the press at least are calling the grave of King Arthur. And now we return to the newsroom for the latest reports on the crisis in the Middle East.'

The picture changed and Hawkhurst, his thoughts still with the tomb, traversed 1500 years in the blink of an eye. He briefly stared at an image of black smoke billowing from the viscera of a bomb-devastated bus then switched the television off. He found himself under Angahrad's smiling gaze.

'So is that where you've been, Thomas? Digging up poor old Arthur. What is the matter with you English that you can't leave a poor Welshman in peace?'

He pulled her close, nuzzling his face against the downy warmth of her breasts.

'Believe me Angie, darling. If I never saw another Welshman again it wouldn't bother me in the slightest. But Welsh woman? Ah now that's a totally different matter.'

Laying her cheek on the tousled crown of his head, she wrapped her arms tightly about him and pulled him close, rocking him like a child in her embrace.

'Will it mean you going back to London, Thomas?' she asked softly.

'No, not often, anyway. I've got all the equipment and reference books I need up at the cottage. I might go up to Edinburgh and ask Old Maloney for a second opinion but I doubt it'll be necessary. To tell the truth, from what I've seen so far, even if the coins don't provide proof positive of the date of the burial, I don't see anything in there to say that it isn't Arthur. No, I think that unless something startling and totally unexpected comes from the other pieces we found, or the laboratories come up with some wildly erratic date for the organic finds, Ms Laura Woods, BA, BSc, is going to go down in history as the woman who found the grave of Arthur Pendragon, the Once and Future King of Britain.' He lifted his face and she kissed his eyes.

'No fame for you then, Thomas the grave robber?' she said, almost sadly.

He shrugged indifferently.

'No. No fame for me, but hopefully enough money to pay off the bank and put a deposit on that new tractor.'

As he took her face in his hands and kissed her, the phone jangled to life, and he sighed.

'That, if I'm any judge of human nature,' he said, 'will be the aforesaid Ms Woods to ask if I watched her performance.' It was indeed Laura.

'How do you think it went,' was her first question, 'do you think I played it down sufficiently?'

'Darling you were wonderful,' he teased, as though he were congratulating an actress on a particularly fine performance. 'You even managed to get my name in without bringing the roof down about your ears.' His sarcasm was either lost or ignored.

'It's about that I'm ringing actually, Tom. The office has already had half a dozen calls. They want to know all about your involvement in this thing and some are asking why I selected an archaeologist of – their words, Tom, not mine – of rather dubious reputation to assist in such an important project. I want you to come down to a press conference tomorrow. We're announcing a special 'Age of Arthur' exhibition to be staged at the museum in a couple of months. It's all going to be a bit of a rush, but the museum directors are mad keen to cash in on all the publicity we're getting at the moment. Thanks to the way the press have reacted they reckon it could be bigger than the Tutankhamun exhibition. Properly organised it will certainly be mega a hit at the box office.'

Hawkhurst considered her words.

'How did Dixey take it – my being involved?'

'Well, as you can imagine there were a few noses turned up when I mentioned bringing you in, not least his, but I managed to get their agreement if not their approval for your involvement. Luckily I'm in a pretty strong position on this one and I made it clear that it would be me and only me who decided who should be on the team. I don't have to tell you, Tom, that you've still got some pretty damn fine enemies on the museum board. Anyway they eventually accepted that it was you or no-one, but they have insisted that you're at the press conference tomorrow to fight your own corner if the press turn nasty. If you're serious about re-establishing yourself you'll have to face them sooner or later anyway.' There was a pause, then she said: 'Another thing, I don't want it getting around that we used to sleep together. It wouldn't be good for my image or for the project. If there's any suggestion of the press getting onto personal ground we stamp on it straight away. Agreed?'

Hawkhurst would have clearly loved to bait her a little on the subject of their long ago love, but, aware of Angie's eyes upon him, he let it go. No point to risk creating jealously or doubt where none was warranted. Laura was yesterday.

'Understood. I'll be with you tomorrow morning. What time is the conference?'

'Four-thirty. We're holding a rehearsal at two and there's a wine and cheese reception in the Egyptian Gallery afterwards. I think a collar and tie would be appropriate in the circumstances.' There was a brief pause as she ran through her mental check list. 'Oh, and Tom do try to get a haircut before tomorrow, there's a dear.'

He looked skywards.

'I'll be with you by midday.'

He turned to Angahrad who, seated on the bed, was now pulling on her jeans. If she had got any gist of the conversation she gave no indication.

'Everything all right, Tom?' she asked over her shoulder.

'Perfect. Can you get someone to take care of those bloody sheep of yours for a day or two?'

'I suppose so. Llew, my sister's husband, will keep an eye on things here if I ask. Why?'

'Because I have to go back to London this afternoon and I don't want to go without you. Is that reason enough?'

She beamed, delighted to find that his new found, albeit probably only temporary, fame was not to exclude her.

'Reason enough and more, Thomas the Grave Robber.'

CHAPTER FOUR

Paul Dixey, the museum's Curator General and Head of Antiquities, looked at his watch and then ran a satisfied eye over the noisy bustling hall. At the rear, beyond the crowded benches of chattering pressmen, technicians tinkered amid the electronic clutter of cameras, sound booms, lights and microphones, making final adjustments to their equipment as the clock ticked closer to four thirty. In front of the rostrum, from which Dixey surveyed the seeming chaos with lordly disdain, photographers wandered to and fro amid an electrical storm of flashing, clicking, whirring cameras. Most of their attention, Hawkhurst noticed, was centred on Laura – academia's pin-up girl. In contrast to her earlier television appearance, her dress today was positively chaste, a simple black two piece suit and white blouse that buttoned to the throat. She also sported a pair of suitably studious tortoiseshell spectacles. Tom smiled. Laura had always had twenty-twenty vision. Appropriately she sat to the right of Dixey while he himself had been seated to the left: just like, so they said, the righteous and unrighteous would sit before God.

'Very well, ladies and gentlemen,' Dixey drained his tumbler of water and then rapped its heavy base on the green baize covered rostrum several times. Eventually the chattering faded to nothing and the fidgeting stilled. 'It's now a little after four-thirty so I suggest we begin.'

He was a tall, austere man in his mid-sixties with a high domed head that was almost devoid of hair. Loops of slack lizard skin hung at his scrawny jowls and the humourless eyes behind the gold half-framed glasses were the colour of faded denim. When the shit had hit the fan in Armenia, Dixey had been in the vanguard of those who had not only demanded that Hawkhurst be dismissed but had also campaigned vigorously for criminal charges to be brought against him. At the rehearsal earlier, their first encounter in three years, he had already made it crystal clear that he did not relish sharing a public stage with Tom one iota. All this was put aside as the bleak features broke into a wintry smile of greeting to the great unwashed of the press. Here they were: arrayed expectantly like swine awaiting the pearls to be scattered before them.

'I think the best way for us to conduct this press conference will be for Ms Woods, who I'm sure needs no introduction from me, to give you a brief update on the current state of our excavations at the Whitenditch site. You should all have been provided with a fairly comprehensive press pack when you arrived and afterwards we'll throw the floor open to allow her and Dr Hawkhurst to answer any questions you might have.' He peered over his glasses, his mien challenging, wanting no doubts about his own pre-eminence among the presiding trinity. 'Any general questions regarding the museum's plans for the exhibits or about our long term policy should be directed to me.' Removing his watch he laid it on the table, perhaps to emphasise just how valuable his time was. 'I think an hour and a half should give us plenty of opportunity to cover our subject adequately after which you are all invited to join us for drinks and a light buffet in the Egyptian Gallery where we will be available to answer any further questions you may have.'

*****

The Egyptian Gallery was abuzz. The conference had gone fantastically well and Laura, media star that she undoubtedly was, had shone especially brightly. She had charmed and educated her audience. She had seduced and informed and entranced. More importantly, she had, without ever once making any unreasonable claims about her discovery, ensured that come tomorrow morning the general public would be clamouring for more. By the end of the session she had them eating out of her hand.

The attendance had been gratifyingly broad-based, with representatives of all the British nationals, tabloid and broadsheets, attending as well as all the major TV channels. The extent of the media's fascination with Laura was emphasised when one journalist, who identified herself as the fashion editor of one of the women's glossies, rose to her feet and enquired, apparently quite seriously, as to what the well-dressed archaeologist would be wearing that year. Never putting a foot wrong, Laura had treated the question with a respect that it eminently did not deserve, not the least hint of sarcasm in her voice.

'Watch my next series.'

There had been only one potentially awkward moment. It had come when the man from *The Clarion* had questioned Tom's presence on the project. The man was weasel-faced with a whining Midlands accent and, perhaps, an eye on the editor's chair. So far as he was concerned it was sleaze not history that sold papers.

'Weren't you, Mr Hawkhurst,' he had asked, 'weren't you once kicked out of this museum for stealing artefacts from graves in Russia?'

Tom felt his face redden yet kept a firm grip on his temper, even managing a convincing smile. He had been expecting something like this and was prepared.

'Actually it was Armenia, not Russia, but yes I'm afraid that is partially true.' He threw a mock-rueful sidelong glance at Dixey. 'I departed the employ of this noble institution at the unanimous insistence of the board of directors just over three years ago. However, and I do hope that in your tireless search for truth and justice you'll find space in your magnificent organ to print this, I can only repeat what I said at the time. If I hadn't smuggled those artefacts out of the country they would have been lost to the world of science forever. They would, like so much else of what we excavated, have been melted down to line the pockets of corrupt officials.' Surprised to find himself on the defensive, the man from *The Clarion* made to sit down but straightened up again as Tom persisted. 'Another thing I'd like you to print is that, not only did I lose my job and my reputation, I never made or expected to make a penny piece out of my actions. My concern was purely for the safety of priceless works of art and in the same circumstances I would do the same again I'm afraid. I may have been a smuggler – I was not a thief.'

To Tom's surprise a light flutter of applause ran round the hall and *The Clarion* reporter took the opportunity to sit quickly down, suddenly concentrating hard on his notes and somewhat discomfited. It would appear Tom still had some friends left in the press, a legacy of the days when as a quite junior field officer he had actively encouraged the demystification of archaeology and issued information on a scale unheard of before. It had been a policy that Dixey and his contemporaries, keen to preserve an arcane mystique, had thoroughly disapproved of. Sensing a certain criticism of the museum creeping in here, and irked that not a single question had thus far been directed at him, the Curator General elected to enter the debate at this stage.

'So far as the museum is concerned we have every faith in Dr Hawkhurst's professional capabilities. He is an acknowledged expert on the Arthurian period and his record speaks for itself. However, in this excavation his participation was invited by my colleague Ms Woods without reference to the directors of the museum and his role, from our point of view, is simply that of a consultant retained by her.' He paused, the next words did not come easily. 'Having made that point I feel I should add that I believe his contribution to the project has already been substantial and will continue to be so.'

He sat down, his gaze sweeping the floor for any further questions that this statement might have engendered. There were none.

'In that case ladies and gentlemen I suggest we adjourn to the more comfortable surroundings of the Egyptian Gallery.'

*****

Taking a glass of red wine that he knew from past experience would be an insult to the palate; Tom cast his eyes around the long marble-walled gallery. The press sidled into the room and formed themselves up into little defensive groups. By now they were largely weary of archaeology and more interested in passing judgement on the museum's largesse. For the occasion the exhibits usually on show in the gallery had been removed and in their place stood five glass display cases containing the inscribed slab that had covered the grave, the sword, the helmet, mail shirt and the bowl. By each case stood a massive uniformed security man.

Despite the almost unseemly haste with which they had been transferred from the tomb to the museum the exhibits had been expertly presented. Each mounted on rich blue velvet they lay beneath carefully positioned spotlights that highlighted the blue-white sheen of the metal and contrasting roughness of the granite. As he stood admiring the bowl, still trying to formulate some convincing scenario for its presence in the tomb, the unmistakable nasal tones of a born and bred New Yorker shattered his reverie.

'Do you believe we're looking upon the actual Holy Grail, Dr Hawkhurst?'

He turned to find himself looking into the deepest brown – perhaps they were black – eyes he had ever seen. She held out her hand in introduction.

'Hi, Mary Lou Berkowitz – I'm the editor of *The Neo-Christian Review*.'

It was not a publication he had heard of but he smiled as if he had. She was an attractive woman, somewhere in her early forties, he guessed. Fully as tall as he was, six foot plus and strongly built, she was nevertheless dressed and coiffured with sufficient style to present an aura of sophisticated if somewhat beefy femininity.

He returned his gaze to the bowl, reflecting that her presence there was an indication of the depth of international interest in the finds. It was also, to his mind, a rather worrying measure of the quasi-religious mystique that was building up around them. Nevertheless, within days, thanks to the fertile imaginations of Fleet Street hacks, people like Mary Lou here were prepared to travel thousands of miles to see them. It augured well for the coming exhibition but represented dangerous ground for a scientist like himself. He addressed her initial question.

'It's highly unlikely. So far as we can tell at this stage it dates from the Bronze Age. To my best knowledge the only other examples that even remotely resemble this one were found in the Balkans a few years ago. They were dated, with a fair measure of confidence, to the early sixth century BC. How or why this example ended up in the grave of a British warrior who lived and died a thousand years later is something of a mystery.'

She appeared not to hear, her eyes remaining fixed on the bowl. It had been carefully cleaned since he had last seen it and with its perfect symmetry and the exquisite modelling of the rim it seemed, even to him, to radiate an unearthly aura. It was difficult to think of it as ancient; it might have been fashioned only yesterday.

'Just to think,' she murmured, 'that it would once have held the precious blood of Christ our Saviour.' She shook her head, as though annoyed at letting herself being beguiled by her dreams. 'Tell me. How much would the museum want for it do you think?'

For a moment he thought it was her idea of a joke but soon saw the dark eyes were totally devoid of humour.

'It's a national treasure, Ms Berkowitz,' he explained gently, fearing he had some mildly deranged weirdo on his hands. 'The museum, or whoever the courts eventually decide has legal claim to it, would never consider selling it. It's priceless.'

'Come on Dr Hawkhurst.' It was her turn to patronise. 'You and I both know that in this world everything's for sale and everything has its price.'

With this she drifted away in the direction of the sword and he gratefully made his way back towards the increasingly noisy little group of pressmen now laying siege to Laura. They were clearly excited at having cornered the star of the show and she, equally fired up, was playing up to them in no uncertain fashion. At his approach she took his arm and smilingly drew him to the centre of the group.

'Now here's the man to ask about the coins,' she told the circle of journalists. 'How is the research going, Tom?'

He hastily swallowed a morsel of cheese and gathered his thoughts.

'Well, I've identified and dated about ninety percent of them. The Roman and Romano-British ones can all be identified with some confidence as originating from between roughly 240 and 450 BC. The remainder seem to have come from a wide range of sources. Coins from Byzantium, Scandinavia and central Europe all appear in the hoard. There are also several which have no precedent so far as I have been able to ascertain thus far – they may not even be coins at all but simply decorative baubles.'

Laura was playing the perfect hostess now, pouring wine for her guests and handing round canapés. The spectacles had disappeared now and the blouse had a couple of buttons unfastened. She put her next question without looking at him, concentrating on filling the man from *The Clarion's* glass.

'Someone was asking if any of your findings suggested a non-Arthurian date for the grave or invalidated the early sixth century date we've tentatively ascribed to it?'

The question was put innocently enough yet he saw within it a clever ploy designed to build up the Arthur hype for the benefit of the news-hungry assembly. He did not want to be drawn into the realms of conjecture and attempted to stall.

'No, I've found nothing so far that suggests it's anything but a very late Romano-British burial. However, that doesn't necessarily mean …'

His words trailed to nothing as Laura moved briskly off towards the exhibits, drawing the majority of her doting audience with her. Only the man from *The Clarion* remained, a heaped paper plate of canapés in one hand and a glass of wine in the other, he jerked his head towards the departing Laura.

'Quite a woman,' he observed absently, 'Looks and brains – I bet she has dozens of men chasing after her. It would make a nice human interest angle to the story. I don't suppose you know if she's seeing anybody on a steady basis?' The ferret eyes looked to Hawkhurst for confirmation or, better still, comment. For the second time that afternoon he was to be disappointed. Tom smiled sweetly.

'Why don't you crawl away and screw yourself?'

At seven that evening, when only the alcoholic hard core of the press contingent remained, Hawkhurst made his excuses and prepared to depart. He had promised to lunch with Dixey and Laura the following day when they would discuss the next moves in promoting the coming exhibition. Before he left Laura had taken him to one side, her tone confidential.

'I noticed you talking to Mary Lou Berkowitz earlier. What did she want?' He smiled inwardly at her interest, she so desperately wanted to have her finger on every pulse.

'Nothing very exciting. I think she's a nutter. She was talking about buying the bowl the way you and I might talk about buying a second-hand car. Did she approach you too then?'

'Yes. She was talking in very much the same vein. Wanted to know who she should negotiate with.' Tom shrugged dismissively, this merely underlining his assessment of Mary Lou Berkowitz as a very naïve religious crank. He smiled wearily.

'She didn't make you an offer did she?'

Laura smiled.

'As a matter of fact she did in a roundabout way. It wasn't one that involved the bowl though.'

He blinked, uncomprehendingly.

'How do you mean?'

She ran her fingers through her hair, pouting seductively as a lingering photographer moved in for a final close up.

'Tom, darling, take it from me. Whatever else that woman may be she's also the biggest dyke since Offa's.'

*****

When he returned to the hotel, a modest, two star establishment in Russell Square that he had chosen because it was both reasonably cheap and convenient for the museum, Angahrad was waiting for him in the lounge. Around her were ranged bags and parcels that suggested a shopping spree of monumental proportions. She smiled as, first planting a kiss on her cheek, he sat down opposite her.

'I thought you'd deserted me, Thomas,' she said pointing to the glass of Chablis before her, 'this is my second.'

'Sorry my love, the reception just dragged on and on. Never mind, I'm here now and all set to eat.' Taking a tentative sip of wine he took in the mound of shopping arranged about her feet. 'How was Oxford Street?'

She drew down the corners of her mouth, recalling the milling crowds. People of every race on earth pushing and jostling, each man's unsmiling eyes fixed ahead of him. In London, she thought, everyone was an alien.

'I'd forgotten how shabby it is – there were drunks and beggars everywhere – and the litter! I went on to Knightsbridge too. That wasn't much better. There was a demonstration outside Harrods, Arabs I think.'

He nodded. Angahrad was well educated and sophisticated to a degree but she would never be a city person.

'It's not the nicest of places, I know, but it does have some advantages.' He indicated the bags. 'Let's take all this up to the room and then grab a cab. We're booked into the Rooftop for eight-thirty – I hope you haven't eaten there before, it's meant to be a surprise.'

'No, it sounds lovely. Oh, I almost forgot, there's a message for you at reception. They wouldn't let me give it to you – said it was marked strictly for your attention only.'

He frowned, perhaps Laura wanted something.

'OK. You take the stuff to the room and I'll see what it's all about. Meet you back here in five minutes.'

The desk clerk, a plump, pink faced young man with eyes that would not have been out of place in a pig sty, was fully occupied trying to explain to a Japanese couple the quickest way to Leicester Square. Despite the fact that their destination was no more than a brisk ten minutes' walk away it was a performance that took almost as long. Notwithstanding its thoroughness it left Hawkhurst with the distinct impression that the couple were destined to fetch up in the suburbs of Irkutsk. As happy, if ill-advised, they went on their way the clerk turned his cherubic, glad-to-be-of-service, smile upon him.

'I think there's a message for me. The name's Hawkhurst.'

'Ah, yes, Dr Hawkhurst,' he spun on his heels to face the pigeonholed wall behind him, 'that's right. In fact, if I'm not mistaken, there's been a second message from the lady since. Now let me see. No, that's not yours, nor that. Ah yes, here we are.' He lay them on the desk: two pink, hand addressed envelopes upon which the clerk had neatly written the time of receipt. Heading back to his table Tom ripped the first missive open as he went.

'Dear Dr Hawkhurst,' it read. 'Following our necessarily brief conversation at the press conference this afternoon it occurred to me that, if you were available, we might usefully get together with a view to discussing the possibility of your producing an article for my magazine. It would, I am sure, be of great interest to our readers and might also, from your point of view, provide a useful vehicle for promoting the coming exhibition. We would, of course, be prepared to pay our standard rate for such an article. This is currently set at 600 US dollars per thousand words. We would be looking for a length of around three thousand words which would mean a fee of eighteen hundred dollars (approximately eleven hundred pounds Sterling at the current exchange rate) plus all reasonable expenses. Please ring me at the number below at your earliest convenience. Kind regards, Mary Lou Berkowitz.'

As he tore open the second envelope, Tom's head was buzzing. Eleven hundred pounds for a single article – an article he could put together in a day – was like manna from heaven. As he scanned the second message his embryonic smile matured into a broad grin.

'Dear Dr Hawkhurst,' the second message read. 'On consideration and in light of the importance of the subject, I feel we could possibly stretch to two thousand dollars for the article. Must speak this evening. Depart for Gethsemane tomorrow morning. Please make contact soonest possible. Kind regards Mary Lou.'

Since Angahrad had still not returned he went directly to the phone booth and rang the number given on the letters. The receiver at the other end was snatched up with such alacrity that he could only assume Mary Lou had been standing right next to it when he rang. Her tone, however, was quite relaxed.

'Hi, Tom, thanks for ringing. Obviously you got my message. Look, it's getting late; can you get a cab over right away? We could discuss the deal over dinner. I fly out tomorrow so I need to get this tied up tonight.'

'Sure. There's only one minor problem. I've got my friend with me, a lady. Can I bring her along?'

'Of course. The more the merrier.'

'Right. We'll be with you in about half an hour – no later than nine at the outside.'

In high spirits he beckoned a waiter and ordered a half bottle of Moet. When Angahrad appeared, having affected a complete change of clothes and looking to his admittedly slightly euphoric eye a million dollars, the contents had diminished appreciably.

'Sorry if I've kept you waiting,' she said, 'but I thought the occasion called for something special.' She turned slowly before him. 'What do you think?'

Without taking his eyes of her he poured out another glass of Champagne. Rarely out of jeans at home, to see her in the simple black cocktail number, a band of sable velvet about her slim white neck, was a revelation. She was absolutely lovely. Already high on his current streak of good fortune and a little drunk, her appearance brought a lump to his throat.

'Sit down,' he said gruffly, 'people are looking at you.'

She smiled, familiar now with his English unwillingness to express any deeper feelings and knowing instinctively that he approved beyond words. Sitting down she sipped at the Champagne.

'So, where was it you said we are going?'

He hesitated, trying to assess how she might react to the news of dinner with Mary Lou Berkowitz.

'Well, there's been a slight change of plan. Instead of the Rooftop, we're dining at the Ritz. That's the good news – I'll tell you the bad news while we're getting there.'

CHAPTER FIVE

'You simply cannot imagine the thrill it was this afternoon, to gaze upon the Holy Chalice.' As she spoke Mary Lou scooped the few remaining shreds of lobster from the scarlet carapace set before her, briefly eyeing the pink flesh before savaging it with undisguised relish. Her tongue ranged over glossy lips to ensure no elusive morsel had escaped.

Despite the scanty evidence and Tom continuing to urge caution in any interpretation of the finds, it was obvious that no doubt remained in her mind. 'The instant I laid eyes on the glorious Grail I was spiritually uplifted. I knew, I just knew, I was in the presence of the Lord.' She lifted her eyes to the heavens, hands raised in oration. 'Blessed are the eyes which see the things ye see: for I tell you that many prophets have desired to see the things which ye see and have not seen them.' She reached for a toothpick, adding briefly: 'Luke 23.'

In the chandeliered elegance of the restaurant a string quartet played Bach and the conversation from the tables about them was a warm, convivial murmur.

Hawkhurst looked up to find Angahrad's gaze upon him, questioning and perhaps a little embarrassed by this middle-aged, perhaps menopausal, woman's ravings. Luckily, amid the noise and bustle of the crowded restaurant, her performance went largely unnoticed. It was, he judged, time to get down to business – he was only here to make some badly needed money.

'What's your deadline for the article, Mary Lou?'

With casual ease she cracked open another massive claw, probing deeply and with real interest while considering his question. She drew forth a succulent gobbet of meat with a smile of triumph and thrust it home. Eating was something Mary Lou was good at.

'I guess so long as we have it by the end of the month it'll be soon enough.' She pushed her plate aside. 'I've been thinking, Tom. Why don't you bring it over to the States when it's ready? I reckon I could fix for you to give a couple of lectures while you were over if you were interested. They pay pretty well.' She looked to Angahrad and Hawkhurst recalled Laura's assessment of her sexual preferences.

'Perhaps you could come too, my dear. I'm sure you'd just love Gethsemane.'

Angahrad frowned.

'Gethsemane? I thought that was in Israel.'

Mary Lou lay aside the cutlery, not something she did lightly, her eyes serious.

'Good heavens, no, Gethsemane, Wyoming it's our headquarters. First Fortress of the Church of Christ the Warrior. You mean you've never heard of us?' She sounded genuinely surprised at this demonstration of ignorance. 'Sherman County, Wyoming, US of A. We laid the first stone out there in the foothills just fifteen years ago. Today it's a community of forty thousand. Forty thousand storm troopers in the host of the Almighty. Around the world our legions number millions.'

Before she could launch herself into the evangelical tirade that the slightly deranged gleam in her eye threatened, the waiter was at the table removing the wrecked crustacean and laying a massive steak in front of her. It was enough to stem the flood, but only temporarily. Sawing at the near raw flesh she returned eagerly to her subject.

'Surely you must have heard of the Reverend James J Whichelow.'

Hawkhurst frowned, thinking hard.

'Whichelow? Whichelow? Yes I think I have. Didn't he set up a commune down in Honduras or somewhere like that a few years ago? I thought the Government expelled him for advocating the use of brainwashing techniques on rich kids he'd lured away from their families.' Becoming aware that Mary Lou might consider these observations about her spiritual leader offensive and having no desire to bite any hand that promised to feed him so handsomely, Tom backtracked. 'Of course, I guess it was only rumours.'

'Worse than rumours, Tom,' she hissed, her black eyes burning as she laid a big hand on his arm. 'Lies. The Reverend is a good and saintly man and an instrument of the Lord but just like the prophets and disciples of old he has Satan's forces arrayed against him.' She took a long pull at her wine. 'Why don't you come to Gethsemane and see for yourself? Reverend Whichelow would welcome you with open arms I know. He sent me here on a special mission to see the Holy Grail with my own eyes and report back as to whether it was genuine.

I have already told him that there is, in my mind at least, no doubt but that it is. I know he will want to meet you.'

Feeling uncomfortable, he held up a restraining hand as he carefully chose his next words. The last thing he wanted in these surroundings was a deep and meaningful theosophical debate.

'The Grail doesn't appear in Arthurian literature until the end of the twelfth century, Mary Lou. I don't think I could ever in all good faith present the bowl we found as anything other than a very fine example of Bronze Age metallurgy. The idea of mystical bowls is older than Christianity anyway – chalices and cauldrons possessed of occult powers feature regularly in pagan Celtic and Norse mythology.'

As a scientist he felt uneasy enough to find himself talking about religious relics in such airy terms, the more so with this clearly neurotic woman. She however was now up and running and not in the least inclined to accept that what she had seen that afternoon was anything other than the Holy Grail. Presumably by the same token she accepted the sword as Excalibur and the skeleton as the mortal remains of King Arthur. Faith might move mountains, he reflected, but in the case of Mary Lou and others of her kind it was equally effective in eliminating logical thought processes. Almost as if she read his thoughts she smiled at him: the smile a Victorian missionary might bestow upon some poor benighted heathen.

'Tom, I understand your reservations. I know you're a scientist and that therefore it's not easy for you to accept things which to those of us who have found the path to true enlightenment shine forth so clear. Believe me, Tom, I'm not some crazy woman – I've thought it all out very carefully. There's nothing in what you say about the bowl that in anyway invalidates its status as the Holy Grail – the sacred cup that held the blood of Christ crucified.'

He stared at her, depressingly aware by now that nothing he could ever say or do would change her mind. She continued to argue her case.

'The bowl, you say, dates to perhaps five hundred years before our Saviour walked the earth. You also say similar finds have been excavated by the time of the New Testament. Joseph of Arimathea, the wealthy Jew who took the body of Christ down from the cross was in the tin trade in Cornwall. It was he who brought the Grail to Britain, to Glastonbury, in the first century. Everyone knows that Glastonbury was once known as Avalon and that Arthur spent much time there. Naturally he would have carried the Grail with him on his campaigns – it's all so obvious.'

He was sorely tempted to correct her in no uncertain manner, to tell her that, far from being historically verifiable, virtually everything she was postulating had no basis in fact whatsoever. One look at the wrapt features told him he would be wasting his breath. Her gaze fluttered to the heavens again. 'Mine eyes have seen the glory of the coming of the Lord.'

Turning his attention to the food before him, Hawkhurst began to eat with rather more urgency than before. Obviously there was nothing more to be said that might change her mind and he was not in the business of acting as Devil's advocate when he might make good money. Just be thankful for the work he told himself and try to get away as soon as possible. However, she had not finished with him yet. She laid her knife and fork aside.

'I've been so impressed with what I've seen over here, Tom, not least by your own frankness, that I emailed a lengthy report to the Reverend Whichelow earlier this evening. I suggested that apart from the articles you've already agreed to write, you might be persuaded to make a couple of live appearances on TVCW to talk about the Grail and the other finds.'

'TVCW?'

'We have our own TV station at Gethsemane, we broadcast to most of the mid-west and west coast states. We also have satellite stations in the Caribbean and Latin America. Fighting the Lord's battles we know the value of a hearts and minds campaign. If you were to come over in a week or so's time we could guarantee you a couple of hour long programmes on prime time. You'd be reaching maybe a hundred million people – and maybe ten times that number if we were to syndicate the shows with other networks. Matter of fact, I spoke to the Reverend on the phone just before you arrived. He thinks it'd be a great idea.'

Hawkhurst shook his head. He had no desire to be used by a bunch of evangelising crackpots.

'Thanks Mary Lou. It's very tempting and I appreciate the offer but I don't think it would be right for me to get involved. I respect your beliefs, of course, but there's no way I'd be prepared to say that what we found was the Holy Grail. Despite all the excitement in the press I'm still not personally convinced that the tomb has anything to do with the Arthur legend at all.'

'You wouldn't be expected to say anything that you weren't happy with, Tom. All you have to do is talk about the 'finds', as you call them, with the Reverend as openly and honestly as you have with me. He will respect your position as a scientist absolutely and guarantees that nothing will be expected of you that might compromise your reputation or professional integrity.'

Hawkhurst considered her proposal. The prospect of a week to be spent in the company of Mary Lou and a bunch of like-minded religious cranks did not appeal. Even so, he had to admit that the opportunity to reach such a vast audience was a tempting prospect. The whole reason for Laura bringing him in the first place was to re-establish his currently badly tarnished reputation. These days there was only one possible way to effectively achieve that and it was via the media. Wasn't Laura herself living proof of that? Even as he weighed up the situation Mary Lou sensed he was weakening and chose the moment to deploy her most effective weapon.

'Although as followers of the risen Christ we embrace the principles of poverty and chastity, we are not a poor Church, Tom. In the ranks of our army we have many wealthy followers of our Lord's campaigns. I've got Reverend Whichelow's approval to offer you $10,000 plus expenses for two TV appearances. We'd be delighted if you'd bring Angahrad here along too. I'm sure she'd find it a most enlightening experience.'

He had almost capitulated, not least if he were honest, because of the money, yet he wanted to retain some semblance of independence. It wouldn't do to appear over-eager. Angahrad remained silent, knowing just how precarious Hawkhurst's finances were and what the money would mean. Finally he nodded.

'All right I'll do it. I have to finish my work on the coins first, but I guess that won't take more than a few days now.' He smiled. If not completely at ease with the situation he was glad to have taken a definite decision. He doubted Dixey would like it much but that was just too bad. Whatever else, his career was, it seemed, on the up-and-up again. 'OK, Mary Lou, you've got yourself a deal. Providing, that is, I have your assurance that I am only expected to speak as an archaeologist and that you understand from the outset that I firmly believe that the finds have no relevance to the scriptures, or for that matter to the Arthurian legends, whatsoever. I remain a sceptic and will be talking as such.'

Delighted to have won him over, Mary Lou, couldn't have cared less about his position. She beamed as she filled up their glasses and raised her own in a toast.

'Congratulations, Tom. You've made a decision you won't regret.' She glanced at her watch: it was nearly eleven. 'We'll make all your travel arrangements from Gethsemane and advise you accordingly. Now I'm afraid I really must be going – my flight out is at eight tomorrow morning so I better grab some shuteye.' He stood up as, a little unsteadily, she rose to her feet and shook his hand, going round the table to plant a chaste farewell kiss on a somewhat surprised Angahrad's cheek. 'I do so look forward to showing you Gethsemane, my dear.' She said, her hands lying lightly on the girl's bare shoulders, 'I think you will be impressed by what we have accomplished and how much more we hope to achieve in the future.'

As she disappeared across the crowded restaurant floor Angahrad reached for the wine, a hand to her mouth to stifle slightly tipsy laughter.

'Well, Thomas. I was obliged to attend chapel until my eighteenth birthday but in all my time I don't think I've seen God bothering brought to so fine a state of the art as that.'

'What do you think?'

She grew serious, a little afraid to see how the discovery of the grave was, so soon, pulling him away from Sarnafon but knowing he must follow his star.

'I think you are right to make the most of her offer. It's a chance to earn good money and to get back into the swing of things.' She reached across the table and grasped his hand. 'I love you, Thomas, and no one is gladder than I that you came to the valley. But you don't belong there. You must get back into the real world.'

'If I do it will only be on the understanding that you come with me.'

'We'll talk about that when you come back from Gethsemane.'

'But you heard what she said. You're invited too.'

'Unfortunately, five hundred blackface sheep and twenty Friesian cows weren't – goodness, just think of the mess they'd make on a 747.' She shook her head. 'They can't feed themselves, Tom, and I can't impose on Llew again, he's got his own farm to run. No, you must go alone and when you get back we'll talk about the future.' Leaning forward she kissed him, her lips warm on his. 'Now, don't you think we should be getting back to the hotel? We don't want to waste that beautiful, big bed do we?'

*****

Laura lay back in the deep armchair, towelling robe wrapped about her, as Dixey's tall spare figure appeared framed in the soft light of the bedroom door. It had not been a successful evening and sensing his mood she was at pains to put him at his ease.

'Do you want me to stay?' she asked gently as he dropped wearily into the chair opposite her, fussily tucking the folds of his dressing gown about his skinny knees. He smiled bitterly.

'I don't think so. I don't think I'm going to rise to the occasion tonight despite all your best efforts. I suppose I just have to accept the passage of the years. At sixty four you can't do what you could at thirty.'

He looked so old and defeated, she thought.

'Nonsense, you're just tired. It's been a long day for all of us.' She smiled reassuringly. 'I bet even Tom Hawkhurst is knackered after this afternoon's session.'

Dixey frowned, this mention of Hawkhurst not improving his mood.

'I sometimes wonder if it was wise to involve Hawkhurst in this, Laura. You have your reputation to think of and I have the museum's image to protect. Collaborating with a thief, does us no good at all so far as publicity is concerned. I'm sure you haven't forgotten that Whitford retires from the board of directors in three months? With your track record and the exhibition under your belt, there's no doubt that you'll be elected to take his place. Think of it, my dear, the youngest director ever to sit on the board and first woman. You've got an awful lot to lose.'

She was never sure if his smouldering resentment of Hawkhurst was genuinely born of a concern for her and the museum's reputation or a more basic sexual jealously. Theirs was a strange relationship and one that they had taken every precaution against becoming public knowledge. Indeed, given the potential danger to both of their careers Dixey often pondered why she had countenanced such an ill matched liaison in the first place. Before the final demise of her relationship with Sujic she had made a point of confiding in Dixey about the unhappy state of her private life. He had assumed initially that she saw in him, a man even older than the straying Sujic, a convenient shoulder to cry on and had been duly flattered. However, it had not been long before he began toying with the at once ludicrous yet thrilling idea that she might find him attractive at a physical level too. After much heart searching and many sleepless nights he had revealed his feelings.

It had not been an easy step for him to take, his age and position in the scheme of things, not least in the hierarchy of the museum, making him very vulnerable. His joy then had been boundless when, one bleak mid-winter evening she had come to his bed and revived passions he had long relinquished all hopes of experiencing again. Although he was no longer physically in his prime, her practised skill and inventiveness, aided by a deal of patience, had succeeded in reviving and sustaining a level of sexual activity that exceeded his wildest dreams. With his joy, however, had also come jealousy and a quiet despair as he came to terms with the unavoidable conclusion that he did not, could not, fulfil her needs.

The forthcoming election for a director to replace the retiring Whitford had been a useful lever, he thought, to unconsciously focus her mind on the position he was in to advance her career. His mention of it now was scarcely needed, however, for the matter was seldom out of Laura's thoughts. She had seen, well over a year ago, that by working her way into the lonely old academic's life, by making herself essential to him in a way no woman had in years, she was as good as on the board already. A few more months and she could get on with her life. She stood up and went across to him, settling herself on the thick sheepskin rug before the flickering gas fire, her head resting on his knee.

'You mustn't worry about Tom. I only brought him into this because he's the acknowledged expert on the period. Who else could have reacted so quickly? The only other possible candidate was Karelian and he's in the States at the moment. I had to act quickly if we were to get maximum publicity.' Her hand caressed his bony knee, sliding up beneath the folds of his dressing gown. 'Tom will do exactly what we tell him and no more. We are the ones who will make the important decisions. When we see him tomorrow everything will be spelt out chapter and verse. He's simply an adviser on this project.' Her hand was now cupping his unresponsive genitals and she smiled up at him as she gently massaged him, pulling back the flaccid flesh. 'Don't worry,' she breathed huskily. 'Everything is under control. Relax.'

The bathrobe slipped easily from her shoulders and he laid his head on the back of the leather chair, his gaze fixed on the ceiling as her magic began to work.

'There, you see it's coming, darling. You just need to relax.' She took his liver spotted hand and lay it on her breast, twisting its soft, heavy warmth deeper into the skeletal, almost claw like grip. 'Mm, that's nice,' she encouraged. 'I love it when you do that.'

Tugging at the cord of his dressing gown she pulled it open, kissing the shrivelled belly and sagging breasts in a fair representation of aroused passion while he continued to stare upwards, desperately willing his body not to fail him again. She looked into his lined features, reading his thoughts and knowing she would have to bring him off quickly or not at all that night. Running a moist tongue across her lips she knelt back to take his organ, the familiar sour smell of his groin on her nostrils. To his joy and her relief, with practised and unhurried skill she once more succeeded, as so often before when he had given up hope, in summoning at least a semblance of an erection and bringing him to his climax. When she looked at him there were tears glistening on the lined cheeks and she kissed his forehead gently.

'There,' she said, 'now you'll sleep well.'

Outside, in the darkness of the Holland Park mews where Dixey lived, Laura smoothed her hair in the driving mirror. It had been a long night and she felt tired. Also she found herself thinking about Hawkhurst. Six months with Dixey, a weary old man who nine times out of ten could only be satisfied orally was leaving her frustrated and fretful. She remembered Tom's lovemaking, long hot foreign nights spent under canvas, luxuriating in the thought of his powerful and tireless body. How much, she thought, how much she envied the anonymous Angie.

CHAPTER SIX

'Just exactly what is it you are trying to say, Dixey?' Hawkhurst's words were loud enough to turn heads fifty yards away down the thronging King's Road, way beyond the confines of the pavement bistro where the three of them sat at what had become, in short order, a very contentious lunch date. Worried Latin eyes exchanged glances as waiters, sensing impending violence, stiffened their resolve or sought the shelter of the kitchens.

'What I'm saying, Hawkhurst, seems plain enough to me. However, since you seem to be having trouble comprehending plain English, I'll spell it out for you.' Dixey's voice was cold but rock steady. 'There is no way that the museum will allow you to appear on TV, whatever it's called, or any other half-baked American network for that matter, before the exhibition opens in the summer.'

Aware of the attention he was attracting, Hawkhurst lowered his voice a decibel or two although he remained adamant.

'What you seem to forget, Dixey, is that I don't work for you or your precious museum. As you were at such pains to point out yesterday, I'm employed as an independent consultant by Laura here. What I decide to do is no concern of yours or any of the other brain dead geriatrics who make up the board.'

'Laura is an employee of the museum and as her employee you are bound by the same terms of contract as she is.'

Hawkhurst, relaxed now, stared across at the older man, a smile of patent disbelief on his face.

'You'll be hard put to find a lawyer who can make that stand up in court, Dixey. The way I see it the museum doesn't, as yet, have any valid claim on the finds. It's treasure trove – it might belong to the farmer on whose land it was found, or the museum or the crown. Until that's decided in the courts you certainly don't have any more control over my writing or talking on the subject than you had over those press hacks yesterday.' He sipped at his beer, eyes defiant as he kept them fixed unblinkingly on his blustering opponent. Dixey, outraged yet well aware that his position was not all that strong, tried another approach.

'Look at it from our point of view. America is a crucial area for our marketing of this thing. We're already negotiating with the Metropolitan for them to take the exhibition for six months next year. We must have control of our media output. If you appear on a tu'penny ha'penny network like TVCW you'll be lessening the authority of the museum and undermining a very expensive PR programme. It could cost us millions in the long run.' He gave a snort of disgust. 'For God's sake, Laura, you try to talk to him.'

Laura's words were low and reasonable. She knew from experience Tom's resistance to pressure, especially when it came from establishment figures like Dixey, a man who, had with casual and self-righteous glee, destroyed his career. Nevertheless, this news of his proposed trip to the States had come as something of a surprise to her. As Dixey had already pointed out at some length, the museum was on the point of signing a £50,000 contract with one of the major marketing companies for a carefully structured public relations exercise that would boost revenue by at least twenty times that amount.

'It could be awkward, Tom, if you started giving lectures even before we've compiled our final report on the Whitenditch finds. OK, I know I've been on TV and radio almost every day since we opened up the grave, but we all know you're a sceptic about the whole thing. That's your privilege, but if you go over there rubbishing the whole idea of this being Arthur's grave even before we've properly analysed the evidence it could mean the people at Metropolitan thinking they can get the exhibition at a cut rate.'

He leant back in his seat, marshalling his words, wanting her to understand that what he was proposing was no threat to her plans.

'I'm not going over there to rubbish the idea, Laura. That's the whole point. I'm just going to give a factual account of the finds and fill in the background with a broad historical and social perspective of the period. So far as I can see the people who have invited me over have already made up their minds that they are, beyond all doubt, the genuine article. You spoke to Mary Lou Berkowitz yourself, Jesus, I couldn't persuade her that the bowl is anything but the Holy Grail or for that matter that the sword might not be Excalibur. They're a bunch of harmless religious cranks who've already made up their minds on the subject. Look, if it will make you feel any happier, I'll give you a personal undertaking not to pass judgement or make any statement on the authenticity of the stuff. You have my word on that.'

He looked at her, confident that she knew him well enough to accept his assurance and she nodded in acceptance of his promise. His words, however, only drew a dismissive snort from Dixey.

'Your word, Hawkhurst? Your word? What good is the word of an acknowledged thief? You go ahead with this and I promise you the museum's solicitors will sue you for every penny you've got. The legal position may be unclear at present but you can rest assured the finds will inevitably come to the museum either by gift or purchase. Any losses we incur....' His words trailed off to nothing as Tom threw back his chair and, hands on the table, leant menacingly over him.

'Dixey, if you were twenty years younger I'd stuff that bottle of claret down your throat here and now. Get this straight. I'm going to the States whether you like or not. Despite the fact that you're a self-righteous, sanctimonious, back-stabbing bastard who deserves everything he gets, I won't do anything to reduce your chances of making the exhibition a success or of ripping off the Met. I doubt you can understand it but it's simply because Laura had the decency to give me a chance with this project.' He turned his gaze on her, his tone softening. 'Sorry, but I'm not prepared to accept any control from the museum on this. Like I say, you have my word that I'll be saying nothing that might compromise the exhibition. Hell, Laura, I hope as much as you do that the tomb proves to be authentic, it'll be a real coup for you.' There was a long forgotten glow in her eyes as he bent forward and kissed her softly on the mouth. 'Trust me,' he said, 'I'm only trying to make a few quid – the glory is all yours.'

She smiled, the touch of his lips bringing a hint of redness to her cheeks and satisfied they were at least parting as friends, he turned and vanished into the sunlight and meandering lunchtime crowds. Dixey's words, the ineffective parting shot of a comprehensively defeated man, came faintly to him.

'What about the coins, Hawkhurst? They don't belong to you. They're the museum's responsibility.'

*****

'How dare he speak to you like that, Thomas.' Angahrad was outraged as she listed to his recounting of the meeting with Laura and Dixey. They were heading northward up the A5, holding a steady seventy under a darkening sky. A few more miles and they would be over the border into Wales.

'It doesn't matter,' he said, 'Dixey's well aware that nothing he can do or say will change my mind. I'm going to Gethsemane and that's final. My only regret is that you won't be coming with me. Are you certain you won't change your mind?'

She lay her head on his shoulder.

'No. I'd like to, Tom, you know that, but I can't just leave the farm.' She clutched his arm tightly. 'I shall miss you though, even if it is only for a week.'

Hawkhurst estimated he had another two days' work on the coins before his report would be complete. After that he would fax a copy up to Edinburgh, for John Maloney, an old friend and numismatician of international renown, to give it the once over. It was a precaution he would not usually have deemed necessary but with Dixey in his present frame of mind he had no doubt that the least inconsistency in his findings would be picked out for special attention. This, together with the demands on his time preparing for his trip to Gethsemane, meant it might be a week or more before they had another chance to spend time together. The thought brought a shadow of depression: she had become central to his happiness.

'Tell you what, why don't we pop into the Griffin and pick up a couple bottles of wine then you can come back to the cottage and I'll cook dinner. You can stay the night and I'll run you back to the farm first thing in the morning – in plenty of time to feed those bloody animals.'

It was dark by the time they pulled up in front of the tatty granite and slate façade of the pub. Inside, their appearance, with Angahrad holding firmly and defiantly onto Tom's arm, drew down the usual cold, resentful silence as they made their way to the bar. A bunch of locals, Glynn Powell among them, were playing crib, forgetting their game at this unexpected visitation. Some half-whispered remarks were passed and she gripped his arm even tighter, willing him to disregard them. This he did, seeking no unnecessary confrontation, keeping his eyes firmly ahead as the publican went to find the wine. Pushing his money across the bar Hawkhurst took the bottles and led her to the door. Before they had reached it Powell was on his feet and anticipating trouble Tom passed the bottles to her, his hands balling into fists. The Welshman's tone was not, however, in the least belligerent. He even managed a half convincing smile.

'Will you take a drink with me, Mr Hawkhurst? When we fell out I was in the wrong – I had been drinking. I'd like to apologise to you and Miss Jenkins.' It was the first time they had spoken in six months, not since the fight, and the man was clearly uneasy at offering the hand of friendship in front of his cronies. Still wary, Tom nevertheless appreciated the effort such a gesture would have entailed and was inclined to accept it at face value. It was an opportunity to let bygones be bygones.

'Thank you, Glynn. I'd be pleased to.'

As the other man, visibly relieved to find his olive branch had been accepted so readily, ordered their drinks he tossed a crumpled copy of *The Guardian* onto the bar. The front page was dominated by reports of a raid by Arab terrorists on a kibbutz close to the Lebanese border. Three Israeli soldiers and one terrorist had been killed. The inevitable retaliatory air strikes by the Israeli air force had killed another dozen or so in a refugee camp in the Bekaa Valley and on the West Bank snatch squads had entered nominally Palestinian controlled territory to lift several prominent militants. In the frenzy of activity since they had opened the grave Tom had lost track of affairs in the wider world but it seemed that the Middle East peace accord was dying on its feet. Islamic fundamentalism was gaining ground and the Jihad, the Holy War, was being called for even by moderate Muslims these days. The only Islamic voice with any influence that still preached moderation was that of Firdasi, Firdasi the mystic, Firdasi The Master.

None of this interested Powell one iota however. He turned to the centre spread which was given over entirely to the press conference at the museum. It was this that had attracted Powell's attention and presumably stimulated his desire to cultivate his erstwhile enemies.

The headline said it all. 'King Arthur's Tomb is genuine says top archaeologist.' Beneath it was a half-page photograph of a smiling Dixey, brandishing the sword above his head like a senile war-lord. Surprised that such an experienced operator, an Olympic class fence-sitter, was prepared to be so definite about the authenticity of the finds, Tom read on with increased interest.

In fact Dixey hadn't exactly said that the finds were definitely genuine. Weasel words like almost certainly, most likely, and probably, appeared in every other sentence. What it added up to was that, while he wasn't personally prepared to say that what he held in his hand was Excalibur, he had laid the evidence before them and they were free to draw their own conclusions. This they had done with a vengeance.

'I saw your name mentioned in there,' said Powell, nodding at the paper as he handed them their drinks. 'I guess this must be pretty important eh?'

Wondering whether the man's desire for a truce was genuine or merely a screen from behind which to pry, Hawkhurst responded cautiously.

'Yes, I suppose so. But don't put too much faith in what you read in the papers. There's no real evidence it's what they say it is. Don't get me wrong, it's an important discovery but it's early days yet.'

Powell quaffed his beer deeply, pausing to blot his lips on the sleeve of his jacket.

'How much do you think those things might be worth? You know – you know – the Holy Grail and the sword.'

'It's impossible to say. As fine examples of Dark Age artefacts I suppose tens, maybe hundreds of thousands. If someone is gullible enough to believe they really are the Grail and Excalibur I guess the sky's the limit. Millions maybe.'

'Millions?' Powell's eyes were wide in amazement. Hawkhurst, however, was tiring of the conversation and keen to be away. Throwing back his drink in one, he brought it down on the bar with a sharp rap of finality.

'Thanks for the drink, Glynn,' he said quickly before any further questions came his way, 'my round next time.' Taking Angahrad's arm he led her to the door and out into the night. The evening air, pushing gently up the darkening valley, came cool and clean after the smoke and stale beer smells within. From high up came the harsh croak of a roosting pheasant settling down for the night. She breathed in the sweetness of it.

'My goodness,' she said, 'that must be the first time in living memory that Glynn Powell has apologised to anybody.'

After lying empty for three days the cottage was distinctly chilly and Tom set about lighting the fire while Angahrad went to the kitchen to fix coffee. In seconds flames danced upwards between the stacked logs in a gently crackling fusillade of sparks. Tossing the match into the flames he stood up and looked around him until Angahrad appeared from the kitchen bearing two steaming mugs of coffee. She noticed he was frowning as though puzzled.

'What's the matter? You look worried.'

'I don't know. I've just got the feeling that someone's been here while we've been away.' His eyes darted about the room, absorbing the minutiae. There was nothing he could specifically identify as justifying his suspicions: it was just a feeling. With a mystified Angie in train he went into the bedroom. Here again everything seemed in perfect order yet the niggling doubts remained. Were the curtains pulled that far back when they had left? Had the carpet been rucked up like that? Somehow he didn't think so.

'Well, I don't think anything valuable has been taken,' he announced half an hour later, having carried out a complete survey of the cottage and outbuildings. 'But I'm bloody sure someone's been here – and quite recently at that – maybe within the last couple of hours or so. There are fresh tyre marks out in the yard behind the garage and traces of damp mud on the floor over there by the front door.' She stared at him.

'But there's never been much crime in the valley before, Tom. It's all too incestuous: everybody knows everybody else. And who would come all the way up here to search an old cottage like this?'

'Someone who thought I might have a hoard of valuable coins stashed away somewhere perhaps?' he mused.

She gasped at the thought.

'Of course. My God, Tom, where are they?'

He smiled at her concern, unbuttoning his shirt and tossing it aside. About his waist was a thick canvas belt. Along its length were rows of small, neatly stitched pockets. Inserting a finger into one of these he produced a twist of soft tissue paper which he opened up to reveal a gleaming silver coin of Byzantium that had first seen light of day in the reign of Constantine the Great.

'I got this idea from Ali Khaleem, an Afghan gun runner of the old school. Ali reckoned paper money, even dollars, represented an unacceptable fire hazard. He dealt only in gold. He showed me a belt just like this shortly before he died. He used it for sovereigns and the like. It seemed a good idea so I had one made for myself. Mind you it killed Ali in the end.'

'Killed him? How was that?'

'Well, back in 1992 Ali was crossing a ravine with a consignment of CIA weapons bound for the Mujahedeen, when his caravan was shot-up by government gunships. The caravan scattered and Ali, understandably but unwisely forgetting the high specific gravity of gold in the heat of the moment, dived into the river. He went to the bottom like a stone. His body was never found. They say you can't take it with you but Ali Khaleem came closer than any man I've ever known.'

Relieved that the coins were safe and suspecting that she was having her leg pulled, Angie busied herself with preparing dinner while he uncorked the wine. As she stood peeling potatoes she reviewed the events of the day.

'It's a funny thing, Tom, but what if Glynn Powell knew someone was up here? Maybe that's why he was keen to delay us down the pub.'

He stared thoughtfully at her, removing a speck of cork from the bottle's neck with a forefinger.

'Could be. As you say he's never struck me as the forgive and forget type and he was certainly very inquisitive about the value of the finds. It's hardly something I'd expect him to be interested in unless there was something in it for him.'

She warmed to the subject.

'What's more, do you remember the car we passed as we came up to the cottage? Once we had left he could easily have phoned from the Griffin to warn whoever was up here.'

'It's possible, of course, but the tyre tracks outside are high performance radials. None of the locals, so far as I know, has a car that would use tyres like that. I didn't really pay much attention to the car we passed. Did you get a good look at it?'

'Not really. It was just a low sports car, I think. I couldn't even tell you what colour it was for sure, although it might have been red.'

He nestled behind her as she stood at the sink, folding his arms about her and kissing her ear.

'Let's forget about it. They didn't get anything. I'll report the whole thing to the police tomorrow. When will dinner be ready?'

'Ten minutes, fifteen at most.'

'Good. That'll just give me time to ring Laura and let her know what my movements are over the next few days.'

On ringing Laura's flat he was surprised when Dixey's icy tone responded.

'Yes?'

'It's Tom Hawkhurst. Is Laura there?'

'Not at the moment. She's down at the ITN studios. She's being interviewed in ten minutes. Why not watch, Hawkhurst. You might learn something about responsibility and professionalism.'

Before a suitable riposte had sprung to Tom's mind, Dixey had slammed the phone down. Switching the TV on he sat impatiently through the weather forecast and commercials before the programme began. While the host went through the usual introductions, Tom poured out two glasses of wine and settled himself in a chair in time to see Laura come tripping on stage to tumultuous applause and a kiss on the cheek from the interviewer.

As usual she looked stunning, this time in a long scarlet number that was split to the hip. As she sat down her smiling attempts to arrange the flimsy fabric into some form of decent covering about her long tanned legs brought good humoured, sympathetic laughter from the audience. The interviewer, getting good vibes about the programme already, was not slow to jump on the bandwagon.

'Right Laura, now you've adjusted your dress, tell us about the way you arrived at the conclusion, after three months of unrewarding work, that something very special lay under that particular burial mound.'

It was a question made in heaven and Laura seized the opportunity with both hands. Without at any time seeming to make special claims for herself, indeed at pains to make it clear how much she owed to the work of her predecessors, by the time the interview was over her beauty, humour and, above all, her humility had the audience on its feet. She was undoubtedly a superstar: she was the woman who had found the grave of Arthur, the Once and Future King.

'It's ready,' Angie carolled from the kitchen. 'Do you want to watch television? Shall I bring it in there?'

He thumbed the remote control, killing an image of Laura, eyes cast modestly down, acknowledging the applause of her fans.

'No. Let's eat out there. I've seen all the television I want for a while.'

CHAPTER SEVEN

Hawkhurst looked around the first class lounge, glad to find that its plush panelled sanctuary, in stark contrast with the pushing and shoving of the terminal outside, was sparsely populated and calm. His departure from Heathrow had coincided with the arrival of an El Al flight from Tel Aviv and the arrival hall had been packed with Israeli women and children, presumably sent to a place of safety in the face of the rising violence at home. Presented with the opportunity to feed off a section of humanity at its most vulnerable, television cameras had been much in evidence, generally adding to the chaos. Thankfully, here in the first class lounge that calm and measured ambience that only the expenditure of sufficient money can ensure prevailed. Almost.

To his right an aged and querulous Jewish-American couple traded complaints about the standard of service in European hotels. He, a Purple Heart veteran of the Inchon River, had been unable to get a copy of *The New York Times* and was thus prevented from keeping up with the latest events in the Middle East. Worse, she'd had to ring reception no less than three times before someone had come to replenish the mini bar. The old pioneering virtues of thrift and self-reliance were clearly spread pretty thin these days. In a corner two young men, darkly Latin and vaguely familiar, pop stars perhaps, conversed in low tones. Their vapid eyes regularly swept hopefully around the lounge, trying to ascertain if someone might have recognised them; possibly even ask for an autograph. If anyone had they were sure as hell not letting it show.

Tom went directly to the lavishly stocked bar where a smartly uniformed, high cheek boned stewardess smiled a lying smile that suggested she was only there to fulfil his every need. Ordering a black coffee he retired to an unoccupied bench seat. It was early and, savouring his drink, he watched with detached interest as his fellow first class passengers drifted in. They comprised a trio of Japanese businessmen, who from their gait and cheerful mien had already, at that early hour, been attacking the sake, and a young, fresh-faced couple who might have been honeymooners. Last to arrive was as a stocky, square set man with a pock-marked face who, succumbing to the temptations of the bar in the shape of a large bourbon, sought shelter behind that day's issue of *The New York Times*. It was an issue whose front page was dominated by comment and detail of unfolding events in the Middle East, and the cosmic unfairness of this was enough to bring the old couple close to apoplexy.

Feeling good and intent on enjoying every moment of the coming trip, Hawkhurst returned to the bar to refill his cup. As she poured, the stewardess enquired if this was the first time he had travelled to the States and he told her no. What he didn't tell her was that while it was true he had visited America several times this was the first occasion he had done so in the luxury of first class. The last time he had stood and queued five hours for a standby flight that had cost him around £200. Today's flight, he knew, would have cost his benefactors six or seven times that amount. Along with his tickets they had also provided travellers cheques to the value of $1,000 dollars for what were described as incidental expenses and $200 in small denomination bills for spending money. Whatever other reservations he might have about them, the Church of Christ the Warrior certainly didn't believe in penny-pinching. For the first time in longer than he cared to remember he did not have to worry about money. As the call for first class passengers came over the tannoy, he picked up his shoulder bag and followed the square set man down the articulated aluminium tunnelway that vibrated underfoot and led into the belly of the aircraft.

Although the flight had started at Frankfurt, the first class section was sparsely occupied and he was shown to a window seat that had empty seats to front and rear. He was pleased with this isolation: inflight small talk was something he could do without. As he rifled through his bag, intent on further polishing his lecture papers, another high-breasted, smiling stewardess was standing over him, this one proffering Krug champagne and caviar canapés. Taking the slim, chilled glass he stretched out as with a melodic chime the seat belt lights glowed above him. A little later, the flight director came in to thank him personally for travelling on flight AV320. This, thought Hawkhurst, is the life.

Two hours later, bored with his papers and the unimaginative muzak on the sound system he made his way to the toilet, carefully timing his visit to ensure it would entail squeezing past the more buxom of the two stewardesses who pandered to their every need. She smiled patiently as he passed.

'Sorry buddy,' It was the square set man who spoke, stepping back into his seat to let Tom pass. It was the first time he had seen the man's face close up and what he saw made him flinch. What at a distance he had taken for pock marks he now realised were scars. The man's face was a mask of coruscated tissue. The scars ran like little tiger stripes, valleys and ridges across his chin, cheeks and forehead, vanishing into the receding ginger hairline. Tom discreetly averted his gaze but the man had evidently come to terms with his disfigurement and smiled easily enough. 'First time I've been to the can since I left the Lebanon.' There were traces of John Wayne in the voice: the way he said Leb-ah-nahn.

'In that case – after you.' Tom returned the smile. 'Your need is certainly greater than mine.'

As the man went gratefully forward Tom took in the broad shoulders and the thick roll of muscle that merged into the bull neck. He wasn't tall, maybe five seven or eight, but one look told you he'd be a real handful in a fight. How, he wondered, had the man come by those terrible scars?

Several glasses of champagne later, stacked at 10,000 feet and circling Kennedy for the fourth time, Hawkhurst was in distinctly liverish mood. Travelling first class could cushion you against almost anything but delays. Now, thanks to a terrorist alert at the airport, all his plans were in doubt. For the next stage of his journey he had to get across to La Guardia to pick up the internal flight that would take him to Gethsemane. Untypically, the schedule provided by Mary Lou and generally detailed to the point of paranoia gave no departure time for his connecting flight. All he knew was that he was flying with St Michael Airlines. It was an outfit he had not heard of before and he assumed it would be one of the small domestic companies that come and go all the time in the US. His first TV appearance was only two days hence and he was concerned that if he missed his flight it might be days before another was available. As he looked down at the brown and green jigsaw of Long Island stretched out below, the captain's voice came over the intercom, soothing and laid back to a degree that Tom felt totally unwarranted in the circumstances.

'You'll be pleased to hear, ladies and gentlemen, that we have been cleared to land at Kennedy Airport and should be touching down in approximately ten minutes.'

By the time he arrived at La Guardia he was in a foul mood. At Kennedy the 'archaeologist' on his passport had been sufficiently intriguing for the young immigration officer, black, disdainful and packing a .38 that made dissent unattractive, insist he open all his baggage. This hurdle overcome the next was provided in the shape of shiny faced Haitian taxi driver who apparently spoke no English. At first Hawkhurst suspected this was no more than a ploy to assist the presentation of an exorbitant fare. Luckily, his French was just good enough to penetrate the driver's thick Creole and, more in hope than anticipation, they set of in search of La Guardia. Despite his initial doubts, on arrival at La Guardia, Tom came to the conclusion that the guy was monolingual and honest. He tipped generously and then went directly to the information desk.

'Where do I go for St Michael Airlines, please?'

The girl tapped deftly at the keyboard, her eyes flickering to the screen.

'St Michael One is being held over at the moment awaiting the arrival of passengers from Kennedy.' She pointed a scarlet nail. 'If you care to wait over there in green section I'll let them know you're here Mr...?'

'Hawkhurst. Tom Hawkhurst.'

As he sat down a familiar voice boomed in his ear.

'Hi buddy. Looks like we're both bound for Gethsemane.' It was the scar-faced man, his hand extended in greeting. Taking it Tom prepared to counter a bone crushing pressure that never materialised. 'Harry Brennan,' the man said. 'Pleased to meet you, Tom.'

St Michael One was a small, twin engine, executive jet. It was white, dazzlingly so in the
mid-afternoon sunshine that made the distant towers of Manhattan shimmer like tinsel as the two men made their way across the tarmac. Stencilled on the tailfin was a flaming red sword: it was the first time Hawkhurst had seen the symbol. St Michael wasn't strictly an airline, Brennan had explained, rather it was part of the Church of Christ the Warrior's transportation infrastructure. Its crew consisted of the pilot, a fit looking, gung-ho type of around forty who introduced himself as Bob, and Sandy, yet another stewardess who, with her tight fitting uniform and carved silicone features, might have been the model for a Cindy doll.

'Can I get you gentlemen something?' – 'gennlemen' was the way she said it – she enquired as they settled themselves thankfully into the air-conditioned coolness of the aircraft. Tom hesitated. His shirt clung damply to his skin and he could smell his own body odour. He would have liked a beer, the champagne having dried his throat and the hurried journey between airports allowing no chance to slake his thirst. However, he wondered if his pious hosts would approve of alcohol. Harry Brennan, clearly an old hand at this sort of thing, solved the problem. He tugged his tie loose and kicked off his shoes.

'Sure thing, honey. The minute we're airborne you can get me a bottle of Jim Beam and a packet of pretzels.'

Sandy smiled with delight at this shameless show of worldly wickedness as the plane bounced gently forward, engines screaming to a crescendo. The fragrance of her perfume reached Tom as she strapped herself into the seat next to him in preparation for take-off.

At 20,000 feet and with a third of Harry's bourbon gone, Sandy disappeared aft returning to his side after a few seconds. In her hand she held a magazine. No that was flattering it. It was a newsletter: the latest issue of *Neo Christian Review* – editor Mary Lou Berkowitz. She pointed eagerly.

'They've given you major coverage, Dr Hawkhurst – you're all across the centre spread.'

And it was true. There was a detailed CV which suggested someone had been doing their homework. However, although mentioning his spectacular work in Armenia it tactfully glossed over the events that culminated in his enforced departure from that place. There was also a picture, a flattering portrait that must have been taken during the press conference, and a snappy trailer for his coming 'face to face' with the Reverend Whichelow. It was nice but somehow worrying. The way it read to him was: 'Coming soon to a nuthouse near you – Tom Hawkhurst, finder of the Holy Grail.' It was the bowl and to a lesser extent the sword that formed the central theme of the article. The identity of the skeleton it seemed was either taken for granted or considered irrelevant as were the other finds. On the facing page a full length article on Grail mythology and its Christian interpretation brought a frown. Scientific evidence was not a priority it seemed. Much emphasis was placed on Arthur, or at least the Christian version, and his band of valiant, pious knights who had suffered so much in the quest for the Holy Grail. Somehow, he could not quite fathom exactly how, the medieval Order of the Knights Templar had got mixed up in all this.

'Tickets were sold out in two hours,' she told him breathlessly. 'I'm afraid I wasn't among the lucky ones, but I shall be watching you on TV.' She hesitated then proffered a ball-point pen. 'Would you mind autographing your picture, Dr Hawkhurst? The girls back in the hostel will be green when they know you travelled on St Michael One.' Distinctly embarrassed, he scrawled across the page noticing as he wrote that the pen bore the same flaming sword logo he had seen on the aircraft's tail. By the hilt of the logo a tiny circled R indicated it was a registered trade mark.

'Hell, honey,' Brennan broke in cheerfully, 'you can have my ticket. I wondered what the hell it was when I picked it up in Frankfurt. No offence, Tom, but I'm gonna be pretty busy for the next coupla days.' Delving into his briefcase he produced a gilt edged ticket, handing it to the delighted girl. He grinned mischievously: 'OK, so what about a kiss for Uncle Harry?' Giggling, she lightly brushed his lips with hers.

'There, Mr Brennan, that's all you get.' Before she disappeared forward into the cockpit she turned and winked broadly at them and Harry slapped his thigh in delight.

'Goddamn it, Tom. I think I just made first base.'

As they flew on across the seemingly endless prairies Tom watched as Brennan, his scarred features growing ever more flushed, began to get to grips big time with the rest of the Jim Beam. His speech was by now distinctly slurred.

'Ever been to Gethsemane before, Tom?' Hawkhurst shook his head. 'It'll be a real eye opener for you. I'm no bible thumper but seeing just what the Reverend has achieved surely makes me wonder if there's not something to the power of prayer.'

'What's your connection with the Church, Harry?'

Brennan blinked and lowered the glass from his lips.

'Me? Oh I'm just a glorified messenger boy. I was a courier in the US diplomatic service until a couple of years back. The job meant I was away from home a lot. My marriage broke up and I guess I started hitting the sauce. The State Department pensioned me off but I was hardly ready for retirement – hell, I'm only forty three – so I took this job. I travel all over, mainly between the colonies.'

'Colonies?'

'Sure. It's what the Church calls their overseas missions. The Church has colonies in maybe thirty countries around the world. Europe, Africa – all over.'

'For half-an-hour Brennan recounted in detail the work undertaken by the Church of Christ the Warrior. From what he said, Hawkhurst gathered it involved the provision of material and technical aid in parallel with some pretty heavy evangelising. Gradually Brennan's speech faltered as the drink took effect and eventually his monologue stumbled to a halt as he drifted off into an uneasy sleep. Later, as the sun was dying in bloody splendour behind the foothills of the Rockies, Sandy reappeared, smiling at the sleeping man as she tucked a plaid blanket about his knees and removed the empty bottle from his unresisting hand.

She switched off the main cabin lights and sat down opposite Hawkhurst again, the solitary reading light that burned at his shoulder lending a soft, almost intimate atmosphere. She had removed her jacket and his gaze settled on the top buttons of her shirt, unfastened to reveal a treasured inch of tanned cleavage. Her tone was confidential, almost conspiratorial.

'Just how much do you think the Holy Grail would be worth, Dr Hawkhurst?'

He smiled. Money again.

'It depends on your point of view. As a few pounds of not particularly high grade silver, a few thousand dollars maybe. As an attraction in a museum, I'm talking about box office appeal, probably millions. Archaeologically it's interesting, of course, but it doesn't add substantially to our sum of knowledge. It all depends whether or not we can convincingly prove that the skeleton in the grave really was the British warlord who became romanticised into King Arthur. Personally I don't see how we are ever going to be able to put our hands on our hearts and say with absolute certainty that is the case.'

'I meant its value as a holy relic.' Her tone was absolutely serious, almost reverent.

'I couldn't even guess.'

'You're not a believer?'

'No.'

She fell into a thoughtful silence and Hawkhurst stared out of the window. Below all was blackness, punctuated by the occasional lights of small prairie townships and isolated farmhouses, while above the stars shone with an icy clarity.

'We should be in Gethsemane in an hour.' She said, stretching out, her feet momentarily brushing his. 'I sure will be glad to hit the sack.'

In seconds she was asleep, head lolling to one side, her arms folded beneath her breasts. He ran an eye over the silky dimpled knees then, feeling like a grubby voyeur, he stood up and went forward onto the flight deck. Bob, drinking coffee, smiled over his shoulder, apparently glad of company. The auto pilot was taking the strain and the pilot waved Tom into the empty seat beside him. All around lights and instruments glowed, lighting up their features red and green like painted harlequins.

'Nice night.'

'Beautiful.'

Hawkhurst craned his neck, trying to pick out the constellations arrayed about them. Along with the iridescent swathe of the Milky Way he could make out Orion and the Plough. The ruddy, menacing disk of Mars was low but rising in the west.

'How long have you been flying, Bob?'

'Since I was eighteen. I was with the Marines in Nam.'

'Topgun?'

'Topgun, shit,' the pilot replied, although without any real venom. 'I was in logistics – transportation. Flying C130s into Da Nang when the gooks had it surrounded: landing ammunition while they were fucking up the airstrip with mortars and 105s. Jesus, I was shitting bricks most of the time. I'm just a flyer, Dr Hawkhurst, not a superstar.'

Feeling distinctly admonished, Hawkhurst fell silent while the pilot, perhaps considering his response might have been a trifle too peppery, went on in quieter vein.

'I know it's fashionable to laugh at the US, the most powerful nation on earth, getting its butt kicked by a bunch of rice-eating peasants, but it wasn't like that. I lost a lot of good friends out there. It makes me mad when I see the army in Nam portrayed as a bunch of junkies who couldn't hack it. I flew seventy missions – some easy, some nightmarish. All the guys I served with believed in what they were doing.' He stared into Hawkhurst's face, daring him to say different. 'I know the losing army in every war says it was betrayed by the politicians at home, but we truly were. Objectives changed overnight because the senators and congressmen back home thought more about their jobs than the lives of the men on the front. OK, Nam was a screw up and we got creamed, but it wasn't the fault of the fighting men. I learnt a lot out there. If it taught me nothing else it taught me that you can't trust politicians. In the end a man has to have something stronger to believe in.'

He paused as if to let this sink in, as if it was the prelude to something more important.

'When I came home I guess you could say I ran wild for a while – liquor, drugs, you name it. Not surprisingly my marriage failed.' He fell silent, thoughtful, for a moment, then continued. 'I got two daughters. Live with their Ma now back in Des Moines. I don't see them much anymore. Yes sir, I was pretty well fouled up at the time. But then I heard The Reverend Whichelow preach and I knew I had found salvation and a firm foundation upon which to rebuild my life. Since then I haven't looked back.'

Hawkhurst sensed a religious discourse coming on and sought to head it off. He wasn't here to dissect the putrefying corpse of war that was now history or to be saved for Jesus. Very little had changed since Bob and his generation had returned from war to find themselves vilified, often by the very people who had cheered them as they went. He remembered the Israeli refugees at Heathrow. Another country, another war. But the same madness. The lesson of history was a hard one to learn it seemed. Perhaps it was un-learnable. He also pondered the similarity between Bob's story and that told by Harry Brennan. The Church would find the flotsam and jetsam of the increasingly rootless and transient societies of the United States and other western countries a fertile hunting ground. He changed tack.

'Tell me about Gethsemane.'

'You'll be able to see for yourself in a few minutes.' Bob pointed ahead and then began to throw switches, going through the routine that would put the aircraft back into manual control. 'There's the airstrip coming up now.'

Stretching away below, laid out upon the velvety blackness of the prairie, burned a huge cross of brilliant light. Gethsemane Field was visible for miles.

CHAPTER EIGHT

At seven thirty the following morning Tom woke to a tentative knocking at the bedroom door. Pulling himself upright he arranged the sheets decently about his naked body and gathered his thoughts as the girl, she could have been no more than seventeen, peered warily around the door.

'Morning, Dr Hawkhurst, I brought your breakfast.' She pinioned him firmly to the bed with a weighty tray bearing coffee, orange juice, ham and eggs, before going to the window and drawing the heavy curtain. Sunlight like syrup flooded in, silhouetting her slim figure on the flawless pastel yellow of the far wall. 'It sure is a nice day.' The girl smiled down at him as she poured out a strong black coffee. 'Mrs Berkowitz said to tell you she'd be in touch around eight. I'm Suzie and I've been assigned as your personal house girl while you're here at Gethsemane.' She pointed to the bedside phone. 'It there's anything you need just ring housekeeping – that's zero zero three zero – and ask for me.'

She wore jeans and a tight gingham shirt against which ripening breasts strained: given fifty years she could have been Doris Day. Well-scrubbed, rosy cheeked and displaying perfect teeth in a seemingly permanent smile, she made Hawkhurst all too aware of his own dishevelled appearance. Arriving at Gethsemane at two in the morning after nearly twenty hours of continual travelling he had fallen gratefully into bed without washing. His mouth still tasted of Brennan's Jim Beam.

'Thanks Suzie.' He looked about him, taking in the simple yet tastefully furnished bedroom and, anticipating his next question, she walked round its perimeter, pushing doors open as she went.

'Bathroom, lounge, dressing room,' she chimed sweetly. 'The fitness suite, sauna and pool are just down the passage on the left.' She stood by the bed, still smiling, hands clasped primly before her and there ensued an uncomfortable few seconds before he realised she was waiting for further instructions.

'Well that's fine, Suzie, thank you. I'll be sure to ring you if I need anything.'

Dismissed, she departed with the mandatory 'Have a nice day.' To Hawkhurst it sounded like a challenge to do otherwise in the wonderful world of Gethsemane. Having eaten, he shaved and showered. At eight precisely the phone by the bed purred softly. It was Mary Lou Berkowitz. After the formal enquiries as to his journey and current wellbeing she got down to business.

'I'm gonna be busy until mid-day, Tom. Gotta meet a Church delegation from Ruanda. Why don't you take the opportunity to spend the morning sightseeing. If you come to the museum, anyone will direct you, at, say, twelve thirty we can discuss your programme over lunch. We're scheduled to see Reverend Whichelow at three. Is that OK with you?'

'Fine. I'll see you at twelve thirty.' As he replaced the handset Suzie returned, keeping her attention firmly on the tray and off his towel wrapped torso as she gathered up the detritus of breakfast. He smiled but having no desire to embarrass his new found ally, pulled on a towelling robe. She relaxed visibly as he sought her advice.

'It seems I'm free to go sightseeing this morning, Suzie. What would you recommend I take in?'

'Today? Well, Doctor, I would suggest you visit the sports stadium; we have the best track and field facilities in the state, the university campus and, of course, the Temple. They're all within easy walking distance but I can arrange a car and driver if you'd prefer it. Would you like me to show you around?' He considered her offer briefly.

'No, no need, Suzie. I guess you've got better things to do. If you can get me a street map I'll find my own way around.' When she had gone he returned to the phone, intent on letting Angahrad know that he had arrived safely. After two abortive attempts his third effort was interrupted by the operator, his tone terse.

'What number are you trying to get, Dr Hawkhurst?'

Hawkhurst read it out, adding. 'It's a UK number.'

'If you replace your handset, Doctor, I'll try to get it for you.'

Setting it down he smiled, hardly anyone called him Doctor back home. Five minutes later the operator was back.

'I'm sorry, Doctor, but that number seems to be unobtainable. I'll try later if you like. If I get through is there a message I can pass on for you?'

'No, please don't worry. I was only letting people back home know that I'd arrived safely.'

*****

As Tom stepped out onto the sidewalk, the warmth of the morning sun took him in its soft embrace. It wasn't too hot, low seventies, but after the fiercely air conditioned hotel it came as a marked, yet not unpleasant transition. The fragrance of jasmine blossom hung in the air. It was all very pleasant he mused. The wide boulevard was almost devoid of traffic and for a moment he wondered if it was Sunday. He readjusted his jet-lagged bio clock. No, it was Tuesday. He could only assume that everyone in Gethsemane must be hard at work in the Lord's vineyard.

The view from his suite had given onto a parking lot beyond which lay a series of unremarkable barrack-like compounds of low buildings. The contrast with what confronted him as he turned the corner to head downtown brought an involuntary gasp.

'The Sacred Temple of the Church of Christ the Warrior,' said the guide book that Suzie had thoughtfully provided, 'is, at 965 feet, the tallest house of worship in the world and an outstanding example of modern architectural and constructional philosophy and techniques.' This was understatement on a monumental scale. It wasn't a church in the accepted sense, of course, but a windowless central skyscraper flanked on either side by smaller buildings, each perhaps half the height of the centre tower. With a little imagination these might pass for medieval flying buttresses. The Temple was surmounted by the now familiar sword cross, this time of gleaming stainless steel, from the hilt of which Old Glory blazed bravely in the prairie winds. 'To the top of the cross,' the guide book added, 'is 1025 feet.' Regaining his mental wind Hawkhurst strode towards the amazing tower of white marble, his eyes screwed up against the reflected glare, a glare sufficient to ensure that any pilgrim kept his eyes cast penitently down.

The sheer size of the Temple gave the impression that it was closer than actually proved the case, for it was best part of a mile distant, and as he lengthened his stride Hawkhurst soon found himself sweating. Loosening his tie, he removed his jacket, throwing it over his shoulder. There were a few more people about here nearer the centre of town. Joggers in pairs laboured past and on the green lawns that ran the length of the broad thoroughfare little instruction groups sat crossed legged in the sun, attentive to the words of their tutors. Everyone he saw seemed to be in their teens or early twenties. Gethsemane seemed a place of youthful enthusiasm and quiet civilisation and Tom found himself wondering if his first assessment of the Church of Christ the Warrior had not been over-critical.

It was as he ambled past one such group that two figures, in uniform khaki trousers and carefully pressed short sleeved shirts, detached themselves and followed briskly in his wake. He was aware of their presence following some fifteen yards behind him, yet unconcerned in this clean and disciplined township. A little later they quickened their pace until they had drawn level with him, one on either side. Tom faced the man on his left. He was young and fresh faced with the earnest, clean cut features that come knocking on doors selling religious tracts. When he spoke Hawkhurst readied himself to gently counter an unsolicited moral lecture.

'Have you strayed from the light, brother?'

'Sorry?' Tom was fully prepared to resist evangelising but found he had misinterpreted their interest in him.

'Where are you going?' The voice was easy, unthreatening, yet firm enough to warrant an equally firm response.

'I'm going to look at the Temple – if that's OK with you!'

'Where have you come from?'

Hawkhurst felt rather than saw the second man moving closer, adding to the pressure on him. There was a distinct air of menace here and he didn't appreciate this style of religion in the least. He would, he thought, give them one more straight answer and then, if they insisted on hassling him, tell them to go to hell.

'From England,' he said, his manner offhand although his heart, preparing for action, had already begun to pick up pace. The other man's mouth dropped open in disbelief, recognition dawning in the dumbfounded features. They had, it was clear, made a mistake though hardly one, Tom thought, sufficiently serious to warrant the abject apologies that ensued.

'Dr Hawkhurst please excuse me,' he stammered, features flushed deep crimson. 'I didn't realise. I mean, we were told you were coming. I – I just didn't recognise you. I just forgot. Please accept my apologies for cross questioning you like that. We get a lot of weirdoes and nosy parkers drifting into town, druggies and other lowlife. Not that you ...'

His words trailed to nothing and the second man, equally embarrassed came around to shake his hand. With his cropped hair and beefy quarter-back physique he could have been a clone of the first. Within seconds they were all the best of friends.

'We're sure looking forward to your lecture tomorrow, sir. Have a nice day.'

It was noticeable he thought, as he continued towards the monolithic temple, that he was the only person who was walking alone. It had presumably been this that had first brought him to the attention of the heavies. If Suzie had accompanied him the incident would probably have never occurred. Couples were the smallest acceptable unit in Gethsemane it seemed and then only when travelling between other group activities. He was aware that his presence often drew uneasy sidelong glances from the other tutorial groups as he passed although no further attempts to query his presence occurred.

Finally standing before the huge vaulted entrance of the Temple with its massive ten metre high teak doors, he joined the short line of sightseers. Over the door, carved deeply in sunlit etched gothic characters were the words: "The Lord is a Man of War." The queue comprised a busload of Japanese and a couple of Native Americans. His presence going unremarked he followed the straggling snake of humanity through a smaller door set in the main entrance and into the darkness beyond. As his eyes became accustomed to the gloom the sense of awe he had experienced on first seeing the Temple from a distance was reinforced by the close up detail. It was a *tour de force* of light management. The interior of the vast – what was the correct term? It was hardly the layout of a traditional church, more of an amphitheatre perhaps, an amphitheatre of encircling wooden pews – seating for 10,000 the guide said. Waxed timber gleamed dully in the subdued, artfully recessed lighting and the visitors shuffled tentatively forward, unsure of what lay underfoot. After the sunlight outside, here all was shadow.

'If you will all stay exactly where you are for a second.' A voice ordered from the darkness, 'I will reveal one or two of the more remarkable features of the Temple.'

For a moment there was silence then an unseen switch clicked and an involuntary gasp of amazement went up. From the rear of the auditorium powerful floodlights played dazzlingly upon a huge mural, fifty feet high, painted on canvas. It was hung upon the wall that rose behind a simple marble altar on which stood the inevitable sword cross.

It was a painting depicting Christ enthroned in Glory, an image like nothing Hawkhurst had ever seen in his entire life, a work of religious art which, while almost crude in its execution, was overwhelming in its impact. It was a portrayal of Christ created to instil the fear of God. This was not Christ, the Lamb of God. This was Christ the Tiger. Beneath brows that knotted in a frown that would tumble kingdoms, eyes of acetylene blazed, pale eyes that would have been cherished by the Waffen SS. The mouth, set within a blonde, neatly cropped beard, was drawn down in a disapproving scowl. The message was familiar. It was a variation of the message imparted by recruiting posters: General Kitchener or Uncle Sam saying "Your religion needs you." In his left hand, blade pointing downwards, Christ the Warrior held forth the sword of divine retribution and death, in his right was the chalice of forgiveness and eternal life.

No wonder the Whitenditch finds had provided Mary Lou with food for thought. Although the sword and bowl they had unearthed bore little physical resemblance to those depicted in the painting, the coincidence would have been inescapable – no, pre-ordained – to someone already convinced of the mysterious ways in which God was known to move. No wonder she had asked for a price. He barely heard the remainder of the tour guide's commentary but stood there in thoughtful silence staring up at the awesome image. His fellow sightseers were similarly affected, their eyes repeatedly returning, uneasily, to the vast mural. No matter where you moved in the vastness of the auditorium those eyes followed, unforgiving and relentless. It was a gaze that said there were only two ways of living life – the way of Christ the Warrior and the wrong way.

'Hell, that sure was something,' said the freckled little American at his elbow as they were ushered out into the sunshine again. Despite his enthusiasm there was more than a hint of relief in his voice, a gladness to be free of the brooding ambience of the Tabernacle. He looked at his equally diminutive wife. 'Whatdya say, honey. I suppose it was worth waiting eighteen months for, but,' he sniffed, as if settling some old domestic score, 'I'd still just as soon have gone down to Costa Rica for the winter.'

His wife, menopausal religiosity heightened by what she had just witnessed apparent on her awestruck features, did not respond. Hawkhurst stared at him, puzzled.

'Eighteen months?'

'Damn right, boy. Eighteen months and five thousand dollars. Seems to me it's easier to get into Fort Knox than Gethsemane – and a damn sight cheaper.'

*****

Mary Lou was waiting for him on the wide steps of the museum, strolling up and down in the sunlight, inspecting the tall Doric pillars of the classical Greek building. In the surrounding gardens, groups of youngsters sat drinking Coke and eating burgers. He was conscious of their interest as he approached. Even before he had uttered a single word in public he was a head-turning celebrity. Mary Lou, in a smart burgundy two piece suit, was at her most effusive in welcoming him.

'Hi, Tom, glad you're early. Let's go and eat.' Remembering the way she had dispatched her food at their last meeting at the Ritz, it crossed his mind that her delight in greeting him again might just mean she was hungry and pleased to eat early. She led him through the sparsely populated galleries of the museum, down quiet polished corridors lined with exhibits he would gladly have lingered over in the normal run of things. Eventually they finished up in a rather grand second floor office, minimalist décor and Japanese prints, overlooking a broad, reed fringed lake where ornamental fowl, widgeon, teal, mandarins and Carolinas, drifted on wind ruffled waters. In one corner a table was laid out for two on crisp white linen with silver cutlery and crystal glass. Sitting down with a minimum of ceremony she began ripping a plate of tiger prawns asunder, delicately fishing a stray leg from between her centre teeth before speaking.

'So? What do you think of Gethsemane?' she demanded, the gleam in her eye showing she had little doubt other than that he had inevitably been amazed. As indeed he had.

'Very interesting, I'm really impressed. How big is it – the whole community?'

She swallowed a prawn, then another, before responding.

'At any given time the town has a population of between forty and sixty thousand. Of that number less than ten thousand are long term residents. The vast majority are here for induction into the Church or for advanced training. The Church owns about three hundred square miles of land around here, most of it cattle country. We lease a lot of it out but most of that immediately surrounding the commune we farm ourselves, livestock and timber mainly. What did you think about the Temple? I take it you saw the altar mural.'

He smiled wryly. How could he have missed it?

'It certainly is a coincidence – the sword and the bowl. I can see now why you were so intrigued by the finds.'

But Mary Lou wasn't prepared to accept any suggestions of blind chance in the discoveries. She thrust the last prawn into her mouth and pushed the plate away from her.

'What you choose to see as coincidence, Tom, we here at Gethsemane see as divine intervention. I guess you must have thought me utterly crass when I mentioned buying the Grail but now you've seen the painting you can see why it's so important to us.' She fell silent as two young waitresses, subdued and clearly overawed by his, or was it her, presence, cleared away quickly and efficiently. Mary Lou's silence hung over them like a sword of Damocles. When they were alone she took up her theme afresh, her tone wheedling this time.

'What do you think, Tom? We want those things real bad – we'd pay top dollar and you could name whatever handling commission you thought fair. What are our chances?'

Hawkhurst stifled a sigh. So that was it. They thought he might be prepared to act as a go between in any negotiations.

'Believe me, Mary Lou, they will never be up for sale – not unless we find something that totally disproves the theory of the tomb being Arthur's final resting place. If that were to happen they'd become less important from one point of view and might, just conceivably, come onto the commercial market. But if we prove the grave isn't Arthur's then the sword couldn't be Excalibur or the bowl be the Grail. From your viewpoint it's a Catch 22 situation. If they're genuine you'll never be able to buy them. If they're not you won't want them. Anyway, to be quite honest, I don't think we will ever totally disprove or confirm their authenticity. We may never be able to provide proof positive of the identity of the man in the tomb but equally I can't see how we will ever be able to say, hand on heart, that it definitely isn't Arthur. So long as there's any doubt the assumption, the general public's assumption that is, if not the scientific community's, will be that we have discovered the tomb of Arthur. They'll be regarded as national treasures and will remain in Britain. Think of it. Would the United States sell the Declaration of Independence or the Liberty Bell?'

Mary Lou smiled a knowing smile, a smug smile that made him uneasy.

'National treasures have been known to cross borders before, Tom.'

He knew she was referring to Armenia and felt his face flush. Perhaps sensing she might have touched a nerve she made quickly to change the subject.

'How's your suite at the hotel? I hope they are making you comfortable.'

As she spoke the waitresses returned, replacing the decimated prawns with a mound of pork fillets surrounded by vegetables on a silver platter and replenishing the excellent Californian Chardonnay.

'Fine thanks. My only problem is I haven't been able to phone home – the lines must be down or something. Your people have been very helpful, they must have tried a dozen times this morning but no luck. The valley's pretty remote and we regularly get cut off in the winter. It's not important; I mailed a post card off this morning so the message will get through eventually.'

'I hope young Suzie is proving satisfactory.'

'Oh yes, she's a nice kid. What's her background?'

'All too familiar in this day and age I'm afraid. Wealthy Boston family, father too busy making money and mother too busy spending it to give her the love and attention a child of that age yearns for. Inevitably she fell into bad company and by the time her parents came to the Church for help she was shacked up with a Puerto Rican pimp. That was two years ago, she was fifteen when she came to us. Thanks to our care, attention and constant prayer today she's ready to be shipped abroad to spread the good word.' As she spoke, she speared a couple of fillets and transferred them to her plate with undisguised relish.

'Yes,' said Hawkhurst, glad to get the conversation away from the artefacts. 'Mr Brennan mentioned your overseas activities. How many colonies do you have exactly?' Mary Lou's eyes gleamed with evangelising zeal and for the briefest of moments the food was forgotten.

'We have established colonies in Brazil, Ethiopia, Uganda, Sri Lanka, Nicaragua and Papua New Guinea. We also have expeditionary forces preparing the ground in Poland, Romania and Albania. The collapse of the godless communist empire has presented us with an opportunity we must not neglect. We have also established Temples in other European countries, the UK included.'

'And the Lebanon?'

Her eyes narrowed, suspicious.

'No, what makes you think that?'

'Oh, just something Harry Brennan said on the plane. I got the impression he had been working in the Lebanon.'

She made a throwaway gesture, a deprecating smile that was not quite convincing.

'I believe Mr Brennan has something of a drink problem. No, we have no current operations in the Middle East. Although we hope eventually to carry the word of God into the heart of Islam we have had some bad experiences there. We find more fertile ground in other parts of the third and developing worlds.' She glanced at her watch, a distinct yet unattributable air of irritability coming to him as she rang for service. 'We'd better get moving. I guess you'd like a look round the museum before we meet the Reverend.'

The museum itself came as something of a shock. In fact it was not a museum at all in the accepted sense but rather a haphazard collection of religious relics and curiosities. Mary Lou, who it transpired, along with her editorial duties was also archivist and curator, seemed happier now, cooing proudly as she conducted him among the assembled exhibits. There were genuine medieval pilgrims' badges, crosiers, papal documents, early bibles both hand-crafted and printed, original copies of Martin Luther's address to the Diet of Worms, Russian icons and Greek Orthodox lecterns. None, so far as he could tell were of any outstanding importance yet she insisted on pointing out each one individually and giving him a comprehensive report on how it came into the Church's possession. In almost every case it came down to purchase at an extortionate sum or by way of a gift from some grateful follower of the Church. The make up of the collection seemed to show that the Church of Christ the Warrior was not theologically a narrow minded Church but respected, or at least recognised, every school of thought that fell under the broad title of

Christian, from the most orthodox Catholicism to the freest of freethinking opponents of Rome, from Copt to Quaker.

'I think you'll find this exhibition especially interesting,' she said, leading him into a side gallery. 'It's quite unique.'

And so it proved. In this long silent hall, where the only illumination came from subtly concealed lights, arranged skilfully to focus attention on the exhibits, were treasures indeed. She pointed to a small carved box.

'Icelandic' she said reverently. 'A carved whalebone reliquary that once held the heart of St Hakir of Orkney. A Viking raiding party murdered Hakir and cut his heart out. They were about to eat it when an eagle, or some say an angel, swooped down and carried it off to the monastery of Reykjavik.'

Ignoring the hagiological claptrap, Hawkhurst nevertheless, had to admit it was an exquisite piece of work and certainly genuine tenth century Scandinavian. Mary Lou anticipated, wrongly, his next question.

'$100,000 and worth every cent.' She said tersely, moving on without another word.

There were many other reliquaries, some lavishly jewelled and fashioned in precious metals. Others were simpler but no less fascinating for that. Some might have dated from the first and second centuries, others from the nineteenth. They came from the world over, from wherever followers of the Christian Church had fought and perhaps died for their beliefs. As they halted before one case she produced a key and, opening up the glass door took out a dark sphere of polished wood, ebony he thought, that rested on a simple silver tripod. Carefully she twisted the top half of the sphere free and held the lower part up for him to see. Inside, lying on a tiny cushion of red velvet, was a crisp coil of dried grey hair.

'I think I find this the most moving relic of all,' she whispered. 'It's a lock of the hair of St Francis of Assisi.'

'Really?' He made great efforts to keep any trace of scepticism at bay. 'How did the museum come to acquire it?'

'The gift of a grateful patron whose wayward son we saved from prison and returned to the path of righteousness.' Returning the relic to its case she continued the tour. It was fascinating for Hawkhurst to see how eclectic the collection was, how, along with the undoubtedly authentic, was displayed the most outrageously spurious.

There was a large splinter of the True Cross and one of the nails that had pierced the hands of Christ. Beside a rusted spearhead that looked to Tom to be clearly medieval, was a lengthy screed identifying it as the lance that had been thrust in the Saviour's side and recovered by the Crusaders at the Siege of Acre. She obviously sensed his doubts.

'I guess you're sceptical about some of these, eh Tom?'

He chose not to be combative.

'Well, I'm no expert on the subject so I'm not really in a position to pass judgement. A lot of it is very interesting though. I will say that.'

'I understand, Tom, you're a scientist – you have to keep an open mind. But I promise you we have had all of these items verified by first class scholars in their field.' Staring at him, she licked her lips as though inwardly coming to some momentous decision. Then she nodded her head definitely. 'Tell you what I'm going to do? I'm going to show you something that I know will just take your breath away.'

Now she produced another key, this one attached by a solid chain to her belt, and went to a panel in the wall that at first sight might have opened onto a fuse box or ventilation shaft. Unlocking it and reaching in she hit a switch and then stood back, pointing to an apparently blank wall at the end of the gallery. There was a faint whirr of machinery and two doors, half way up the wall, slid aside to reveal a hidden cabinet. Stepping forward Hawkhurst moved closer, his eyes wide with disbelief. As he approached within a couple of feet she lay a restraining had on his arm.

'Don't get too close, Tom. You'll trigger the alarm system.' After a moment's triumphant pause, she added. 'Well, what do you think?'

'If it's what I think it is, I am truly amazed.'

'It is. It's the reliquary of St Bernadino.'

It was a casket, perhaps eighteen inches square, sheathed in beaten gold and inlaid with electrum, its domed lid surmounted by a solid gold cross. Both cross and casket were liberally adorned with rubies and emeralds. His eyes locked on the reliquary Hawkhurst ran a thoughtful hand across his chin. He chose the next words carefully.

'I thought this had been stolen. 1987 wasn't it? There was a terrific hue and cry when it disappeared.'

She smiled.

'That was for the benefit of the press. No, we didn't steal it, we didn't need to. We bought it, fair and square for $20 million – I can show you the receipt. The monastery of St Bernadino was falling apart at the seams and the only way they could raise the necessary cash for reconstructions was to sell their greatest treasure. The Vatican wouldn't help so they helped themselves. We heard about their problems and offered to buy it from them. The story of a theft was put out for the benefit of the Pope and the politicians in Rome.' She smiled. 'We did hear later that San Bernadino had the reliquary insured for $5 million so I guess the story of a theft suited them pretty well.'

'I'm impressed, Mary Lou. As you say, I'm not entirely sure about some of the things you have here, but anyone who has the organisation and finance to pick up an item like that gets my vote. Pity is you'll never be able to put it on exhibition.'

She seemed to think that of little account.

'Oh, in ten or twenty years we may be able to bring it out of the closet. Anyway, things have a value beyond mere historical interest. It's the same with Excalibur and the Grail, when you say they'll never be up for sale. I hear what you say of course but that doesn't mean we can't explore alternative means of acquiring them.' She looked at her watch. 'Three fifteen, Tom. Guess we better be going – don't want to keep the Reverend waiting, he's a busy man these days.'

With a rumble the doors slid shut across the gleaming reliquary, throwing his features into shadow as she closed and locked the switch panel.

CHAPTER NINE

'Tell me, Tom. Has your time with us here at Gethsemane brought you any nearer to a belief in the existence of God?'

Hawkhurst, groaning inwardly at this latest phase of the Reverend Whichelow's interminable inquisition, took comfort in the fragrance of the brandy glass in his hand and maintained his easy smile. At times his jaws had physically ached and the smile was in danger of becoming a permanent fixture after the past week's frenetic activities. In spite of everything, his resistance to their incessant evangelism and lobbying for ways of obtaining the Grail, remained as rock steady as his smile. Come the morning, please the God who featured so prominently in even the most mundane conversations in Gethsemane, he would be outward bound for Britain and free once and for all of this endless theological harassment.

'No. Not in a personal God, I'm afraid. I've never found any evidence of a deity who took any interest in me as an individual.'

The Reverend, his massive back turned to his audience, Tom and Mary Lou, sighed audibly. Staring out at the Wyoming night, hands clasped behind his back, he shook his huge head.

'Have you never considered that your presence here in Gethsemane today might be the very evidence you seek? That the Almighty first revealed his wonders to you in that tomb and then guided your steps here? Guided you to where you can best serve His purpose?'

It being Hawkhurst's last night in the commune he had half expected they would throw everything into converting him to their beliefs like this. Throughout his stay in Gethsemane he had been obliged to fend off their persistent lobbying. However, while it was tiresome, they had, nevertheless, treated him like royalty and, more importantly, were prepared to pay handsomely for the privilege. In the circumstances he felt honour bound to treat their continual evangelising with politeness at least.

'I'm not sure I'm looking for any evidence,' he pointed out gently, 'and remember I have never accepted your basic assumption about the Whitenditch finds. You see the hand of God in the discovery of the grave and the finding of what many, yourself included, choose to believe is the Holy Grail. I only see a chance archaeological discovery and Dark Age artefacts.'

In the shadows of the Reverend's vast and gloomy office his acolyte, Mary Lou, laid aside her pretzels to take up the cudgel on her spiritual leader's behalf.

'We believe the Lord has chosen you, Tom, as an instrument to make his divine will manifest to the world. We believe he wants you to use the power represented by the Grail to further his mighty work.'

Tom shook his head.

'But you know I have never accepted the bowl as being anything other than an example of early Celtic silver smithing. I cannot and will not interpret it as anything I cannot prove or deduce.' It was time to dig his heels in. 'I'm sorry. I recognise what you say as being strongly held opinions and I have nothing but respect for the work you do here, but I cannot pretend to share your beliefs.'

The Reverend turned to face his heresy. Somewhere in his mid-fifties, he was a big man in every way. Six feet if he was an inch and probably close on 300 pounds. Despite the expensive, carefully cut suit, nothing could disguise the great sack of a belly that strained over his belt or the rolls of fat that welled up above the starched dog collar. Nevertheless, even such grossness could not detract from the man's awesome presence. Above the wild patriarch's beard, black eyes smouldered like the coals of hellfire and his lank, iron grey hair hung down, shoulder length, like an Old Testament prophet. About his neck, suspended on a heavy silver chain, the sword cross looked like nothing less than an assassin's dagger. The beetling brows were knitted; he was clearly saddened by this continuing show of scepticism.

'Sweet Jesus, Tom, it's so clear. Why can't you see it? Why do you insist on thinking it's just coincidence that, as we stand on the brink of a new Millennium, these sacred objects have been revealed to the world after lying hidden in the earth for so long? The Lord is holding out his hand to you.' Whichelow's voice was bass rumble, sonorous and straight from the deep south yet surprisingly gentle. 'By this revelation of the Grail he's calling on you to enlist in his mighty host. He wants you to take up arms alongside us and serve among the ranks of the righteous in the coming battle with the Prince of Darkness and the armies of the godless.'

Distinctly embarrassed now, Hawkhurst drained his glass. Politeness was one thing but there was a limit to what even he was prepared to accept. He had experienced a growing personal unease with all things pertaining to the Church of Christ the Warrior ever since his experience with the heavies on day one. Since then he had witnessed at close quarters the fervour that his presence in Gethsemane had generated and had no desire to be any further part of it. Both of his televised meetings with Whichelow had been packed to capacity and, Mary Lou had joyfully informed him, in the world beyond had yielded chart topping viewing figures on the west coast and in the midwest. Videos of both meetings were at that very moment winging their way to every colony.

This pleased him not at all, in fact he was dismayed that the impact of his TV appearance had been so dramatic. He felt used. Each hour on screen had been preceded by the audience spending twice that period in prayer and hymn singing, bringing them to a high state of excitement long before he appeared on stage. In spite of his determination to bring a coldly analytical approach to his subject and a strict insistence on rationality, both meetings had ended in scenes of hysteria. His every remark and word had been given an unintentioned interpretation by Whichelow who could summon quotations, biblical, hagiological and mythological with consummate ease. During the proceedings there had been spontaneous outbursts of psalm singing and chanting. Some had fainted under the broiling heat of the television lights and these had been hailed as clear examples of possessions by spirits. Others had claimed to have seen visions while some gibbered like apes and were declared to be speaking in tongues. Afterwards, when he had attempted to leave the Tabernacle, he found himself mobbed by hundreds of young zealots, pushing and jostling in their eagerness to shake his hand or slap his back. On the second occasion it had taken some very
un-Christian baton wielding by the security guards to force a way through to the waiting limousine. Heads had been busted to restore discipline.

Of course, he recognised that it wasn't all bad news. While back in Britain Laura might envy his hogging the limelight like this, both she and Dixey would, he knew, be delighted by the hype that was building up around the finds. But it had been irritating to find his deliberately pragmatic and low key approach totally upstaged by Whichelow's ability to quote some obscure tract which inexorably pointed to divine intervention and the hand of God. To impressionable youngsters like

Suzie, many of them deeply world scarred and desperately seeking some sense of direction in their lives, it was a possibility that inevitably held infinite attraction. Already thoroughly indoctrinated in the ethos of the Church of Christ the Warrior they had been fertile, unquestioning, ground for the Reverend's interpretation of the finds. Disturbed by the, to him rather distasteful, hysteria he seemed to have stirred up, Hawkhurst had already vowed never to undertake such appearances again and now longed only for the flight out tomorrow. It appeared, however, that the Reverend had still not abandoned all hope of recruiting him to the cause. He settled his bulk behind the massive oak desk, his face bathed in the soft yellow glow of the angled reading light. Prominently displayed on the desk were three silver framed photographs showing Whichelow outside the White House alongside Presidents Reagan, Bush and Clinton.

'Well, I'll be honest, Tom, I'm bitterly disappointed that we haven't been able to convince you but I'd like you to take a little longer to think this thing through. We've seen these past days the power you have to move people, to inspire them. You would be a powerful warrior in the host of the Lord. With the Holy Grail going before us we could smite our enemies hip and thigh. Once and for all we could end the dominion of Satan over the benighted tribes of the earth. Use your power, Tom. Use it in the coming battle.'

Hawkhurst smiled dutifully but, draining his glass and glancing pointedly at his watch, made to get up. He'd had just about enough.

'We're deadly serious about obtaining the Grail, Tom.' Mary Lou's voice had a distinct edge to it. 'It belongs here where its true meaning and purpose is recognised. Here, where its divine power for good can be properly utilised.'

Hawkhurst recalled her thinly veiled reference to treasure crossing borders.

'That, I'm afraid, is quite out of the question. You must be realistic. Even if I was interested in joining your Church, which with all due respect I'm not, I have absolutely no control over what happens to the finds. They will almost certainly stay in Britain. Even with the vast resources the Church of Christ the Warrior evidently has at its command you couldn't hope to obtain an export license for something like that. I'm afraid you just have to accept that. While we may never know for sure what the origins of the bowl really are it will never be up for sale.'

The short silence that followed made Tom hope they had finally accepted the inevitable and that he now had an opportunity to depart without appearing ungracious. The Reverend, however, had one last card to play.

'OK, Tom, I guess we have to accept what you say but ...' he bit his lower lip thoughtfully, as though in some dilemma. Then the deep set eyes flashed. 'Look, I know you're flying out tomorrow but, before you go there's something I'd like you to see. It won't delay your departure and it may give you a deeper insight into what we are trying to achieve here. What do you say? I'll pick you up from the hotel at six. We'll arrange to have any luggage you may have to be taken direct to the airfield. OK?'

Tom groaned inwardly. Would they never give up? Still, so long as it didn't delay his flight out, what the hell. He nodded his assent.

*****

The breeze stirred the nets and Heydar felt its cool kiss on his cheek. He liked the times they stayed at this remote house high in the mountains above the broad plain of the Euphrates. He did not know who owned the house but imagined it would be some senior government official in distant Damascus, perhaps a relative of the Syrian President. From the first floor window he looked down on the verdant lawns where peacocks wandered among the rainbow casting sprinklers, their plumage iridescent blues and greens in the early sunlight. Heydar always imagined Paradise would be something like this. Deep in thought he did not hear Firdasi enter the room and seat himself behind the ornate walnut desk that was a relic of the days of the French mandate over the country. He smiled at the younger man's reverie.

'Good morning, Heydar,' he said softly and the young man turned to face him.

Firdasi was thirty three years of age, of medium height and slim. He wore a simple white woollen robe and his dark hair was cut close, as was the neatly trimmed beard. In the olive skinned face the deep brown eyes twinkled with good humour.

'Good morning, Master.'

To his closest followers Firdasi was always The Master although he himself had never sought any such title. Indeed he had carefully avoided any title or mark of rank that might make him unacceptable to any of the several, often conflicting, Islamic sects. He would not be Imam, Mullah or Ayatollah, nor Sheikh or Caliph. Nor was he overtly Shia, or Sunni, Ismaili, Wahhabbi or Sufi. While his name, Firdasi, might suggest Iranian birth, his manner of dress tended towards the Arab and was always so austerely simple as to defy categorisation. Some said he was The Mahdi, the God guided one sent to heal the rifts that had split and weakened Islam for so long but Firdasi laughed at such talk. He was, he insisted, Firdasi, a simple slave of Allah.

Yet for all his modesty he had truly achieved much success in healing the running sores of Muslim history and his influence was growing everywhere. He was as welcome in the rabid Western-hating capitals like Teheran and Tripoli as he was in moderate Cairo. Throughout Islam the struggling democracies, the military dictatorships and the feudal aristocracies were as one to Firdasi. To Allah and Allah only did he bow down. On the Haj last year he had drawn crowds to his tent outside Mecca that had numbered hundreds of thousands. In the same year he had met with Jewish and Christian religious leaders in Jerusalem and had embraced them as brothers and People of the Book. The Americans and Israelis had their doubts about him for although he was regarded as a voice of moderation who had never advocated violence, he had an unsettling ability to reconcile the irreconcilable and as such posed a clear threat to their traditional policies of divide and rule.

'You will be sorry to leave here, I think.' As he spoke Firdasi kept his eyes on the open file at the centre of his desk. The boy, he was little more, shrugged.

'As Allah wills, Master.'

'As Allah wills indeed,' echoed Firdasi absently. 'Has Boujera arrived yet?'

'The man is downstairs now, Master.' Try as he may Heydar's dislike of Boujera could not be disguised in his voice. 'I will summon him.'

When Boujera appeared the boy's contempt was reinforced as he contrasted the appearance of the Palestinian and The Master. Today, Boujera wore a smart navy blue suit, a dark red silk tie and a pair of hand crafted Italian shoes that glowed darkly. On every finger a gold ring flashed and at his wrist a heavy gold watch. He might be an Arab but the West and its corrosive culture had eaten into him. As if sensing his disapproval Boujera remained standing and eyed him in cold silence. Firdasi made all clear.

'You may speak openly, Akbar. I have no secrets from Heydar.'

Boujera, unhappy, frowned. His relationship with Firdasi was an odd one for he received no payment for the information he supplied. It was his need to have a foot in all camps that brought him here. Where he sold information to the Americans, Israelis, French and British for dollars with Firdasi he bartered in kind. Seeing the boy would not be asked to leave he shrugged and sat down, carefully arranging the immaculate creases of his trousers so as not to blunt their edge.

'I believe The Reverend Whichelow is preparing some move in the near future.'

Firdasi's features remained impassive.

'What makes you think that?'

'His people have been asking many questions recently, raking up the matter of the hostages again.'

'The dead hostages?'

'Yes.'

'The hostages he knows full well are dead yet he persists in trying to get them released?'

'Yes.'

'And why do you think that is, Akbar?'

'He is picking an old sore to stir trouble. To encourage his warmongering supporters in Washington to initiate aggression against us.'

'Us, Akbar?'

'Islam.'

'Ah, I see.' Firdasi smiled sagely. Like Heydar he had little respect for the man before him. Boujera was devious, of uncertain loyalties and driven by a dangerously passionate love of material things. Yet he had his uses and now it was time to make sure the man continued to keep him informed. 'Thank you for that insight, it agrees with what my other informants tell me.' The smile died. 'Now, no doubt, you will want something to tell your other clients about my plans, Akbar.'

Boujera looked at him, uncomfortable at this plainness of speech and its implications of double dealing, but said nothing. What The Master, as they were calling him in the Souks, did and said was carrying growing importance these days. Everyone was interested in Firdasi's thoughts and actions and first-hand information about these things was at a premium. Firdasi looked at him directly.

'You can tell them that I am going into the desert to commune with Allah. When I learn what he wants of me I shall give a sign to the whole of Islam. Another thing. Tell your contacts at the Church of Christ the Warrior that God sees into their hearts and that nothing is hidden from Him.'

His gaze dropped back to the file before him and Boujera, realising he would get no more than this cryptic offering stood up and left. As he went Heydar looked wistfully out of the window again and savoured the soft zephyr that rose up from the flood plain. So it was to be back to the desert, to the heat, dust and flies, the stench of obstinate camels and the flapping of wind tossed tent canvas. So be it. It was the simple, hard nomadic life that had inspired Abraham and Mohammed. It was the life where man came closest to Allah. He turned to find Firdasi watching him. The Master smiled.

'Taqiyya, Heydar. You know what that means?'

The boy nodded.

'Yes Master. That at times of great danger the heart's dearest beliefs should be concealed from the enemies of Islam until the danger has passed.'

'These are such times, Heydar. We shall remain here for several weeks yet.'

*****

Back in the quiet sanity of the hotel Hawkhurst made another abortive attempt to phone Angahrad. Again advised that the number was unobtainable he took solace in the fact that he would be home in two days and, his head a little muzzy from Whichelow's brandy, decided to take a swim before turning in.

Like everything else at Gethsemane the facilities were impressive. An Olympic length pool with a separate diving pool, all in immaculate cerulean blue tiles that stretched upwards into the shadowy darkness of the unlit viewing stand. At nine in the evening it was predictably deserted, the mirror-like surface of the water shattering as he plunged into its balmy, soothing embrace. At home he regularly swam in the broad pools that formed in the mountain streams as they cascaded down to the valley and contrasted the invigorating bite of their waters to the oily, sybaritic warmth of the pool. The sound of his efforts echoing in the empty hall, he swam steadily for half an hour until his arms began to ache gently and he felt he had done sufficient penance to exorcise the effects of the surfeit of food and alcohol that had been such a feature of the Church's hospitality. Hauling himself out of the pool he took up the towel and began drying himself off, chafing his arms and torso roughly until a satisfying glow of wellbeing began to spread through his body.

'Good night, Doctor Hawkhurst.'

It was Suzie's voice, ringing out hollowly from the shadows of the stands above him. He craned his neck, eyes straining to penetrate the upper gloom. Slowly she materialised, her slim form solidifying as she came into the light, swaying gracefully down the steps towards him. Across the blue water between them she waved a book at him. He guessed it would be a Bible.

'I hope I didn't disturb you. I like to come here to study at night – it's so much quieter than the reading room.'

He smiled. In the days since he had arrived in Gethsemane she had shed much of her initial shyness.

'No, you didn't disturb me, Suzie. And you're right, it is very peaceful here. Goodnight.'

With a wave, he padded back down the long, plushly carpeted corridor to his room, intent on an early night, the girl watching thoughtfully as he went.

Having packed his few belongings in readiness for tomorrow he switched on the television, just in time to catch CBN News at Ten. So completely immersed had he been in his business at Gethsemane it was his first contact with the real world in six days. Little it seemed had changed. The Middle East still held centre stage. Suicide bombers had blown up a bus carrying Israeli schoolchildren, killing dozens and maiming more. The Israeli Prime Minister had announced that the peace process was now on hold indefinitely and had sent troops back into areas only recently handed over to Palestinian control. A major conference of all Islamic States was to be held to consider an appropriate response. Firdasi had decided not to attend. According to those who knew about such things, sensing a slide towards war, he had held aloof and had vanished into the desert with his closest followers to seek divine guidance. The news from elsewhere was equally depressing. In Central Africa evidence of continuing tribal genocide among refugees was shown. Hawkhurst briefly took in the images of bloated, fly infested bodies, strewn haphazardly along the margins of some godforsaken Rwandan mud track like so much litter, and switched off. It was nearly ten thirty. Tomorrow would be a long day, the more so now he had allowed Whichelow the chance to delay him further. He'd best get some sleep. As he switched out the light there came a tentative tapping at the door. Pulling on a robe he went to the door and, to his surprise, found himself looking down into Suzie's eager fresh features. She seemed nervous.

'I'm sorry to disturb you, Doctor.' She looked up and down the empty corridor. 'I just wanted to tell you how much I enjoyed your lectures.'

'Thank you, I've enjoyed being here.' He lied. 'You've all been very kind.'

Even as he spoke he sensed this was something more than a simple leave taking, that there was more on offer here than an exchange of pleasantries. It had been over ten days since he bid farewell to Angahrad during which time he had enjoyed no female company save for the rather marginal Mary Lou. It would, however, be akin to sacrilege to push this particular situation too far, he decided. Yet the matter was to be taken out of his hands, when after an embarrassing pause in the conversation, she slipped past him into the room and firmly shut the door behind her. A little bemused Tom watched as she went through to the bedroom, suspecting that for all her expressions of Christian piety Suzie was just as subject to the pagan temptations of the flesh as he was. By the time he stood in the doorway of the bedroom she was sitting on the bed. Naked save for a pair of yellow briefs through which her pubic darkness showed clearly, she leant back the better to display the heavy, dark bossed breasts. The decision it seemed, had been taken for him.

'Are you shocked, Doctor Tom?' Her voice was child-like, she was a naughty little girl, fearful of a stern rebuke or maybe physical punishment. Taken aback, Hawkhurst's first feelings were for the girl's feelings, although there was no denying the allure of her ripe young body.

'No, not shocked, Suzie, just a bit surprised I guess. Why me?'

'Because I trust you. Because I think you're the only one in this whole sick township who won't report me. I guess because you seem to tell the truth, whether or not it's what people want to hear. I saw the way the Reverend tried to make you say that old bowl was the Holy Grail but you wouldn't. A lot of people here swallow anything they're fed so long as they can convince themselves that God wants it that way, but some of us still have a brain left, we're not all the zombies we must look like to you.'

He stood by the bed, stretching out his hand to stroke her hair. He half wanted to tell her to go back to her own room, that he was not interested, but knew that was not entirely true. Already his body was overriding his conscience. Sensing his ambivalence she smiled up at him, gaining confidence.

'I'm not a puritan maid, you know. I guess Mrs Berkowitz will have told you I worked the streets for a while. She makes sure she tells all the men who come here that – make them worry I might be carrying a dose of clap. She also tells them that I've been saved by the Church – that's so their conscience will stop them trying to lay me. She's jealous as hell of anyone who even looks at me.'

'Why should she be jealous?' Hawkhurst asked, at the same time recalling Laura's cryptic reference to Mary Lou's sexual proclivities.

'Cos she thinks she owns me. Cos she thinks she's turned me into a raving lesbo like her.' She ran a wet tongue across her lips and her bright blue eyes, grown bold now, flirted with his. 'She'll never know how wrong she is. Do you have a wife, Doctor?'

He considered the question and thought of Angahrad. It was a fine distinction. He could tell the truth and still be lying. This he did.

'No. I'm not married, Suzie.'

Perhaps reassured to find that, whatever other commandments she might be about to break, technically at least adultery would not be amongst them, she stood up. Slim arms went about his neck, pulling his mouth down onto the heat of her own. Her tongue slithered like a scarlet serpent into his mouth and, feeling his body respond, she smiled up at him, her hand sliding across the muscled plane of his stomach under the folds of his robe, finding and gently caressing his swelling manhood.

'Mm. It's nice to feel the genuine article again. Rubber strap-ons can be a real turn off.' Now she was being deliberately forward, trying to shock him with her worldliness.

Thoughts of resistance fading fast, Hawkhurst was nevertheless determined to stay in control of the situation. Behind the easy coquettishness he sensed the whore's contempt for her mark. Taking her nipple between thumb and forefinger he twisted the puckered flesh sharply, bringing a yelp of pain from the girl. He smiled at the outrage that flared in her wide eyes as she writhed to escape his cruel grasp. Finally releasing her, he held her at arm's length then pulled her close, listening to her defeated panting against his chest.

'Now, Suzie,' he said softly. 'Let's start again.'

'What do you like?' she asked weakly. 'What do you want me to do?'

In answer he lay both hands on her soft shoulders, applying just enough pressure to indicate that she should kneel. The sullen features melted into a sultry smile, she was back on familiar ground again. Dropping to her knees she twined her arms about his strong thighs and he curled his hand about the smooth nape of her neck, pulling her onto him. At first she made a token gesture of resistance, arching her back against his pull, her eyes defiantly on his, although her smile never faltered. Then her gaze moved down to his penis and in one hungry movement she took it in her mouth. For several minutes her head plunged rhythmically, all the while expertly regulating the speed and pressure of her lips and tongue. Each time she sensed he was approaching his climax she would slow down her ministrations, easing back to delay the proceedings. Suddenly, disengaging with speed that took him by surprise, she ran to the bed, laughing aloud. Removing her pants in one easy movement and tossing them aside she lay back, legs spread wide.

'Right, Doctor Tom. How let's see what sort of head you give.'

For two hours they continued the remorseless proceedings. Deprived of an outlet for her natural needs for so long, Suzie was determined to make the most of this opportunity. She teased and cajoled, dominated and submitted. Each time he came and his organ flagged she would produce another variation from her repertoire that would bring him willingly back into the fray. She knew how to use to maximum effect every weapon of love that Venus had bestowed upon her. Slim hands like silk, the hot wet mouth, the tight muscular vagina, and in extremis, her plump buttocks were all called upon to sustain and accept his fire. Eventually, totally spent she lay, soft and still, in his arms.

'I guess you think I'm a real slut, eh Tom?'

'Certainly not. Why should I?' He kissed her damp forehead. 'Sex is the most natural thing in the world. To feel shame about it is to deny our own nature. If people spent more time making love and less making money or war the world would be a much happier place.' He knew his words were glib but also that it was what she needed to hear.

She snuggled closer, happy to have been granted absolution so readily.

'I'll never forget you, Tom. You're a good man. When you leave tomorrow I shall come down to the airstrip to see you off. I hear you're going out to Reachwood with the Reverend first though – I heard his chauffeur saying they were getting the chopper ready.'

This mention of the morrow brought him back to reality.

'Oh yes, I'd forgotten that I was promised. What goes on at Reachwood anyway?'

'I don't know. It's strictly off limits to all but the high command. I never heard of any ordinary foot soldiers being allowed up there. To be honest I'm not exactly certain where it is – only that its way back up in the hills someplace.' She took his hand and kissed it, her eyes sad. 'Please, Tom. Will you make love to me once more before I go?'

CHAPTER TEN

'God's own country, son.' The Reverend was shouting to be heard over the drumming of the Chinook's twin rotors. Hawkhurst nodded, looking down at the herds of caribou that scattered in terror below them at the helicopter's approach, swirling like living liquid between the pines. All along the ridge ahead electrical storms danced among the basalt clouds. They had been in the air for fifty minutes and Tom's ears were ringing under the reverberating assault of the engines.

Since leaving Gethsemane Field at first light Whichelow had, without once giving any real intimation of what he was to expect, maintained a non-stop barrage about the importance of what was about to be revealed. Two things were much to the fore in Tom's thoughts. When the Reverend spoke of God's own country, it wasn't simply the understandable pride of a patriotic American in the beauty of his country. It was a literal statement. Every acre of prairie, foothills and mountain that they had flown over belonged, courtesy of the Church of Christ the Warrior, to the Almighty. The other thing was the almost imperceptible shift in their relationship. When he had arrived in Gethsemane Whichelow had greeted him as Doctor. As they had got to know each other better it had become Tom. Now it was son. Well if that was the way he wanted to play it, it was fine by Hawkhurst. He made an effort not to sound over-impressed.

'It's beautiful, Jim. How much further?'

'No more than five minutes. I've put them on alert that we're on our way, so you'll be able to see what Reachwood is all about in short order and get back to Gethsemane pronto. St Michael One is all fuelled up and ready to go so don't worry about that. Just relax and enjoy the show.' He grew studiedly sincere. 'What I'm hoping to do, Tom, is give you something to think about on your way back to the UK. Fact is, son, for better or for worse, what I'm going to show you will change your entire life.'

Eventually the dry beat of the engines relented, throttles easing back, and the chopper banked steeply giving Hawkhurst his first glimpse of Reachwood. It looked like a military camp. Standing in a broad clearing hacked out of the surrounding carpet of sequoia, one half consisted of a tarmac parade ground around which stood a number of administrative buildings. The whole perimeter was delineated by a high triple razor wire fence at each corner of which stood a watchtower. From the air Reachwood looked deserted.

In one corner of the parade ground a large white cross had been laid out and as the helicopter floated into position above this, Whichelow pulled a camouflaged combat jacket over his dark cleric's jacket and set a black beret, complete with silver sword emblem, upon his head. Seeing the question in Hawkhurst's eyes he smiled but offered no explanation. With the gentlest of bumps they settled on the tarmac. Exiting rapidly they hurried across the landing pad, heads down against the down draft of the main rotor. A small knot of khaki fatigue clad figures came forward to receive them. Salutes were exchanged and Whichelow made the necessary introductions.

'Tom, meet Colonel Brett McNaughton. Brett's top honcho here at Reachwood. Brett, this here's Doctor Tom Hawkhurst. Countering the slightly over firm handshake, Hawkhurst assessed the newcomer. A little under average height, McNaughton sought to compensate for his lack of inches by an excessively stiff backed posture, his chin drawn in. He was somewhere in his late thirties and wiry rather than solid in build. Tom noticed that the Colonel and his small entourage who held back at a respectful distance during the introductions all wore the reversed silver sword insignia in their berets. He also saw that on their sleeves, picked out in red silk on white shield shaped badges, red for blood, white for purity, they bore the splayed tipped cross that had first been carried to war by the Knights Templar, the fearsome soldier priests of the Crusades. Having briefly introduced his aides McNaughton got down to business, his speech rapid fire.

'Sure am glad to make your acquaintance, Tom. Just loved your TV programme – the Almighty has certainly showered his blessing upon you. The Reverend tells me you're in something of hurry so if you'll just follow me to the review rostrum we'll get this show on the road. Pity we didn't get more warning, we could have laid on something really spectacular.'

It was an odd feeling, sitting there on the raised podium looking out across the deserted parade ground, the whisper of the breeze that tugged at his hair the only sound. Hawkhurst, flanked by Whichelow and McNaughton, stared out across its emptiness and imagined King Canute must have felt much like this. This immediate lack of action did not seem to trouble his hosts in the least. It was all very quiet. For what seemed like hours, although it was probably no more than three or four minutes, they sat in expectant silence. Then, from far off, came the distant drumming of engines, many engines. His eyes searched the grey, overcast sky but could make out no sign of any aircraft. Nevertheless, the hum was growing in intensity all the time, slowly swelling to a throbbing growl. Then McNaughton pointed.

Over the dark profile of the ridge, nose down and hugging the undulating contours of the timbered hills, came a squadron – no, an armada – of helicopters. They were twin rotored machines similar in configuration to the one that had brought them to Reachwood. That, however, had been painted in the same white livery as St Michael One, these were camouflaged and bore the Templar cross. As they lifted clear of the intervening crest, the raw power of their engines sent out tangible vibrations that Hawkhurst felt rippling on his face. Onwards they came, more and more warbirds materialising from beyond the distant mountains, driving towards the camp in a thunderous symphony. Long before the rearmost had cleared the ridge the leaders were already hovering above the parade ground. Forming up into a regular formation, they swayed gently, almost elegantly, as they kept station with each other. Above these other choppers, smaller more manoeuvrable escort machines bristling with cannon and machine guns, circled continually in a protective umbrella. By the time the last machine was in position Hawkhurst estimated there could have been no less than one hundred and fifty aircraft in the air and the noise of engines was physically painful. The Colonel laid his hand on his arm, shouting to be heard over the din.

'The big bastards are Vertols, Tom, Boeing CH-47s – best damn troop transportation in the world. The others are Apaches, front line attack choppers, latest version straight off the MacDonnell-Douglas production lines. Carry a whole range of weaponry – pack a hell of a punch. If we ain't got anything else we've sure as hell got the hardware. Thanks to our contact in the Pentagon we can sometimes even get priority over the army.'

Slowly the bulky transports began to descend, touching down on the parade ground in almost perfect unison, rotors seemingly only inches apart in their deadly scything. As each machine sagged down onto its undercarriage, doors were thrown open and files of rhythmically grunting soldiers disembarked, running at the double to form up in front of the aircraft that disgorged them. What, minutes earlier, had been a deserted expanse of tarmac was now occupied by three battalions of heavily armed combat troops. Arrayed before him, Hawkhurst estimated were perhaps two thousand well trained and equipped fighting men. So sudden and unexpected had been the appearance of the gunships and so disciplined the marshalling of the troops he had been reduced to a stunned silence. The Reverend had been right in one thing, he reflected grimly. What he had just witnessed would certainly change his life forever. For them to lay on a demonstration like this meant the Church of Christ the Warrior was playing for very high stakes indeed. He considered Whichelow's tunnel-visioned obsession with the bowl – the so called Holy Grail. What, he wondered, could be the connection between that and this blatant demonstration of military power? Whatever it might be, he grimly recognised that this show was not laid on for the benefit of his health.

    As the last troops filed into position, the leading helicopter was already lifting off, followed in quick succession by the rest. Within two minutes the whole fleet was airborne once more, circling the camp, filling the sky like angry dragonflies. Gradually discipline was brought to the aerial melee, the craft slowly forming up into the unmistakable sword formation. Black against the basalt cloud, drumming like thunder, they maintained the symbolic configuration until The Reverend stood and gave an acknowledging wave while McNaughton stood to attention and saluted stiffly. Then, peeling off with immaculate precision, they growled away, line astern, to vanish over the ridge from whence they had come.

    The sound of engines fading to nothing, the stunned Hawkhurst returned his attention to the array drawn up before them. Already they were formed into marching order and at a signal from McNaughton commenced to parade past the podium. All wore standard US Army steel helmets, flak jackets and full combat gear. On each helmet was stencilled the Templars' cross. As they passed at the double, feet crunching in perfect time on the concrete, he saw they were, in the main, armed with standard Armalites. Some of the specialist units, however, were equipped with heavy machine guns, antitank missiles and hand-held surface to air missiles. At the double they filed past the Colonel who saluted each company as it went, eyes snapping right in polished unison. When the last ranks had vanished from the parade ground into the barrack compound he sat down and looked at Hawkhurst.

'So, what do you think, Dr Hawkhurst?'

'Incredible, but ...'

The Reverend laughed aloud at his obvious confusion, a rumble of mirth from the depths of his vast body.

'I guess you could use a drink, eh Tom? Let's go over to the bunker and I'll explain.'

The bunker was a concrete command complex and sunk fifty feet below ground and extending beneath the parade ground. Tom guessed it would be proof against anything short of a direct nuclear hit. At the entrance guards, bearing machine pistols, snapped smartly to attention as, with Whichelow making the pace, they swept through and proceeded down the stairs to
solid-looking steel inner doors. Within, in an ambience of cluttered desks, computer screens and softly ringing telephones that reminded Tom of a busy newspaper's editorial offices, young men in drill fatigues went about their business – whatever that might be. Finally, McNaughton ushered them into a slightly more opulently furnished room where three heavy leather armchairs were drawn up before a large wall-mounted screen. Behind the chairs a projector stood ready loaded with a carousel of transparencies.

'Sit down, Tom, make yourself comfortable.' The Reverend poured out black coffee from a dyspeptic percolator, handing paper cups to all present. 'No doubt you've got lots of questions. Well, just sit back. All is about to be revealed.'

As Hawkhurst eased himself into the chair, the strip lights dimmed and McNaughton took up position by the screen, pointer in hand. With a nod of his head he indicated that he was ready to proceed and a dry click brought up the first image; three faces, young, smiling faces.

'In July 1994, nearly four years ago, while on a mission of mercy in Southern Lebanon, three of our soldiers, John Grantly, Joe Edberg and Patrick McNally, were seized by Hamas terrorists outside a Red Cross medical station. For some eighteen months, through intermediaries, we negotiated with the kidnappers to secure the release of these fine young men. We offered ransom money amounting to $2 million per hostage or, alternatively, whatever non-military aid they cared to name, we even offered to use our good offices to speak out on the Palestinian cause. We might as well have saved our breath. Throughout the negotiations the terrorists refused to allow us access to the hostages or even to confirm that they were still alive.

Our last contact was four months ago when they informed us that the talks were at an end. We believe they were acting under orders from the top echelons, the Ayatollahs, in Teheran. The US and Iran have been at daggers drawn ever since the overthrow of the Shah for a number of reasons – compensation for damage to American assets during the revolution, freezing of Iranian support for international terrorism. Anyway, the negotiations came to nothing and since then all bets have been off.'

He nodded and the next image slid into focus. This time is was single face, darkly handsome Arab features behind a carefully tended Saddam-style moustache. About his head was a chequered head cloth.

'Throughout, all our contacts with the Shiites,' the Colonel, perhaps deliberately, pronounced the word 'Shites', 'has been through this man. Akbar Waleed Boujera. Boujera's a twenty eight year old Palestinian who was born in a Gaza refugee camp. He's as artful as a barrel-load of monkeys and has been, at some time or the other, associated with just about every Islamic fundamentalist faction in the Middle East. It's worth remembering that because he was prepared to spread himself so unselectively, his credibility as a freedom fighter began to wear a little thin. Perhaps because of this credibility gap, sometime in the early nineties he turned his considerable talents to less dangerous and more lucrative pursuits. Within the last few years he has been instrumental in negotiating the release of several French and Italian hostages. He has a good pedigree for this line of work and was certainly involved in getting Waite and the other Brits out in '92. Whatever his motives may be, his credentials are impressive and he's cornered the market – we need him and so do the terrorists – if anyone can pull strings it's Boujera. Three weeks ago he contacted our agents in the Lebanon with important information about the hostages.'

The lights flickered on and Hawkhurst, still assimilating the talk of hostages, frowned as Whichelow stood up. Surely there was more to it than this?

'OK, Tom,' The Reverend's tone was curt: he was in a hurry now. 'Show's over and you've got a plane to catch. I'll tell you the rest on the way back to Gethsemane.'

*****

Airborne again Tom waited impatiently for further explanation of what he had just seen. But the Reverend it seemed was in no great rush.'

'So what did you think of Reachwood?'

His tone was smug but Hawkhurst, worried by the wider implications of what he had witnessed and deeply concerned about the turn events had taken, was in no mood to stroke inflated egos. The combination of an armed force of the size and quality he had just seen and hostages in Lebanon added up to potential disaster.

'I found it a bit disturbing to be honest, Jim,' his tone conveyed a casualness he did not feel, 'Are you seriously thinking of launching a rescue bid?'

The self-satisfied smile on Whichelow's features grew broader.

'Something like that. Well? What do you think? You saw the hardware, you saw how well prepared we are. Are you with us?' His eyes narrowed and he hissed the next words. 'Will you get us the Grail? We want it born aloft at the head of God's host when we smite the infidels. Deliver it to us, Tom, and we'll be ready to strike home.'

Hawkhurst stared in disbelief. Suddenly things began to fall in place.

'I thought I made it clear that I have no control whatsoever over what happens to the Holy Grail.' Despite the firmness of his words he cursed inwardly to find he was using the term now. The Reverend, folding his beret into a neat roll and tucking it away in his pocket, ignored his protestations.

'Why sure you do, Tom, don't be so modest. You're the world champeen on this sort of things. Why the hell do you think we invited you over in the first place? If anyone can move valuables across borders you can. God knows – you're the best grave robber in the business – that's why He sent you to us.'

Flushing with anger Hawkhurst stared directly into Whichelow's puffy features. It was time, he decided, to spell things out once and for all for the benefit of this increasingly ill-mannered fanatic.

'Out of respect for your cloth Whichelow I'll moderate my language. But the more I see of you and your Church, the less I like it. When I fly out of here today I sincerely hope it will be the last I ever see of you and your sick society.' The Revered smiled without humour, easing his bulk deeper into the bucket seat.

'Well it sure pains me to hear you talk like that, son. I had hoped we could do business together.'

Hawkhurst looked out of the window with studied indifference.

'Forget it, Reverend. Just pay me what you owe me and we'll go our separate ways.' Even as he spoke he wondered if he would be allowed to escape that easily after what he had seen. Whichelow, silent for a moment, studied the archaeologist's features thoughtfully. When he spoke next, some of the overwhelming certainty had left his voice, and his manner was a shade more accommodating.

'You must understand, the world is changing fast and the rate of that change is accelerating all the time. Tell me, what do you see when you read the papers, when you watch television, when you talk to your friends? You're an intelligent, educated man, Tom, knowing what you do, how do you see the world developing in the next Millennium?'

Hawkhurst hesitated, his eyes locked on the Reverend's unflinching gaze. The question, he decided, was a serious one. He thought of the television news the previous evening, the mindless savagery, the shattered bodies, the squalor of the refugee camps, the pitiful humanity. He pushed the images from his mind.

'In the last ten years we've seen the end of dictatorship in eastern Europe. We've seen apartheid disappear along with the Berlin Wall. Fanatics and dictators have been kicked out on their arses all round the world. The threat of any major nuclear war has virtually disappeared. That's not a bad record to my mind. I hope it's a sign of the way things will go in the future. I know it's not all good – the Middle East, Africa, Afghanistan, the Balkans – there's a lot to do. But I see a world where hostages are released thanks to patient negotiations. Face it Reverend; you and your private army are dinosaurs.' He continued to eyeball the other man until, with a shrug, Whichelow looked away.

'I guess that's what a lot of people see, son. That's because it's what they want to see. Fact is, it's a load of bullshit. Fact is, the world's going to hell on a handcart. In twenty years the population of the world will be around eleven billion. With the climatic changes that are already screwing up the ecosphere, and believe me there's no hope of reversing them in the foreseeable future, the chances of feeding that many mouths is a big fat zilch.' As he warmed to his subject he rocked slightly to the fro within the confines of his seat.

'Why the hell do you figure every goddamn politician these days is growing greener by the day? I'll tell you. It's because in a very few years, within the first decade of the Third Millennium, everyone will be able to see just what a –' The Reverend hesitated, he was not a naturally profane man and an expletive needed careful consideration – 'what a monumental fuck up the politicians have made of things. When what small part of Africa isn't a dust bowl it's a colony for AIDS victims, when skin cancer's guaranteed for two people out of three, even in the temperate zones, when two billion Chinese start looking for serious Lebensraum, people are gonna turn real nasty. The human race is just like rats in a laboratory; subject them to stress and overcrowding and they become hyper-aggressive. What we're doing to planet Earth, what we've been doing for the last two hundred years, is just replicating laboratory conditions.'

'Global warming is irreversible, just so long as we keep burning fossil fuels and believe me, like it or not, economic considerations dictate that we'll do just that for the foreseeable future. We're gonna see hurricanes like you never dreamed of, we're gonna witness floods and plagues, droughts and famine and most of all we're gonna see wars. Through greed and weakness we have broken our covenant with the Almighty. The Lord is angry with his people. This is how he makes his anger manifest. He's done it before. Remember Moses and Pharaoh, the Lord is a Man of War.

'You think a raid into Lebanon is going to change things?'

'Look ahead, Tom. Stop thinking like a scientist for once and have a little vision. When the whole kit and caboodle starts falling apart who do you think they'll come running to?'

'You think they'll turn to you and your kind to save them, Reverend? Is that what you think?' Hawkhurst smiled bitterly. 'Somehow I doubt it.'

Whichelow returned his smile in trumps, fingering the sword about his neck.

'Oh no, Tom. Not to me. People like you and me don't figure in this in the long term. They'll turn to God. They'll turn to God because there'll be no one else to turn to. Look at the Middle East; the Muslims have seen what's coming. They are on the march already. Firdasi and his followers may talk peace but they know well-enough what's coming. Where we, the Church, come in is to prepare the way. Prepare ye the way of the Lord. We've been told what to do – the

Church of Christ the Warrior and its allies have taken up the challenge.' Whichelow looked at Hawkhurst, trying to assess the impact of his prophecies. The dark features remained impassive as The Reverend took up his theme anew. 'Tell me, Tom, you're an archaeologist, what do you know about the Templars?'

'Probably a damn sight more than you,' Tom thought, recalling the symbols worn by McNaughton's men, but said nothing.

Whichelow drew breath as he prepared to lighten his perceived darkness.

'The Knights of the Temple of Solomon were formed in 1118 to guard the Holy places and the pilgrims who visited them. They were disciplined like monks and trained like warriors – lambs in peace and lions in war. That's the way I like to think of the Church of Christ the Warrior. But the Templars became much more than simple tools of Rome. They became diplomats and traders. They became bankers to the whole of the western world. They became the makers and breakers of Kings and kingdoms. They worked to Holy ends in worldly ways. That, too, is my dream for the Church.'

As Hawkhurst assimilated this cryptic observation the co-pilot appeared in the doorway to advise them that the field was coming up fast. As the chopper banked into its landing position, things bothered him more than somewhat. The Reverend had revealed his hand in no uncertain manner. Surely he would require some assurance that Hawkhurst would not breach the security about Reachwood. As they settled back for the descent Whichelow laid a hairy hand on Tom's knee. The man was deadly serious now, menacing.

'There's a war coming, Tom. Armageddon, the war to end all wars. The war that will establish the Kingdom of God on Earth for all time. Only He can save this polluted, benighted planet and we must prepare the way for His coming. Think about what I've just said and all you've seen here. We'll contact you in a few days. Until then don't mention anything to anyone else.'

Before he could muster a suitable response, the door was opened and Whichelow pointed out across the airstrip. 'Your flight's waiting, son. I should get moving if I were you.'

*****

'Good trip, Tom?' Brennan's interest seemed no more than a polite conversation opener, yet, with the Reverend's parting words much in mind Hawkhurst was tense enough to see conspiracy everywhere. He hadn't expected to be travelling back with Brennan and if the man was on the Church's payroll, it would pay to be careful. He tightened his lap strap and smiled easily.

'Sure. It's a very impressive place.'

Brennan already had a broached bottle of Bourbon in hand, holding it up questioningly. Tom shook his head.

'Not just yet, Harry, a little later maybe.'

Sandy appeared from the cockpit, smiling in unashamed joy at having the pair of them in her power once more. For all her angelic appearance she seemed to have no qualms about aiding and abetting their descent into purgatory.

'I sure loved your programmes, Dr Hawkhurst,' she said, sitting down opposite him. 'I watched both of them. What will you do when you get back?'

His thoughts in turmoil, Tom's response was guarded. He could do without small talk. He needed to think.

'Well, there's a lot of work to be done. I haven't completed my research on the coins yet.' It was a lie but he needed to keep the thing open and subject to some doubt. 'It only needs one coin to date from a later period and the whole theory of it being Arthur's grave goes out the window.' He didn't voice his growing conviction that this might be no bad thing. 'How long before we take off?'

Sandy peered out of the window.

'Shouldn't be too long now. Just as soon as the ambulance has moved off the strip we can get rolling.'

'Ambulance?'

Brennan broke into the conversation.

'Yeah, nasty business. Seems some kid from the hotel walked into a propeller.'

CHAPTER ELEVEN

The first part of the flight from Gethsemane to New York slipped past in a kind of nightmare limbo. Numbed, first by The Reverend's revelations at Reachwood and then by Brennan's casual remark about the accident at the airfield, Hawkhurst remained largely oblivious to what was going on around him. Without having to ask he knew instinctively that the incident at the airstrip had involved Suzie. What was even worse to contemplate was that it was almost certainly a direct result of the madness into which he had been unwittingly drawn. 'I'll come to see you off,' she had said. Now she was dead.

It was with La Guardia less than an hour away that Brennan, the obligatory bottle of Jim Beam in his outstretched hand, broke into his grim reverie.

'You sure are quiet, Tom. Everything OK?'

Hawkhurst's eyes narrowed. Was the man fishing? Was he a party to what went on up at Reachwood? There was only one way to find out. He took the offered bottle and poured a healthy measure into a crystal glass before responding. No, whatever Brennan's relationship to The Reverend and the Church, it seemed unlikely that he would know what was going on up in the mountains. He decided to play it straight.

'Sorry, Harry, didn't mean to be unsociable. Got a lot on my mind at the moment. My feet have barely touched the ground these past few days.' He tried to change the subject. 'What about you? Where are you off to next?'

Brennan shook his head and blinked stupidly: the bourbon had really got to grip by now. His scarred face was flushed and his tie hung crookedly below the unbuttoned shirt collar.

'Don't really know. The Reverend told me to stop over in NY and that I'd get my orders from there.' He snapped his fingers. 'Hell, I almost forgot. I got something here for you.' He pulled a battered brief case from the overhead locker and rummaged through it, finally producing a large manila envelope. Handing it across the aisle to Hawkhurst, he grimaced. 'I guess that old dyke Mary Lou would have my balls for breakfast if I forgot to give it to you.'

Peeling back the adhesive flap Tom slid his hand inside. It contained three smaller envelopes, white numbered with large stamped letters; one, two and three. With fingers grown clumsy in his haste to learn the worst he opened number one.

It was a cheque for thirty thousand dollars, three times his agreed fee. They had either been very impressed with his efforts or, more likely, were trying a little bribery and corruption. There was a note in Mary Lou's neat hand clipped to the cheque.

"Dear Tom," it read, "I hope most sincerely that you will accept this as a small token of our appreciation of your sterling efforts while in Gethsemane. In the other two envelopes you will find other things relating to our work at Reachwood and our future plans. I believe the Reverend has already spoken briefly to you about these." The next sentence had been underlined in red for emphasis. "Be warned. Mr Brennan is not party to any matters relating to Reachwood, nor are the crew of St Michael One. Under no circumstances should you discuss Reachwood or the contents of the accompanying envelopes with anyone. With the exception of the cheque, I recommend you destroy everything else by burning at the earliest opportunity. This is for your own protection as much as ours. Open envelope number two next."

The second envelope contained another letter, this time in a flamboyant scrawl. It was from Whichelow.

"My dear Dr Hawkhurst," it read, "I imagine your visit to Reachwood will have provided you with much food for thought. You will, I am sure, be in no doubt whatsoever as to the sincerity of our beliefs, of our determination to carry out our plans. I spoke of a time for action, that time has arrived. By the time you reach London the Church of Christ the Warrior will be on the march and the task force will have embarked on its historic mission. It is irrevocable and unstoppable. His truth is marching on.

You have ten days in which to deliver the Holy Grail into our possession, preferably with the sword although this is not essential. On receipt of the sacred chalice you will be paid the sum of one million US dollars or its equivalent in any currency of your choice. We will also be happy to provide any assistance you may need to evade or placate the authorities. I suggest you take five minutes to consider our offer. If after that period you decide you are with us, do not, repeat, do not open the third envelope but destroy it at the earliest opportunity.

If you feel you are against us, however, and do not choose to fight on the side of right in the coming battle, then you are to open it, inspect the contents, and then review your position. May the Almighty guide you in your deliberations, Doctor."

Hawkhurst stared at the remaining envelope, wondering what it could possibly contain that might change his mind about Whichelow and his maniac plans. It could, he thought, although with little conviction, be a letter bomb. He certainly wouldn't put it past Whichelow and his cohorts to blast St Michael One out of the sky if they thought it would ensure their plans were not compromised. He ran an exploratory hand lightly over the smoothness of the creamy paper. What a letter bomb actually felt like he hadn't the least idea but assumed it would be wired up to batteries and therefore bulky. In fact he couldn't feel anything unusual although it was fairly stiff, as though it might contain a card. Reassured, he slit it open with his thumb. It was a sheaf of black and white photographs.

He flicked through them, his mouth tightening at what he saw there. It was Suzie, kneeling among the tangled sheets of his bed, her head thrown back in delight, her eyes slits of lust. The corners of her moist lips were pulled down in sheer abandon as he went at her from behind. Mounted like two dogs in the street, his hands clutched at her heavy breasts, his face set in a smile of salacious concentration. The camera must have been in the digital alarm clock.

The others, there were eight in all, were in much the same vein. It was noticeable that in every photograph, in every position, his face was always recognisable. No doubt these were only a selection. Ashamed and mortified he thrust them hurriedly back into the envelope, his eyes going to Brennan, fearful the man might have seen. His fears proved unfounded for Brennan was by now fully preoccupied with draining what little liquor remained in the bottle. Clipped to the photographs had been another message from Whichelow.

"Dear Tom, The fact you are reading this can only mean that you have been tempted to throw your hand in with the forces of darkness. It will also mean you have seen the photographs and are now fully aware that you have no other choice than to deliver the Holy Grail into our hands. I suggest you make your plans swiftly. Our agents in London will contact you within three days. At this late stage any attempt on your part to involve the police or other authorities can have no effect whatsoever on our plans. It will, however, automatically result in the photographs being despatched to all major newspapers in Britain and the United States. Even if such filth is not fit to print it will certainly make a good story. Sleaze is always so popular with the gutter press. If you are still not convinced of our determination I think you should know that young Suzie was involved in a nasty accident down at the airfield this morning. Seems like she committed suicide. I guess the kind of depraved treatment she received at your hands must have turned the poor child's mind. Anyway, it'll be another juicy angle to a story that the papers would just love to get their hands on. It should just run and run, as they say."

Tom considered this final twist of the screw suspiciously. How, he wondered, could Whichelow have known about Suzie's death in time to include it in the letter? The accident had only happened while St Michael One, and Brennan with the letter in his briefcase, were waiting on the airstrip. His initial shame and discomfiture slowly hardening into anger, he seethed at the callous ruthlessness of Whichelow. Having presumably ordered, either directly or through Mary Lou, the dead girl to seduce him, the man had then casually had her killed to strengthen his hold over Hawkhurst.

A slow red glow of anger began to pulse at the centre of his brain. It was humiliating enough to recognise the ease with which they had duped him. But, even so, he knew for all the embarrassment it would have caused, he would not have bowed to the pressure of sexual blackmail. Now the rules had changed. An innocent girl, a child who had trusted him, had been used and then killed to further a crazy man's religious mania. Someone was going to pay, but first he needed information. He ran through a mental list of potential sources, the time for caution had passed.

'Any of the Jim Beam left, Harry?'

Brennan, half dozing, opened his eyes and examined the empty bottle in some dismay.

'Afraid not, Tom.' His face brightened. 'But if I'm any judge, young Sandy will have another stashed away somewhere. He pressed the button on his armrest bringing the stewardess to his side in seconds. She smiled down at them like a couple of naughty schoolboys but was, nevertheless, quick to produce the necessary elixir. Perhaps weary of the tight-arsed puritanism of Gethsemane she was relentless in her determination to send them on their way as drunk as possible.

For the present that suited Hawkhurst just fine. Nor was Brennan displeased at the prospect.

'Ain't for me, Hon, honest,' the scarred man insisted wide-eyed. 'It's for the good doctor here, though maybe I'll help him out a little. Truth to tell, I've never been one to let a man drink alone – it's always seemed downright rude to me.' He was delighted to be presented with the opportunity to crack another bottle, unaware that Hawkhurst intended to make the most of his good humour and inebriated condition.

'You ever been up to Reachwood, Harry?'

'No. I never really found out what goes on up there. Guess it's some kind of retreat, huh?' He smiled. 'Somewhere they go to commune with God?'

'Something like that.'

Hawkhurst remembered a sky dark with growling death and three battalions of crack assault troops. If what Whichelow had written was to be believed they were already on the move, already embarked on whatever madness he was planning. It made sense. Once they had revealed their hand to him they wouldn't hang around, just in case he did decide to blow the whistle on them.

Sipping his bourbon carefully he considered the situation. He was no military expert but even he could see the task force didn't make tactical sense for a hostage rescue. Two thousand men to bring out three? It was a crazy concept. For all the undoubted excellence of their training and equipment, any direct attack on a heavily defended urban area like Beirut had to expect twenty, maybe thirty per cent casualties.

That would be an optimistic figure, knowing the fanatical courage of the Muslim fighters it might well be much higher. Even assuming that, possessing the element of surprise, they did manage to establish a bridgehead, they would have to be pretty quick if the hostages were not to end up with their throats cut.

On top of this, the international repercussions were too awful to contemplate. The Middle East was a tinder box. In Iraq, despite his humiliation in the Gulf War, Saddam Hussein was still in power seven years on, licking his wounds and looking for any opportunity for revenge. Iran remained as anti-western as ever in its fundamentalism, a fundamentalism that through Hezbollah was spreading like a virus to previously stable states like Egypt and Algeria. In Israel the Intifada dragged on, and the situation there was little short of open warfare already in some areas. To many in the West, Islamic fanaticism was already on the march while to many moderate Muslims it seemed their most dearly held beliefs were under siege by the decadent, sex-obsessed and money driven culture of the Great Satan America. Any apparent aggression by a western, nominally Christian, force could have the most dreadful repercussions. It would bring the polarisation that the fanatics, on both sides, longed for. War seemed a distinct possibility. A bunch of Christian mercenaries, for whether they had got religion or not, that's what they were, were to be inserted into the world's most unstable region. It would not just be war, it would be a Holy War – the Jihad that Khomeini and Gaddafi and others of that ilk had urged so often, yet been unable to ignite. Whichelow was about to provide the ayatollahs and imams with a cause that every decent Arab would be quick to rally to, while pariahs like Saddam and Gaddafi would be eager to fan the flames. Even the, thus far, benign influence of Firdasi would be unable to stop the slide towards war. There was a potential for disaster here that appalled and fascinated.

The more Hawkhurst considered the matter, the less he was inclined to see the task force assembled at Reachwood as having the hostages as its prime concern. Something similar had been tried before and the lessons of history did not make for happy reading. In 1980 the United States had mounted a similar operation, intending to rescue 50 hostages held by the revolutionary government at the US embassy in Teheran. Operation Eagle Claw, which had the advantages of unlimited resources and first class intelligence, had been an unmitigated fiasco. Despite the best efforts of the crack Delta Force, in the end ten American servicemen had died, expensive equipment had been shamefully abandoned in the hasty pull out and the hostages quickly dispersed across Iran by their captors, ruling out any further rescue attempts.

Whichelow was undoubtedly mad, yet it was the perverse, unturnable madness of the fanatic that allowed him to rationalise everything. In his scheme of things there wasn't anything, no matter how evil or destructive, that you couldn't do – always provided it was done in the name of God. He was the mirror image of some Islamic leaders. Tom threw back his bourbon in one, half refilling his glass and generously topping up Brennan's.

'Where're you staying in New York, Harry?'

'I've got an apartment over on the East River, on 23rd and FDR.' He winked broadly. 'A lady friend keeps it for me while I'm away.' He produced a card. 'That's the address, look me up next time you're over. Tell you what, why not stop over tonight? You look as though you could use some shuteye.'

Tom shook his dead.

'Thanks, Harry, but no. I've got too much work waiting for me back at the museum. I have to be in London by tomorrow at the latest to submit my report on the coins. I'll be on the first Heathrow flight out of Kennedy.' He smiled conspiratorially. 'May just have time to buy you a farewell drink at La Guardia though.'

*****

Dropping his cab just short of 23rd, Brennan went straight to the nearest liquor store and bought two bottles of bourbon for himself and a half of gin for Sinead. Then he went to the all-night flower seller at the corner and bought her a big bunch of red roses. It wasn't going to be enough and he knew it: he was in deep shit.

She would have been waiting for him at the apartment since early evening, he knew, and he felt guilty. Why the hell had he let that son of a bitch Hawkhurst get him into a session in the bar at La Guardia. He shrugged philosophically. What the hell? They'd had a good time and, for a Limey, he hadn't been so bad. What's more the guy could certainly drink. He looked at his watch. Shit, it was nearly eleven, that had been three hours ago. Falling asleep in the airport lounge he had been moved on by security in no uncertain terms. He didn't mind, in fact he was grateful: but for them he'd have been there now.

He felt tired and hungover. What he needed right now was his bed and Sinead in it. Cursing softly, he struggled to get his key in the front door lock, roses and bottles tucked awkwardly under his arm as he made his way up the darkened stairs. On the second floor, panting slightly from the climb, he rang the apartment bell. He didn't need to for he had a key but he wanted to surprise her. He rang a second time. There was still no response and he began to suspect that she had abandoned all hope of seeing him that day and gone back to her own place. Cursing his luck he fumbled again with his key and the door swung inwards. The lights were on.

She was in the lounge, tied with her own tights into the big colonial rocking chair that was Brennan's pride and joy. The eyes above the taped mouth were wide, outraged, and he held a finger to his lips, fearing her struggling might betray his presence. Carefully putting down the now irrelevant gifts he drew the snub-nosed Smith and Wesson from his shoulder holster and held it, double handed, arms extended as he moved warily through each room.

All around was chaos. Drawers pulled out and tossed aside, cupboards ransacked, their contents scattered across the floor. In the kitchen, likewise everything lay strewn about, ketchup and Thousand Island dressing oozing across the linoleum. It had been a scrupulously thorough job but, by his standards, hardly a professional one. He approached the woman, gently peeling away the plaster across her mouth.

'Are you OK, honey? They didn't hurt you?'

Sinead was indeed unharmed but her Irish blood was well and truly up. She had always known Brennan was something of a rough diamond and with a rather dubious reputation. It was, if she was honest, part of the attraction he held for her ever since that night he had wandered, stoned out of his skull, into the Bronx restaurant where she worked as a waitress. Even so, this was too much. She made her feelings transparently clear.

'Jesus Christ, Brennan,' she spluttered. 'A girl comes round to cook a romantic supper for two and ends up trussed like a fucking chicken herself.'

He smiled, relieved to find, judging by her tone, that she had not been mistreated.

'Who was it? Did you get a good look at them?'

'Sure I did. It was only one guy. He was big. Late twenties, maybe early thirties, black hair. He had an accent – I think he was English.' Her outrage mollified somewhat as she chafed the circulation back into her wrists. 'He was quite a charmer really.' She mimicked an English stage accent. 'Said he was awfully sorry to inconvenience me like this. I think he took something from your desk.'

Brennan moved quickly to the roll-topped desk, sliding out a false bottom that Sinead had not been aware of before.

'Fuck it,' he shouted, bringing his clenched fist smashing down onto the desktop in uncontrolled fury. The woman fell silent; she had never seen him like this before. He drew a deep breath, trying to regain control of his emotions, then he went to the phone punching out a number with a stabbing forefinger.

'Control. This is Brennan. I think I've been blown. I want a driver and a plane to the UK straight away. I'll take an Air Force flight if I have to. I also want a complete security profile on a Doctor Thomas Hawkhurst. He's British, an archaeologist. I don't know the full story but I heard a whisper he was deported from one of ex-Soviet republics a few years back for smuggling, so you should have a file on him somewhere.' He hesitated, gathering his thoughts and, for Sinead's benefit, pointing to the bourbon. 'I don't know how bad this is. It may not be the opposition – in fact I'm fairly sure it isn't, but we can't take that risk. I'll report back once I've reached London. Let the office there know I'm coming and that I'll need plenty of back up.'

Ringing off, he turned to Sinead, a little crestfallen at allowing her to see him lose his temper like that. She passed him his bourbon and he handed her the flowers.

'Sorry, honey. Looks like this is going to be a short stopover.' He pulled his wallet from his hip pocket and peeled off a wedge of notes. 'Do me a favour, will you? Get someone to clear this mess up while I'm away.'

She took the money, tucking it down her ample cleavage and moving close, kissing his ravaged features. She was a big-boned woman of maybe forty or so, dark haired and with a rather over-ripe body. Harry liked her because she never mentioned his disfigurement, because she made love like she really meant it and because, unlike any of his three ex-wives, she never once lectured him about his drinking.

'Come on, Harry. You know me. I never ask questions about what you do for a living. But surely you can take an hour or so off. Take a look at yourself in the mirror; you look like shit on a spoon. Let me run you a bath while you fix us both another drink.' She smiled. 'Tell you what, I might just get in with you.'

Her lips brushed his eroded cheek and his eyes twinkled. What the hell? It would take control hours at least to fix up his transport and get the printout on Hawkhurst. Also, there was no chance of overtaking his quarry, probably somewhere over the Atlantic by now, anyway. He pulled her close, his hands on her full buttocks.

'Sounds good to me, honey.'

CHAPTER TWELVE

When he arrived back at the cottage, Hawkhurst's first thought was to contact Angahrad. To his annoyance, when he had attempted to ring from Heathrow, her number remained stubbornly unobtainable. Having dumped his travelling bag and hidden the papers taken from Brennan's desk beneath the bedroom carpet, he headed for Sarnafon Farm. Although he had come to terms with the situation he remained uncertain how, if she were to find out, Angahrad would react to his brief fling with Suzie – a casual unthinking, indiscretion that had cost the girl her life. He wanted desperately to see Angahrad again yet his anticipation was spoiled by the situation he had been drawn into and, worse, the knowledge that he had betrayed her.

He was in no doubt whatsoever that the Reverend's men would make contact very soon and that they would not hesitate to release the photographs if he resisted their demands. He desperately needed to discuss the situation with someone yet, if he were to be totally open with Angahrad, how would she react?

Another thing that troubled him was the documents he had taken from Brennan's apartment. As an attempt to learn more about Whichelow's crazy schemes it had to be considered a partial failure. Far from throwing light on the task force and its objectives they had suggested the situation was even more convoluted than he had suspected. The papers were cryptic yet threw a new and unsuspected light on the American's role in Whichelow's plans.

At the farm he switched off the engine then sat and waited outside in the car for several minutes. A fine rain was falling, the only sound the rhythmic hiss of the windscreen wipers. He stilled this and waited in silence, frowning. He was puzzled and worried. Angahrad would never have left the front door hanging open like that: it would have been an open invitation for the semi-wild cats that prowled the barns and sheds. Also, she normally came out to welcome him when she heard his car approach. Today only the idly swinging door greeted him.

Eyes narrowed he climbed out of the car, closing the door quietly behind him, and headed towards the house. His hands balled into fists and his palms felt distinctly moist as he stepped warily into the shadowed passage. All was quiet, save for the persistent drip of a tap into the big stone sink in the kitchen off to his right. Stepping into the low, oak-beamed lounge he moved to the centre of the room. A frisson of fear ran down his spine.

'You can count yourself fucking lucky I'm not a man who bears grudges, Hawkhurst.'

Brennan's words came soft and easy from the inglenook. He sat, the statutory glass of whisky in his left hand, the .38 in his right pointing directly at Hawkhurst's head. Despite being taken completely unawares, Tom's voice was rock steady when he answered and there was an undisguised menace in his words that made Brennan's finger curl a fraction tighter about the trigger.

'Where is she? Where's Angahrad?'

The American nodded at the table. At its centre, lying alongside the post card he had mailed from Gethsemane, was a scrap of pink notepaper. Picking it up Tom scanned it briefly. Unhappy at what he saw he tossed it aside impatiently and voiced his doubts.

'This was supposedly left for Llew, her sister's husband. She says she's gone down to London to meet me and would he take care of the farm for a day or two. But this is a load of bull. She wouldn't have left the farm just like that and she couldn't have met me, even if she wanted. She had no idea when I was arriving back. I haven't spoken to her in over a week, her phone's been out of order.'

'I'm not too surprised about that,' Brennan waved his pistol at the skirting board where the telephone cable had been ripped from the junction box. His eyes came up slowly. 'Where are the papers you took from my desk?'

'Safe,' Tom snapped. Just now the papers were of little consequence so far as he was concerned. 'Where's Angahrad?'

'I don't know. I only got here myself an hour ago. Could be the boys from Gethsemane are holding her.' Perhaps sensing that, with this news, Hawkhurst had enough to occupy his thoughts Brennan put his revolver to safe and slid it back into its holster. 'I think you and I should talk, Tom. I think we can help each other.' Quitting his seat, he drew up a chair to the table, setting another across from him he indicated Hawkhurst should sit.

'Did you read the papers, Tom?'
'Of course.'
'And?'

'I'm not sure. But I don't think you're what you say you are – I don't think you're a simple leg man for the Church of Christ the Warrior, Harry.' He eyeballed the American. 'I'll be honest, first off I thought you were keeping an eye on me for that fruitcake Whichelow, but from what I could glean from your reports you're more interested in his activities than mine.'

Brennan's face remained stony; he was not best pleased to find his cover blown by this persistent archaeologist. It was time to reassert himself, to put the pressure back on Hawkhurst.

'What do they want from you anyway? More to the point, what have they got on you?'

Inclined, from what he had read in the stolen papers, to accept the American as a potential ally, Hawkhurst still had reservations about being too open, too early. Once his usefulness as a source of information had been fully exploited he and Angahrad would rapidly become expendable – expendable in the eyes of both Brennan and Whichelow.

'Let's just say they've got pictures of me that I wouldn't like printed in the national newspapers. They intended to blackmail me with those. It wouldn't have worked. I wouldn't have gone along with it. But that's neither here nor there now they may be holding Angahrad.'

'So, you fell for the honey trap, uh. Well you're not the first one.' Brennan's eyes narrowed. 'What do they want?' Hawkhurst looked to the ceiling in frustration and disbelief at what he was about to reveal.

'The damned bowl we unearthed. Can you believe it? They've got it into their heads that it's the Holy Grail. They're fanatical about getting their hands on it. I told them it would never be up for sale and, with the kind of logic that seems the norm in Gethsemane, next thing I know they're trying to blackmail me into stealing it for them.' He smiled grimly. 'As I imagine you're already aware, I've got something of a reputation in certain circles.'

The American's faces remained impassive. He could see a certain pattern evolving. The agency's files on Hawkhurst had been detailed enough about his alleged smuggling activities. No doubt Whichelow would have seen someone with that kind of track record as a soft target for either blackmail or bribery. His next question was just a little too casual.

'Any idea why they want it so bad?'

'Yes, I think so.'

The shutters came down on Tom's eyes and there was a silent pause as Brennan waited for clarification. When he realised it was not to be immediately forthcoming, he snorted impatiently.

'For Christ's sake. Hawkhurst, wise up. There's a couple of dogs out back with their throats slit, that's the sort of people you're messing with here. The best chance you've got of seeing your lady friend again is by co-operating with us. Level with me, tell me all about what you saw at Reachwood and I promise to put the Agency's resources to work to locate her.'

Rising, Hawkhurst went through to the flagstoned kitchen. Taking a tumbler from the dresser he returned to the table, setting the glass before him. Things were happening so quickly; he needed time to think. He poured himself a stiff one and topped up Brennan's glass. The man was drinking slowly today, he noticed, well in control. He took a gulp of the fiery spirit, inhaling the pungent vapour. Despite his reservations, Tom knew he had very little option other than to be totally open. Like it or not, he needed Brennan.

'I know it sounds crazy but I think they're planning a commando raid somewhere in the Middle East, probably Lebanon. I think they're intent on rescuing some of their men who are being held by Shiite gunmen. If that isn't scary enough for you, they want the bowl – the Holy Grail as they call it – as a talisman. They are absolutely obsessed about taking it with them on the raid. They're treating the whole thing as some kind of modern crusade.'

He stared across the table at the American, searching for some reaction, but the scarred features reflected not the least emotion at these revelations. Perhaps he knew these things already.

'Precisely what did you see up at Reachwood.'

'A small army.'

Brennan leant forward his eyes hard as flints.

'Details. I need details, Tom. What kind of equipment have they got?'

Hawkhurst racked his brains, trying to recall what McNaughton had said about his hardware. Was it only yesterday morning?

'There were an awful lot of helicopters. I think they called the troop carriers Vertols, something like that, I couldn't be exactly sure how many there were, but thirty or forty at least. There were some smaller ones too, gunships I think, over a hundred I would estimate. I can't recall what McNaughton said they were called, but I think he said they were built by the McDonnell-Douglas company.' He looked at Harry. 'Does that make sense?'

'Sure it does - Apaches - I guess.' Brennan was thoughtful now. 'How many men did they have?'

'About two thousand, I thought, although I could be wildly wrong – I wasn't really counting. It seemed like a hell of a lot to me. But what I saw might have only been part of their total force, it was a demonstration that was put together at very short notice for my benefit.'

'Did you get any details about the operation? Dates? Targets? Anything that might help.'

'Only that according to the blackmail note you handed me on the plane yesterday the task force is on the move already. They mentioned the Lebanon and the hostages but the more I think about it the more I think that was let drop just for my benefit. That scenario just doesn't seem to make sense. The terrible thing is that, on the evidence of what I've seen so far, they're capable of just about anything.'

Hawkhurst wondered whether he was giving Brennan useful information here, anything he didn't already know. He said as much, wanting to be as forthright as possible in the circumstances. Brennan was equally open.

'Reachwood's been sewn up tight as a mouse's anus for two years now. After the Davidian fiasco down in Texas the FBI keeps a close eye on the weirder cults and sects but they haven't been able to get a man inside the place and aerial and satellite surveillance has come up with absolutely nothing. From what you say there must be best part of a hundred and fifty choppers up there at least. Well that's news to me and my superiors. They must have kept them below ground or well dispersed in the timberland around the camp. Trouble is, there are so many born again pilgrims in Washington these days – Whichelow's brothers under the skin – that any surveillance was probably compromised anyway.' He ran a hand across his eyes. He looked tired.

'The deeper I get into this thing, Tom, the more I get the feeling the Reverend has friends in high places. He's the figurehead, but there have to be people, powerful people, in the Pentagon and

Congress aiding and abetting the lunacy. It's almost as if someone at the highest level actually wants this raid to take place. I'm not saying it's coming from the White House, but it sure is someone with plenty of clout.' He shook his head as though to clear it of troubled thoughts. 'And you say you think they've left the States already?'

'According to Whichelow. That's all I know.'

Brennan assimilated what he had heard in ruminative silence.

'Did they say anything about contacting you with further instructions?'

'Yes. Within a couple of days, they said.'

'When they get in touch what do you intend doing?'

'Anything I have to do, to get Angahrad back.'

*****

They drove back to London that afternoon. Brennan had rented a battered Mondeo and by five they were on the fringes of north London, where the Hertfordshire countryside gave way to a shabby concrete wilderness and the traffic flow faltered and eventually coagulated. Before they had crossed the border into England the American had phoned his London contacts advising them of the situation and setting in train the search for the missing Angahrad. On the journey, probably realising that Hawkhurst would, in his determination to rescue Angahrad, fall in with their plans, he opened up a little.

'We only found out about Whichelow's set-up thanks to a whisper from one of our men in the Lebanon.'

'Boujera?'

Brennan's eyes widened.

'That's right. You've heard of him?'

'Only in passing. McNaughton, the military commander at Reachwood, mentioned him. I understand that Boujera was acting as a go between in the hostage negotiations. I may have been fed false information but I was told he had revealed where the hostages were being held. Whichelow only said they had received important news, but it would tie in with launching the operation now, before they can be moved.'

Trapped in traffic Brennan's beefy fingers drummed an impatient tattoo on the wheel. Tom guessed he was in a difficult position, not sure how much he should reveal. His own original suspicions about the American's motives and loyalties now allayed, he was well aware just how much he needed the man and his Agency's resources if he was to see Angie again. They hadn't hesitated to kill Suzie, whose part in things had been so minor and unwitting, and he knew Angie was only safe so long as she was useful to them. He decided to spell things out.

'I've given you everything I've got, Harry. What are you going to do for me?'

Brennan considered the matter.

'I'm gonna buy you dinner, buddy.'

*****

In the deserted Bayswater pizzeria, Hawkhurst examined the stained menu with little enthusiasm and wished Brennan would come to the point. The American, however, was in no rush. The young Asian waitress with the gold nose stud stood patiently over them, trying to translate his minutely detailed requirements.

'Oh yeah, and easy on the pimientos,' he yelled at her retreating form. She did not acknowledge this final instruction but continued to stare in disbelief at the list of specials he had ordered as she disappeared into the kitchens. Hawkhurst had little interest in food.

'For God's sake, Harry, we should be out looking for Angahrad. Not hanging around places like this.'

Brennan held up a pacifying hand.

'OK. I know you're in a hurry, Tom. In your position I'd be in a hurry too. But look at it from our point of view. Once she's free I imagine you intend to blow the whistle on Whichelow, Gethsemane, the whole caboodle. Am I right?'

Hawkhurst nodded.

'They've still got the pictures of me and once they are released I can say goodbye to any career I might have had left in archaeology. But, one thing I didn't mention, the girl who appears in the pictures with me was the one who was killed at the airfield. She was murdered, Harry, on Whichelow's orders, just to spice up the story. The pictures would have been nasty enough but I could have handled that. But I don't see why they should get away with murder, do you?'

'No. No, I don't, but there are other considerations in this, Tom.' He fell silent, smiling up at the waitress who lay before him what even a cursory glance told him could have been no more than the vaguest approximation of the culinary delight he had been anticipating. Suspecting as much she beat a hasty retreat as he tentatively poked a carrot. Having made his protest he got down to business.

'The Middle East situation is going down the tubes, Tom. All America can do is to try to influence developments as best it can. With an election just round the corner the government doesn't want to get involved in any situation where it might have to send in troops. So it tries to influence things through diplomatic channels, by offering and withdrawing aid, by sending peace envoys to try and get the various parties around the table. It is a prudent, pragmatic and statesmanlike approach. After the Lebanon and Somalia no one wants to see any long term military involvement, especially of ground forces, anywhere in the area, least of all Joe Public. However, there is a tacit understanding that the State of Israel is to be supported, and if necessary defended, at all costs. The Jewish lobby is very powerful in Washington but that's not the only reason. Israel is the only real ally in the region we can rely on. Therefore, the official policy is to work towards an Israeli rapprochement with the Arab states, especially those states with oil reserves, and to encourage Tel Aviv to give some measure of self-determination to the Palestinians. But make no mistake in the final analysis we would be obliged to go to war if the future existence of the Israeli State was ever seriously threatened.'

'Is that time coming?'

'Until yesterday I would have said no. Now I'm not so sure. OK so there's daily rioting on the west bank and in Gaza, but the Jews can keep the lid on that without our help. The majority of Arab states make no secret of the fact that they would all love to see Israel bombed to rubble, they say as much regularly in the UN, but they won't make any moves because they all hate and distrust each other with equal venom. They also know the Jews have the capability to go nuclear if they want to. No, our political advisers all see the thing staying much as it is for the next five years at least. There may be an escalation of riots and terrorism from time to time, that's only to be expected, but no one predicts a major conflict in the area.'

'Do these political advisers know about Whichelow and the task force?'

'Do they hell.'

'But I just don't see it, Harry. Whichelow regularly ranted on about an ecological disaster, about the world falling into chaos and the Church taking over and picking up the pieces. He seemed to think that time wasn't far off. Maybe his pals in Washington are thinking of giving the status quo a little fine tuning, just to speed things up a tad. I can't see three hostages justifying an operation on this scale.'

Brennan's next words were delivered dead pan.

'Nor me. Especially when we know for a fact that all the supposed hostages have been dead for over two years. We know that Whichelow knows as well.'

Hawkhurst looked up from his food.

'What?'

'Grantly, Egberg and McNally were seized by a Shiite splinter group about four years ago. It happens all the time. Someone with nothing better to do comes up with a new interpretation of the will of Allah or maybe at that time it was the will of Khomeini. Once someone's dead there's no end to the way people will screw around with his philosophy. One sees the light then convinces a few like-minded zealots that they should form a breakaway group. To prove they mean business they then proceed to kidnap a few westerners to get media attention. Sects like that come and go all the time in the Middle East. Most are religious, but some are ethnic and some are political – some are all three.' He pointed to his ravaged face. 'See this? This was a letter bomb in '88. To this day I don't know if it came from the PLO, Hezbollah, Islamic Jihad or the Mahomet Fan Club. Anyway, Grantly, Egberg and McNally were lifted by a group that was presumably so short lived it never got given a proper name. I guess in the interests of discipline the orthodox hard line Shiites would have been keen to see them back in the fold or, failing that, in the ground. What it comes down to is that by early 1996 the hostages were surplus to requirements and probably a damn nuisance. Boujera, our only reliable source, says they were then being held at a refugee camp in the Bekaa. Then the Israelis, suspecting the place was being used to launch attacks on northern Kibbutzs, launched a surprise raid on the camp. Our guess is that before the kidnappers pulled out they took the opportunity to relieve themselves of the embarrassment of the hostages and killed all three. At least that's what the Jews said happened although there's always the possibility it might have been friendly fire.'

'So why doesn't everybody else know this? If you can prove they're dead it would show the whole operation up as a sham. Surely any support Whichelow has in Washington would disappear overnight.'

Brennan pushed his barely touched plate away with evident disgust. Producing a silver hip flask he poured a solid slug of bourbon in his coffee by way of compensation.

'Unfortunately the Israelis weren't prepared to bring back the bodies and subsequently they disappeared, probably buried out in the desert somewhere. The only evidence we had was a set of photographs taken by the Israelis. They showed three bodies we could fairly confidently identify as being the American hostages. At that time, US policy towards any Iranian backed terror group was, to put it mildly, hawkish, and no doubt hoping to encourage a fairly brisk punitive response, MOSSAD agents were only too happy to hand the pictures over to the CIA. There's no love lost between any of the intelligence services, even those supposedly on the same side. The Israelis would only have handed the pictures over in the belief Uncle Sam could be relied on to respond with some pretty tough action. They take a broad brush approach when it comes to reprisals. So long as someone on the other side gets their head busted they're happy. With the President coming up to the end of his term in office they knew they could, politicians being what they are, expect some positive action to keep the voters happy.'

'So what happened?'

'Nothing. Anything as sensitive as reprisals for murdered hostages needs rubber stamping by a whole load of government departments. Well, somewhere between CIA headquarters and the Pentagon, before there had been any official comment or press interest, the pictures went missing. Not only that but, at precisely that moment, the Reverend Whichelow appears nationwide on TV and announces, Alleluia, that he had received evidence that the hostages were alive and well and negotiations were once again under way to obtain their release.'

'Are you saying that he's kept the myth of these three hostages alive since then? That he's been planning whatever it is he's up to since then?'

'Sure looks that way. I guess it made a pretty good cover story. He could count on getting support from a whole range of people who wouldn't necessarily agree to a wider use of force. We've got files on maybe fifty people at the Pentagon, senior people mostly, who have had contact with Whichelow during the past year. We also know of at least twenty Senators and Congressmen who have visited Gethsemane over the same period. We've got nothing to say it's a conspiracy but they're sure as hell not getting together for the sake of their health.'

Hawkhurst shook his head. It was all becoming too complicated.

'So what is he doing? What is the mission the task force has been set up for if not a rescue bid?'

'That's what I need your help to find out, Tom. But before we can count on your help I guess you'll expect us to find Angahrad.'

'You better believe it, Harry.'

'OK we'll see what we can do.' He smiled wryly. 'Apropos nothing in particular, Tom, this is going to be dangerous enough but, should you ever come across a lady called Sinead Mulroony, you better be loaded for bear.'

CHAPTER THIRTEEN

'Nice to see you back, Dr Hawkhurst.'

Tom, inwardly cursing this unexpected interruption, looked up from the microscope and smiled amiably at the ancient security guard who stood outlined in the vault door. Even in the shadows he recognised the man's face from the old days, although the name escaped him.

'Thank you, it's nice to be back.' He nodded at the coins spread out on the bench before him. 'Nearly there, I should be finished with this lot in fifteen minutes or so I'll call you when I'm ready to put them back into the safe.'

The guard nodded.

'Just ring the desk, sir. Either me or Bert will come and lock up after you.' He jangled the keys in his hand. 'Suppose I better be getting on – check none of the mummies has tried to escape.'

It was a well-worn joke. In all his forty years at the museum no-one had ever attempted to break in. The only excitement security had enjoyed in all that time had been provided by a down and out who, far from wanting to break in, had woken to find himself locked in and been extremely keen to break out. To be fair, the museum had been equipped with the latest electronic security technology and was closely monitored by cameras and alarms from a remote HQ somewhere on the other side of London. The least cause for concern and the police would be on the scene in minutes. It was the administration's confidence in this that allowed them to indulge their feudal sensibilities by keeping on a handful of long serving retainers whose limited value was reflected in their derisory salaries.

As the man went on his rounds, Hawkhurst returned his attention to the microscope, bringing the coin under examination into crisp edged focus with a twist of the milled brass ferrule. Even after the wear and tear of fourteen centuries it was in near mint condition and he regretted having had to drill the hole that would make it match the genuine coins from the tomb. No one could mistake where or when this particular example had first seen light of day. King Penda, the pagan Anglo-Saxon who gave the world the penny, would have been proud of his mint. Sliding the coin from the viewing table he laid it away among the others and made the final entry in his report. With a sigh of relief, he closed the folder and pushed back his chair. As he did so the phone at his elbow jangled, making him start.

'Dr Hawkhurst?' The caller was English and cultured.

'Yes.'

'I'm a friend of the Church. I understand from the Reverend Whichelow that you wish to make a donation to the fighting fund.'

'That's correct.'

'Bring it to Cleopatra's Needle, any time after ten tomorrow. A car – a black Ford Escort with a roof rack – will pick up you and the donation. This is just a preliminary examination you understand. Once we are satisfied it is the genuine article it and you will be dropped off at Kings Cross station.'

'I believe you will have something for me in return.'

'The answer to that is in the positive,' the voice at the other end gave an inane giggle, 'or rather, in this case, the negative.'

'You can stuff the photographs. Where's Angahrad – Miss Jenkins?'

'The woman is another matter. Once I have passed the photographs back to you there will be further instructions. Please don't try to be clever Dr Hawkhurst. Just show us you are in possession of the Grail and the pictures become no more than an unhappy memory. Follow our further instructions precisely to the letter and the woman will be released unharmed. Goodnight.' The line went dead.

Tom's face was grim as he contemplated the situation. Far from bringing the affair to a conclusion, delivering the Grail was to be no more than a preliminary and they clearly intended to use Angahrad as a lever to embroil him further. To be honest, it had not come as a total surprise; he had half expected for some such development knowing the kind of madmen he was up against. His best hope was that Brennan, with his shadowy intelligence contacts, would locate her before he delivered the Grail. However, he recognised Brennan's priorities were not identical with his own and he had no intention of relying solely on the American. He had plans of his own.

Gathering up the coins he laid them back in the green velvet lined case, dropping each into a shallow recess against which was a neatly inscribed adhesive label giving date and source. Closing and locking the lid, he reached towards the phone, intent on calling the guard to lock it away. Before his hand had reached the dial, however, another figure stood silhouetted in the door. This time it wasn't the security man but an altogether softer form. Laura, her hair backlit in an auburn halo smiled down at him.

'Working late, Tom?' Her voice was husky, he noticed, as though she had been drinking.

'Just finishing up,' he said briskly, his plans now in jeopardy and his mind racing through the options. It was an eventuality he hadn't planned for. 'I was just about to call security to lock all this stuff away for the night.'

Holding up a bunch of keys, she tinkled them like bells.

'They told me you were still here, so I thought I'd look in to see how you were getting on. I can lock the vault.'

She was dressed in a short cerise cocktail number with a deeply plunging neckline.

'Don't tell me you're working in that sort of thing these days.' His gaze fell approvingly on the gleaming swell of her golden breasts. 'Mind you, it's very becoming.'

She smiled, pleased he had noticed.

'I'm on my way to a reception. I wondered if you'd care to come along?'

The fragrance of expensive perfume came to him as she stepped out of the shadows into the warm circle of yellow light cast by the desk lamp. What she did not tell him was that she had come straight to the museum from another futile evening spent with Dixey. The culmination had been his peevish refusal to accompany her to the reception. She lay a cool hand on Hawkhurst's arm.

'Come on, Tom. Loosen up a little. You used to like parties – remember the night we wrecked the British Consul's car in Alexandria?'

He smiled, recalling all too well an event that had served to set the pattern of his relations with the museum's establishment. In the eyes of some; Dixey and his minions, it had signalled the start of a rake's progress that had culminated with satisfying predictability in the Armenian scandal. It was, perhaps, only to have been expected. His success in the field at such an early age – by twenty seven he was recognised as a, if not the, leading authority on Celtic and Anglo-Saxon Britain – had inevitably fostered professional jealousy. This had been especially vitriolic among those like the Curator-General who, despite a long, unblemished if unremarkable career, was still as far away from the coveted knighthood as ever, and had become little more than an administrator.

'Or the time we flew your panties from the mosque in Al-Quddifi?' He countered laughingly.

'A blow for women's liberation.'

Collecting up the case containing the coins he moved towards her, his manner relaxed.

'But won't it damage your reputation – being seen on the town with me?'

She moved closer and her fragrance came to him.

'Let me worry about that. One thing's certain – the party's being thrown by the Arts Council, by the way – it won't do your reputation any harm to be seen moving in the right circles again. Melvyn will be there and the Lords P and G.'

The right circles for Laura meant those people who could do you most good professionally. He sometimes wondered if she had any friends who she liked for themselves rather than the social cachet they carried. Nevertheless he nodded.

'OK, why not? If you'll just unlock the safe again I'll pop these away and we can get moving.'

The vault in which they stood was a massive affair, fifty metres square and entered via a single heavy steel door that was a masterpiece of Victorian metallurgy. Inside it were arrayed ranks of drawers and cabinets that held the museum's more valuable exhibits while they were not on display. Smaller items, such as coins, were locked away in individual safes and cabinets but larger pots and statuary, too bulky for such storage were stacked high on either hand. From one upper shelf a row of gap-toothed skulls grinned eyelessly down. In a corner, crystal coffined and curled into a dry foetus, the leathery cadaver of an Egyptian fellahin, four thousand years dead, slept peacefully on.

At the far end of the vault stood the heavy, grill-fronted cabinet containing the bowl, sword, chain shirt and helmet. It was to this cabinet that the coins should now be returned. As Tom pulled back the clumsy lattice he felt the warmth of her body standing behind him, perhaps a little closer than was strictly necessary. The softness of her breast brushed his elbow. He prayed he was reading the situation correctly.

Sliding the tray of coins away he turned to face her, his arms going about her slender waist and pulling her close. Momentarily there was the merest hint of resentment in the emerald eyes but it was the briefest of rebuffs, the instinctive reaction of a high born lady being pawed by a servant. This, as he had suspected, had been precisely what she had come for. Melting, her arms went about his neck, pulling his lips down to hers, the wet tongue probing expertly. As she moulded her body to his, he slid one shoulder of the flimsy dress down her arm exposing a flawless breast. Her eyes closed and her head rolled back as his lips moved down across her throat and to the pink flower of the offered nipple.

'Wait,' she breathed, pulling away. 'I'll lock the door – we don't want to be disturbed.' Hitching the dress back up over her shoulder she drew away and walked swiftly down the length of the vault. Watching as she went, Tom quickly reached into the half closed cabinet and retrieving the bowl dropped it into the battered leather briefcase. Laura returned, kicking off her shoes as she came close, the lattice had been drawn across and the cabinet's solid wooden outer doors shut and locked. Fortunately for him, archaeology was the last thing on Laura's mind at that moment.

Like a princess she turned her back to him and his fingers went to the zipper, sliding it down to reveal smooth tanned shoulders and curved hollow spine. As the dress slipped easily around her thighs to the floor he saw that she was naked beneath save for a black silk garter belt and stockings. Turning to face him, one cool caressing hand went to his trouser fly, unzipping and expertly easing him free, while the other curled serpent-like about his neck. In seconds he was naked.

She was as hot as hell, the cumulative frustration of the months spent with Dixey coming to the boil as, gasping in her passion, her hands ran over his hard naked body. There was little subtlety in her approach and he responded accordingly. Placing his hands beneath her satin buttocks he lifted her effortlessly from the floor. Her face was a mask of unbridled desire as she guided his organ home and her legs locked about him. Hawkhurst stared up at the skulls that looked down on their frenzy like macabre voyeurs, and his fingers bit deep into her soft flesh in a grip that made her gasp. For maybe five minutes he held her aloft as she groaned and threshed, writhing in delight on the shaft of flame that filled her entire being. Her nails raked his back and sharp teeth brought blood to his lips as she ground and rotated her soft stomach against his. Suddenly her body tensed and her head went back, the scarlet mouth wide.

'Ahh, oh yes, oh yes,' she hissed, jerking convulsively as the bolts of ecstasy struck home. Her lips found his in one final lingering kiss as her body relaxed and softened in his arms, spent, totally exhausted. 'God, Tom, I needed that,' she murmured as he lowered her gently to the floor, steadying her as she regained her composure. The emerald eyes opened lazily and she smiled up at him, the first genuine smile he could recall since she had arrived at the cottage. 'You haven't come, have you?' she said, her hand grasping his persisting erection, still slick with her own juices. 'Still, how long has it been, three years? I guess we must be out of practice.' A scarlet tongue strayed wetly across the generous mouth.

'Never mind, I expect I can do something about that.'

*****

'Goodnight, Rafferty,' Hawkhurst waved as, briefcase in hand, he swept past the desk, pleased he had succeeded in recalling the man's name. 'Miss Woods is locking the vault now. Perhaps you'd like to check that she's OK, that door weighs a ton.'

'Certainly, Dr Hawkhurst,' Rafferty smiled up from his desk, equally pleased to be remembered. 'I'll get down there right away.' He unlocked the door to allow Hawkhurst out into the night, watching approvingly as the tall figure strode away down the wet shining street. Now there was a real archaeologist, he thought. A bit on the wild side, of course, but someone who knew the business from the bottom up. Not like that sour old windbag Dixey or that flighty Madame Laura Woods. It was the thought of Laura and her, at times, acid tongue that sent him shuffling off down the shadowy galleries in the direction of the vault. Standing in front of the steel door he frowned. It was locked yet there was no way she could have passed him. Unlocking, he slid the heavy steel levers free and pulled back the massive door, amazed to find himself facing a rather red-faced Laura.

'Has Dr Hawkhurst left yet?' she demanded sharply.

'Yes, Miss. Five minutes ago ….'

She thrust past him without another word and as he stepped back to allow her to pass, Rafferty noticed that her copper hair was far from its usual perfectly groomed state and that her dress had somehow collected a fair amount of dust. He smiled to himself; that Dr Hawkhurst.

Locked in her office, Laura drew deeply on a rare cigarette and looked down at the scrap of paper in her hand. 'IOU one Holy Grail – love Tom,' it read. The bastard! He'd made love to her like he'd really meant it and then locked her in the vault although – the final insult – not until she'd fully gratified him. Bastard! What on earth was he up to? More importantly, how the hell was she going to explain it? Her eyes went to the phone. Biting her lip as she picked it up, she punched out Dixey's number. His voice, irascible as ever, came sharply down the line.

'Dixey here.' She contemplated the precariousness of her situation. Once the world knew the Grail had been stolen the press would be down on the museum like a swarm of bees. How could she explain that she had been in the vault with Hawkhurst? She couldn't deny it, Rafferty had seen them. 'Hallo, who is this?' Dixey's impatience was plain to hear. Softly she placed the handset back in its cradle.

What she couldn't understand was why Tom would have done such a thing in the first place. He could never have hoped to sell the Grail in a million years and anyway she knew him well enough to dismiss personal financial reward as a motive. She paced up and down in the confines of the office, trying to make some sense of these bewildering developments. Tom had recently returned from America and now he had stolen, or at least borrowed, the Grail. The two events must be linked, she felt certain, yet knew instinctively that he wouldn't have countenanced selling out to Mary Lou Berkowitz for monetary gain. There had to be something more to all this, but what?

Tomorrow was Saturday, she reasoned, so although the museum would be open to the public no-one would be working in the laboratories or reference rooms and therefore it was unlikely that the Grail would be missed until the Monday morning. She would have to find Hawkhurst by then or her career could end up much as his had done. Worse, knowing what chatterboxes the security men were, the fact that she had been alone with him in the vault would certainly be common knowledge in the space of a few hours and interpreted accordingly. How would Dixey view such a thing? Bastard! Bastard! Bastard! Where would he go? She wondered. Back to Wales? It hardly seemed likely but it was the only thing she could think of. If only she could locate his woman, what was her name, Angahrad? She might know something. As she irritably stubbed out her half smoked cigarette, the phone rang. She stared at it hesitantly for several seconds before picking it up. It was Hawkhurst.

'What the hell do you think you're doing,' she stormed.

He was unmoved by her anger, terse and to the point.

'I can't tell you everything – it's too bloody complicated – but if you want to see the Grail again, here's what you have to do.'

*****

About the base of Cleopatra's Needle, the tourists swarmed like flies, necks craned skyward, photographic equipment to die for recording the granite obelisk from every conceivable angle. Beyond, the Thames at low water pervaded the atmosphere with the rank smell of sun-dried mud and decaying vegetation. Coach after coach, bus after bus, drew up in succession, disgorging their culture hungry cargo, mainly Japanese. Each group lingered for maybe ten minutes before being herded back on board and driven away in pursuit of other cultural quarry. As each vehicle drew away it was immediately replaced by yet another. After two hours it had become a performance that had lost a lot of its charm for Laura.

Dressed in faded jeans and shapeless sweater, eyes hidden by stylish wrap around polaroids, she felt positively ill at ease in her unaccustomed anonymity. Seated on a bench across from the obelisk, the video camera Hawkhurst had given her lying at her side, she cursed herself for ever involving him in the first place. He sat facing her across the broad thoroughfare of the Embankment, the bag containing the Grail in his hand.

How could the bastard look so cool and unconcerned, she fumed to herself? At a time when nothing less than her entire career might be at stake. When he had first made contact and very briefly outlined the situation he had got himself into, her immediate reaction was to report the matter to the museum authorities. From there it would certainly have been rapidly handed over to the police. It had only been when he had gone on to describe the precautions he had taken to deter any such move that she reluctantly agreed to go along with his mad scheme. She picked up the video camera and zeroed the view finder on to his dark features like the telescopic sight of a hunting rifle. If only she could send a bullet across the space between them!

'There's just one thing you should know,' he had said, almost as an afterthought. 'I've added an extra coin to the grave hoard we found. It's a hundred years later than the grave and if anyone who knows what they're looking at gets to see it, it will certainly put paid to any more silly talk of Arthur and Holy Grails. Once this mess is settled I shall remove it and destroy the photographs I took of it lying among the others.'

It had been this that had finally forced her into helping. Any coin of Penda's reign would have meant putting the dating for the grave back beyond the possibilities of any Arthurian burial. No way would it retain any credibility after that. She felt her face flush with anger at the way he had used her, firstly making love to her like he cared and then compromising the whole exhibition, not to mention her reputation, by introducing the aberrant coin.

She twisted the zoom lens again, bringing him so close she felt she could almost reach out and slap his stupid face. Unabashed, he stared back down the lens of the camera, winking broadly as he did so. Furious, she lowered the camera as the black car drew to a halt between them and she hurriedly returned it to her shoulder and set the video tape running.

The driver, a heavily built individual with a shaven head, was clearly nervous. As Hawkhurst went forward and climbed in next to him, his gaze darted about, alert for any treachery. Satisfied she had succeeded in recording good profile and full face shots of the man, Laura stood up and turned her attention to the red pillar of the Needle, the morning sun picking out the hieroglyphics on the obelisks' weather eroded facets. When she looked again the car had gone.

CHAPTER FOURTEEN

'So what do they want you to do?' Brennan, shirt sleeves rolled lightly up around beefy biceps, ran an easing thumb under the strap of his shoulder holster. Hawkhurst sat down on the bed and poured himself a Scotch, his eyes running round the run down Paddington hotel room that the American had made his temporary headquarters. It was very basic, seedy even, and in the street outside the traffic fumed and growled. He took a thoughtful pull at his drink. He was feeling hot, tired and distinctly uncooperative.

'Have you located Angahrad?'

'We think so. Thanks to the video the other woman took the police were able to identify your contact as Simon Mallinson, a former con man and petty thief who saw the light a few years back and got into religion in a big way. He must be well trusted by the Church because US immigration records show he's made several visits stateside recently. We put a trace on him and he led us to a house in west London. We're pretty sure that's where they're holding your lady friend.' His eyes narrowed. 'What about the woman who took the video, Laura Woods. I did a little research – she seems like a pretty smart cookie but she's too high profile for this sort of work. How much does she know about this business?'

'I told her as little as possible. She just knows I'm in some kind of trouble and need to borrow the Grail.'

Brennan raised a quizzing eyebrow.

'And she handed it over - just like that?'

'No, it wasn't quite that easy. I had to twist her arm a little, metaphorically speaking. So what happens next?' There was cool edge to Tom's words suggesting that while they might be, of necessity, allies, it did not mean that trust was absolute.

'I can only tell you that when I know what Whichelow is planning.'

'Once Angahrad is free I'll tell you exactly what they want, but not until I'm one hundred per cent certain she's safe. You say you know, or think you know, where she's being held. The CIA, if that's who you work for, can easily pull strings in this country. Tell the police where she is, get her released, and I'll cooperate right down the line,

Brennan. But until she's out of danger I'm not prepared to get involved in anything that might leave her at risk.'

For several seconds the American stared hard at him, their eyes locked. Then he looked away with a sigh.

'It's not that simple, Tom.'

'Convince me.'

'OK. So we know where she's being held and we've got the place under surveillance day and night. I only need to say the word and we – in this instance 'we' means the anti-terrorist branch of Scotland Yard – can bust the place wide open and release her.'

'That's very comforting to hear. So why are you wasting time and money sitting there watching me drink your Scotch, Harry? Why not just get on and do it?'

'Have you read the papers lately?'

'No, I've had more important things to think about.' This was not entirely true but Hawkhurst, already in too deep for his own liking, was inclined to be only as helpful as was necessary to find Angahrad.

'You must know what's happening in the Middle East. The peace talks are dead in the water and all around the Mediterranean Islamic fundamentalists are stirring the pot. Suicide bombers in Israel, attacks on foreigners in Algeria, Libya and Somalia, riots in Cairo, and that's just in the past two days. The ayatollahs and the imams are preaching Jihad, Tom.' Hawkhurst nodded, he knew what was going on. It would only need the least provocation to start a war. Brennan pressed his point. 'And it's not just foreign policy that's involved. Back home a lot of people are looking forward to a long hot summer and we all know what that means. We've got a lot of Muslim black activists who would just love an excuse to go on the rampage. Even in Europe riot police are standing by in countries with large Muslim minorities – not least of all right here in Britain. The whole thing could go up like a torch. The only moderate voice at present is Firdasi and no one seems to know where the hell he is.'

'On top of which Whichelow and the task force are out there somewhere, intent on God knows what madness.'

'If we don't stop them it'll mean a bloody holy war. And it won't be confined to the Middle East, Tom.'

'Seems to me, from the sort of help he seems to be getting, Whichelow and the Pentagon are much of a mind on that matter.'

'Don't be such a smart ass, Hawkhurst, you're not that dumb.' Brennan's patience was wearing thin. 'The whole region is a fucking powder keg.'

Hawkhurst sighed, he was sick with worry for Angahrad's safety and burdened with a foreboding that the labyrinth of deception was likely to wind on forever. Yet he felt a glimmer of sympathy for the American. While he was worrying about one woman this man was thinking on a global scale. Sensing he was making progress Brennan persisted.

'Help us, Tom. You're our only way to get to them. If we don't stop them it could mean millions of casualties.'

'OK Harry, but I don't see why that means you can't get Angahrad out.'

Brennan slopped another inch of Scotch in each glass.

'Did you get the negatives?' He asked casually.

'Yes, and I shredded and burned them.' Hawkhurst smiled. 'I guess you and your agency wouldn't have minded having a copy, eh?'

Brennan matched his smile letting out a deep chuckle.

'Fucking A, Tom. Save me having to appeal to your better nature. So tell me, what do they want you to do now?'

'I'm not sure. I was told to pack for a journey, a journey to a warm country. I would be away for several weeks, possibly a month, Mallinson said. I'm to be picked up tomorrow night at Cleopatra's Needle again. That's all I know. Returning the pictures was just a gesture to let me know they are people who keep their word, I imagine. While they're holding Angahrad I guess they figure they've got me over a barrel.' He patted the briefcase lying on the bed at his side. 'That's why they even let me hold onto the Grail once they had checked I actually had it. I think they want me to go along to provide provenance, to tell Whichelow's crusaders and the rest of the world that it really is the Holy Gail.'

'You prepared to go through with something like that?'

'If you spring Angahrad I don't see why I should have to,' he said, taking a long pull at his drink, 'but somehow I get the feeling that you're about to come up with several good reasons why I should.'

Brennan nodded. Not many men would be prepared to get any deeper in this thing than Hawkhurst was already.

'The only way we're going to avoid a war is by giving the diplomats a chance to turn the gas down. So Whichelow may be getting help from somewhere in the Pentagon, that doesn't mean the US wants a Middle East war, Tom. America's had its fingers burnt too many times before in the region. Lebanon, Iran, Somalia – there's no mileage in it. Even when we dumped Saddam on his butt back in '91 none of the Arab leaders were really grateful. They hated and feared Saddam and took great delight in watching troops that bore the brunt of the fighting. Most ordinary Muslims, the man in the street, supported Baghdad in its defiance of the West. Any involvement by the US in the area is seen as unprovoked aggression and wins us few friends. Nevertheless, make no mistake about it, if at any time the existence or even the independence of Israel was seriously threatened America would come in with both feet. We're still only guessing, but it's likely Whichelow is planning something that might bring about just such a scenario with the inevitable results. We have to stop him.'

Hawkhurst listened in grim silence, knowing what Brennan said was true. Beyond this remained the matter of Suzie. He found he still wanted revenge.

'Get Angahrad out and I'll do anything you want.'

Brennan shook his head.

'Look at it logically. If we spring Angahrad, Whichelow will know we're onto him. We can't let that happen until we've at least located the task force. Even if we manage to do that we've still got plenty of problems. Who's to say there's only one task force? Who's to say Whichelow's the real leader? There are so many fruitcake cults about these days this could be a world-wide thing. He's got influence at the highest level at home, that's for sure, but he's got plenty of powerful friends around the world too.'

Tom stared out through the dirty windows at the evening sky. He could see all the awful potential of a situation so finely balanced. If they raided the house it would send unmistakable signals to Whichelow that his cover was blown. It could lead to him unleashing the task force before there was any chance of forestalling it.

'Surely you must have some idea of where the task force is? A force that size would need a whole fleet of aircraft or ships to move it.'

Brennan smiled ruefully.

'Every surveillance satellite, naval vessel and reconnaissance aircraft at the Pentagon's command is on round the clock alert. The coast guard has checked every sailing from the US in the past week and the airport authorities have done the same. They've all come up with a big fat zilch. Every warship in the Eastern Mediterranean, Red Sea and Persian Gulf is on the look-out. American, British, French, Italian, Spanish, you name it. Just about every major nation with a navy has ordered its fleet to find the task force. I can't see how Whichelow hopes to get close enough to launch a ground attack, even with choppers, yet somehow I have a nasty suspicion he's planned for every possibility. Our only hope of locating the task force is for you to infiltrate their organisation. We want you to go along with them, Tom.'

'You want me to hand the Grail over to them?' Tom was incredulous. 'We'd be giving Whichelow exactly what he wants, a talisman that transforms his lunatic schemes into a holy war. It would be giving the fundamentalists on both sides exactly what they want, too.'

'They could easily have taken it off you this morning, Tom. Did you think about that? Along with his other failings Mallinson has a list of convictions for assault and grievous bodily harm. If they had taken it you'd be sitting there now with your thumb jammed firmly up your ass and no cards to play.'

It was Hawkhurst's turn to smile as he pulled back his jacket to reveal a big service style revolver under his left armpit.

'I wouldn't have made it easy for them, Harry. I've also got a switchblade down my boot and a can of mace in the bottom of the case. I think to let the Grail fall into their hands would be one big mistake for all concerned until I've seen Angahrad alive and well.'

Brennan looked at the Englishman with new respect.

'We won't be giving them the real Grail, Tom. It'll be a replica. We haven't got time to have a proper copy made, silver beating is a pretty time consuming business they tell me, but the agency's metallurgists reckon they can make a casting that will fool all but experts like yourself. We're going to put a homing device into the base of the thing so even if we lose visual contact with you we'll be able to keep track of you from a distance. I can have it ready for tomorrow morning and you can hand the original back to the museum.'

'Isn't there a risk that word will get out? Archaeologists are the worst gossips in the world and I've got a lot of enemies in those circles. We could be compromised before we start.'

'No. We can handle that. Only the top people will know. Someone very high up in the British Government will have a quiet word with the top people at the museum. They'll be read the official secrets act and told to put out a story that the Grail's been stolen – presumably by you. I'm afraid it'll be another stain on your reputation but you'll just have to live with that. If the museum has the genuine article and an official assurance that what you're doing is vitally important, it'll save you a lot of trouble when you get back.'

Hawkhurst smiled broadly. He could imagine Dixey's reaction to such a turn of events. The word apoplexy sprung to mind. It would be worth it for just that, he thought.

'OK, Harry, you've got a deal. Deliver the replica and I'll take it to Whichelow.' He frowned. 'But only on the understanding that you spring Angahrad the moment I'm out of the country. If they've got me and the Grail, even if they find out she's been released, they won't think it's got anything to do with me. Anyway, accepting he's planning to stir things up in the Middle East, where do you think he'll strike?'

'I don't know. Israel possibly but more likely a sensitive area, a refugee camp or hospital. In all the time I was on Whichelow's payroll I never learnt anything of real value about their long term plans. In his shoes I'd hit some soft target that would produce a major outcry from the Arabs. Killing a few woman and kids is always good for the networks. A refugee camp maybe, some undefended township. A few atrocity stories would certainly keep things on the boil. Three battalions, even with air support, can only achieve so much, so he'd have to be in and out pretty sharply. What he wants is a knee jerk response from the hotheads. Saddam would love a reason to flex his muscles again. We've done our best to draw Iraq's teeth with arms control teams and imposing no fly zones but we know for a fact there's at least a dozen Scuds still unaccounted for and probably stocks of chemical agents hidden in the mountains. If they start flying you can bet Israel would go nuclear. Once that happens everybody would be dragged in. It's up to us to stop it.'

*****

Even her high moral outrage could not disguise the relief in Laura's voice as Hawkhurst handed the Grail back to her. However, the coldness of her manner said she had still not forgiven him for having got the better of her in the museum vault.

'It seems undamaged,' she said stiffly. 'I suppose we should be grateful for small mercies.'

He was unrepentant, aware his life depended on attention to detail from now on.

'You know what you have to do?'

'I have to keep it here at the flat until further notice and on Monday we tell the world it's been stolen. I don't know who's in this with you, Tom, but they certainly carry plenty of clout with the museum board. Dixey's furious at being told what to do, of course, but they've made us sign the official secrets act and hinted at all kinds of official retribution if we don't go along with the charade. Truth to tell, I think in the long run it'll make for marvellous publicity for the exhibition and so does he, but he's always had the knives out for you and he'll be sure to make the most of it to blacken your name.' She smiled sadly. 'Pity, Tom, you were on your way back there for a week or two.'

He shrugged, indifferent.

'The old twat can make all the fuss he likes just so long as he doesn't jump the gun. The story of the theft mustn't break before I'm out of the country.'

After locking the Grail away in the wall safe Laura stalked into the kitchen and his gaze
settled on the tight buttocks that clenched and relaxed beneath the thin fabric of her skirt as she went. Returning with two mugs of coffee she handed one to him.

'I don't suppose you can tell me what this is all about.'

He shook his head.

'Not really. You'll just have to trust me when I say my life depends on you playing your part. That's no exaggeration.'

'Play my part? In the same way you played your part in the vault, you mean?'

His face grew serious. He could imagine how she must have felt to be used like that.

'I'm genuinely sorry about what happened, Laura. If you had turned up ten minutes later I wouldn't have had to pull a rotten trick like that.'

'You made love to me to divert my attention, so you could steal the Grail.'

'That's right. I'm sorry.'

She considered his apology in silence and when she spoke next the frostiness in her voice had thawed a little.

'Who was that man I videoed yesterday on the Embankment?'

'One of the bad guys.'

'And you're one of the good guys?'

'I like to think so.'

Realising that she was unlikely to glean anything of value, Laura let the matter drop. To ask about the scarred man who now sat in the car outside, his eyes on the window where she stood, would be equally fruitless she guessed.

'OK, Tom. Tomorrow morning we tell the police that you've done a runner with the Grail. What happens then?'

'I haven't the faintest idea. But I can't see this business dragging on for long. You'll have plenty of time to announce that you've recovered the Grail. It'll have them flocking into the exhibition.'

'What will become of you when this is over?'

'I haven't the faintest idea.'

To his surprise she leant across and kissed him softly on the cheek.

'Take care. You may be a bit of a bastard but I'd hate you to get hurt.'

He smiled grimly at this almost convincing show of concern. Whichelow had murdered an innocent young girl just to increase the pressure on him. He was realistic enough to know that once he had delivered the Grail he would be surplus to the Church of Christ the Warrior's requirements and totally expendable. He took her smooth cool hand in his.

'Thanks, I'm glad we're still friends, Laura, and I'm truly sorry about taking advantage of you the other night.'

It was her turn to smile, curling an arm about his neck and kissing him warmly.

'Don't be,' she breathed in his ear, 'it was terrific.'

After he had gone she watched from the window until the car carrying Tom and Brennan disappeared around the corner. Then she stood in front of the hall mirror, absently smoothing her hair, her gaze thoughtful. At least the Grail was safe now, she thought, but Tom's report on the coin hoard and the maverick Penda mark still posed a threat to the provenance of the grave. With Tom likely to be out of the way for some time, she picked up the phone to call the Smithsonian in Washington.

'Hello, I want to speak to Professor Max Karelian, please.'

He would remove the Penda mark and commission a new report

CHAPTER FIFTEEN

'Exciting times, Dr Hawkhurst.' Mathews lit a cigarette, exhaling noisily and filling the car with foul smelling smoke. He was a thin, rat-faced individual who carried a liberal dusting of dandruff on both narrow sloping shoulders of a threadbare suit. He was also a chain smoker and an extremely nervous one at that for the ashtrays had spilled over onto the floor of the car and several empty packs lay about his feet. Hawkhurst made to lower his window an inch or so in the hope of clearing the air. When the handle refused to budge Mathews explained apologetically, the cigarette between his lips jerking as he spoke.

'Sorry, Doctor. Everything's been locked solid. Orders from the high command. Everyone's very conscious of the inestimable value of the Grail.'

They were heading south, mainly on back roads, and from the few road signs he had glimpsed Tom reckoned they were somewhere on the Sussex Hampshire border. It was nearly dark, the headlights of the car flickering ahead of them along the hedgerows that flanked the narrow lane. Rabbits scampered for cover at their approach and once a fox, eyes blazing red in the beam, stared at them boldly before slinking away into the undergrowth.

On several occasions since leaving London they had stopped and pulled off the road, waiting for ten minutes or so to check they weren't being tailed. At other times the driver, Mathews, had punched out a number on the telephone at his side, nodding at what Tom assumed would be reassuring reports from a second escorting car probably following at a safe distance to double check there was no subterfuge and to provide assistance if there was.

'Exciting times, Dr Hawkhurst,' Mathews repeated parrot fashion.

'You could say that. Where are we going anyway?'

'To Radstone airfield. It's not far now. The Church keeps a couple of aircraft there. I'm to pass you over to one of our pilots.'

'Where am I bound after that?'

'I really don't know. My job ends at the airfield.' He fell silent for several minutes and Tom reflected that for a kidnapper he was remarkably relaxed, friendly even. When he spoke next it became clear that the man's grasp of what was actually going on here was not all it might have been. 'You must have faith, Doctor. With God's help your wife will overcome the curse of drug abuse. I have seen it happen many times. I too have been a slave to noxious substances in my time; alcohol, and was cured. Prayer and fasting are most efficacious in these cases. I will make special mention of you both in my prayers.'

Tom decided it would be best to go along with the charade.

'How long do you think it will be before she's back on her feet again?'

'The specialist seems to think a week or so, maybe two, before she is completely detoxified.' He sounded genuinely concerned. 'By the time you get back she'll be up and about again, I'm sure.' His next question further reinforced the general air of unreality. 'Oh, I forgot to ask. Were the photographs Mr Mallinson passed to you sufficiently detailed to allow a definite identification?'

The man was obviously under the impression that Angahrad was a junkie taking a spell of cold turkey in one of the Church's rehabilitation centres and that the pictures of his session with Suzie had been photographs of the Grail. It seemed that very few of the Church's people in Britain were allowed to know what was really going on.

'Oh yes, excellent quality.'

'And tell me, is it – is it really the Holy Grail?' The question was delivered in a tremulous whisper. 'We were told that Reverend Whichelow had no doubt but that it was. Did the laboratories at Gethsemane provide clear evidence then? Is it the sacred chalice from which our Saviour and the apostles took wine at the last supper?'

'Oh yes,' said Tom quickly, 'I'd say it was beyond all doubt now.'

While Mary Lou had thought the Grail had held the blood of Christ on the cross. Mathews had embraced another equally ancient, equally unprovable, tradition. Zealotry clearly placed little emphasis on consistency. The man had become quite agitated now, placing a bony hand on Tom's arm.

'Alleluia, brother. The Lord has raised you up. He has called you to be a mighty warrior in His war against the Evil One.' Mathew's eyes glowed.

'Alleluia,' echoed Tom with what little fervour he could muster.

For another ten minutes they drove on through the night in silence until, after a final check over the telephone, the car drew sharply off the road. Bouncing easily over about half a mile of roughish pasture they finally came to a halt in front of a long low building where a solitary light glowed dimly behind the slats of a venetian blind.

'Please, Doctor,' Mathew's voice was small, awestruck, 'before you go would it be possible for me to see the Holy Grail?' He looked down at his hands, the sinewy fingers knotted together. 'I have been a sinner, Doctor, but through our Saviour Jesus and the Church of Christ the Warrior I have been redeemed. If I were only granted a sight of that precious vessel I would know I am saved for all eternity.'

Tom stared at him, then, reaching down into the case at his feet, he drew out the bowl, folding back the layers of tissue paper in which Brennan's metallurgist had wrapped the phoney relic. Switching on the light Mathews reached forward with hands that shook visibly and taking it from Tom he lifted the bowl up like a priest making an offering at the altar. Struck dumb, there were tears brimming in his eyes as he brought it to his lips and kissed the ornate rim. He handed it back, sitting in silent meditation as Tom returned it to his case. It was several minutes before he had sufficiently recovered his composure to speak.

'Thank you, Doctor. I shall remember today for the rest of my life.' He glanced at his watch. 'I think we'd better go in, Mr Potgeiter doesn't like to be kept waiting – he's not a nice man.'

Not a nice man was Tom's assessment too – in trumps!

'You took your bloody time.' The Afrikaner's staccato words were almost spat out as he stepped from the shadows. He was huge, as tall as Tom and fifty pounds, all muscle, heavier. Mathews, standing dwarfed and cowed between them, made to explain.

'I was told to be careful. We couldn't afford to take chances with the ….'

Potgeiter came forward, pushing the man effortlessly aside with the back of a contemptuous hand, until his face was inches from Tom's. He was about forty with cropped blond hair and a mouth that drew down in a permanent sneer. He wore a fur lined leather flying jacket against the evening chill.

'So you're the famous Hawkhurst?' The pale blue eyes bored into Tom's. 'Well, have you got the bloody thing?'

Mathews drew breath audibly at this blasphemy. Tom ignored the question.

'Any chance of coffee?' he asked indifferently. 'I'm parched.'

Potgeiter blinked, he was not accustomed to being spoken to in such a casual manner. Hawkhurst tried to imagine his thoughts. He wouldn't like Englishmen on principle, a race of pinko liberals and faggots who slept with Kaffirs when they weren't buggering each other. Most of all he wouldn't like educated Englishmen like Tom. They would make him feel uncomfortable. However, whatever the man's prejudices he had his orders and the Reverend had made it clear that this particular passenger was to be treated with kid gloves. He looked away.

'Sure, there's a thermos flask in the plane. We'd better get moving.' He turned to Mathews, whose gaze was still held by the case in Tom's hand, the spell only broken when Potgeiter snapped out his last orders. 'Make sure you clear up in here before you go, OK? No one must know we were ever here.'

Outside Tom followed the bulky figure of the pilot through the darkness to the aircraft. A waning moon hung low in the west, its crescent obscured by a gossamer film of thin high cloud. The aircraft was small, single engined, and painted, so far as he could tell in the gloom, a drab olive colour. It didn't look like one of the Church's regular fleet and Potgeiter hardly seemed the religious type. Probably a mercenary, he guessed.

'Throw your gear in the back,' he was instructed tersely, 'and get in. I'm gonna grab a crap before we go – we've got a long night ahead of us. Coffee's under the seat. I won't be long.'

It was about three in the morning when they finally took off. The South African, clearly a very experienced pilot, waited on the ground for twenty minutes in total darkness, engine idling, to bring his night vision up to scratch. He made one final check of his instruments and switches before easing the throttle open, taking them forward into what seemed to Tom like a solid, impenetrable wall of blackness. Unable to see a thing ahead he felt his palms sweating as they rolled inexorably down the strip. Then, just as it seemed they must run out of time, the rumble of the undercart over the rough grass ceased and they lifted effortlessly over the shadowy outline of the trees marking the field's perimeter. As with a solid thump the undercarriage retracted beneath them, Tom breathed out his tension and Potgeiter laughed harshly.

'Scared?'

'You could say that.'

'Don't worry. I've never lost a crate yet.'

As his heartbeat settled down, Tom decided it was time to start gathering such information as he could. Knowledge was power, they said. If so, he was currently in a particularly frail condition.

'Where did you learn to fly?'

'South African Air Force for eight years, Buccaneers and Mirages, then I did some bush flying in Kenya and Tanzania. Taking tourists and fat cats out to the game parks. Rich bastards mainly – medallion men who wanted to play the big white hunter but couldn't hack living rough. I wouldn't have given most of them house room – a couple of them even wanted me to let them shoot elephant from the plane. But, like I say, it had its advantages: the money was good and that kind always has a few nice looking woman in tow.'

'Sounds fun.'

'It was.'

'So why did you quit?'

'There was trouble – a woman.'

In normal situations Hawkhurst would have discreetly changed the subject at this point but now he needed to find out all he could and the niceties would have to go by the board.

'What happened?'

'It's a long story, but we've got time.' He grunted and Hawkhurst detected that he was starting to soften.

'A group of American tourists with ambitions of shooting trophies for their beach houses in Captiva hired me for a ten day safari. They wanted the whole jungle experience and I set up an overnight camp in the bush whilst their women stayed over in a hotel enjoying relative luxury. I settled the guys and returned to the hotel to check in on their families. One of the wives, the particularly overweight Martha had other ideas. She'd planned a night of passion or at least a few hours and when I rejected the offer of a blubbery fuck she cried foul and accused me of trying to force myself on her. Her screams woke the daughter who came flying in from the attached room with a Swiss army knife ready to defend the honour of her dearly beloved mother.'

'Well, my commando training kicked in and I tried to push her away with an open palm to the face but caught her full on the nose. This forced her nose into her skull and she was dead before she hit the floor.'

'The husband, another fat and overbearing bully, didn't believe me and Martha fabricated a story to clear herself of all blame. I was arrested and tried in the States. Fortunately my lawyer had close links with the Church of Christ the Warrior and the rest is history. Bloody no-good, overfed Disney-lovers settled out of court.' His wry smile hinted at a story of what settling out of court could entail.

Hawkhurst wanted to dig for any nuggets of information to see if Potgeiter had any doubts about the cargo or himself, he was particularly nervous about the homer. To his relief it quickly became clear that the South African harboured no such suspicions. His interest lay in other directions.

'How much is it worth, d'you reckon? In negotiable form.'

'You mean melted down?'

'How else?'

Tom felt that it would be wise to discourage the awesome man at his side from pursuing this line of thought. His tone was throwaway.

'Nothing like the ten thousand you'll get from Whichelow for delivering it, and me, in one piece.' The pilot laughed, getting his drift.

'Relax. I don't double cross my customers. Anyway, what would anyone want a thing like that for? Wouldn't even make a decent piss pot.'

*****

Brennan looked at the Flying Squad man, one eye raised questioningly. Things weren't happening fast enough for his liking.

'Well?'

Inspector Bullivant, a man of roughly Brennan's age yet who contrived to manage an air of positive antiquity, shook his head.

'The place was deserted. No sign of Mallinson or any of the Church's people and no sign of any woman.'

The two unmarked police cars were parked in the muddy entrance to Radstone airfield, shielded from the low control tower by a hedge of blossoming blackthorn that tossed fitfully in a cold morning breeze. Brennan pushed the dew beaded foliage aside with the barrel of the Smith & Wesson, peering out across the frosted field beyond.

'That's Mathews' car parked outside,' he said. 'He's not likely to be armed but tell your men to be careful – you can never tell what people will do once they've got religion.'

At a signal from the Inspector both cars slewed out across the intervening mire, lights flashing, sirens wailing. Brennan, trying to keep out from under the officer-in-charge's feet, followed on foot, stumbling over the rutted earth. His mind was troubled. The raid on Mallison's flat half an hour before had revealed nothing. If the Jenkins woman wasn't being held there, where the hell was she, he wondered? He thought of Hawkhurst, sticking his neck out because he thought she would be safe. It was too late now for any change of plan. They just had to play the cards as they were dealt.

He took some comfort in the fact that they had at least been able to keep a trace on Tom. From the moment his aircraft had taken off it had been tracked by an RAF Nimrod, right up to the edge of Spanish territorial waters and from there to the airstrip high in the Cordillera mountains. Now a US Air Force AWACs was cruising off the coast awaiting its next move. With their powerful radar neither tracking aircraft had needed to come closer than fifty miles of their quarry. There was no way their presence could have been detected.

Still, the thought of the woman still being in Whichelow's hands was a disturbing one. He had developed a lot of respect for Hawkhurst, the guy was sharp, could think on his feet, and had plenty of balls, but if there was anything likely to throw the plans, Angahrad's disappearance was at the top of Tom's list. Inspector Bullivant emerged, the gun in his hand hanging loosely at his side. He was pale.

'Anything?' Brennan snapped impatiently.

Without a word the policeman moved back to let him pass and Brennan stood in the door, his eyes going to the ceiling. From the cross members of the hut roof hung the body of Mathews. Tight about his neck was the flex of the shattered desk lamp that lay in one corner. His face was black with blood and his swollen tongue protruded obscenely between rolled back lips. The bulging eyes were open, staring heavenward like a martyr in ecstasy. On the floor beneath the body lay one pathetic shoe.

Brennan moved outside, standing next to the Inspector who stared out across the grey fields where the first early crows were flocking in to feed. He took a lungful of cool air.

'Messy.'

'Very. I've put a call out to get a forensic team here asap. I guess we'll be here most of the morning waiting for them.'

'Have you checked the car?'

'Clean as a whistle so far as my men can see. Of course forensics may come up with something.'

'Mind if I take a look?' The American's tone was deferential, he was just an observer here, but playing the diplomat was playing hell with his nerves. Luckily the inspector was not a tight-arse.

'Sure, go ahead, but I don't think we'll find anything worthwhile. That poor bastard in there was just small fry. I reckon they topped him before we could put any pressure on.'

Brennan slid into the driver's seat, his eyes running over the dash as he reached in and shuffled through the contents of the glove compartment. At first sight the RAC handbook and road maps it contained offered little hope of anything useful and it was only as he returned them that he noticed that on the back of the handbook someone had scribbled the number 49. He looked cautiously over his shoulder. The inspector was out on the airstrip examining the tread marks of the aircraft. Lifting up the telephone he punched out the number, although with little hope of receiving any response. To his surprise, after a moment's delay, it began to ring and his face grew grim as the phone at the other end was taken up. It was a woman's voice. He listened for a moment then, without acknowledging the voice at the other end, laid the handset back in its cradle. He stared out across the windswept airstrip for a second before, licking a forefinger; he rubbed the number into an illegible smear.

'No luck?' The inspector was anxious he hadn't overlooked anything obvious.

'No,' lied Brennan. 'Nothing at all, I guess I'd better be getting back to town. Any chance of fixing a cab for me?'

*****

In his eagerness to be rid of Brennan, the inspector had allocated him one of the police cars and within a couple of hours he was back in

London. He now sat basking thankfully in the late morning sun outside the Eight Bells, the ornately tiled Victorian pub across from Laura's Chelsea town house, a large bourbon in hand, a copy of *The Times* obscuring his features. The red Porsche stood in the open garage beneath the house and once he caught a glimpse of a pale face at the first floor window, sipping his drink slowly he settled down for a long wait.

At a little after three she came skipping down the tiled steps that led from the big black Georgian front door. Twirling the key in her hand she strode lightly to the car. When the vehicle had disappeared around the corner Brennan drained his glass and quit his seat. This would have to be a very quick job – there was already an air force plane warming up at Lakenheath, awaiting his arrival.

CHAPTER SIXTEEN

The sun was coming up behind the western Cordillera Cantabrica as the plane, banking steeply, dropped down towards the miniscule slip of greenness that lay along the otherwise barren flank of the mountainside. As the little craft levelled out into its approach run Hawkhurst felt none of the nervousness of their earlier night departure. Throughout the journey, hour upon hour, he had watched Potgeiter pilot the plane unerringly through blackness and turbulence to make this landfall. A few hours ago they had flown over the Ushant light at the extreme western point of the Brittany coast. For Hawkhurst it had been the last identifiable mark he had seen until the Spanish coast had come up at dawn. Somehow the South African had arrived precisely where he wanted to be. Although there was a sophisticated satellite navigation system on board as far as Tom could tell he had not once used it, preferring to fly by compass and the stars. The man was good.

Now he throttled back and with only a modicum of bumping they were down, rolling to a standstill in the coarse, uneven grass with a low rumble. He cut the engine and, glad to be free of the cramped cockpit after so long, they both jumped down, joints protesting, ears ringing in the welcome silence. It was cold, their breath crystallising on the thin high sierra air, for the sun had not yet touched this side of the mountain and frost rimed the grass. The small mountain flowers at their feet still held their petals closed against the night's chill and there was no birdsong. The only sign of life was a lone lammergeier carving wide circles high overhead in the cool blue of the morning. Hawkhurst's eyes ranged the boulder strewn heights above and below while behind him Potgeiter urinated noisily, winding up his performance with a sigh of relief.

'Christ I needed that.' He said with evident sincerity, coming to stand at Tom's side, his eyes searching the crags above. 'Now, where the hell are they?'

'Who?'

'The sons of bitches who are supposed to meet us here with fuel and provisions. We've still got a ways to go and the tanks are nearly empty.'

For ten minutes they stared in vain, the only sounds the hiss of the wind and the sporadic clicking of the aircraft engine as the hot metal cooled rapidly. Then something moved just below the ragged fringe of the crest.

'There,' Tom pointed up the mountainside. Far off and high up, an unsteady caterpillar of donkeys and men were making a slow and precarious descent towards them. Potgeiter produced a pair of Zeiss 10x50 binoculars from the cockpit, scanned the approaching caravan briefly then handed the glasses to Hawkhurst with a disgusted sniff.

'Bollocks. They should have been here waiting for us. I wanted to get away from here before the sun is over the crest. Once the frost melts, the strip will stick like shit to a blanket.' He shrugged. 'Oh well, I guess we've got an hour or more before they get here, I'll fix breakfast. Eggs and bacon OK with you?'

From a locker at the rear of the aircraft's fuselage he produced a Butane cooker and a set of lightweight cooking utensils then busied himself preparing the food. Tom continued to track the progress of the approaching party. Initially he thought the men wore mountaineer style cagoules, as they drew closer he saw they were garbed in long rough habits. The newcomers were, it seemed, monks. Nine of the animals bore large jerry cans strapped to panniers on their backs. This, no doubt, would be the fuel for the next leg of their journey. On the rearmost donkey, however, rode a man, his head cowled like his companions. All looked weary and Tom wondered just how far they had trekked to reach this remote rendezvous. Occasionally man or beast would stumble sending a little avalanche of scree clattering away into the abyss that fell away below the narrow path they trod. Despite Potgeiter's annoyance at the delay in their arrival it was obvious that any attempt to undertake such a journey in darkness would have been tantamount to suicide. Eventually the party reached the terrace, filing down onto the level of the strip where the aircraft stood. As they drew near Potgeiter looked up from the bucket of cold water in which he was scrubbing the cooking traps. Setting his work aside he stared at the newcomers.

'We're going to have company for the rest of the journey, Hawkhurst.'

Tom frowned. More complications.

'Who?'

'I don't know for sure. It was a last minute thing. I got a message from the Church's people just before we left the UK. I think it's a priest of some sort, a cardinal something or other, Martini? Some wop drink it sounded like. Believe me it's not my idea. It gives us real payload problems but I guess for the money they offered it's worth it. Those bastards at the Church always play their cards close to the chest but I get the distinct impression that this guy is pretty important.'

Tom brought the glasses to bear again, bringing the mounted figure into hard-edged focus. There could be no mistaking the gaunt features, the pale witch-finder eyes that glittered from within the shadow of the hood like some feral beast in its lair, the beak-like hoot of a nose. He lowered the glasses.

'Not Martini,' he said softly, 'Martinette. Monsignor Martinette of St Germaine – the heretic cardinal.' Even Potgeiter was impressed.

'Shit. I read about that guy. Didn't the Pope excommunicate him a couple of years back?'

'Not quite but it was a close run thing. He's a hyper-traditionalist. He'll only celebrate mass in Latin, has always taken a very hard line on abortion and birth control and has advocated the repatriation of immigrants from France, especially non-Christian immigrants. He's a real right winger and goes hand in glove with La Pen's nationalists. Back in '91, before the Gulf War, he was right up the sharp end with the French Army's Daguet Division during the build-up for Desert Storm. He was virtually preaching a holy war, a crusade, against Saddam, something that didn't go down too well with the Saudis and the other Muslim contingents. It was pretty obvious that he had powerful friends amongst the French military but the Americans found him too much of a liability and eventually he was ordered back to France where he was given a hero's welcome. Since then, despite threats from the Vatican, he's continued with his campaign for a return to traditional Catholic values. He's very popular with grass roots Catholics in France as well as the whole political right wing. Nevertheless, the Vatican didn't like what they were hearing. The liberal faction was talking of the possibility of a black Pope within the next ten years and here's Martinette preaching what amounts to racism. It could easily have led to a major schism in the Roman Catholic Church and, like you say, rumour has it that he was at one time threatened with excommunication if he didn't shut up. The message must have got through because he's been pretty quiet since then. Word is, though, he is still very popular in the Catholic Church, especially in Europe and the States, and whatever the official line may be it's rumoured he's still got a lot of support in Rome. Despite everything he's got to be a strong contender to be the next Pope.'

The South African, impressed by what he was hearing, stared hard. Then he laughed.

'Just as long as he doesn't expect me to kiss his ring.' Ignoring Martinette he strode towards the monks and their animals, pointing towards the plane. 'Unload the gas over there,' he hollered. 'I'll show you how to fill her up.'

Tom watched as the Cardinal dismounted, steadying himself against the pommel of the saddle he arched his back, stretching aching joints back into action. In the saddle he had seemed tall but dismounted proved to be small, diminutive almost, no more than five feet in height. Intrigued, Tom walked towards him to make an introduction but the priest, his thin, lined face grave and unsmiling, raised a silencing finger to his lips before dropping to his knees on the dew-moist grass, bony hands locked in prayer. From the rosary he held, dangled a small gold sword. Unlike the simple silver symbol Whichelow wore about his neck this was studded with tiny jewels and semi-precious stones but there was no mistaking the inference. This too was a crusading priest. His unexpected appearance could only mean The Reverend had succeeded in setting up a powerful alliance in support of whatever lunacy he planned.

As Martinette knelt in prayer, a burly monk stepped forward, placing himself firmly between them and indicating to Tom that further attempts at communication would not be welcome. With a shrug he turned and made his way back to the aircraft where the contents of the jerry cans were being transferred into the aircraft by means of a small hand powered rotary pump. It was a slow, laborious business and Potgeiter was clearly getting impatient. Doubtless the Spanish security forces patrolled the area looking for Basque separatists and other antisocial and criminal elements. The contents of less than half of the jerry cans had been transferred to the aircraft's tanks when, having examined the gauges, the South African called a halt to the proceedings.

'That'll do,' he snapped. 'We're going to be overloaded as it is and this strip is too damn short for my liking.' His eyes went to Martinette who, surrounded by a knot of monks, watched from a little way off. He beckoned the Cardinal to get on board with a peremptory sweep of his arm, at the same time grunting to no one in particular: 'Not very friendly is he.'

As Tom helped Potgeiter stow away the fuelling equipment the monks led the donkeys clear of the runway, Martinette climbed into the aircraft and settled himself into a folding canvas bucket seat to the rear of the pilot. Now staring fixedly ahead, the rosary sliding between his fingers, he had, since his arrival, neither spoken to or acknowledged the presence of either of them. The priest's aloof indifference seemed to rankle with the big pilot. Either His Eminence considered himself above communicating with menial beings or he was worried about the coming take off. Whatever, Potgeiter was determined to exacerbate any unease he might be experiencing.

'Strap yourself in Tom boy and hold onto your hat,' he said grimly. 'I'm going to give her the gun.' He gave a jerk of the head to indicate the priest sitting behind them. 'That motherfucker's really going to need his goddamn worry beads.'

Smiling grimly Hawkhurst steeled himself for the coming ordeal; Potgeiter started up the engine and opened the throttle wide, bringing it to a screaming pitch that made the aircraft shudder on its undercart. Tom looked out of the window. The monks now knelt in a tight semi-circle at the edge of the strip, their tired, untethered mounts grazing unconcernedly beyond. He sensed rather than saw the Cardinal's raised hand making the sign of the cross, a departing benediction on his faithful followers as the aircraft began to move down the uneven sward.

Again it seemed to Hawkhurst that Potgeiter could not possibly get the plane airborne in such a confined space, the rock face rushing inexorably towards them, closer and closer. There was nothing he could do. He shut his eyes and as he did so felt the nose wheel lift and they turned steeply away to starboard, still so low the tip of the inside wing brushed through the grass, throwing up a delicate spray of dew. When he opened them again they were soaring above the crest and sunlight was splintering on the perspex of the cockpit cover. Potgeiter was grimly silent and Tom guessed the take-off had been a pretty close run thing. Despite the man's unsavoury past and his over aggressive approach to life in general, Tom could not deny a growing respect for his flying skills and seemingly nerveless courage. He looked over his shoulder to see how his fellow passenger had dealt with the ordeal and smiled; His Eminence had fainted.

Now they headed due west, skimming down the long stegosaur spine of the Cordillera, flying just below the crest to confuse any radar, and crossing the coast once more this time just to the south of Corruna. Along the whole length of the mountain range they had been constantly buffeted by invisible thermal currents that swirled and billowed up from the warming slopes below and Tom was glad of the calmer conditions they now encountered. He thought of the homing device Brennan's people had planted in the phoney Grail and wondered about the tracking aircraft, probably hundreds of miles away, that were, hopefully, following their every move.

Once over the sea Potgeiter brought the plane onto a more south-westerly heading. Away to their left the headland of Cape Torinana melted into the morning mist and within minutes they were out of sight of land. The sun had gone now and a low layer of slab-like slate cloud was sliding in from the Atlantic. Aware it might be vital later and trying to keep some estimated check on their position Tom kept a discreet watch on the compass and hoped they had taken enough fuel on board to get them back to shore again if the rendezvous was to prove unsuccessful. Potgeiter could have been reading his thoughts.

'I hope I've got my navigation right,' he said. 'Cos if I haven't we're sure in for a long swim back. Keep your eyes peeled, according to my reckoning we should be over the RV position very soon now although the GPS puts us well to the north.' He consulted the satellite navigator again, then switched it off in disgust. 'Never did trust those damn things anyway.'

Hawkhurst's gaze swept the desolate vastness around them.

'What are we supposed to be looking for?'

'The biggest fucking ship you've ever seen in your life.'

For maybe five minutes they flew on, then Tom pointed. On the horizon, away to port, was a long low smudge, apparently heading south into a gathering storm.

'Could that be it?'

'I sure hope so.' He tapped the glass face of the fuel gauge. 'We are well down into the red already. I reckon we've got no more than fifteen minutes flying time left at best. I just hope I haven't cut things too fine.'

The ship grew in size and clarity as they drove low and fast above the long Atlantic swell, the aircraft now being hammered by rain that smacked into the windscreen like machine gun fire. As to the vessel's size the South African had not been exaggerating. She was truly enormous. A ULCC and once the largest oil tanker on the Kuwait to United States run, the Nagasaki Maru had weighed in at nearly half a million tons when she had been launched from the Tokyo shipyard in 1972. While the Suez Canal was blocked she could earn her owners a small fortune carrying vast cargoes of oil down the long haul around the Cape of Good Hope. Then she had been an engineering masterpiece, now she was a dinosaur. Too big to operate efficiently once the canal was reopened in 1974 she was now, at nearly twenty six years old, an environmental disaster just waiting to happen. Her rust scabbed hull with its dented and battered plating told its own story. It occurred to Tom that if this was the flagship of the Church of Christ the Warrior's navy they were being untypically coy about it for the only flag he could make out was the rather threadbare Panamanian ensign that fluttered at her stern.

As they flew down the length of her port side, each man grimly aware of the precariousness of their position, Tom could see that all the normal loading fittings and cargo handling gear had been removed to leave the vast expanse of deck forward of the bridge clear and flush. This area, the length of three football pitches, had been marked out with white lines running down its entire length and transverse markings delineating every twenty five metres. It seemed as though they were going to maintain strict radio silence, making no attempt to establish contact with the mother ship. However, it was clear that their approach was being tracked from the ship for from the wind deck of the bridge a brilliant white light winked spasmodically and he saw the huge vessel begin to swing ponderously onto a new course.

'Will they stop for us?' Hawkhurst asked. The pilot shook his head.

'Not a chance. Even if they went full astern a thing that size takes hours to come to a standstill. We'd be out of fuel long before then. No. The only help they can give us is to come onto the wind which, I hope, is what they're doing right now. I'm going to make one dummy run and then we'll go for broke.'

Unlike their previous landing and take-off this approach presented no problem insofar as the length of the runway available was concerned. However, perhaps aware of their precarious lack of fuel, the tanker's skipper had turned too hard, heeling the vast vessel over the waves, bringing her beam on to the growing swell. The result of this was that by the time she had achieved the required course, the ship had built up a noticeable sway. Potgeiter rocked the plane from left to right and back again as he tried to match the motion of the Nagasaki Maru. As the aircraft banked away at the last moment to avoid the towering structure of the bridge it was apparent to Tom that this was no easy task.

'This time's for real,' the pilot grunted, throwing the switch that would lower the undercarriage and waiting for the confirming light to indicate it was locked in position. 'If I foul up we'll probably go over the side. If that happens be prepared to unstrap damn quick and, once I release the cockpit canopy, swim like fuck. Good luck boys.'

Hawkhurst prepared himself, looping his arm through the handle of the case containing the Grail. It was a whimsical thought but the last thing he wanted was for it to meet a watery fate after all this. He looked back to see if the Cardinal was fully aware of the urgency of their situation. The fervour with which the rosary was running through his fingers suggested he had. Potgeiter smiled.

'If he keeps that up he'll end up with rope burn.'

But the priest's fears were to prove well founded for they were still several hundred metres from the vessel's bulbous bow when the aircraft engine coughed dryly and the propeller faltered. For a few seconds or so it picked up again as the last dregs of fuel were burned up but then coughed in a hollow death rattle, this time to die completely.

'Oh, shit.' Potgeiter said softly. 'Why didn't I study harder? I could have been an accountant.'

The only sound now was the sigh of air over the wings and the slap of rain on the misted cockpit. They began to lose altitude quickly as the South African, eyes slitted in concentration, struggled with the controls, fighting to maintain sufficient height and speed to glide the last desperate metres between them and the improvised flight deck. Feeling the sour bile of sheer terror rise in his gorge Hawkhurst gritted his teeth and prepared himself for death. If they smashed into the bow of the ship it would at least be quick. If they ended up in the sea it would be a long futile struggle with no hope of survival.

They made it but only just for the undercarriage was only inches above the deck level as the seething bow of the Nagasaki Maru swept beneath them. Mercifully they touched down mid-roll when the ship was on an even keel and Hawkhurst breathed out forcibly as they trundled to a halt scant metres short of the rusting plates of the bridge superstructure. Potgeiter laughed aloud, suddenly affable.

'Well, Tom, I don't want too many like that.'

Tom breathed his tension out and nodded, in total agreement with the sentiment, then pointed to the pungent pool of greenish liquid that was forming beneath their feet on the cockpit floor.

'I'd say the Cardinal doesn't either.'

CHAPTER SEVENTEEN

Across the deck, heads bowed against the worsening weather, a group of white boiler suited deck hands ran towards the aircraft as the three of them climbed out, Tom and Potgeiter half carrying Martinette between them. Their leader, a young Phillipino, had to shout to be heard above the rising wind.

'Please, gentlemen, follow me to the bridge. My men will take care of the plane.'

Grateful to feel the solidity of the deck beneath their feet and keen to be out of the buffeting elements they headed for an open door at the base of the towering bridge superstructure. As the thick steel door swung closed behind them and securing clips bolted home, Hawkhurst shook the rain from his hair and looked around. The interior of the ship was in complete contrast to her battered external appearance. Here the freshly painted bulkheads and gleaming brass work were more reminiscent of a luxury cruise liner than the rust bucket oiler she had appeared from the air. They were led down pastel carpeted corridors where tasteful prints adorned the bulkheads and up several flights of steps, finally arriving on the bridge where Whichelow and Mary Lou, both dressed in white boiler suits bearing the sword motif, waited to greet them. The watch officer, helmsman and two lookouts who shared the bridge with them kept their attention firmly on the business of handling the vast ship. Whichelow was affable while she was coyly triumphant. He stepped forward and bowed briefly to the Cardinal, now somewhat recovered from his ordeal, his huge bulk towering over the little priest. It was a sign of respect but a measured one and there could be no doubt as to who was pre-eminent here.

'Welcome aboard, your Eminence.' He rumbled. 'Your accommodation is all prepared. No doubt you will be weary. We shall talk later.'

Martinette, composed now after the ordeal of the landing, nodded gravely and when he spoke, for the first time since he had joined them in the mountains, his voice was strangely high pitched, adding to the overall bird-like impression. His English was almost perfect.

'Indeed, it has been a long journey.' He turned to Hawkhurst. 'Forgive me for being such a boorish travelling companion, Dr Hawkhurst. Until we were safely aboard I felt it was essential that I remain silent. Had we been intercepted it could have compromised the entire mission. I am free to travel where I will but you are a wanted man in your own country and if the two of us were taken together it would certainly suggest to even the most stupid of our enemies that something was afoot. Now we have arrived may I say how glad I was to learn that you are with us in this historic enterprise.' Tom raised a questioning eyebrow, wondering who 'our enemies' might be, but said nothing as the priest grew increasingly agitated. The piping voice dropped to a whisper. 'Please, before I retire to my prayer, show me the Grail.'

Tom produced the dummy chalice that Brennan's people had manufactured so swiftly. He knew there were minor flaws in the reproduction but felt it unlikely that the Cardinal would be able to detect them. Mary Lou, who now stood at his shoulder, however, might be another matter. She was a historian and antiquarian of sorts. To his relief her unwavering smile as Martinette took the chalice between both hands, kissed the cool metal and raised it to the light, said she suspected nothing.

'Magnificent. On that glorious day when the Holy Grail is used to perform the Blessed Sacrament in Jerusalem, the whole of the Christian world will be in your debt for all eternity, Doctor. Until then, until we proclaim the coming of the new Messiah to the waiting world, it shall be carried at the head of his earthly forces. This sacred chalice is the symbol that will tell the world we come in the name of God to claim the Third Millennium for Christ.'

With the briefest of nods to the others he turned on his heels and was ushered away by a brace of stewards. Tom watched him go, pondering on the cryptic remarks about Jerusalem and a new Messiah. Nothing these people said surprised him anymore, nothing they might be planning could seem too outrageous. The sheer scale of the operation , the vast resources available to the Church of Christ the Warrior, the level of support and cooperation they seemed to enjoy in high places, the unturnable, ruthless conviction with which they carried out their plans, all pointed to a conspiracy that must inevitably have global repercussions.

He had already recognised that his only chance of learning enough to be able to affect their schemes was to appear to go along with them, to appear as if he had been seduced by their lunacy. Just so long as Brennan and his agency were following his progress there was time yet for the Nagasaki Maru to be intercepted and for the whole mad hatter's tea party to be put behind bars. They were now off the coast of northern Spain with, he estimated, maybe seven or eight hundred miles to the Straits of Gibraltar. Unless they had installed new, more powerful engines, an old tanker like this would take at least two days to cover that distance and even then they would still be a long way from the Middle East. Anywhere in the Mediterranean they would be within easy striking distance of powerful air and naval forces, especially the US Sixth Fleet, however, if their mischief making was destined for the Persian Gulf...'

'What the fuck's going on?'

Potgeiter's oath shook Tom from his reverie and he walked to where the man stood, staring down in disbelief at the vast expanse of deck below, just in time to see the aircraft that had brought them being pushed towards the ship's side, the intent obvious. Manhandled, with some difficulty at first, by half a dozen deck hands, the pitching of the ship soon took her and, once in motion, she rolled easily to the side where, after a moment's hesitation, she lifted her tailplane and toppled gracefully into the sea. The South African turned to Whichelow, anger etched into every line of his craggy face. The Reverend raised a pacifying hand.

'Calm yourself. You will be handsomely paid for the loss of your aircraft, Mr Potgeiter. Unfortunately we have no room below decks on the Nagasaki Maru for another aircraft and to leave it on deck would have invited questions.' He smiled slyly, his eyes going to Hawkhurst. 'After all, who knows who might be out there looking for us? You will be recompensed and put ashore at the first convenient opportunity. Until then why not just enjoy the Church's hospitality?'

Potgeiter snorted in disgust but said nothing and it occurred to Tom that maybe the intention was to keep the South African on board where they could keep an eye on him until this thing was over. Perhaps the same applied to him, Mary Lou broke into his train of thought.

'Sure glad to have you along, Tom.' She made to take the briefcase containing the chalice from him. 'I'll just slip this into the safe and then we'll get down to brass tacks. You'll want to wash up I guess. I've assigned you a most attractive cabin.'

Tom ignored the prissy ministrations, grasping the case tighter and eyeballing Whichelow.

'Have you released Angahrad?'

Whichelow smiled. His bass voice rumble was reassuring, friendly almost.

'Why sure we have, son. What kind of people do you think we are? You've kept your part of the bargain and we've kept ours.' He clicked his fingers and one of the lookouts handed him a mobile telephone which he passed to Tom. 'Ring the farm. I think you'll find she's safe and sound at home once more.'

Tom rang the number. After a few moments she came to the phone.

'Angie? It's me, Tom. Are you all right, darling? They didn't hurt you?'

'No, they didn't hurt me. I'm fine, everything's OK, but where are you?' Her voice was small and distant but she sounded all right he decided.

'I'm ....' Before he could utter another word Whichelow reached forward and snatched the phone from his fingers.

'Your lady friend's OK, Tom. That's all you need to know. We can't allow lengthy transmissions of any sort – satellite surveillance is so sophisticated these days.'

Tom bit back his anger and nodded acquiescently. For the moment he was quite prepared to accept any petty display of power The Reverend chose to indulge in. Now he was certain that Angahrad was safe, the tamer he appeared the better chance he had of learning something useful. The closer he could get to Whichelow the better chance he would have of killing the man when the time came, for he knew in his heart that nothing short of a blood fee could decently atone for what had been done to Suzie.

'Right,' Mary Lou's tone was bright and breezy: they were all friends again. 'Just let me have the Holy Grail, Tom, and I'll show you and Mr Potgeiter to your cabins.'

He handed it over without further dissent.

'Dinner at eight, boys,' Whichelow was addressing both Hawkhurst and Potgeiter now. 'We'll shoot the breeze then. I bet you've got no end of questions.'

*****

His cabin was small but comfortable. There was a single bed, a desk, an en suite shower and a lavishly stocked bar from which he quickly plundered a healthy shot of Scotch before examining his new home in detail. One small brass porthole, too small for a man to climb through, looked out over the port quarter of the Nagasaki Maru. He stared out. The weather conditions building up outside were reflected in the rain flecked glass and sluggish roll of the ship and he could make out no sign of land through the greyness.

    Tom meandered about the room, looking innocently befuddled but actually searching for any sign of bugging. There was a solitary fire sprinkler in the deckhead which he suspected might be a listening device and a shaving mirror over the washstand which could have been two way. Whether Whichelow would consider it necessary to spy on his unwilling house guest he couldn't say, but it had to be a possibility. Tom considered the possibility that he was a prisoner, however, and he found the cabin door was not locked and he was, apparently, free to wander around the ship at will. He looked at his watch, it was four thirty pm UK time, and he assumed they were still in the same time zone here, running down the coast of Spain and Portugal. Four hours to dinner: time for a shower and a spot of shuteye, he thought. As he headed for the shower there came a loud rapping at the cabin door. It was a distinctly peeved Potgeiter.

    'What the hell's going on here?' he demanded. Hawkhurst, his back to the mirror, pointed to the sprinkler overhead. The South African looked up, frowned then nodded.

    'I really couldn't say. I was just going to take a turn around the deck for a breath of fresh air. Fancy joining me?' Getting his drift the other man nodded.

    It was hardly ideal conditions for a stroll. Outside the weather had really turned nasty, a near gale screaming through the radio antennae and heavy rain slapping down in wind-driven surges that stung their faces. Above the bridge the radar scanner hissed in its endless pirouette, throwing off a swirl of spray. They stood huddled in the lee of the huge orange lifeboat that hung in its davits at the stern of the vessel. Although they were unlikely to be overheard here Tom still wasn't sure he entirely trusted this huge airman. Potgeiter's anger at the loss of his aircraft had been real enough and he clearly hadn't been expecting to be held on board like this. Nevertheless, he reminded himself that he would do well to remember that this man was, above all, a mercenary and aboard the Nagasaki Maru information was as valid a currency as flying skills. It would not do to be too open too soon.

'All I know is they're a bunch of religious maniacs who plan some hare-brained scheme in the Middle East. That, plus the fact that they've killed in the past and won't hesitate to do so again. If we want to come out of this alive we need to stay on our toes and keep our heads down when the shit starts to fly. What do you know about them?'

Potgeiter turned the fur-lined collar of his flying jacket up against the rain, thrusting his hands deep into the pockets, and pressed closer into the shelter of the lifeboat.

'Apart from the fact they pay well and I've never had trouble with them before, the square root of fuck all. I was due to refuel on board and fly from here down to Algiers for another pick-up.'

Hawkhurst considered this. It was just possible Whichelow had others intending to join him later on the voyage. For whatever reasons those plans had been changed. He looked at Potgeiter thoughtfully.

'Can you fly a helicopter, Mr Potgeiter?'

'Sure. Why?'

'Because unless I'm very much mistaken there are a lot of them stowed below decks and we may need to get off this ship in a hurry. I reckon we've got a few days before things start to happen so we'll just keep our eyes and ears open for now. If you see any chance to grab a chopper and get the hell out of here let me know. I'll do the same.'

Potgeiter smiled and held out his hand.

'You've got a deal – and the name's Piet.'

*****

Dinner, served punctually at eight by a young black steward formally attired in white ducks and bow tie, was almost a friendly affair. Whichelow held court with Martinette and Mary Lou doing their best to include Hawkhurst and Potgeiter in their discussions. To Tom's annoyance, however, it was only generalities, platitudes and inanities they were prepared to offer rather than the hard evidence he sought. The food, a succulent leg of roast lamb carved at the table and accompanied by generous quantities of an excellent Californian red, could not be faulted and as the wine flowed a generally relaxed ambience soon filled the dining saloon. Conversation mainly centred about the state of the world, especially the crisis in the Middle East and the supposed threat to the Christian world posed by the rise of Islamic fundamentalism. Iran under the ayatollahs was clearly regarded as the main threat to global stability and was roundly castigated, but their fears and suspicions seemed to embrace the whole of the Muslim religion. Even the pacifist Firdasi was not spared their suspicion, indeed as it was, The Master's apparent commitment to peace made him all the more suspect in their eyes.

It was a subject on which Tom had only a passing knowledge but even he realised they thought and debated in the broadest of terms. They seemed to make no differentiation between sects, Shia or Sunni, or race, Arab, Iraqi, Iranian or Afghan, in their general loathing. It was also noticeable that, in the eyes of the Church of Christ the Warrior at least, Christianity and the western world were regarded as synonymous. Their interests were regarded, unquestionably, as being universally mutual and self-supporting. As the steward cleared away, Potgeiter, struck the first slightly discordant note of the evening.

'Well, it's all been very interesting but just where are we headed, Reverend? I don't want to sound ungrateful or anything but the Middle East isn't on my list of priorities. If it's all the same to you I'd rather not get involved. If you'll just pay me what you owe me I'll be on my way just as soon as you can put me ashore.'

The room went silent, only the muffled throb of the engines many decks below and the hiss of the screws as they carved through the Atlantic swell came to them as Whichelow stared hard at the South African. Smiling through the smoke of the fat cigar that lay in the ashtray before him he nodded.

'I understand your eagerness to be away, Mr Potgeiter, but I would ask you to exercise a little patience. A cheque that more than adequately covers the inestimable services you have provided to the Church has already been paid into your burgeoning Swiss account. Another to reimburse you for the loss of your aircraft will be paid in tomorrow. If my arithmetic serves me correctly you will, all told, be richer to the sum of one hundred and twenty thousand US dollars.

Surely with that in mind you can afford to relax a little, take a short sea cruise. What I'm offering is, at minimal risk to your person or pocket, a chance to watch history in the making.' He stood up sharply, pressing down on the arms of the chair to heave his huge form erect. 'Follow me, gentlemen. I'm going to give you a preview of what we are all about here on the Nagasaki Maru and just what our plans are.' He turned to the other two, both deep in debate about the Grail and its historical relevance. 'Mary Lou, Your Eminence, if you will excuse us for a short while.'

From the dining room he ushered them into a small adjoining cabin about four metres square. It was dark, the only light reflecting from the half-dozen television screens ranged along the forward bulkhead. There were three rows of cinema style seats facing the screens. Whichelow sat himself down in the front row and produced a remote control, peering closely at it in the semi darkness. Tom sat next to Potgeiter as Whichelow spoke.

'Right, although she may not be much to look at we've got some pretty fancy communications installed aboard the Nagasaki Maru. Thanks to the wonders of modern technology we can keep abreast of world events, hour by hour, as they happen. Even here, hundreds of miles from land we can still, at any time, go directly to where the action is. From this room we can watch history in the making – watch history even as we make it.' He clicked randomly at the control pad in his hand and each of the screens flashed briefly before settling down to an image of a different newscaster. The sound was way down and they read mutely to the cameras as Whichelow continued. 'Thanks to satellite broadcasting we can receive just about every major news channel in the world. Of course, I don't have time to sit through each newscast so the communications officer and his team edit everything that comes in. Each night I get a digest of all relevant news – anything that might have an impact on our plans.' He turned his head towards Hawkhurst. 'There's a piece here from the BBC I think you'll be interested in, Tom.' He clicked once again and the oval features of Angela Rippon materialised before them. Whichelow thumbed up the sound.

'Police and customs officers are keeping watch at all ports and airfields following the theft of the so-called Holy Grail from its museum in London at the weekend. A police spokesman said they wanted to interview Doctor Thomas Hawkhurst about the missing bowl which was recently unearthed at Whitenditch in Wiltshire. A spokesman for the museum said it could not explain how such a valuable item could be stolen so easily and has offered a large reward for information leading to its recovery. Churches throughout Europe and the USA have also expressed their dismay at the loss of what they regard as one of the most important relics of the Christian faith.' The brief item was accompanied by a photograph of Tom. The screen went black.

Whichelow chuckled evilly.

'What did I say back in Gethsemane? Best grave robber in the world? Looks like we've made you a star, Tom.'

Hawkhurst grunted non-committedly. While it was hardly helping his case back home, such broadcasts would hopefully go some way to assuring Whichelow that he had delivered the genuine chalice and that he had burned his boats once and for all. The Reverend was hardly interested; he was keen to get on.

'But that's just a very small part of the picture, gentlemen. Obtaining possession of the Holy Grail was just one small part of an ongoing program, a global strategy that will change the course of history. The culmination of twenty years planning is now only days away.' He brought another screen to life, this time it was rioting Palestinians somewhere in Israel, probably Jerusalem, using slingshots and rubber bullets. It wasn't what he wanted and he clicked anew, replacing it with a long range shot of a modern city that Tom instantly recognised as Alexandria. 'Egyptian State Radio, this was yesterday's big news.' Whichelow said briefly. The shot of Alexandria changed to a darkly attractive woman newscaster and he took a long draw at his cigar as he settled back to listen.

'Security officers are continuing to examine the wreckage of the luxury river cruiser Rameses the Third, sunk by terrorists on the Nile yesterday, twenty kilometres south of Luxor. At least two hundred and fifteen tourists and ninety crew were killed in the explosion which occurred just after midnight. At least another fifty have been injured, some seriously and others are still missing. A full casualty list has yet to be issued but it is understood that guests aboard Rameses came mainly from the USA, Europe and Japan. It is also believed that there were a number of school parties aboard and that many children are amongst the dead. No group has claimed responsibility for the outrage, although the US ambassador to the United Nations has insisted publicly that Iranian backed terrorist groups lie behind this and other recent atrocities. The Egyptian President has sent his condolences to the families of the victims and promised that every effort will be made to bring the perpetrators to justice. It is understood that a team of American forensic experts is on its way to Cairo to assist in the investigations.'

The commentary was accompanied by pictures of the smouldering hulk, burnt down to the waterline and lying midstream, black smoke still dribbling low across the muddy yellow ooze of the ancient waterway. Along the nearer bank, police and emergency workers, faces masked, walked amongst rows of sheet-shrouded bodies neatly laid out beneath a brazen sun. Above, helicopters hovered low, wet suited divers searching for others still in the river. At this point Whichelow peremptorily switched off the screens, stood up and without a further word returned to the dining room. Hawkhurst looked at Potgeiter, eyebrows raised in question. The South African shrugged, obviously equally bemused, and they followed The Reverend back to the table where Mary Lou and Martinette sat savouring another brandy. Whichelow puffed his cigar back to glowing life with satisfaction and resumed his discourse.

'What you just saw in there, gentlemen, was just another example of the barbarity of our enemies. It has been going on for hundreds of years, growing stronger and more arrogant each year while we in the West, blinded by our natural democratic desire for peace and progress, have slept. Today Islam, grown contemptuous of our Christian meekness, has taken up the sword and is on the march again. Next time you hear Firdasi quoting the Koran and talking about Allah the Merciful remember the people on that boat. That is why the Church of Christ the Warrior has, in alliance with other likeminded Christian Churches such as His Eminence's, decided to take up the challenge.' He looked to them for comment.

'You reckon you can topple one of the great religions of the world with just this ship?' Hawkhurst asked. 'I've seen your hardware and it's pretty impressive, but I don't see Hezbollah or whoever it is you're proposing to hit, running away from that.'

Whichelow shook his head.

'You're still thinking small, Tom. That's the problem with people like you. You lack depth of vision. Like the Grail, this ship is only part of a much wider strategy. It, you, me, all of us here, have small but vital roles to play in the strategy.' He spread his arms, the huge hands palm up. 'Think of it, let the wonder and majesty of it sink in. As we approach the Millennium we are on the brink of fulfilling the aims of two thousand years of Christian endeavour.' He looked around the table. 'You want to know what our plans are? They are simple. We are dedicated to spreading the gospel, the word of God, in the only way the twentieth century understands. With the Bible and the Sword we are committed body and soul to preparing the way of the Lord. The time for the Bible, for words of wisdom and the binding of wounds, will come in due course – but not yet. First must come the time of the sword.'

*****

'You are troubled, Heydar?' Firdasi tucked the folds of his cloak tighter about him as he spoke.

They sat in the garden close by the tinkling fountain, the coolness of evening on their faces. It was a full moon, its silver face forming and shattering on the water's blackness.

The boy looked up from The Book, his eyes sad.

'I was thinking of the people on the boat, Master.'

Firdasi nodded. He had guessed as much.

'Only Allah lives forever.' The boy did not answer and Firdasi grew solemn, sad almost. 'You wonder why I have not publicly denounced that act? Understand, Heydar, all men die – it is as Allah ordained. The violence you see today is the child of yesterday's evil, and that evil was the spawn of the day before. What I say or do not say is as nothing in the face of His will. Tell me, can you recite all the ninety-nine names of Allah?'

Heydar blinked but without hesitation launched himself into the litany.

'Allah the Compassionate, Allah the Merciful, Allah the King, Allah the ...'

Firdasi held up a silencing hand.

'What is the eighty-first name of Allah?'

The boy hesitated, mentally running through the list.

'Al-Muntaqim, Master. The Avenger.'

Firdasi smiled.

CHAPTER EIGHTEEN

The following morning found the Nagasaki Maru steering a south-easterly course and making a steady fifteen knots under clear skies and a balmy southerly breeze. All that remained of the previous day's gales was a low bank of cloud far away to the north. Hawkhurst, refreshed by his first proper night's sleep in three extremely stressful days, woke early, shaved and in high hopes of finding out more about Whichelow's intentions elected to explore a little. He now stood on the weather deck, balancing himself against the slight roll of the ship, and scanned the eastern horizon. As yet there was no sign of land but he knew that somewhere out there to the east lay Cape St Vincent and that if they continued to hold this course they would be transiting the Straits of Gibraltar sometime later that day. Taking a deep final breath of the brisk morning air he went below to the dining saloon and breakfast.

The saloon was empty apart from the steward and a smiling Colonel McNaughton who beckoned him over to the table.

'Hi, Tom. Good to see you again. Sorry I wasn't here to welcome you aboard yesterday, what with round the clock weapons training and briefing schedules my time's not my own these days. Haven't hit the sack in sixteen hours.' He sounded exhilarated rather than troubled by his busy schedule, a man hard at work doing what he did best. Dabbing his mouth with a napkin he stood up and with great precision set his beret squarely on his shaved head. 'I'm gonna grab a couple of hours shut-eye right now but The Reverend has asked me to show you round the ship sometime later today.' He consulted his watch. 'Let's say we'll meet here for lunch at around twelve-thirty and then I'll give you the full tour.'

Once McNaughton had gone the steward came to the table, standing at his side, a steaming coffee percolator in his hand. Like most of the domestic staff on the Nagasaki Maru he was black, young and very efficient. Hawkhurst had noticed there was always a cool reserve maintained between the elite and the lower orders, presumably these were newer recruits to the Church and as such expected to know their place until they had been fully indoctrinated. As he poured out the coffee Tom looked up. This might be an opportunity to learn something.

'Lovely day out there.'

'Sure is, sir.'

'The name's Tom.'

'Yes, sir.'

'Been with the Church long?'

'Two years, sir.'

Sensing he wasn't making any progress, Tom tried a more direct approach.

'Looking forward to the next few weeks?'

'Yes, sir, I sure am.'

'What will you be doing exactly when things get started?'

'My duty to God, sir.'

Tom sighed. If the stewards were this close-mouthed what chance did he have of getting the senior officers to open up? Was it religious zeal, military discipline or just plain old fashioned fear that motivated these tense, defensive youngsters, he wondered? Maybe the steward didn't know what would be required of him. He let it go.

'I'll have orange juice and the ham and eggs, please.'

'Yes, sir.'

As he ate in silence Hawkhurst planned out the day ahead. The afternoon was given over to McNaughton when, hopefully, he should learn something useful about the men and weapons carried aboard at least. The problem was, even if he did succeed in getting hard and fast evidence of what was going to happen, how could he pass it on to the outside world? The radio shack would be somewhere up by the bridge, he guessed. After breakfast maybe he'd wander that way and see what sort of security they had in place. There was always the possibility of transmitting a message if he could overpower the operator although he recognised that, even if he got a message away, it would be all up for him afterwards. He desperately needed allies and so far as he could see the only possibility that presented itself was Potgeiter. As the steward cleared his plate in silence the South African appeared in the saloon. He was in a relaxed mood, wearing a brightly coloured shirt that strained over his barrel chest, white shorts and desert boots. He smiled as he sat down, though always keeping one cautious eye on the door to the galley from whence came the clatter of cooking.

'Well, I've had a look round. So far as I can see unless we can grab a chopper the only way of getting off this rust bucket is the lifeboat. I've read the instructions and it'll take at least two of us to launch it. Even so, it'll be so slow we'd be sitting ducks – they'll be able to blow us out of the water or run us down before we've gone a mile.'

Tom was surprised and not a little suspicious that the other man should be thinking along lines so close to his own – and so open about it. Nevertheless, the time for caution had passed he decided. If he wanted assistance from Potgeiter it would be best to reveal his own hand.

'I'm going to take a look at the radio shack later. If we can get in there we might get a message off. We're getting pretty close to Gibraltar. If we got lucky the Royal Navy could have a frigate or aircraft here in a couple of hours. Trouble is, from what I saw earlier, I guess most naval vessels will be heading for the Eastern Mediterranean right now.' Potgeiter shook his head.

'Forget it. There are two guards with Uzis on the door. I tried to get forward of the bridge but every hatchway has at least one guard, and all of them armed.' He looked at Hawkhurst. 'Are you carrying, Tom?' Hawkhurst frowned, initially mystified, then, comprehending, he nodded.

'Hardware, you mean? I've got a Webley service revolver and about thirty rounds in my cabin. There's that and a can of Mace hidden under my mattress. I've got a switchblade down my boot as well. I was amazed they didn't search us when we came aboard.'

'Me too, seems like they're only human after all. I've got a Berretta and a couple of full clips of ammunition. Let's hope they don't search our cabins. So far as I can see this is the first mistake they've made. Let's hope it's not the last.' The shades came down on the South African's eyes as Whichelow entered the saloon, and he reverted to his old abrasive persona, clicking his fingers loudly to attract the attention of the absent steward. 'Where is that bloody kaffir?'

Whichelow was in high spirits and, after politely enquiring as to what sort of night they had passed, invited them into the information centre to view the latest batch of newscasts. Potgeiter pleading a rumbling stomach, declined, preferring to eat, but Tom was quick to follow.

There were three news items in all. The first was a follow-up on the cruise ship bomb story they had viewed the previous night. Here, the horror grew with the dead now numbered at more than five hundred and it seemed unlikely there would be any more survivors. Experts agreed it had been an extremely powerful device, probably around twenty pounds of Semtex or something similar, that had ripped the entire starboard side out of the vessel, causing her to capsize and settle on the river bed in a matter of seconds. Timed to explode at just after two in the morning meant most of the guests and crew were asleep and had no chance to escape. Of those not instantly blasted to pieces by the bomb, most had drowned in their cabins and divers were still recovering bodies.

The Egyptian security forces had reacted quickly to the outrage and a number of leading Islamic fundamentalists had been arrested attempting to cross the border to the Gaza Strip. However, their arrests had sparked off riots and looting in Cairo and other major cities with troops opening fire on several occasions, killing some and wounding dozens of rioters. It may well have been this popular backlash that had pressured a very shaky Egyptian government to sanction a prompt release of the suspects, within hours of their being picked up. The NBC newscaster suggested as much but a spokesman for the Egyptian government rejected any such suggestion of bowing to public pressure vehemently and assured the world at large that the perpetrators would be brought to justice.

'In a pig's eye they will, Abdul,' grunted Whichelow.

The next newscast reported the sailing of major units, several aircraft carriers included, of the United States Sixth Fleet from a number of Mediterranean ports. This was as well as the appearance of a combined American, British and French force in the Gulf of Oman. This latter was now effectively in a position to blockade the Persian Gulf although 'routine and pre-planned exercises' was the official reason given for its presence in the area. Americans and Europeans had made up the bulk of the Rameses' passengers and these nations were now flexing their muscles in response to the outrage. The report, with laudable even-handedness, then went on to relay the inevitable reaction in the Middle East, showing the mobilisation of the armed forces of several Islamic states. Jordan, Algeria, Iran, Syria, Libya and Sudan had all announced the introduction of a high state of alert. Iraq too, despite still being under a whole range of United Nations' sanctions and restrictions had seen Saddam Hussein parade the hated Republican Guard through the streets of Baghdad. In Israel the Likud, well aware where the gathering storm would most likely break first, had warned that any violation of Israeli borders or airspace would bring 'devastating retaliation'. It was a timely reminder, if such were needed, of that nation's nuclear capability. Only the oil-rich Gulf states such as Saudi Arabia, Kuwait and the Emirates, the fat cats who didn't want to rock the boat, were preaching moderation now, although money from their vast coffers still continued to swell the war chests of a multitude of more aggressive groups.

Watching these latest developments Tom could see with an awful clarity how a madman like Whichelow, now sitting at his side calmly evaluating this latest information in a kind of abstract musing, might see himself as God's messenger. As the world powers strutted and rattled sabres, this bloated self-satisfied priest, this murderer, was sailing in complete security towards an Armageddon he believed he could unleash at will, as and when he so chose. The anger grew in Tom's head but he remained silent as Whichelow gave a satisfied nod of approval to all he had seen.

'All coming to the boil just dandy. Wait for this next one, Tom, I know it'll interest you.'

It was British television, Channel 4. The saturnine features of John Suchet reporting from Bradford.

'Claims by a previously unknown Muslim Group, the British Brotherhood for Islamic Purity, are said to have stolen the so-called Holy Grail from its museum in London, were phoned through to our studios yesterday afternoon. The group claims that the whole concept of the Holy Grail and the crucifixion and resurrection of Jesus is anathema and an insult to Muslims. The Islamic faith recognises Jesus as an important messenger sent by Allah but, importantly, not as the Son of God. A spokesman for the BBIP said that to exhibit such an item was to profane the name of Allah and could not be allowed. They claim that the bowl has already been melted down and the proceeds from the sale of the silver will be donated to Muslim charities. Police, who have interviewed a number of Muslims in the Midlands and North of England, were previously keen to interview Doctor Tom Hawkhurst, an archaeologist closely involved with the discovery of the Grail and who disappeared at the same time, but this new claim must raise questions about his safety. Whatever the outcome of investigations into the theft of the Grail, the incident has certainly raised the ethnic temperature in towns which have a large Asian minority population. In Bradford there were at least eight cases of suspected arson overnight, all at Mosques or the homes of leading Muslims, and a protest march by all the Christian communities in the city is planned for the weekend.'

Whichelow killed the image with a deep chuckle.

'Guess that gets you off the hook eh, Tom?'

Hawkhurst was taken aback. Did Whichelow know he was only holding a replica of the Grail? Had his deception been discovered? He stalled.

'But how can they ....'

'They can't. But only we know that. It's just a little window dressing, Tom, just a little harmless fun. There's no such group as the BBIP and even if there was we know they haven't got the Grail because we have it right here aboard the Nagasaki Maru. But you see what I mean by the power that emanates from the Sacred Chalice. It only takes one phone call to the television people and, hey presto, Muslims are getting barbecued and the Christian Churches are coming together in protest and for mutual defence.'

Tom sighed.

'So do I assume the phone call came from followers of the Church of Christ the Warrior?'

'Indeed so. And, believe me, the Church's soldiers will be very much to the fore in the protest march this weekend. Mr Mallinson has proved a most energetic organiser. Why, it wouldn't surprise me one bit if there wasn't violence on the streets of British towns and widespread damage to property. Cardinal Martinette's followers are working on something similar in France and I imagine guest workers in Germany and elsewhere are in for a rough ride too. We are on the march at last.'

Tom watched in silence as images of smouldering houses collapsed and outraged Muslims, young, old, men and women alike, spilt out their understandable anger for the benefit of the camera. He thought of Whichelow and of the gun hidden beneath his mattress. Should he not go, right now, bring it back here and kill this monster? He considered the ramifications of such action. It would certainly mean his own death and, even if he could accept that, would it change anything? Everything now had an awful inevitably about it and it seemed unlikely that, even if Whichelow died, the Nagasaki Maru would calmly sail ahead on her mission while there were men like McNaughton and Martinette aboard. No, the only way was for the whole task-force to be taken out and neutralised at one fell swoop. Yet how could they hope to accomplish such a thing while all the world had its eyes fixed firmly on events in the Middle East? He prayed that Harry Brennan still had his eye on the ball and was out there somewhere tracking their progress.

Later that morning he stood with Potgeiter, staring out over the stern of the vessel. The sun was warm on their backs and both men had removed their shirts. Tom recounted what he had seen in the information centre.

'It's coming, Piet. It's sure as hell going to be war unless we can do something about it. The people who bombed that cruise ship want it as badly as the Church of Christ the Warrior. We've got to get a message off before this ship gets within range of the Middle East. McNaughton's supposed to show me what goes on beneath decks this afternoon. I'll see if there's anything helpful I can find out, some way to hijack a chopper maybe, but so far as I can see that lifeboat is our only chance. If we launched it at night perhaps, we could be miles away before they missed us.'

'I don't think so. There's usually an automatic alarm on the bridge that show the state of the lifeboat. The moment we release it from the davits it would tell them something was going on. We've either got to get away very fast or not at all. In the water in that thing we'd be sitting ducks.'

'Any other ideas?'

The South African turned his face to the sun, closing his eyes against its glare.

'Well, it did occur to me that if we could get down into the engine room we might indulge in a little sabotage. I managed to smuggle a couple of pocketful's of sugar from the dining saloon and I've made a point of collecting any small pieces of metal or grit, anything that's small enough to be dropped down a dipstick tube, I can find lying on deck. I recommend you do the same, if we could get a little of that into the engine sump or into the reduction gearing it would seize the engine solid within an hour or so. Once stopped they'd either have to call up assistance or miss whatever their deadline is, either way they'd be back-footed.'

Hawkhurst smiled approvingly, Potgeiter was clearly thinking a long way ahead. Yet why, he wondered? As a mercenary why should he take sides? It was out of character. The other man seemed to read his thoughts.

'Don't worry about my motives, Tom. I'm here for reasons very much like your own. The tale I told you about killing a girl? It's not true, any of it. My reasons for being here are personal. I did a pick-up for the Church five years back, I was chartered to fly a girl, Sarah Cathbertson, from Pretoria up to one of the Church's rehabilitation centres in Britain. From everything they told me she was a pretty wild little bitch and she'd got herself into trouble with the police – the usual thing – drugs and alcohol. Although, as it turned out, that wasn't how she really was at all. Anyway, her old man, who was a diamond broker and a real shit, wanted her kept out of the way until things quietened down and, if possible, she was cured of her anti-social tendencies. "Tamed" was the term I remember he used. In those days I didn't ask questions, I just took the money and was grateful. Anyway we were forced down by a dust storm on the way north and I had to make an emergency landing in Botswana, right out in the middle of nowhere. It was three days before we could get airborne and during that time we got to know each other pretty well.' His voice dropped as he recalled that time.

'She wasn't in the least how I had expected her to be, not bad at all, just young and full of fun. Well, by the time we finally arrived in Britain I'd got it pretty bad and I was having real problems coming to terms with handing her over to the Church. Anyway I told her I'd write and we'd get together once she was back in the republic. She said she'd like that. I wrote maybe a dozen times, under an assumed name of course to prevent the Church thinking I was getting emotionally involved with the customers. But I never heard a word from her afterwards and I swore I'd find out what became of her if it was the last thing I did.' His eyes came up. 'That's why I still work for the Church, Tom. I intend to find out what happened to her. However, first and last, I'm a survivor and I can see which way the wind is blowing. Once this thing is over, providing it goes their way, we'll both be surplus to requirements. We need to be planning ahead.' He ran a hand through his thick yellow hair. 'There's just one thing. We don't move until tomorrow at the earliest if we can help it.'

Hawkhurst frowned.

'Why not?'

'Because,' he said, smiling, 'If Whichelow's to be believed there's a big fat cheque being paid into a Basle bank that won't clear until then.' He shook his head in mock sadness as he considered the wicked ways of the world. 'I've read about megalomaniacs before. They're all the same; Hitler, Stalin, Genghis Khan, thwart their dreams of world domination and they'd cancel a cheque quicker than that.'

Tom smiled too, no doubt the man was a mercenary and no better than he ought to be, but beneath the hard-bitten veneer there was sharp intelligence and not a little humour.

'Understood. Look out, Whichelow's just come on deck!'

They both turned towards the huge figure who now stood on the weather deck, neck craned, taking in the blue skies above until his eye fell upon them and he came across to where they stood.

'I hope you're enjoying the cruise, boys,' he rumbled genially. 'Not often you get the chance to see history in the making,' He didn't wait for a response but pointed out to port. There, distant but clear, rose the unmistakable peak, a long feather of cirrus cloud streaming from its summit. 'Gibraltar,' he said portentously. 'One of the Seven Pillars of Hercules and another milestone on this journey towards our destiny.' He seemed so smug, so completely at ease or perhaps oblivious to the misery and destruction fulfilling his destiny would bring down upon millions of innocent people. Hawkhurst's anger flickered.

'It was Jabal-al-Tariq before it was Gibraltar, Reverend.'

Whichelow blinked, aware he might have been upstaged. 'What?'

'Jabal-al-Tariq, the Rock of Tariq, the Muslim general who spearheaded the Islamic invasion of Spain in 711. If you intend to make history you should first learn from it. You don't want to get the idea these people are going to be a pushover.'

CHAPTER NINETEEN

Brennan sipped his coffee and ran his eyes up and down the crowded souk. He would have dearly loved a good slug of something stronger in it but felt exposed enough in this Arab market on the southern fringe of Cairo's sprawling slums without upsetting the locals. Things were so damn tense right now it was a risk for a westerner to be here in the first place. He wished Boujera would hurry up. Sun filtered down into the dust of the narrow street and around him the locals, newspapers spread on the tables before them, spoke in guarded tones of the threats and counter threats now flying between the world's capitals. As those around him drank their thick bitter coffee and smoked the hookah, few seemed excited about the prospect of war, they he noticed, were older men with few illusions about what war would mean. It would be the young hotheads who responded to the presidents and ayatollahs, to the senators, generals, colonels and imams. It always was.

He glanced at his watch. He had sat there for thirty minutes now and began to wonder if Boujera was going to show. Then, pushing his way through the throng, the man appeared, hurrying up to the table where Brennan sat. He wasn't his usual enigmatic self today. The chequered head cloth was a little awry and there was a thin film of sweat on his dark features and hands. Brennan beckoned the ancient waiter, ordered more coffee and waited while Boujera composed himself.

'Problems?'

Boujera shrugged.

'It is difficult. It is the month of the Haj – the sacred pilgrimage. Many of my contacts are in Mecca.'

Brennan smiled.

'Sounds to me like a real good place to be right now.' The rich, always a target for fundamentalists and now facing the prospect of a major war, were quitting the city for the capitals of the West in droves. It was happening all over the Middle East. For the faithful yet circumspect Muslim of more modest means a lengthy pilgrimage to Mecca must seem like a good idea in the circumstances. 'So what's the word on the street?'

'It has been difficult, you understand. There is a price.'

Brennan shrugged non-committedly.

'Have we ever been tight with money?'

'The price is doubled. This is important information for the United States I have.' Brennan considered the offer. He was out on a limb here and for all the Arab's assurances he knew the information might prove to be useless. He shook his head.

'No. The price stays the same as we agreed. $2000.'

Boujera smiled from behind his coffee. He was a child of the refugee camps. Haggling was in his blood.

'$4000 or no information.'

Brennan sighed.

'No information and I'll just have to reconsider our relationship, Akbar. I know how important the money is to your friends in the camps. Kalashnikovs don't grow on trees. But if you go back on our deal there'll be no more money and ......' He fell silent, thoughtful, and Boujera felt a frisson of fear. He had dealt with Brennan before and knew something of the man's past. He might carry those Arab inflicted scars easily enough but perhaps, even after all these years, he harboured thoughts of revenge.

'What?'

Having ensured he had his man's full attention Brennan took a sip of coffee, savouring its acrid flavour.

'Funny thing, Akbar. That last payment we made into your account you know, the monthly grand we pay you to let us know of any approaches from the Church of Christ the Warrior? Seems like some of the money was picked up by the US Coast Guard, they told my agency about it and they told me.' He smiled cruelly. 'I said, no, it wasn't possible. You were a Palestinian freedom fighter, an idealist. All the funds we paid you went straight into the Hezbollah fighting fund.' He shook his head. 'But then they showed me the money and, know what, the serial numbers matched. You made a big mistake, Akbar, I don't have to tell you what the boys on the West Bank would do if they found out you were doing a little freelancing with company funds.'

From a distant minaret a Muezzin called the faithful to prayer, the haunting wailing briefly stilling the bustle of the souk. Boujera stared. The sweat was flowing freely now, hanging in droplets from the handsome moustache. His bluff had been called. He tried to retain as much dignity as the circumstances would allow, an uneasy smile on his lips, his eyes shifting sideways, fearful that Brennan's words had gone beyond the table.

'OK, Harry. $2000 it is.'

Brennan twisted the knife a little.

'Give me the information. Then we'll decide what it's worth.'

The Palestinian's words came in a rush.

'There is to be no war, at least no Jihad. Even the most extreme of the Islamic leaders have reached a consensus that a war at this time is unwinnable and not in their interests. Tehran is for it as usual, but, again as usual, none of the other leaders will respond to any call for war from that quarter. Hezbollah will certainly initiate many raids and terrorist activities but it will stop short of out-and-out war. However, you must recognise it is essential that the United States does not overreact to these provocations. Any retaliation, and we know it will come, should be measured. There must be no more bombings like the raids on Libya.'

Brennan stared hard at his man, as if he did not welcome unsolicited advice on what US foreign policy should or should not be.

'What is Firdasi saying?'

The Arab took a tissue from the dispenser at the table's centre, dabbing at his face and fanning himself with the limp paper.

'Firdasi has gone into the desert. No one knows where. My contacts tell me he has been much troubled by recent events, that he is considering renouncing politics and the worldly life. They say he may follow the path of the Sufi.'

Brennan knew Boujera of old. When he didn't know anything he'd bullshit. He was bullshitting now.

'My contacts tell he's been in touch with Tehran and Tripoli several times over the past weeks. That doesn't sound like someone seeking spiritual guidance to me. Will he sanction violence?'

Boujera shook his head firmly, sending droplets of sweat flying from his moustache.

'No, The Master and his followers know the Surahs. It is written: Begin not war for Allah loves not an aggressor.'

'Admirable sentiments, Akbar, but what if the West takes action over the Rameses?'

Boujera shrugged, leaving Brennan to draw his own conclusions.

'Anything else?'

'Yes, something very important.' Boujera's smile gained confidence and he held out his hand. '$2000?' Brennan shook the hand and nodded. No money would change hands here.

'OK, Akbar, you've got a deal.'

'There is to be a new peace initiative. The Saudis will offer to broker it on behalf of the Palestinians. They want the United States to put pressure on the Israelis to ensure the initiative at least gets a fair hearing.'

Brennan's eyes narrowed. This was important.

'Any idea what the Saudi proposals are?'

'No details, it's all very vague as yet, but my friends understand it will require the establishment, of full self-government in certain Palestinian areas and in return for an end to the Intifada, guarantees of non-aggression by all the states sharing borders with Israel as well as, and the Jews will just love this,' he smiled spitefully, 'up to a billion dollars of oil revenues from the major oil producers over the next three years, just to oil the wheels of diplomacy.'

'When is this new initiative to be announced?'

'In two weeks. If the Americans hold off until then we could have a viable peace process. If they don't, what happened to the cruise ship will just be a beginning and it won't be confined to the Middle East. Think you can convince them, Harry?'

Brennan reached inside his jacket and produced a silver hip flask, tipping a hefty tot of bourbon into his coffee. Head back, he threw it down in one. The time for caution was gone.

'I don't know,' he said softly. 'I just don't know.'

*****

The guards slapped their machine pistols in salute as Hawkhurst and McNaughton stepped through the steel door that lead into the forward section of the Nagasaki Maru. Inside, Tom craned his neck to the lofty deckhead and looked around him, taking in the bustling activity. For as far as he could see stretched rank upon rank of helicopters, their rotors folded back and packed in so tightly that there was barely space for the maintenance crews to move between them. The only clear space was at the centre of the deck where four solid steel pillars mounting hydraulic ramps marked out the lift that would deliver the choppers to the flight deck when the time for action arrived. This upper deck had been converted into one huge aircraft hangar.

Everywhere, white boiler suited men worked on the choppers. Some engines were being run up, reverberating in the steel belly of the ship and belching clouds of blue exhaust that billowed about the harsh strip lighting. Others were being stripped down, while yet more were occupied with armourers who, Tom guessed, would be carrying out final adjustments to the awesome armoury of machine guns, cannon and missiles each gunship carried.

It was noisy, painfully so, and stank of gasoline and exhaust fumes yet there was a quiet discipline about everything he saw around him. He tried to assess the number of aircraft but gave up after counting to sixty, knowing there would be others stowed elsewhere on board. The fire risk in such a situation was inevitably considerable and around each craft whose engine was running stood a three man crew of asbestos-suited firefighters their equipment ready and trained on the roaring monsters. McNaughton yelled to be heard over the din.

'We can't use the flight deck for maintenance for obvious reasons; that means we can only run half-a-dozen engines at a time. The air-conditioning can only safely handle a certain level of exhaust fumes at one time which means we have had to develop a rolling maintenance schedule. It means the fitters have to work right round the clock but our record for serviceability is as good as the US Army's, or any other army's for that matter. Believe me, I know.'

The Colonel was proud of his command and Tom decided this might be the time to probe a little deeper although he kept his tone suitably disinterested. He deliberately underestimated.

'It's incredible, Brett, you must have at least fifty choppers here.'

McNaughton snorted good humouredly.

'This is just Alpha Flight, Tom, we've got over three hundred helicopters on board all told. There are four hangar compartments like this one, all running forward towards the bow. Each compartment houses a single flight and each has its own lift to the flight deck. The flights are self-contained each with a transport section and a ground attack component. There's a lot of healthy competition between the flights which makes for efficiency – we can get the whole force in the air in less than half an hour. We've got a flight simulator on board so the pilots can keep their hand in while we're at sea. I'll show you the others, Bravo, Charlie and Delta flights, if you like but they're all much the same. I like to keep a pretty low profile down here. The men know their jobs and don't need me looking over their shoulders all the time. Let's go and see how the grunts, the infantry boys, are doing.'

They descended a flight of steel stairs into the deck below. Here the deckhead was much lower than in the aircraft hangers, only inches above his head, and space much more restricted. As McNaughton led the way down a long narrow corridor, Tom marvelled at the way the ship had been converted. It would have required nothing less than rebuilding the entire interior. He was impressed and said as much to the Colonel.

'We've kept her moored up a creek on Puget Sound, Washington State since the late eighties. In theory she was obsolete when we bought her and too expensive for the Kuwait oil run once the Suez Canal reopened. But she was plenty big enough and that suited our purposes just fine. The Church has some pretty powerful friends in shipping circles, London, Piraeus, Seattle, so it wasn't difficult to place some discreet, and lucrative, orders for refitting her. If anyone had become suspicious the official story was that we were intending to use her as a floating home for refugees in South East Asia. Of course, some of the specialist work, strengthening the flight deck and installing the hydraulic hoists for instance, had to be carried out by people in the know but, as you've seen for yourself, nothing is impossible if God wills it.'

At the end of the corridor another steel door, again guarded by two soldiers in full combat gear, barred their way. These came smartly to attention but nevertheless insisted on inspecting McNaughton's ID. Even when he, their commanding officer, explained Tom's presence there and how there had been no time to issue him with proper identification, he detected a distinct reluctance to allow him through, their suspicious eyes boring into his. This was a very tight ship indeed.

'Sorry about that, Tom,' he grunted apologetically after it had taken a phone call to Whichelow's quarters to resolve the hiatus, 'but they're only doing their job. If they hadn't they know I'd have bawled them out.'

The door led into another broad expanse of deck space, maybe a hundred metres by fifty, and here groups of men, of platoon strength, were stripping down carbines and other light weapons. Seeing McNaughton's arrival, a powerfully built black sergeant bellowed an unintelligible order and the entire deck sprung to attention. The Colonel waved an airy salute and another barked order sent the men back to their duties. As they made their way between the pre-occupied groups from the distance came a dry crackle of automatic gunfire.

'We have a firing range, a gymnasium and an assault course on this level. It's pretty hard on the men, being confined below decks for the best part of two weeks but they're handling it well. Anyway ass ache can be a pretty good motivator – I reckon by the time we go into action they'll be meaner than junkyard dogs.'

'How many men are there? Where do they all sleep?'

'We have four full strength battalions aboard, 2,500 men. It's a hell of a lot, even for a ship this size. We've had to convert just about every spare inch of space to accommodate them. Even so, a lot of them are hot bunking; using camp beds and hammocks on a rota system. It's not ideal, but these are fine young men and they don't complain. They all believe in the just and divine nature of our cause and won't be found wanting when the time comes.'

After about an hour walking through the ship watching men drilling, weapon training and engaged in unarmed combat, Tom estimated they must now be approaching the bow section of the Nagasaki Maru. Here, before a massive watertight door, McNaughton halted.

'Sorry, Tom, this is where the tour terminates. Even I need permission from The Reverend to go forward from here. It's very, very delicate, the equipment we've got stowed up there, so admission is restricted to the high command and then only in special circumstances.'

Tom stared. Here the guards wore little strips of plastic on their lapels and across the centre of the heavy doors at their backs was stencilled a huge grinning death's head, black on a yellow background.

'What's up there?' He asked and McNaughton smiled at his naivety.

'You wouldn't want to know.'

*****

Brennan lay on the bed and took in his opulent surroundings. The Hilton had seemed a sensible choice in the current situation although he knew there would be hell to pay when he put his monthly expenses through. Here he would just be one westerner among hundreds of others and security was usually good at this class of establishment. The possibility of another massacre was much on everybody's mind in Cairo right now and the presence of armed police in the foyer was a bonus so far as he was concerned. Swinging his legs to the floor, he went to the mini bar and was dismayed to see that bourbon was not among the contents. He cursed softly and consoled himself with two of the small bottles of Scotch in a tumbler, adding a little water to ease his conscience. Drinking on active service was frowned on in the agency but most operatives still indulged.

Going to the wardrobe, an item of furniture ebulliently styled on finds from the Valley of the Kings and far too voluminous for his modest needs, he produced a mobile phone from his jacket pocket. As he slid the mirrored door closed he examined his battered visage. He hadn't shaved in three days and had to grab such little sleep as he could on the RAF flight, sprawled on the floor of a freezing, rattling C130, from Lakenhurst to the RAF base at Akrotiri. From there he'd taken a commercial flight to Cairo for his meeting with Boujera. He had advised the agency of what he had been told about a new peace initiative but had added that he no longer entirely trusted Boujera and it might be wise to draw up plans for neutralising the Palestinian at some time in the future. That done he could now turn his attention to the pressing matter of the Reverend Whichelow and his crackpot schemes. He activated the scrambler on his phone and punched out the agency's London number.

He could imagine, De Soto, the local head, sitting in that dusty Victorian office overlooking Sloane Square, his feet on his desk and probably daydreaming of the expensive little love nest he'd rather foolishly set up just down the road in Fulham. Brennan reflected that if De Soto had been aware that the New York office had a thick and almost pornographically detailed file on all his many affairs, he'd certainly have been a good deal less relaxed. The more so if he knew, as they did, that his latest paramour worked for Section P of the French secret service. The thought brought a smile to Brennan's lips and he shook his head ruefully, there would be a vacancy in the London office soon, he guessed. Still, the man would get a decent pension and there was always work for ex-intelligence people.

'Dave, it's me, Harry Brennan. What's going down?'

'Hi, Harry. Is this line secure?' The voice at the other end was guarded and Brennan instantly felt the stirrings of concern. His phone, like all agency issues, was scrambled and the codes changed at frequent intervals: such a question should have been unnecessary.

'Sure it's secure. What's the word on the bucket?' Bucket was the code word for the Grail. 'How's the surveillance going?'

There was a brief silence.

'Surveillance was withdrawn at 1100 hours yesterday.'

'What?' Brennan was incredulous. 'How the fuck did that happen? On whose orders?'

'Pentagon, High Command. I argued with the bastards best I could but, things being the way they are right now, they reckoned any AWACS was more use on station in the Eastern Mediterranean than trailing some old rust bucket just because she might or might not be a bogey.' He became defensive and Brennan suspected he hadn't argued his case over strongly. 'I have to say, Harry, with World War Three brewing I think they do have a point.'

Brennan snorted impatiently

'That, Davey boy, is because you're a fuckwit with his brains in his bell end!'

He rang off and then punched out the New York number with a finger that shook with anger. This was breaking protocol, London were supposedly heading up the surveillance, but things had taken a distinctly nasty turn and action was needed. Valdes was on duty in New York, a good man, calm and clear thinking. He listened to Brennan's tirade in silence.

'We know, Harry. We've lodged protests at the highest level but it hasn't done us any good. Fact is we don't have the faintest idea of what we're looking for now. The radar signature suggested a large vessel but what type we can't tell. It could be a liner, a container ship, a tanker or a bulk carrier. We don't even know for sure where it's heading either. Common sense says she'll enter the Mediterranean but the course she was steering last was due south so she could just as easily be heading for the Cape. We've got a couple of small high speed vessels available in Southern Spain, Harry. They're out patrolling the Straits right now but hundreds of ships go through that stretch of water every day so it's like looking for a needle in a haystack.' Brennan sipped his Scotch, composed now.

'The surveillance, who called it off?'

'It came from the top, that's all we know for sure. But word is General Cornelius Beauregard was most insistent the AWACS was withdrawn, even though there are a dozen similar aircraft a whole lot closer to the action.'

'I take it the general's file is lying on your desk right now. Correct?'

'Sure is, Harry.'

'And?'

'Seems like he got religious in a big way back in the seventies. This would have been after he was captured by the Viet Cong in Cambodia.'

'That sure doesn't surprise me none, Billy.' He considered the situation. 'I've finished here, Bill. I think I should get to Spain, I might be able to help and anyway there's no point in my coming back Stateside – there's going to be plenty to do out here whatever happens about the peace initiative.'

'Fine by me, Harry. Just keep in touch. OK?'

Brennan laid the phone aside and, drink in hand, went out onto the balcony. The sun was hanging low in the western sky and the air was rapidly cooling. Away to the south, beyond the sprawling shanty towns, the peaks of the pyramids were just visible. In the hotel gardens below, the last bathers were quitting the swimming pool and contemplating dinner while the hotel attendants were clearing away the sun loungers. Silhouetted against the purple twilight sky, kites circled soaring lazily like huge black moths. Brennan took the scene in dispassionately and thought of Hawkhurst. Had Beauregard, with all his contacts in military and civil intelligence circles found out about the homer and the phoney Grail? Had he informed Whichelow? If he had then the Englishman was as good as dead.

A plaintive wail rose above the darkening city and at first Brennan assumed the faithful were being called to prayer for the fifth and final time that day. But it wasn't. They were testing the air raid alarms.

CHAPTER TWENTY

At dinner that evening, Whichelow was in high spirits. It may have been the fact that the confined waters off Gibraltar, with their increased likelihood of detection, were now astern, Tom thought. As the broad expanse of the Mediterranean opened up before them the possibility of being intercepted was reduced significantly. Whatever the reason, the huge cleric had visibly relaxed and, having drunk the best part of a bottle of Monterey red on his own, had now turned his attention to the brandy. He lay back in his chair, a cigar nestling between his thick fingers, eyeing the assembled company with a benign eye. Colonel McNaughton had returned to his duties and Potgeiter, feigning tiredness was, in fact, out somewhere between decks assaying the possibility of gaining access to any of the vital machinery spaces. Only Martinette, Mary Lou and Hawkhurst remained. Hawkhurst found the company irksome to say the least but was all too aware that he still needed to find out more about their plans. He also knew that if he could divert their attention it would buy the South African time.

'We have received encouraging reports from France, your Eminence,' Mary Lou offered at one point when Whichelow had drifted off into a pensive reverie and the conversation faltered. 'There have been at least fifty serious incidents in Paris and Marseilles. Rioting and looting in the immigrant quarters. Several hundred casualties, some dead. Christians everywhere have been outraged by the Rameses incident. We have the latest reports on video if you would like to …'

Martinette raised a claw-like hand in horror, closing his eyes as if to shut out the awful reality that lay behind the divine plan.

'No. I do not think such things should be glorified. However necessary these measures may be, they are distasteful in the sight of the Lord.'

'There's been action in Germany, too.' Mary Lou, positively gleeful, obviously didn't share His Eminence's sensitivities and gushed on regardless. 'A whole bunch of Turks fricassed in a Dortmund guest workers' hostel – we got pictures of that too.'

Her words brought Whichelow growling out of his dreaming.

'Phase One certainly seems to have exceeded our best hopes – the bombing of that cruise ship couldn't have come at a better time if we'd arranged it ourselves. Let's hope Phase Two goes as smoothly,' he rumbled. 'But His Eminence is right when he says we shouldn't take pleasure in inflicting suffering on our enemies. When this is over there will be a time for reconciliation but until then we must be merciless in the execution of the Lord's will.' He laid his cigar aside and clasped his hands in prayer, eyes closed. 'Oh Lord of Hosts, strengthen these thy soldiers as they prepare to enter battle. Grant us victory in the coming conflict that the whole of mankind may enter the coming Millennium under the shield of your awesome power, the light of thy wisdom and the benevolence of thy everlasting mercy. Amen.'

'Amen,' carolled Mary Lou and Martinette, the Cardinal making the sign of the cross. Only Tom remained silent sickened at such callous hypocrisy. Whichelow refilled his brandy balloon and stood up a little unsteadily. He stretched his arms, stifling a yawn.

'Well, I'm going to look at the latest reports before turning in. Care to join me, Tom?'

In the information centre Tom sat through a series of depressingly similar reports on anti-Muslim outrage across Europe and America and the inevitable reactions in Islamic countries. Even stable, secular states like Turkey had been shaken and angered by the unprovoked attacks on their citizens abroad and as a result the influence of extremists had been strengthened in such countries. Yet the violence had even wider effects. In India, the burning resentment between Hindus and Muslims, always simmering beneath the surface, had erupted into attacks on Mosques and Temples with massacres in many areas. Pakistani tanks had been moved up to the Kashmiri border in response.

Commercial considerations and the interlocked interests and destinies of the major industrial powers were also hardening attitudes. Japan, whose mighty economy was almost wholly dependent on the Middle East for its oil, had sought, and received, assurances from the United States that supplies would be guaranteed. Exactly what such a guarantee meant was couched in diplomatically vague terms but undoubtedly inferred the possibility of military intervention should the need arise. What the industrialised world was saying was: we stand together or we stand alone. Despite the provocation of the industrialists' posturing, by and large the Arab oil states had responded moderately by reassuring all major oil importers that supplies would continue although no intervention in their internal affairs would be countenanced.

'Looking good,' Whichelow remarked as he clicked off. 'Tomorrow should really put the cat amongst the pigeons.'

'What happens tomorrow?' Tom's tone was even. He no longer tried to please his captors by pretending to support their aims and they no longer seemed to care one way or the other where his loyalties lay.

'By midday tomorrow, boy, we'll be just west of Sicily. It gets real narrow there so we'll be vulnerable, but once we get South of Malta there's plenty of space. More importantly we'll only be a couple of hundred miles off the Libyan coast and then we're going to put on a real fireworks display for that lunatic Gadaffi.'

Tom frowned. Could Libya and Colonel Gadaffi be the target for the task force? The man's blatant support for terrorism, not only in the Middle East but also in Northern Ireland and the Basque region of Spain, had made him an implacable enemy of many western establishments and few tears would be shed if he were to be punished. But Gadaffi had his own internal problems these days. In the eyes of many militants he had gone soft and any provocation would have to be responded to vigorously if it were not to mark the beginning of the destabilisation of Libya and an incoming regime capable of almost any fanatical excess. No one could tell what repercussions might follow an unprovoked incursion into Libyan airspace.

'You intend to attack Libya?'

Whichelow laughed aloud. As the days passed he took increasing pleasure in patronising Tom's incredulity and it was beginning to irritate him more than a little. As he had told Potgeiter: "The fat bastard is beginning to give me the shits."

'Hell, no. We ain't gonna attack anybody, Tom. We're just gonna light a very long fuse and stand back. What happens after that is anybody's guess. Wait until tomorrow. There'll be plenty going on, believe me.'

*****

Back in his cabin Potgeiter was waiting for him, laying on the bed with a whisky in his hand. Tom smiled and poured one for himself. He turned on the wash basin taps to confuse any electronic eavesdropper but still kept his voice to a whisper.'

'Any luck?'

'Some. I got into the engine room OK. I've cultivated the chief engineer, who is something of an old soak, and he's very proud of his ship. For the modest price of half a bottle of gin he gave me the full Cook's tour. While he was showing me round I located the sump oil filling points on both engines and on the reduction gearing. Getting at them unnoticed won't be easy though. The engine room crew, there are four on watch at any time, are very professional and the engineer officer of each watch carries a sidearm. We'll just have to bide our time. If things get really desperate we may have to shoot our way in, pour whatever crap we can lay hands on into the sump and hope the engines seize solid. Thank God this is an old tub. Most modern tankers have their engines monitored from the bridge and the machinery spaces are kept sealed.'

Tom looked at him hard.

'Something's going to happen tomorrow, Piet. Something really bad. Whichelow's intending to do something that involves Libya. I don't think it's an actual invasion but it's something big, some kind of provocation I imagine.'

The South African nodded.

'It all fits with what you say's going on around the world. Any more news?'

'More of the same. Anti-Islamic riots and counter riots. Outrages around the world. Not surprisingly the Muslim countries are closing ranks. With the pressure that's building up they're finally coming together. Where they've been split in the past there is now the real possibility of a unified Arab front. It only needs the least thing now and the shit will really hit the fan.'

Potgeiter took a reflective pull at his drink and rolling off the bed onto his feet went to the small porthole, stooping to look out into the darkness beyond.

'We mustn't make our move too soon, Tom,' he said. 'If tomorrow's going to be bad who can say what's to follow. We may well be the only ones who can stop these madmen. If we show our hand too soon and fail they'll just sail on regardless. What I suggest is that for the time being you keep on trying to get more information out of Whichelow and I'll stay in the background looking for any other way to stop the ship.'

'You've thought of something?'

'Well, it strikes me all those choppers are going to be very thirsty for fuel and Avgas is a very inflammable commodity indeed. If we can find where it's stowed we might just be able to indulge in a little arson. If I see McNaughton in the morning I'll ask him if I can have a tour of the hangars. He knows I'm a flyer so it's only natural I'd be interested. If I can locate the storage tanks it could be very useful when we have to make our move.'

*****

The following morning dawned fair with a light northerly wind and the sun was already warming the steel deck below his feet as Hawkhurst stared astern at the ship's wake. Above the tattered ensign a few gulls hung motionless on the air mewing sadly while away to the north a scattering of small fishing vessels went about their business, keeping well clear of the lumbering tanker now toiling her way down the Sicilian Channel. On the horizon larger vessels, the morning sun highlighting their superstructure, carried on their trade regardless in a world that now teetered on the brink of Armageddon. Full of apprehension as to what the day might bring he went into breakfast to find the Reverend already eating. His ebullient mood of the previous night seemed to have evaporated and he looked hung over, his sallow sagging cheeks puffy under slitty eyes. His welcome however was friendly enough, too friendly for Tom's liking, in fact for he suspected the man had been revived by the prospect of baiting his unwilling guests.

'Morning, Tom. Looking forward to Phase Two?'

'I might be, if I knew what it involved.'

Whichelow took a long drink of orange juice, belched softly and then chuckled.

'Well, why not? Seeing as how you're here for the duration it can't do any harm, I guess. How's your geography?' Tom frowned as the man continued without waiting for answer. 'Ever hear of the Gulf of Sirte? It's a stretch of sea that's claimed as territorial waters by Libya. That claim has always been disputed by other neighbouring countries and also, especially so, by the United States. Ever since

Gadaffi came to power there has been a series of incidents and provocations initiated by both sides. There have been actions at sea and in the air and every so often, just to let Gaddafi know who's boss, the US puts a naval force into the area to assert its claims to free access to those waters and to underline its capacity to go where it goddamn likes. All and all it's a very touchy situation down there.'

'And you've got another incident arranged?'

Whichelow beamed.

'That's right, nothing too drastic, something tailored perfectly to exploit the current situation. We knew long ago we wouldn't want to unleash anything too big, too soon. Until we get on station in two days, at which time we commence the third and final phase of the operation, we just need to keep things nicely on the boil.'

'How do you propose to do that?'

Whichelow took an orange from the piled fruit bowl and began to peel it with a thick thumbnail. His hands trembled slightly, Tom noticed.

'What with the trouble that's going on, all American naval forces have been moved further east. According to our latest information the only western warships in the area at present are two Italian frigates, Fiume and Salerno, and they are both patrolling well outside the disputed waters. Nevertheless, despite their peaceful proceedings, if everything goes to plan they will suffer an unprovoked attack by Libyan aircraft this afternoon.' He broke the orange down into segments and laid them on the plate before him. 'Ever hear of a PTD, Tom?' Hawkhurst shook his head. 'Pilotless Target Drogue – it's a small unmanned aircraft that's used for missile and gunnery practice by most navies. It can also be used for remote, low level surveillance work. In its basic state it's pretty low tech equipment, flies at around 500 miles an hour and can be pre-set to navigate virtually any course on the GPS system. Because of the type of work they are used for their operational range is normally limited. However, we've introduced a few sneaky modifications and our babies can now cover well over a thousand miles before the fuel runs out.'

'You intend to attack the Italian ships with these PTDs and hope the world will think it's the Libyans?'

Whichelow shook his head sadly at such lack of sophistication.

'Nothing so crude, my boy, nothing so crude. We're going to launch twenty PTDs directly at the Libyan capital Tripoli. We've optimised their radar signature and incorporated one or two other electronic gimmicks to enhance the overall effect. When Gadhafi's air controllers see 'em coming in over the skyline they'll think it's Pearl Harbour all over again. Given the international situation we can expect the Libyan Air Force to be at a high state of alert and to respond to any threat immediately. However, having infringed territorial waters and ensured the bait has been taken the PTDs will then change course and head directly for the Italian ships. The Libyans have had their butts kicked so often by the West that, if they think our boys are running away, they won't be able to resist a chance to get a little of their own back. We estimate that once the frigates pick up the PTDs heading straight for them they'll call for air support from the Italian mainland — luckily for them there's a squadron of Tornadoes based on Sicily that's probably just as trigger happy at the moment as the Libyans are. Should be a hell of a show and, just think, we'll be able to follow it minute by minute on the TV.'

Tom stared, incredulous.

'Don't you ever think about all the people who are going to die because of your grand design?'

Whichelow grew grave at this rebuke. It was as if he couldn't understand Tom's lack of enthusiasm, that he was saddened by his lack of vision.

'We've all got to die sometime, Tom. You, me, everyone. What we have to do is to make certain that our death fits in with God's great plan. I saw that plain as a pikestaff back in 1978.'

Hawkhurst looked at him.

'1978? What happened in 1978 that was so important?'

Whichelow grew thoughtful, his eyes distant. 'I would have been about your age then, new to the ministry and second in command to the Reverend James D Jones of The People's Temple down in Jonestown, Guyana. Why, we'd been chased from pillar to post by the authorities in the States and in Guyana – every man's hand was turned against us – God only knows why. We lived clean and broke no laws but because we were different we were persecuted like the apostles of old. Then, one morning Jones called me into his office. I remember that meeting as clear as if it had been yesterday. There were flowers in a vase on his desk. "We're going to Jesus," he said. "We're all going to Jesus." Then he told me what he planned – just exactly how we were all going to get to Jesus. I swear the man had received a revelation.'

'It seemed so logical when he spelt it out to me. That night I mixed bottles of Kool-Aid with cyanide while the Reverend James held his last meeting out there on the fringes of the jungle. He told everyone exactly what he planned, there was no deception: that the only way we would get to see Jesus face to face was by dying. Out of a thousand souls only a handful slid away into the darkness, afraid of death. More than nine hundred Christian souls drank the potion I had mixed and ladled out. Most took it away in plastic cups to drink in the privacy of their homes. Some drank it back in front of my eyes then walked a little way off, lay down and died. For couples with young children we provided syringes to ensure they didn't retch it up and suffer a lingering death. I administered the poison myself in a couple of cases when parents became distraught. It was all very calm and very beautiful. Everyone went to see Jesus.'

Tom, numbed by what he was hearing hardly heard his own next words, and when he did they were sad, reproachful, rather than angry, although exactly why he couldn't say.

'Everyone except you apparently. Promotion comes pretty fast in your line of work doesn't it?'

Whichelow did not respond at first, he was still back in the Guyana jungle twenty years ago.
The Reverend scraped his chair back with a snort and for a moment Tom thought he was going to be attacked. Then the anger subsided and he sat back with a sigh, shaking his head.

'Don't you see you miserable benighted scientist, that I am only here because God willed it. So that I could continue the work begun and carried on by others. I didn't refuse the poison down there in Guyana because I was afraid. Can't you see that? Can't you see that I knew the fight wasn't over – could never be over until victory was ours? Sitting here now, knowing that in a few days I will have been the instrument that prepared the way for the second coming and the Kingdom of God on Earth, more than justifies all the recriminations and insults that have been heaped upon me ever since the happenings in Guyana.'

'Supposing things don't go your way tomorrow? Supposing the Libyans don't react as you expect, and even if they do supposing the Italians show restraint, what then?'

Tom's concern about the morrow clearly pleased the Reverend and his ire receded as he settled back into his chair and the self-satisfied smile returned. He gave a dismissive shrug of his massive shoulders.

'Believe me, Tom, it doesn't matter in the least. All this is just window dressing. Phase Two is just a preliminary; Phase Three is the important one. It will be launched from this vessel and will be devastating. Anyway let's not spoil the surprise, let's wait until this afternoon before we make any judgement on Phase Two. Who knows how it will go? I still think we're in for some pretty dramatic action.' Swallowing down the last segment of orange, he looked at his watch. 'Changing the subject, we're due to pick up another passenger after lunch, I hope you'll join the welcoming committee on the bridge. It's someone real special – I'm sure you'll be impressed.' He hauled himself to his feet. 'Right now I'm going in to look at the latest reports. Care to join me?'

'No thanks. I think I'll get some fresh air.'

CHAPTER TWENTY ONE

The first flight of PTDs was launched at 1600. Brought up to the flight deck via the aftermost lift they were quickly and efficiently fuelled and activated to be flown off in four groups of five aircraft with an interval of about ten minutes between each group. Looking down from the bridge Hawkhurst watched as the tiny craft, at that distance seeming little bigger than models, bounced uncertainly across the deck. In tight formation each group trundled forward, clumsily at first but gaining speed to at last lift lightly away and then dip low over the sea, soon to be lost against its restless vastness, the thin scream of their engines fading to nothing. Once out of sight they would continue to fly at very low level, undetectable by radar, until they were well within the disputed area of the Gulf of Sirte, then they would climb to 2000 feet and activate the pre-set electronic systems that would give them a radar signature indistinguishable from an incoming flight of F18 Tomcats. The timing of the launch had been calculated to the nearest second. The Libyans would have about ten minutes to react and get their MiG-25s airborne by which time the PTDs would have turned away towards the unsuspecting Italian vessels.

Within minutes the fuelling and launch teams had disappeared below decks and as the last flight vanished from sight the Nagasaki Maru came slowly round onto a more northerly course that took her closer to the Sicilian coast. Having unleashed God knows what havoc Whichelow was prudently putting himself closer to the protection of the NATO air bases there. As the launch crews disappeared below and the aircraft lift slid smoothly back into place Tom looked down on the deserted flight deck, grimly aware that, whatever the outcome, no one would ever be likely to suspect this battered old hulk as being capable of instigating a major international incident. Phase Two had been initiated and the countdown to the third and final phase seemed unstoppable now, yet he still had gleaned no hint of what it would involve. If this was the overture he had little doubt that the finale would be cataclysmic. Potgeiter stood at his side, his eyes on the horizon and both men knew that unless they acted soon it would be too late. It was Whichelow who broke the silence coming to stand behind them and clapping a huge hand on each man's shoulder in genial fashion.

'Well, boys, what say we take in a little television?'

In the now familiar half-darkness of the information centre they sat in silence as the Reverend programmed in. 'Let's go over and see what's happening in Tripoli,' he grunted. The image of the Libyan newscaster – coming to them live – fragmented, bounced, then settled down and Whichelow brought the sound level up, yelling for the steward as he did so. 'Johnny, get in here son and tell us what this camel driving son of a bitch is saying.'

The steward to whom Tom had spoken the previous day now sat by Whichelow's side and began, haltingly at first, to translate the Arabic commentary.

'There has been a happening – an incident. Libyan airspace has been violated. People should not panic but go to a place of safety. The Libyan Air Force has been ordered to respond. The American aggressors will be punished. God is great.' The steward frowned then continued. 'In the interests of internal security all foreigners are to be placed under house arrest. This is a temporary measure and will be rescinded once the emergency is over. God is great.'

Whichelow switched off. He was smiling.

'So far so good.' He turned to the boy at his side. 'Thanks for the translation, Johnny. I guess this calls for a little celebration. Bring us a bottle of the Dom Perignon, will you, and put another on ice for later.' They returned to the saloon where he handed foaming flutes of Champagne to Tom and Piet as if hosting a garden party. 'I guess it'll be an hour or two before we can evaluate the full effects of Phase Two but I've asked the monitoring team to have a full brief ready for 1900. It'll be a longish session I guess so we'll eat dinner in the information centre while we watch – it'll be a TV supper with a difference so to speak.' He looked at his watch. 'Now, if you'll excuse me, I mustn't neglect my spiritual duties. I'm holding a special service for the men tonight. As the time for action approaches something morally uplifting won't go amiss. Perhaps you'd care to come along?' Neither man responded and he smiled. 'Well in that case, I'll see you gentlemen later then.'

When he had gone Hawkhurst and Potgeiter moved out into the sunlight of the starboard wing deck. The South African shook his head grimly.

'We're going to have to make our move pretty soon, Tom, or not at all. We can't rely on your friends to still be tracking us. Surely they would have acted before now if they were in contact?'

'I think you're right, Piet, but what can we do? So far as I can see we've got three options. We can try to bugger the engines, start a fire with the aviation fuel, or we can take over the bridge and try to run the ship aground. Whatever course of action we chose there's no guarantee we'll succeed and every likelihood we'll end up dead.'

Potgeiter shook his head impatiently.

'But we can't just let them carry on towards whatever the culmination of all this is. Hundreds, thousands have died already. I know we haven't a snowball's hope in hell but we've got to try.'

'OK, I'm with you, but let's give it until tomorrow morning. If by then we're not any closer to finding out what Phase Three is we'll make our move.' He took a cautious look over his shoulder, checking none of the bridge watch were around, then turned his face towards a sun that was now dropping low in the sky. 'I reckon taking over the bridge is our best bet. So far as I can see there's no remote steering position on this ship so, as long as we can control the vessel from there, we may be able to run her aground or at least delay her long enough to get someone's attention. If possible we need to get a look at the charts to see where the closest shallow water or rocks are.'

'I also think, when we do make our move, we should take Whichelow and Martinette as hostages. We'll take McNaughton and Mary Lou too if possible. If we keep them close to us it'll discourage any trigger happy bastard who might be tempted to take a pot shot at us. If we take them at breakfast we'll have our best chance of scooping the lot. Let's hope that can of Mace I've got stashed away is still in date. If we can get them sitting close together I'll give them a long burst that should put them out of action for a minute or so. That'll give you a chance to deal with the steward – bust him over the head or something similar, we only want the aristocracy. We'll need something to tie them up with, two of us won't be able to keep an eye on them all the time. Then we'll move them up onto the bridge, order the crew off the bridge and secure ourselves inside. Hopefully the bridge crew will think twice before putting their masters at risk but if they do decide to make a fight of it we shoot to kill, OK?'

'Agreed, and ….'

Tom looked at the big South African.

'And?'

'There's a good chance we're not going to come out of this alive, Tom. That's OK – I can live with that,' he smiled wryly at his inappropriate choice of words, 'I mean I can accept it, but I don't want it all to be for nothing. If there comes a time when it looks like everything is turning to rat shit we kill Whichelow, Martinette, and McNaughton, in that order of priority, before we get the chop. Agreed?'

'Agreed.'

*****

There was an almost electric tension in the information centre that evening. Earlier, in the hangars below, Whichelow had delivered a powerful sermon on the theme of fighting the good fight and Martinette had celebrated the mass for the considerable number of Catholics among the men. He had used the Grail to serve the consecrated wine, probably, he said, the first time it had been employed for such a purpose in fifteen hundred years. The effect had been electric. As the diminutive priest had held the chalice up to the altar every eye had been fixed upon it. The soldiers were strung tight as a fiddle string as the operation gained momentum and action beckoned and they had roared their alleluias until they could be heard reverberating throughout the steel corridors and hangars of the Nagasaki Maru. It seemed to have produced a galvanic charge of energy in the men. A sign perhaps that the final act was at hand, Hawkhurst wondered. Now they all, McNaughton and Mary Lou included, sat in the cramped blackness awaiting news of the outcome of that afternoon's launch. The effect had indeed been dramatic.

As intended, the Libyan pilots, exultant at seemingly having the enemy on the run for once, had pursued the decoy PTDs until the latter had run out of fuel and dropped harmlessly into the sea. Unable to locate any enemy air forces the frustrated Libyans had then attacked the Italian frigates, seriously damaging the Fiume and causing a number of casualties among her crew. Before this, however, signals had been sent by both ships advising the Italian Naval Headquarters of the approach of unidentified aircraft and requesting air cover. Now, out of ammunition and short of fuel, the Libyan MiGs had turned for home only to find themselves under attack from Italian Tornadoes. Heat seeking missiles had sent eight Libyan planes plummeting into the sea. The western media, even that diminishing part of it which still prided itself on trying to retain some objectivity, were hailing it as a great victory. There were pictures of the crippled Fiume limping back towards Taranto harbour under tow, her paintwork scorched and blistered. Interviews with jubilant Italian pilots now safely back at their base were shown several times.

But as with every victory there was a price to pay. The enigmatic Libyan leader had declared that all foreigners were now hostages. There were several thousand Italians in the country and these were singled out for special attention. They had been dispersed around a number of strategic military installations where in the event of any further aggression they would be used as a human shield. A few, those who were lucky enough to be close to the border at the time, had been able to slip the net and escape into Egyptian territory. They told chilling tales of murder, beatings and rape at the hands of Islamic fundamentalist groups, allegations indignantly denied by the Libyans.

An emergency meeting of the United Nations, called within hours of the incident, had revealed the increasingly dangerous polarisation of attitudes. The western powers, along with Russia whose eye was firmly on the threat to their borders posed by those former Soviet republics with large Muslim populations, and Japan, worried by the possibility of oil embargoes, issued a declaration condemning the attack on the Italian ships as 'an act of flagrant aggression'. For all its implicit menace, it had a hollow ring to it and was rejected with contempt by all the Muslim states, along with almost the entire third world, most of whom saw the whole thing as a Western plot to set up Colonel Gadaffi. Following the UN meeting the United States and a majority of European states, seeing there was little hope of getting wider agreement for any military move against Libya, had emphasised their right to freely move in international waters. To underline this they were now in the process of assembling yet another multi-national naval force that would within hours be steaming towards the Gulf of Sirte.

As Whichelow had intended the incident had served admirably to ferment the turmoil around the world. In Europe intimidation, arson and general resentment had fuelled the beginnings of a reluctant exodus of not just Muslims but other minorities too, Asian and black, who now found themselves at the mercy of an increasingly unselective xenophobia. The airport lounges were full of families fleeing the taunts and torments of people who until a few months before had been their neighbours. In the main the men would remain, hoping to keep the small businesses they had painstakingly built up over the years running despite all the omens, sending the women and children away from the festering hate all about. Usually they were boarding planes that had just been quit by European workers who, sensing the gathering storm, had left lucrative jobs in the Middle East and Africa. Nurses, oil workers, engineers were flooding back home. Jobless and with uncertain futures these ex-patriots were disgruntled and resentful, blaming their former Muslim employers for every misfortune that befell them.

In this climate extremist politicians, people who had been treated with contempt up until then, were now assured of an attentive audience when they preached racism, nationalism and chauvinism. As they came out of the woodwork with them came a new political concept – Pan Europeanism. Pan Europeanism went way beyond the concept of a European Community united for commercial and political advantages. Pan Europeanism emphasised the need for a return to a Europe that was essentially white and Christian. It was a concept that struck an echoing chord in America too, especially in the states of the mid-west and Deep South.

There was a glimmer of hope. At the same UN meeting the United States Ambassador had announced that new Middle East peace proposals had been put forward by the Saudi Arabian government and these were described as 'interesting' and were being studied with 'some urgency' by the Israeli and American governments. In the light of these new moves the United States urged 'restraint' on all parties, although, even when acting the peacemaker, The American Government could not forbear to stress its right under international law to 'respond appropriately to any acts of terrorism or aggression.'

And still the Nagasaki Maru steamed east.

*****

Having agreed to join up with Potgeiter at seven the following morning for a final council of war, Tom decided to take a walk around the deck before turning in. His head was spinning. Tomorrow they were, most likely, going to die. In the normal run of things such a thought would have been hard to assimilate, here, however, on this ship of madmen bound for Armageddon, it seemed a strangely acceptable price to pay. There was neither moon nor stars and the wake of the Nagasaki Maru, a long trail of churning phosphorescence that faded to nothing, was the only light on the black waters. He thought of Angahrad, at least she was safe back home in the peace of the farm. A few weeks ago he had been a poverty stricken archaeologist, a man with serious money problems and no future. Yet, with her, he had undoubtedly been a happy man. What had brought him to this? Had he been tempted and succumbed to evil? Had the lure of riches and fame brought him to this? Had it all been preordained? He shook his head savagely, he was beginning to sound like The Reverend. As if summoned up by this thought – speak of the Devil and he's bound to appear – the bass rumble of the man's voice came out of the darkness.

'Frightened, Tom?'

Hawkhurst, all his doubts and fears dispelled in that instant, turned to where the glow of the man's cigar etched his gross features in the shadowy lee of the lifeboat.

'Of what?'

'Of the enormity and inevitability of all that is to come. Of the vast sweep of events – the majesty of God's plan unfolding before you. Don't tell me you're unmoved by all you've seen, by all that's going on around you? You're an intelligent man, Tom, one who God, or if you prefer the whims of fortune, has placed in a uniquely privileged position. When all this has come to fruition, when the final battle has been fought and won, you and I will be able to say we played our part in that victory. Don't tell me that thought doesn't move you at all?'

Tom moved closer. He considered there and then running at the man, perhaps seizing him about the waist, wrestling his huge bulk to the ship's side and hurling him into the hissing spume below. No, it was not yet the time for violence. That time was close but first he must make one final effort to learn about Phase Three. The Reverend read his thoughts.

'I guess you're wondering what comes next, eh, Tom?'

'Yes.'

'I know how you feel, it's got a real fascination about it, ain't it – wondering what Armageddon is really gonna to be like.'

'What is it going to be like?'

Whichelow's features faded into blackness for several seconds then glowed again as he drew on his cigar.

'It's going to be swift, terrible and bloody. Just like the Good Book told us it would be.'

'What's going to happen?'

'Come back into the saloon, Tom, and I'll reveal everything.'

Grateful to be back in the bright warmth of the comfortable saloon Tom saw that a large multi-coloured map now hung on the forward bulkhead. It covered an area that stretched from Greece to India and from the Horn of Africa up to the southern borders of Russia. Evidently Whichelow had, all along, planned to enlighten him when the time was appropriate. Pouring two very large brandies he handed one to Hawkhurst and moved towards the map.

'Make yourself comfortable boy. This won't take long.' He pointed at the Suez Canal, taking a long pull at his drink as he did so. 'We are expected to arrive here, off Alexandria at the northern entrance of the Suez Canal, in a little over two days from now. Then, according to our manifest, we are scheduled to transit the canal with the first available southbound convoy. The Nagasaki Maru is ostensibly bound for Pakistan to be broken up for scrap – at least that's what it says in *Lloyd's List*. In fact, we'll be going no further than the entrance to the canal – that's where the fun really begins.' He looked to Hawkhurst. 'Know much about Islam, Tom?'

'Not a lot.'

'Well, to your average Muslim the three most holy places in the world are Mecca, Medina and Jerusalem,' he tapped his finger lightly on the map to indicate these three points. At this time of the year they all go on a pilgrimage to Mecca, to parade around some heathen chunk of rock they call the Kabah. Every Muslim is expected to go on pilgrimage at least once in his lifetime. A lot of them look in at Medina too. Right now, talking ball park figures, there's about a million and half pilgrims in Mecca and several hundred thousand in Medina.'

Tom was tiring of the lecture. He wanted to know the facts.

'You reckon your men can take 'em then, Reverend?'

Whichelow slapped his thigh and bellowed in delight at such a display of ignorance.

'Take them? Hell, Tom, we ain't gonna try and take them. We ain't that dumb. No, we won't try to take them – we're gonna nuke 'em.' Hawkhurst stared, appalled. Surely this was some kind of sick joke? Even as he considered the matter he knew instinctively it was no joke. Whichelow returned to his diatribe. 'I bet you were wondering what we've got stashed up forward on this ship, weren't you. I told Brett to let you have a peek at that end of the ship – just to whet your appetite.'

Tom remembered the guards and the plastic strips they wore on their lapels. Of course, they would have been radiation indicators. What the hell had they got stored up there? He tried to keep his growing tension from becoming too evident, keeping his words slow and calm.

'As a matter a fact I did wonder. What are they?'

'What we've got up there, Doctor Tom, is three Tomahawk cruise missiles, together with launch systems and nuclear warheads. I can see you're impressed. Just like something out of a James Bond movie, eh? You'd be surprised just how easy it is to buy nuclear weapons these days. The SALT treaties meant literally thousands of them were to be dismantled or destroyed, of course, under strict supervision by multi-national teams but I guess a few of them just disappeared off the inventories. We could have had Soviet missiles if we wanted – they were a darn sight cheaper – but we wanted guidance systems we could rely on. Good old American know-how, that's what counts. The Tomahawk's always gonna drop within twenty metres of its target. If we'd bought SS20s we could have ended up zapping Disneyland.' He took another sip of brandy and looked to Hawkhurst. 'So, what do you think of the plan so far?'

When he had gathered his thoughts Tom's tone was flat, all emotion drained away.

'You seriously intend to hit Mecca, Medina and Jerusalem with nuclear weapons?'

The Reverend shook his head.

'No, not Jerusalem. That is a sacred site. We're just going to occupy part of Jerusalem, those parts held by the Templars of old, and reclaim it for the Christian faith. It won't be such a big deal as you think. We've already established links with groups of Messianic Jews living in Israel so we're not without influence. Once we take out Mecca and Medina, and the recriminations and retaliations begin, believe me, the Israelis will be glad of all the help we can give them. For a few days or so it'll be complete and utter chaos, no one will have the least idea of what the hell's going on. By the time they do no one's going to take much notice of us. Peace will be a dirty word and the final battle will have started. Hell, if the US comes in quickly enough it may be all over by then.'

Hawkhurst stared. When, shaking his head in disbelief, he found the words there was undisguised contempt in his voice.

'How do you sleep at night, Whichelow?'

Staring at something a long time and distance away, Whichelow shrugged at the question.

'Sleep? Hell, I ain't slept more than twenty minutes at a stretch since 1978.'

CHAPTER TWENTY TWO

Brennan, his stomach not yet entirely in tune with the queasy motion of the MV Lucia, gripped the guardrail and concentrated hard on the horizon. At his side Silvio, the boat's darkly handsome young Sicilian skipper swayed easily enough to the pitching and rolling, scanning the distant sky with equal intensity.

'It was right here, Signor Brennan. The GPS is very accurate and I marked the position off on the chart. The main radar contact was about 25 kilometres to the west – a very big vessel. It was the purest chance that I should be on watch at the time. I cannot tell you exactly what it was I saw, maybe boats, maybe aircraft, but I am sure something was launched from the vessel at around four o'clock yesterday afternoon. I saw it with my eyes. Just for a moment there was another contact on the screen – a smaller one moving away to the south from the main one – then another, then another and another. But they vanish within seconds. I am a member of the Italian Naval Reserve so I naturally take an interest in anything unusual, anything that might involve drugs or arms running. I report what I have seen to the Coast Guard and the next thing I know I am told you are flying in within two hours and that I am to give you every assistance. This is important, I think.'

Brennan nodded, his eyes still on the horizon. So much hung on this chance report.

'It could be, Silvio. I can't tell you everything, it's very sensitive, but we're looking for a vessel, a large vessel. If we don't find it could be very bad for everyone.'

'I think this has something to do with the fighting yesterday. Yes?'

The young fisherman was clearly no fool and Brennan knew it would be a mistake to treat him as such. Like most of his countrymen he was filled with patriotic pride at the beating their airmen had inflicted on the Libyans and keen to be part of the unfolding drama. However, there was a limit to what he could be told.

'It could do.'

'The radar echo I saw was certainly a large one. But that was twelve, thirteen hours ago. She will be a long way to the east of us by now. She was moving at about 12 knots so she'll be maybe 200 kilometres away, assuming she held her original heading. That would put her somewhere in the eastern Sicilian Channel by now, probably between Malta and Cape Passero.'

'Show me on the charts.'

They returned to the wheelhouse where Silvio pointed.

'It is still a very large area of sea, Signor and many big vessels pass down this channel. A needle in a haystack I think you say.'

Brennan stared down at the chart. This might well be a wild goose chase. He had still been in Cairo waiting for a flight out when Silvio's suspicious sighting had been reported to NATO's Mediterranean headquarters. Typically, locating the task force had been downgraded as a priority for no one had been prepared to spare a regular naval patrol boat to search for the vessel. Whether the hand of General Beauregard, now appointed Commander in Chief of the allied land forces, was behind this or not was hard to say for in the circumstances it was only to be expected. All eyes were firmly fixed on the big game that was developing at a frightening pace and warships were being carefully husbanded. Luckily, Valdes in New York had heard a whisper of a chance sighting and got straight onto Brennan. There might just be a connection between the report and the inexplicable behaviour of the Libyans, he had said. Look into it. Brennan went to the wheelhouse door and stared to the east. The task force, if it was a task force, was long gone but at least now he had something to go on.

'How fast can this boat go, Silvio?'

The young Italian glowed with pride as he answered. He had hoped he would be asked such a question.

'I can make thirty five knots, perhaps a little more in an emergency. Also I take the precaution of taking extra fuel abroad – at that speed my Lucia she drinks and drinks.'

Brennan nodded approvingly.

'Then give her the gun – we've got to find that ship. While you're working for me I can pay you double what you'd earn fishing.'

The young Italian stiffened, his feathers a little ruffled at this mention of monetary considerations. Without a word he elbowed the helmsman aside and took the wheel. As he brought back the throttles the powerful twin Yamahas beneath their feet growled like angry beasts and the bow of the Lucia lifted to meet the swell. She slammed a little at first, sending Brennan lurching, but then, gathering speed she steadied and skimmed like a hurled stone across the hammered glass of the sea, the ensign at her stern cracking in the wind.

'Signor Brennan,' said Silvio. 'Is not a matter of money. Is a matter of honour.'

*****

Angahrad stood on the crowded concourse of Paddington station and looked about her. She hated big cities, the bustle and noise, the shabby untidiness of it all. The unintelligible boom of the loud speaker system hurt her ears and the furtive, squalid beggars and winos that haunted the fringes of the station offended her sensibilities. About her feet diseased, drop winged pigeons pecked at the remains of a discarded burger that oozed cheese like yellow vomit. In her eyes London seemed to perfectly epitomise the concept of urban decay and already she longed for the peace of Sarnafon. And why was she here? What she hoped to achieve she hardly knew herself, yet had been unable to sit idly at the farm while Tom might be in heavens knows what danger.

Her abduction by the Church's men had been a terrifying ordeal. She could still smell the acrid chloroform pad they had clamped to her face; recall her reeling senses and the hands that roamed over her body as she laid bound and helpless in the back of the car. Then there had been the claustrophobic room with the barred window that overlooked a scrapyard in the heart of Birmingham. Her captors were clearly under orders to take no chances. Taking her clothes they had dressed her in a pair of men's striped pyjamas that were several sizes too large and continued to keep her sedated. Not satisfied with these precautions, her wrists had been bound with webbing straps to the bedhead leaving her virtually crucified on the bed. She was continually watched, three men sitting with her in four hour shifts. Every six hours or so they would administer an injection that kept her docile and escort her to the toilet or feed her with a sandwich and a little liquid. Apart from these times she lay bound and helpless, drifting in and out of a drugged sleep that brought dreams and nightmares.

Two of her jailers had been older men, both of whom spent their hours on watch reading the Bible. The third was a younger man, perhaps thirty, powerfully built with a shaved skull and she grew to dread his times on duty. At first he had simply sat, thick arms folded, staring at her lying there, either asleep or staring vacantly at the ceiling.

Then boredom had set in and he began to take a closer interest in her. She had kept her eyes shut, feeling him fumbling with the buttons of the pyjama jacket then tugging loose the cord of the trousers. On his first assault on her he had been content to stroke and paw her thighs and breasts, kissing her unresponsive mouth, his foul breath almost making her retch. At no time did he speak but wore a fixed humourless smile, taking cruel pleasure in her total helpless submission to his will. Before he went off duty he had administered an extra dose of sedative to prevent her making any protest to the next man.

After that the man had become ever more inventive. On the final day of her captivity she had struggled to consciousness to find him, naked, sitting astride her, his swelling penis hanging inches from her face. His intentions were obvious. No doubt aware she was to be released shortly he had decided to make the most of his last opportunity. Outraged, she had clamped her mouth tightly shut and turned her head away but he had simply smiled and pinched her nose until she had no option but to gasp for air and allow him to thrust home. Eyes glazed he had squealed like a farmyard beast, ejaculating within seconds, leaving her choking and sobbing in distress. For several minutes he had stared down at the distraught woman as she gagged, desperately swallowing to clear the vile fluid from her throat. Then he had calmly dismounted, adjusted her clothes and administered another injection.

When the Church's people had released her she had been instructed to tell no one about what had occurred or it would be the worse for Hawkhurst. Initially, fearful for him, she had followed those instructions to the letter. They had killed her dogs and these she had buried on the slopes of Cwmdower. As she piled a low mound of stones over the graves she had wondered what kind of people would do such a thing and worried the more about Hawkhurst. Then, for two days that seemed like an eternity, she had sat at home and listened to radio reports about the Holy Grail. These had been brief and uninformative and were soon ousted by others telling of the growing tension in the Middle East, although at the time she had made no connection between the two.

That there had been no word from Tom since that brief phone call and the conflicting rumours circulating now, about the whereabouts of the Grail and his own safety, had encouraged her to fear the worst. Now she had arrived in London to do a little investigating of her own. As she stood there, lost and unsure among the crush of commuting office workers, it seemed a forlorn hope. She had only one likely source of information and that was Laura Woods. Luckily Tom had scrawled down her address and telephone number when she had first made contact weeks back. If Laura couldn't help then the only other option was to go to the police and risk whatever repercussions that might bring. Picking up her case she strode purposefully towards the phone booth, eyeing the explicitly worded prostitutes' business cards on display there with incredulity. She punched out the number.

'Hello, is that Miss Laura Woods?'

'Yes.'

'Miss Woods, you don't know me. My name's Angahrad Jenkins, I'm … I'm a friend of Thomas Hawkhurst. I'm very worried about him. I wondered if you knew anything about his whereabouts or anything that might help me find him. I just want to know he's safe. Can I see you?'

There was a momentary hesitation at the other end of the phone as Laura assimilated this. It was an unwelcome distraction from her own plans but one she would ignore at her peril.

'I don't know if I can help but, yes, do come here. I'm as worried about him as you are.'

As Angahrad went in search of a taxi Laura put down the phone and then took it up again. She spoke quickly but there was steel in her words.

'There's a problem. I have to fly out this afternoon. Make the arrangements. I may have a travelling companion, a Miss Angahrad Jenkins. She'll most probably not have a passport on her so we may have to spend some money when we get to Istanbul. I expect you to ensure we don't get held up. I don't have to tell you that Mrs Berkowitz would be very unhappy if anything went wrong now. No screw-ups at this stage, OK?'

She went to the kitchen and prepared coffee. At that time of the morning it would take Angahrad at least half an hour to get through the rush hour traffic and reach the flat. Then she went to the bedroom and picked up her clasp bag. She reached in, drawing out the small revolver she had kept there ever since Tom had disappeared. Returning to the lounge she slid it behind a cushion on the chaise longue where it would be to hand if and when the need arose. Looking thoughtfully around the tastefully furnished room she gave a final approving nod and went in search of the beckoning aroma of coffee now coming from the kitchen, twenty minutes later Angahrad arrived. As she settled herself into a comfortable armchair, a mug of steaming coffee on the table before her, Laura, knees tucked under her on the chaise longue, appraised Hawkhurst's woman with an expert eye.

Angahrad was a little embarrassed initially, it was not in her nature to impose on people at such short notice, but there was no doubt in Laura's mind about her concern for Tom.

'I've been worried sick these past days. If you can't help me Miss Woods I'll have no option but to go to the police. I was warned not to by the men who held me but what else can I do?'

Laura looked thoughtfully at this open, simple mannered young woman who was so clearly deeply in love with Hawkhurst. She could understand: she had been there herself.

'What would you say if I told you Tom was perfectly safe? He's in big trouble but he's alive and well.' Angahrad's eyes widened.

'You know where he is?'

'Yes. I can't reveal his whereabouts yet. But he's alive.'

'You say he's in trouble. Who with? The police?'

Laura shook her head.

'No, not the police.' She took up her coffee. 'I can't tell you anymore.'

'How do you know all this? Why haven't you told the police about what you know? They think Tom is a thief – which he isn't.' She was becoming annoyed now, angered by Laura's sophisticated veneer of indifference. 'It isn't fair. Why don't you tell them whatever it is you know?'

Laura slid a hand behind the cushion and curled it round the solid butt of the revolver. She had hoped it wouldn't come to this.

'Because Tom has unwittingly become caught up in something so big and so important that nothing can be allowed to interfere. There are things going on, things so far-reaching that you cannot possibly comprehend. God willing, in a few days, perhaps a week, he'll be released but until then nothing can be allowed to put those plans at risk. Go back to your farm and wait. Whatever you do, don't go to the police – that could be really bad for Tom.'

Angahrad's head buzzed with what she was being told. She had already made her decision: since Laura would not help she would go to the police. She was not bound by any promise to secrecy to this cold, self-satisfied bitch. Her only concern was for Tom. As she pushed herself up out of the softness of the chair she noticed how the room had grown very warm and that her senses were beginning to swim. Laura released her grip on the pistol as the drugged woman made unsteadily for the door, her legs buckling under her after a couple of steps. Getting up, Laura stood over the younger woman watching carefully as the china blue eyes fluttered upwards and finally closed with a sigh. She went to the phone.

'I'm ready to move now. Bring the car round in ten minutes time. I'll need a couple of men to help with my travelling companion. She'll be out cold for hours from the dose I gave her so I'll need help getting her to the car. If they ask questions, it's just another case of drug abuse the Church is handling. Tell the airfield we're on our way too. We should be there before midday.'

Hauling the inert Angahrad into the chair Laura placed a hand under her chin and rolled the lolling head upright, staring into the blank, drowned features. A nice looking girl, she thought, and with plenty of guts. Not many women would go through what she had and still come back for more – all for the sake of a man. Bloody Hawkhurst, how did he do it? She smiled grimly: she knew damn well how he did it.

*****

Tom sat across the table and stared at the bulk of Whichelow slumped in the chair opposite. The Reverend nodded, dozing fitfully for a few minutes every so often then jerking awake to look, blinking, around him and take another pull at the brandy. It was, Tom imagined, the only way the man could achieve even the briefest periods of unconsciousness. The saloon was deserted apart from the two of them now, only the small overhead lamp throwing a dim circle of light on the table's centre. It was past one in the morning and they had talked for hours about the coming cataclysm. Hawkhurst had argued, reasoned, pleaded and begged with Whichelow to consider the enormity of what was planned. But it was clear there could be no question of any turning back now.

For a man who had calmly recounted how he fed cyanide to children in the Guyanan jungle because he had believed it was the will of God, nothing, no matter how awful, was unthinkable or forbidden. Just so long as he believed God sanctioned it. Within two days the Tomahawks would be launched and millions of innocent people would be exterminated. War would follow as surely as night follows day, a war in which no weapon or tactic would be considered too terrible so deep would be, already was, the hatred. It would drag on for years because surrender would be impossible to contemplate. Vast tracts of land, cities, towns, would be laid waste. Nor would the destruction be confined to the Middle East. Whichelow had told him, with visible satisfaction, how numbers of former Soviet ballistic missiles had been retained by some of the Islamic Republics after the breakup of the 'Evil Empire.' Not many, but enough to encourage the US to consider a pre-emptive strike. Nowhere was safe. The destruction and desecration of their holy places would be an outrage for which even the most moderate Muslim would demand a bloody vengeance.

The distant thud of the engines far below, driving the Nagasaki Maru eastwards, made Hawkhurst grimly aware of how quickly time was running out. Tomorrow they must attempt to take control of the ship or abandon all hope of affecting the relentless countdown to destruction. If he and Potgeiter couldn't buy sufficient time to disable or delay the ship then it would all be up to them. He knew their chances were slim and even if they did achieve some success they would inevitably be killed. He looked up to find Whichelow's eyes upon him, swirling the brandy in his glass. He was smiling.

'I guess you've had a lot to take in over the past few weeks, Tom.'

'That is something of an understatement.'

'Know what I've found? If you just let God into your life everything becomes simple. Stop fighting it, just go with the flow and stop looking for explanations. The Great Architect of the Universe is working out his mighty plan and it's not for us to try to understand or approve, only to obey.'

Tom didn't reply. No words would move this man from his maniac plans, he had to be killed. He made to stand up but before he could move the telephone on the bulkhead jangled harshly and

Whichelow hauled himself to his feet. Taking up the handset he listened intently for several minutes.

'Right,' he said shortly. 'Let me know when they come aboard and I'll receive them on the bridge. As for the radar contact if it gets any closer than two miles send for me. If it's a naval patrol we may have to take action to deal with it. Make sure Colonel McNaughton is advised of its presence.' He turned to the table and replenished his glass his manner suddenly pensive. 'Well, it seems we're gonna have company for tomorrow, Tom. I won't spoil the surprise but it's someone you'll be real pleased to see.'

This was his second mention of visitors but Tom was not interested. Another religious crank at breakfast was something he could do without, another complication. The mention of a patrol was something else however. Perhaps Brennan had been keeping tabs on them after all. Even so, he wouldn't know they had nuclear weapons aboard and might decide not to intervene until it was too late. Still, for the first time it gave him a certain satisfaction that Whichelow looked concerned. Tom continued to needle him.

'Perhaps they're onto you at last, Whichelow. Maybe that raid yesterday was just a bit too good to be true.'

The Reverend considered the matter.

'It's always possible. They've been steering the same course and closing on us fast for the last hour or so. But most likely it's just some fishing vessel. Even if they do decide to take a look at us we're OK. Remember this ship is officially an obsolete pile of rust that's on its way to Pakistan for conversion into razor blades and that's exactly what we look like. Our ship's papers and credentials are impeccable.'

'Perhaps they won't be satisfied by that. What if they put out a boarding party? What then?'

'Don't raise your hopes, Doctor Tom. We've got contingency plans for any eventuality. We can deal with boarding parties and anything else they may try. Nothing will be allowed to delay us. In less than twenty four hours we'll be within range of all our targets.'

Tom sighed. No doubt they would have weapons aboard that could blow any small vessel to kingdom come and any boarding party would be easily overcome by the McNaughton's men. He wondered again about Harry Brennan and then put the thought aside. All the signs said it was wrong to count on receiving any help from outside: it would be up to him and Potgeiter now; they had to rely on themselves.

He stood up, intent on heading back to his cabin and snatching a few hours' sleep. As he made to leave Whichelow spoke.

'Oh. One other thing, Tom. Seems like we slipped up somewhere along the line and let you and Piet Potgeiter bring weapons aboard.' He smiled ruefully. 'Sorry, son, but it's a rule of the house that no unauthorised weapons are allowed on board. Someone might get hurt. I've had to confiscate your toys, I'm afraid. Let you have them back once you leave the ship.'

Hawkhurst's spirits sank as he realised that Whichelow had been playing with them all along, allowing them to make their futile plans only to thwart them at his leisure.

CHAPTER TWENTY THREE

After leaving their cabins the next morning Piet and Tom held a final council of war out on the stern deck. It was a distinctly gloomy gathering and both agreed that without guns they had little hope of seizing Whichelow and his cohorts and even less of taking control of any vital section of the ship. The possibility of sabotage was also increasingly remote since they would undoubtedly be carefully watched whenever they were in the vicinity of vulnerable equipment or stores. The only hope, it seemed, now lay with the possibility of outside intervention. Tom told the South African about the shadowing vessel that the Nagasaki Maru's radar had picked up earlier that morning. It was unlikely but it was something to hold on to. Before they went in to breakfast Tom laid a hand on the South African's shoulder.

'According to Whichelow the prime targets, Mecca and Medina, will be within range of the cruise missiles late tonight, so time is running out. We've lost our guns but I've still got the switchblade down my boot. If nothing happens before then, providing I can get them together in one place I intend to try and kill Whichelow and McNaughton. It may not change anything but it'll make a big hole in their chain of command. The best thing will be for you to keep well out of it, Piet. If it doesn't work maybe you'll get a better chance later. There's no point in putting all our eggs into one basket.'

Potgeiter stared at him then nodded in agreement.

'OK. Let's give each other a wide berth from now on. If I see any opportunity for mischief before then I'll make the most of it. If alarms start to ring we'll meet back here by the lifeboat. It may be the only chance of escape and it'll take the pair of us to launch it. Take care of yourself, Tom.' They shook hands and headed for the saloon.

There was a distinct air of excitement around the table that morning. Whichelow, today dressed in khaki fatigues, was holding court. Everyone was present, even the usually elusive Martinette. His Eminence was exchanging religious small talk with Mary Lou who, as usual, was making merry amongst the corn flakes. Despite the matter of the weapons he had confiscated Whichelow greeted them affably enough.

'Sit down, boys, grab yourselves a good breakfast – it's going to be a long day.'

With the exception of Martinette, all of them, even the steward, now carried a pistol at his hip. Hawkhurst poured himself a glass of orange juice.

'What's on the programme today, Reverend? The Apocalypse?' The sarcasm was ignored.

'Well, Tom, we're arming the Tomahawks right now and their guidance systems have already been pre-set, so they can be launched at ten minutes notice. Anything's possible but no, probably not today. We need to get closer in to the Israeli coast before we can airlift the task force into Jerusalem. The whole thing has to be closely co-ordinated with our people ashore. Mind you, by about ten this evening we will be able to hit Mecca and Medina so if there's any hitch or any sign of outside intervention, we'll do just that. Two out of three will be good enough to get the show on the road. If you care to join me in the information centre later I'll be happy to give you a full run down on the operation.' He dabbed his mouth and laid his napkin aside. 'Now, if you'll excuse us, the colonel and I have a tour of inspection to complete.'

As he rose from the table Tom looked up innocently.

'What about that radar contact last night, Reverend? Is it still there?'

Whichelow smiled.

'Nope. It turned north at around five this morning. Like I said, it was probably just a fishing vessel heading back to Greece. Better face it, Tom, the cavalry aren't coming this time. You'll save yourself a whole bunch of disappointment if you just sit back and enjoy the show. It's gonna be spectacular.'

After breakfast Potgeiter and Martinette also quit the saloon. The priest to his prayers, the South African doubtless in search of mischief. Tom, happy to keep her distracted, was now left alone with Mary Lou. She seemed pleased to have him all to herself, her tone smug and secretive.

'We picked up a couple of fellow travellers in the night, Tom, they choppered in from Turkey. They're sleeping just now, both dead beat, but there's a little welcoming ceremony scheduled for 1300 hours so do try to join us, I'm sure you'll be impressed.'

Tom looked at her. The possibility of meeting the new passengers interested him not at all yet he had often wondered about Mary Lou's place in the scheme of things. She was clearly a trusted member of the Reverend's staff and a clever and diligent aide de camp. She had worked as hard as anyone in support of the Church of Christ the Warrior's mad crusade and was clearly every bit as ruthless as her masters in achieving her targets. Yet he had always felt that there was something that didn't quite fit; something not quite compatible with her religious fervour, or her voracious appetite for food, drink and, allegedly, other women's bodies. Like her leader, he doubted that she would be vulnerable to logic so he decided to try a more oblique approach.

'Do you really want all this, Mary Lou? The destruction of holy places and the murder of millions. Whichelow is barking mad, you're not. How can you be part of something so evil? What have Muslims ever done to you to deserve such treatment?'

She took a lump of sugar from the silver bowl before her and popped it into her mouth.

'It isn't what they've done to me, Tom. This isn't personal. It's what they've done and are still doing to women in general that earns my hatred. At best the Muslims treat women like second class citizens, at worst like beasts of burden. No civil rights, no education, virtual imprisonment in some areas and sexual mutilation in others. After this women everywhere in those benighted regions will have new hope, new freedoms.'

'If you launch those Tomahawks you'll be murdering hundreds of thousands of women. How do you square that with your feminist ideals?'

She took another lump of sugar, examined it briefly, then dropped it back into the bowl.

'They will be martyrs, Tom. There's always a price to pay and women have suffered for their beliefs since the beginning of time. As I say they will be martyrs and they will not die in vain. Their deaths will signal an end to centuries of servitude and abuse at the hands of men.'

Frustrated at his inability to convey the enormity of what was planned or to turn her aside from it, Hawkhurst got personal.

'Like Suzie back in Gethsemane? Was she a martyr?'

Mary Lou's black eyes glowed like coals.

'That poor child's death was none of my doing. If you hadn't been so weak as to let her seduce you she would be alive today. If you'd simply turned her away when she came to your room she would have had no part to play.'

She stood up and stalked from the saloon in angry silence, leaving a frowning Hawkhurst alone with his thoughts.

*****

In the information centre Whichelow was just beginning his daily review of the previous day's events. There had been sporadic violence in Israel, suicide bombers had decimated an army patrol in Nablus and half a dozen Katyushas had been fired across the border. An Israeli retaliatory incursion had been launched into southern Lebanon killing, according to Hezbollah sources, thirteen civilians. Further west the Italian/Libyan standoff continued, with accusations and counter accusations of unprovoked aggression flying between Rome and Tripoli. There had, however, been no further incidents in that area and the Libyan leader had announced that as a concession to peace the foreigners he now held would be allowed to leave the country. In the countries of Europe, voices of moderation were calling for an end to ethnic violence and the police now seemed to have at least brought a temporary halt to the arson and violence in most areas. It seemed to offer a glimmer of hope: the world had stepped back a pace.

Yet if it seemed as if the rush to disaster, if not halted, had at least slowed significantly, everything now rested with the new Saudi peace initiative. Everybody paid lip service to the new moves and they had, apparently, brought a brief period of comparative calm to the region. But it was obviously a very fragile peace indeed and none of the interested parties had relaxed their military state of readiness one iota. Whichelow seemed well pleased with the situation.

'That's just about perfect. They're talking peace and we are nearly in position. When we hit Mecca it'll go down as another day of infamy in the annals of history. Once we strike home it'll be war to the knife.'

War to the knife. As they moved back to the saloon Hawkhurst's thoughts strayed to the switchblade in his boot. The Reverend stood now within a metre, one long arm's length, of him, unsuspecting and relaxed. He could if he chose draw the weapon there and then and thrust it up into the man's heart in the flash of an eye. Yet he hesitated, unsure, wondering about the technicalities. He had never killed a man before, had never seriously contemplated doing so. Given the man's huge girth, was the heart his best target or should he go, slashing rather than stabbing, for the throat and jugular vein? Equally important, was now the best time or should he wait until later when, presumably, McNaughton would be present at the welcoming reception and he might be able to take them both out? As he pondered these matters he continued to keep Whichelow occupied.

'So tell me Reverend. Exactly when do you intend to launch your attack? You can be perfectly open now, there's nothing I can do about it anymore. I'd just like to know what's going to happen.'

Whichelow produced a cigar and waited for the ever attentive steward to bring a light. Leaning down to the offered match he drew deeply, exhaling a blue cloud of perfumed smoke that hung about his head and shoulders.

'OK, Tom. Why not? Let's step out onto the wing bridge and I'll fill you in on everything. It's a lovely morning.'

For a few minutes they paced the deck but it was hot outside and the Reverend was soon sweating. Mopping his brow, he eased his bulk down onto one of the huge mooring bollards and stretched his legs. All about the sun sparkled on what for Tom was a seascape depressingly devoid of other shipping. Lounging at the ship's rail Hawkhurst decided a little flattery wouldn't go amiss.

'I won't say I admire what you're about to do Reverend, but I'll say one thing, you sure can organise. How did this all get started?'

Whichelow gave an appreciative nod.

'Why thank you, Tom. It hasn't been easy. Setting this up has taken twenty years and one hell of a lot of blood, sweat and tears, but I've only played a modest part in it really. I have merely been God's agent, nothing more than a divinely inspired catalyst if you like. All I have done is to draw other likeminded people together and made use of their talents in fulfilling God's will. Like I told you, I saw the truth of the matter back in the jungle; I saw then that the meek might inherit the earth – but only six feet of it. It was there I saw the only feasible way to ensure God's rule on earth was by fire and the sword and, to do that, I had to become ruthless, merciless and, most important of all, infinitely patient. Well, after I'd seen to the decent disposal of the bodies down at the People's Temple and convinced the authorities that the mass suicide was nothing to do with me, I returned to the United States.'

'I didn't know exactly what I was going to do next but, luckily, I wasn't entirely without funds. The People's Temple may have had a rough ride but Reverend Jones was no fool when it came to fund raising and had squirrelled away the best part of half a million dollars in a tin trunk under his bed, money for which he no longer had any need. I decided it was to be used as bread upon the waters and I began to organise. I changed my name to Whichelow and baptised myself James in honour of Jones, for he was a man I much admired. Then I started by launching a preaching tour in churches all around the southern states. I soon recognised that to succeed in this world a good preacher needs an angle and it was at this time I began developing the concept of Christ the Warrior. There were a lot of very disillusioned young men around at that time, mostly veterans of the Viet Nam war. They hadn't wanted to stop fighting when the US pulled out. They felt betrayed and cheated, they wanted another chance to serve and this time they wanted a leader they could trust. I saw that through The Church of Christ the Warrior I could give them the promise of that.'

'It was hard work, as a fisher of men I have to admit I made very little progress in gathering followers in the first years. Then, by the grace of God, I met General Cornelius Beauregard at a church meeting in Washington. I recognised then – he was only a colonel at the time – that he wasn't entirely stable and that his vision of the future wasn't exactly the same as mine, but I could see how he might fit usefully into a wider plan. He saw the potential of a militant, campaigning Christ. Of course, embittered by his treatment by the Viets, at that time he thought God was only concerned with destroying Communism – which of course, in his own good time, he had done – but by then I was looking beyond that, I was already planning for the final battle. Beauregard had been captured in Cambodia and spent five years in the Hanoi Hilton. That was where he found God. Thanks to him, things really picked up for the Church of Christ the Warrior after that. Beauregard comes from a very influential family down in Louisiana and had useful contacts in Congress and, naturally, in the Pentagon. He brought converts, Brett McNaughton among them, influence in high places and plenty of cash.'

Tom stared. Brennan had suspected the Church had friends in high places. They didn't come much higher than a five star general.

'Are you telling me this is being funded by the Pentagon?'
Whichelow shook his head.

'No, Tom. They would shut us down if they could, like you they don't have the breadth of vision for this kind of thing. But with a few well-placed friends and God on your side it's amazing what can be achieved. Gethsemane, the task force, everything, it all began when I met Cornelius Beauregard back in eighty one. As we progressed with building up the Church's influence and the Cold War ended, he was, with a little help from me, quick to see where our destiny would lead us next. It was all so logical: establishing the Kingdom of God on Earth was just a natural progression from bringing down the Evil Empire. That's the thing you have to recognise with military men, politicians too. If they haven't got a mission they haven't got anything. I didn't just offer Cornelius Beauregard a mission, I offered him a crusade.' He took a reflective drag on his cigar and looked to Tom for comment.

'Right. So here we are a few hours away from the culmination of all your plans. Assuming everything goes to plan and you destroy the holy cities of Islam and occupy Jerusalem. What do you intend to do then? Step in and offer to clear up the mess? Start preaching peace and reconciliation?'

'No, Tom. Once the Nagasaki Maru is on station and the Tomahawks are launched; once I have seen my soldiers safely embarked on their historic mission, I intend to disappear for a while. From then on it'll be up to Cardinal Martinette to provide spiritual leadership for the task force and a focus for the whole Christian world. He'll get all the glory and, eventually, probably the Papacy, but I shall retain the power. When the ordure strikes the fan I intend to be a long way from here, somewhere safe from where I can observe the working out of The Almighty's plan. Then I shall fast and pray and wait for divine direction.'

'I thought you would want to enter Jerusalem at the head of your army, Whichelow. Hold a prayer meeting in the Al-Aqua Mosque maybe – something like that? Have all the worlds' press there to see your triumph.'

'You're quite wrong about me, Tom. I don't seek any publicity or personal glory. I intend to leave that kind of thing to Cardinal Martinette – that's why we brought him into this in the first place. Whatever happens in Jerusalem it will ensure Martinette is elected the next Pope or, if things go badly, becomes another glorious martyr for the cause. Either way it can only serve to strengthen that cause. I think the Catholics are so much better at that kind of thing, don't you? All that ritual, the robes, incense, the whole bit.' He fell silent, staring out to sea.

When Whichelow spoke like that, Tom thought, it was hard to think of him as being mad. What he said about not seeking personal glory was true, for he had for twenty years kept a very low profile, shunning publicity and ostensibly working to altruistic ends. Yet all the while he had been working tirelessly for the execution of the most obscene outrage of an obscene century. Had it not been for Laura's chance discovery of the tomb and all that had followed he himself would never have known of the existence of the Reverend James Whichelow or guessed about Gethsemane and all it stood for out there on the prairie. It seemed quite likely that, in global terms, very few people indeed knew of Whichelow's existence and of those few only a handful would have the least hint about his crazy schemes. Yet, when it was all over, it seemed depressingly inevitable now, and millions lay dead, he would still be out there somewhere, gloating over the misery and rubble and waiting for further instructions from on high.

Hawkhurst was rapidly running out of time, of patience, and of ideas. He bent down, apparently brushing his trousers free of some speck of dust, but actually to press a testing hand against the hilt of the switchblade, to feel it's reassuring solidity against his palm. He wouldn't get a better chance than now: Whichelow, under the heat of the noonday sun was growing drowsy and beginning to nod, the great head slightly back, laying open his fat neck to the blade. Hawkhurst drew a deep breath, trying to slow his racing pulse. It had to be now. If he could kill the man and throw the body over the side he might get a chance at McNaughton later, just so long as nobody missed The Reverend for an hour or so. He pulled his trouser leg up, fingers caressing the bone handle of the switchblade. As he did so the steward stepped out onto the wing deck, his shoes ringing on the steel deck, and Whichelow started, blinking, from his dozing.

'Mrs Berkowitz asked me to advise you that your guests are up and about, Reverend. They'll be in the saloon in about five minutes.'

Heart pounding, Tom casually gave his trousers another brush down and followed Whichelow inside.

CHAPTER TWENTY FOUR

Taking a glass of champagne from the offered tray with as much aplomb as his trembling fingers would allow Hawkhurst stood in silence, nerves ajangle, awaiting the appearance of the latest arrivals aboard the Nagasaki Maru. Thirty seconds before he had been on the brink of committing bloody murder and despite this distraction he knew he must be prepared for the next opportunity. Although he had hoped that McNaughton would attend the gathering and so present a choice of target he was to be disappointed for there was no sign of the colonel. Only himself, Whichelow and Mary Lou, foraging through a bowl of pretzels, made up the welcoming committee. He glanced at his watch, it was now a little after one, and wondered where Potgeiter was at that moment.

'Hello, Tom.' The words were low and mocking and as he turned, his mouth dropped open to see Laura and Angahrad ushered into the saloon. As he struggled to find words, Whichelow stepped forward, gallantly bowing to kiss first Laura's and then Angahrad's hand. Seeing Tom, Angahrad pulled away and ran to him, throwing her arms about him, burying her face in his chest.

'Thank God you're safe.' She breathed, as he hugged her close, kissing the crown of her head. As he struggled to adjust himself to this latest development Tom looked to where Laura, flanked by the Reverend and Mary Lou, stood smiling at them. He was angry now. A few seconds ago everything had been so cut and dried. He had accepted the need to kill bloodily and if necessary to die in like manner to thwart Whichelow's mad schemes. Now, with the appearance of Angahrad, everything had changed. He looked to Whichelow who stood smiling patronisingly at this display of emotion.

'Is this the way you keep your word?' He snarled. 'I kept my side of the bargain. You've got the Grail and you've got me, it wasn't necessary to bring her into this again.'

It was Laura who responded.

'It wasn't The Reverend's idea, Tom, it was mine. Angahrad came looking for you and luckily, luckily for us that is, she came to me first. She was very persistent and I couldn't risk her going to the police at this stage and messing things up so I brought her along. Don't worry, you're both perfectly safe.'

She was totally composed, standing there with one hand resting on Mary Lou's shoulder, a glass of champagne in the other. Dressed in cotton slacks and a short sleeved shirt no one would guess she had only recently flown several thousand miles by plane and helicopter. Her serene indifference rankled with Tom, the more so as it began to dawn on him that he been duped all down the line, right from the moment she had turned up at the cottage with the temptation of fame and fortune.

'I didn't have you down as the religious type, Laura? Guess I was wrong.'

'Religion doesn't come into it, but I've been a supporter of the Church of Christ the Warrior for a few years now, Tom. Michael introduced me to Mary Lou around the time you were packing your bags at the museum. I have never advertised my loyalties because I felt I could be of more use to the cause if I kept in the background. Events have proved me right.'

'So the tomb was a fake after all,' he said bitterly. She shook her head.

'No, that's the wonderful thing about all this. Everything I told you about the way I came across it was perfectly true. It never crossed my mind that the Church would have a use for it until you decided to steal it. Seems a leopard can't change its spots.'

Hawkhurst was puzzled. He had watched her lock the original Grail away in her safe. Why was she continuing with the charade? He decided it would be safer to keep the conversation off the Grail. If Whichelow thought for one moment he had been tricked it might bode ill for them.

'So you're actually part of this sad, sick company are you Laura? Tell me, are you happy about what's going to happen over the next few days. The death and destruction?'

She shrugged.

'The hostages must be released. I was up at Cambridge with Pat McNally – I knew him before I knew you. It's inhuman that people should be held like animals for so long.'

Tom frowned. Perhaps she wasn't as au fait with what was going on as he had first imagined. He was about to say as much when

Mary Lou cut across the conversation perhaps not wanting Laura to know more than was necessary.

'Well, Laura, my dear, I think we need to talk – so much has happened since we last met – why don't we go back to my cabin, it's quieter there. You can give me all your news and I'll put you in the picture.' Encompassing all present with a wide smile Mary Lou took Laura's unresisting hand and led her away. When they had gone Whichelow let out a low chuckle.

'I guess Mary Lou's pleased to have some fresh meat aboard.' He threw back the last of his champagne and laid the glass aside. 'But if you'll excuse me now, I'll be about my business. No doubt you'll have plenty to talk about. Help yourself to more champagne.'

Alone, Tom took Angahrad in his arms and kissed her eyes, her cheeks, her mouth.

'I'm so sorry I got you involved in all this, darling. They've made a bloody fool of me all down the line. When they found they couldn't buy the Grail they blackmailed me through you – all to get possession of it. But that's only a small part of their plans. They're planning to start a war in the Middle East – you can't imagine just how utterly evil they are. We've got to stop them, but first I've got to get you off this ship.'

She pulled away.

'We leave together or we don't go at all. I won't go on my own, Tom.' She said firmly, her pale features softening into the ghost of a smile. 'After all this I'm not letting you out of my sight. You're not safe to be out on your own.'

Back in her cabin, she had been accommodated just across the passageway from his, he told her all of what had passed, omitting the episode with Suzie. This done they discussed their plans. When she heard he was contemplating killing Whichelow in cold blood, Angahrad's eyes grew wide in disbelief. It was a side to him she had not seen before, dark and ruthless. But he remained adamant.

'We can't have any scruples in this, Angie. Within a few hours they will have Mecca and Medina within range and once that happens there'll be very little we can do to stop them. Millions of innocent people will die. Unless something drastic happens before then I intend to kill Whichelow at dinner tonight – meals are something of a ritual aboard the Nagasaki Maru. That's as late as we dare leave it. When I do all hell will break loose and you must make the most of the confusion to get away. When Piet gets here I'm going to ask him to get you away in the lifeboat.'

There came a soft tapping at the door and Potgeiter, who had not been present on the bridge, entered, surprised at Angahrad's presence there showing on his sun tanned face. Hawkhurst made the necessary introductions and then related what had happened and how he now intended to kill Whichelow and McNaughton at dinner. Potgeiter looked at him pensively.

'OK, but launching that lifeboat manually isn't going to be easy. It'll take five minutes at least to winch out and then lower her away. We'll have to be pretty quick once you make your move.' He looked to Angahrad. 'How do you feel about all this Angie?'

She was less than enthusiastic – not frightened but searching for other less drastic options.

'It seems so desperate and with only a slim chance of success. If you think it's the only way I'll go along with it, but surely there's something else we could try, something that would give us all a chance to get away. I noticed The Reverend was wearing a gun. He's such a fat man, so slow moving, surely the three of us could get the gun off him and take him prisoner. With a gun we could hold the others off for a while at least.'

Hawkhurst considered her suggestion.

'Well, he doesn't often move far from the saloon and information centre and the stewards are all armed now. But it's an idea. We'll keep our eyes open. Let's go back up now and see if a chance presents itself.'

*****

Again their plans were to be thwarted for there was no sign of Whichelow all that afternoon. Having discreetly searched the sections of the Nagasaki Maru that were accessible to them, it became apparent that the Reverend was attending to his duties elsewhere. Eventually Potgeiter drifted off below decks to continue his thus far fruitless search for some weakness in the ship's defences. He left Tom and Angahrad strolling in the warm sunlight at the stern of the vessel. As the sun began to drop and the cool caress of the Meltemi began to blow down from the Adriatic to the north, Tom felt her shiver and suggested they go below and get some rest. There was an hour to go to dinner.

Having showered and shaved Tom dressed and only pausing to check the switchblade remained easily to hand, went across to Angahrad's cabin. She wore the same simple dress she had arrived aboard in but her hair shone and she smelled of soap as she ran to him, laying her hands about his neck. She was crying.

'Don't do it, Tom,' she pleaded. 'Please. Even if you do manage to kill Whichelow they'll kill you afterwards. What will that achieve? There're too many of them. Why not let things take their course. Maybe it won't be as bad as you think. Oh God, I don't want to lose you now. Not after all this.'

He kissed her warm tears, holding her close.

'Don't worry, little one. I shall be all right.'

Even as he spoke he knew it wasn't true. He was, almost certainly, going to die within a couple of hours. The awful thing was that, since her arrival, he had for the first time begun to doubt his ability to go through with it. Before, the enormity of what was going on about him had been sufficient to keep his natural fear of dying at bay or at least to make death an acceptable price to pay. Now, with her there to worry about, nothing was simple anymore. For the first time he wondered, even if Whichelow made it easy for him, whether he could perform such a bloody act or; more importantly, whether he was prepared to leave Angahrad at their mercy afterwards. As he wrestled with his fears there was a gentle tap at the door and Potgeiter's tawny head peered in.

'Sorry to impose folks, but I think we need to talk before we go in to dinner. I've been doing some thinking.' His eyes went to the mini bar. 'Any chance of a drink?'

Tom poured a couple of stiff Scotches and a glass of wine of Angahrad. The South African was unusually reticent, he noticed, almost shy in Angahrad's company. The man's attitude had been transformed dramatically since their first clash at the airfield. The old arrogance had gone now, perhaps it had always been a façade, and Tom knew this was a man he could grow to like and respect. Potgeiter threw his drink back in one and held it out for a refill. He smiled.

'As I say, I've been doing some thinking, Tom. I find the odd drink helps the process sometimes. I also think I may have managed to slow them up a bit.'

Tom's heart rose at this: perhaps there wouldn't need to be any killing after all.

'What's happened?'

'Well, since it wasn't possible to get near the engines, I began to think about other possibilities. This afternoon I managed to get down into the shaft space right back aft, there's a big bearing in there that supports the shaft. Well, I poured half a kilo of sugar into the sump. In normal circumstances that should mean the bearing will start to overheat within an hour or so and they'll have to reduce revolutions or risk seizing the whole thing solid. The trouble is I don't know how effective it will be. There may be a filter system fitted that will clean the oil up before the sugar can get to work. We'll just have to wait and see what happens.'

He fell silent for a moment, looking first to Angahrad and then Tom before continuing.

'I've also been thinking about the idea of killing Whichelow. We'll still have to go ahead with it if nothing dramatic happens to the engines during dinner. If nothing's happened by, say, Eight thirty, we must assume I haven't been able to bugger the shaft bearing. In that event we go ahead with Plan B – the knife. OK?'

Tom nodded. There was at least hope now, albeit slight.

'OK. Piet. Eight thirty it is. Let's hope it isn't necessary now.'

Potgeiter sipped his drink and licked his lips.

'I think I should be the one to do it, Tom.'

Hawkhurst stared.

'What?'

Potgeiter leant forward, intense.

'Listen. You've got this young lady's safety to think of now. Whoever does the act is going to be full of lead within minutes. Face it Tom, it's a suicide mission. OK, hopefully we'll have the satisfaction of fouling up their plans and taking a couple of them out but you should be thinking beyond that. If you kill their leader they'll take it out on Angahrad. I'm on my own, a loner. It's less likely there'll be reprisals. Look, we both have our reasons, damn fine reasons, for hating Whichelow but mine are better, I think. What do you say?'

'Not a chance, Piet. You've done enough. It's my turn to perform.' Tom's voice was firm but the South African would not be denied.

'Listen you stubborn bastard. Forget the stiff upper lip and start thinking of the lady here. Once this thing starts, whatever happens, we'll all be surplus to requirements. I've seen you operate and, with luck, the pair of you may just be able to escape or at least stay alive. Once you stick that son of a bitch you're a dead man and so is she.'

Tom felt Angahrad's eyes upon him. Everything Potgeiter had said was undoubtedly true yet he couldn't simply hand over the knife when to do so was tantamount to signing the man's death warrant. It also had a whiff of cowardice about it. Potgeiter produced another solution.

'Tell you what. Why don't we spin a coin? Heads for me, tails for you. Whoever comes up gets the knife.' He had already produced a coin, and balanced it on his thumbnail. 'Come on, Tom, surely there's nothing wrong with that.'

Reluctantly, Hawkhurst nodded in agreement.

'OK, Piet. Spin.'

Potgeiter flicked his thumb and the silver disc spiralled towards the deckhead, to drop to the floor at their feet. They all leant forward to see what fate had decreed.

'Heads it is,' Potgeiter gasped triumphantly, scooping the coin up, almost as though he had won the toss at some football match. 'Hand it over.'

Tom slid the switchblade from his boot and passed it across to the South African who, clearly no stranger to such toys, opened and shut it with practised skill, the six inch silver of steel blade darting in and out like a viper's tongue.

'Right,' he said, sliding the deadly blade out of sight down his right desert boot. 'Why don't we go and join the others?'

*****

The galley had made special efforts that evening, roast quail followed by a choice of sirloin steak or langoustine, and the wine flowed freely. Given the circumstances it made for a strangely convivial atmosphere and by eight the conversation was flowing as freely as at any suburban dinner party. Tom and Potgeiter had been seated directly opposite Whichelow with Angahrad between them. This was a bad configuration for a murder attempt, putting as it did at least two metres between the South African and his quarry. To Whichelow's left sat Martinette and McNaughton, the latter a slightly easier target, while Laura and Mary Lou sat side by side, their hands touching on the table.

From the moment they had sat down Tom had been straining his ears to catch the throb of the engines, hoping at any minute to detect the first indication of any relenting in its pulse. As the meal had worn on his hopes began to fade and he watched with growing tension as the large digital clock mounted on the forward bulkhead blinked away the seconds. The sabotage plan, it seemed, had failed. He listened to Potgeiter, now making polite conversation with McNaughton, and wondered at the man's courage. How could he be so relaxed, he wondered, when in less than twenty minutes, he would be attempting to kill two men, including the one he now held in conversation, and very soon afterwards would probably be dead himself. Tom marvelled at this display of icy nerve and prayed his own tension wasn't obvious. At his side Angahrad, silent and withdrawn, picked unhappily at her food.

'I'm sure you'll all be glad to know we've been making excellent time and by midnight we'll be within range of our primary targets.' It was Whichelow who threw this offering into the general conversation and McNaughton took it up with obvious pleasure.

'That's right. Nothing can stop us now. We shall smite our enemies hip and thigh. Even if we were intercepted we'd still have plenty of time to get the Tomahawks aloft now. Mind you if my boys don't get a chance to bust a few heads they'll be sick as dogs. They're just itching to rock and roll.'

Hawkhurst looked to Laura, questioningly. Until then she had been largely preoccupied with the attention of Mary Lou and by her smiling reactions was in no way adverse to her advances. Laura Woods, he had decided that night was sexually a far more complex personality than he had previously suspected. However, instead of the challenging and slightly mocking gaze she had offered him until then, Tom now saw the first hint of doubt setting in. She turned to Whichelow.

'I understood there would only be a minimal likelihood of actual fighting on this raid, Reverend,' she said. 'I thought your men were just going in to pick up the hostages and bring them out. A surgical operation was how it was described to me – clean and quick. Has something happened to change your plans?'

Clean and quick, thought Hawkhurst. Clearly she had no idea of the manpower and equipment that was stowed up forward. As the Reverend considered her question Tom saw the clock behind him click away another minute: it was eight seventeen.

'Well, it's a little more than just a raid, Ms Woods,' he smiled modestly. 'Yes, it's certainly more than that. But don't you worry your pretty head about it. You'll be safe as houses aboard the Nagasaki Maru.'

This kind of conversation was not to Laura's liking at all. She looked to Tom who shrugged his shoulders easily, pleased to see her shaken for once.

'Good Lord, Laura, you mean you didn't know? You've won the jackpot, or do I mean crackpot? You've been instrumental in launching the third and, most probably, the last World War. The Revered here and his fruitcake friends, your new girlfriend among them, are about to obliterate the holy sites of Islam.'

She stared at him in sheer disbelief while Mary Lou slid a consoling arm around her shoulders.

'Take no notice, Laura baby,' she cooed. 'Dr Hawkhurst is not sympathetic to our cause. He naturally paints everything black.'

Hawkhurst persisted.

'The hostages, your friend McNally included, have been dead for years, Laura,' he continued. 'The myth of their imprisonment has been used as the justification for something so horrible I doubt you could comprehend it.'

'That will do Hawkhurst,' Whichelow barked, as the clock at his back snapped off another minute. Tom was unabashed: a bit of a fracas might give Piet a better chance.

'Go fuck yourself, Whichelow.' He rasped. 'Tell the silly bitch the truth. Tell her about the nuclear weapons you've got aboard, all ready to go. Tell her about how you're going to send the Middle East, and elsewhere, up in flames.'

A shocked silence reigned around the table at his unseemly outburst in the excitement of which Potgeiter had apparently dropped his napkin. He reached below the table to retrieve it. When he straightened up Tom could see that the knife, already open, wrapped in the folds of the linen of his knees. Below, the engines thumped on inexorably; there were two minutes to go.

Tom knew at that moment that he could not let Piet go in alone, to allow that would be rank cowardice. His hand curled round the steak knife – he would have preferred the langoustine but was more interested in the cutlery than the food – testing its edge with his thumb. Although it was sharp he recognised it was not much of a combat weapon, a thin short serrated blade that would snap if it met bone. However, he judged that if Piet took McNaughton, the South African's closest and easiest target, he himself might get across the table in time to do Whichelow serious injury before the stewards could draw their guns and finish the pair of them. He looked briefly into Angahrad's eyes, eyes wide and fearful yet resolute. It might be the last time he would ever look on her face again. Another minute clacked away and he drew a deep intake of breath, preparing himself. It was precisely as he sensed Potgeiter steeling himself for the first move that the bulkhead telephone grated harshly to life and Whichelow, oblivious to just how tenuous his hold on life was at that precise moment, rose and lifted it to his ear. As he listened his face darkened.

'Right,' he snorted. 'We're on our way.' He looked to McNaughton who, already sensing problems, was on his feet. 'Brett. We've got company, a whole lot of it. Bring the ship to action state Zebra, put the Tomahawks on five minutes standby to fire and then join me on the bridge.' He looked around the table. 'I suggest for you own safety that the rest of you return to your cabins,' were his departing words although it sounded like a suggestion rather than an order.

Hawkhurst looked to Potgeiter, who lifted a questioning eyebrow as the clock registered eight thirty precisely.

'Oh well,' he said breezily. 'Looks like we're not wanted on voyage anymore. Maybe it's time we were thinking of moving on.'

He cocked his head, listening and both men fell silent, smiled, then laughed aloud as deep in the bowels of the vessel the throb of the Nagasaki Maru's engines faltered for the first time.

CHAPTER TWENTY FIVE

As they quit the saloon Potgeiter clapped Hawkhurst on the shoulder.
'Let's go up on deck and see what's happening.'
Throughout the ship klaxons were shrieking and along the decks the crew, struggling with flak jackets and helmets, were running to their action stations. In all this activity no one took the least notice of them and when they arrived on the stern deck it was quite deserted. It was dark now and both men scoured the merging sea and sky in vain for any sign of life. They could make out nothing save the loom of the light on Cape Passero, the south-easterly limit of Sicily now far astern and fading rapidly.
'What do you think has shaken them up like this?' Tom asked.
Potgeiter shook his head.
'I don't know. They must have picked something up on radar. Whatever it is it couldn't have come at a better time for us: just as they've had to reduce revolutions because the shaft bearing is overheating.'
There was, as yet, no visible evidence of the Nagasaki Maru losing speed apart from the subtle change in the engine pitch. But Tom knew they wouldn't want to risk going astern with the shaft bearing in its present delicate condition and that the ship's huge bulk would maintain her momentum through the water for a good while, possible hours, before she finally came to a halt. He looked aft to the shadowy bulk of the orange lifeboat, still hanging in its gallows-like davits. It offered their best hope of escape and surely they should take their chance now and try to slip away under cover of darkness while the rest of the ship was preoccupied?
It certainly made a lot of sense. Once they were clear of the Nagasaki Maru the crippled tanker was hardly likely to give chase in its current perilous situation. Then he recalled the missiles stored up in the bows of the ship, armed and ready to go. If Whichelow thought his plans were now compromised he wouldn't hesitate to cut his losses and cause as much havoc as possible. True, they were still at the very extreme limit of their range but he knew that if his schemes looked threatened Whichelow would not hesitate to fire them come what may. To him it would be of little consequence where they fell so long as they

caused massive damage and created an international incident sufficiently serious to provoke war. Even if they could not reach their original targets, they need not necessarily fall at random. If there was time to reprogram their guidance systems there were numerous Islamic targets, densely populated capital cities, vast oil installations, nuclear power stations, even the Suez Canal, all well within range to the south and south west. As he yelled his intentions to Potgeiter he was already at the foot of the companionway leading up to the bridge.

'Piet. You and Angie get the lifeboat winched out and get inside. Give me ten minutes. If I'm not back by then take her away. I'm going up to the bridge – unfinished business.' Potgeiter would have liked to argue but, seeing to do so would only waste precious time, stooped and produced the switchblade from his boot, tossing it lightly to Hawkhurst.

'You may need that. Good luck.'

There was an armed sailor on guard at the bridge door but Tom's face had become so familiar aboard that he stepped aside to let the Englishman pass without question. Hawkhurst made a mental note that the sentry would have to be dealt with when he made his escape. Inside the darkened bridgehouse, all thoughts were elsewhere and no one took the least exception to his appearance there. Whichelow, McNaughton at his side, and the crew were totally preoccupied, night vision binoculars trained ahead. Tom kept in the background, trying to give off an air of relaxed indifference he did not feel, but all the while edging his way closer to Whichelow and McNaughton, the hilt of the knife concealed in his pocket sweaty in his hand. Among the bank of lights on the bridge control console he noticed the lifeboat alarm was now an urgently winking red eye. Now, however, all eyes were elsewhere and no one appeared to have noticed it. Potgeiter was obviously wasting no time. At that moment Whichelow lowered his glasses and seeing him there smiled. It wasn't an entirely convincing smile.

'Hi, Tom. Come to see the fun?'

'What's happening?'

Whichelow turned his massive back on Hawkhurst and resumed his watch.

'Seems we've got some kind of mechanical problem with the engine, had to reduce speed. Chief engineer is down looking at it right now. Also there's a formation of half a dozen or so ships just come into radar range to the north. They're travelling fast and heading our way.'

Despite these problems Whichelow didn't seem to be overly worried, Tom thought. He was standing about three metres from the man now but his path to the target was blocked by a couple of lookouts, both armed. To move too soon would be futile. He needed space and so played for time.

'What are you going to do?'

Whichelow kept his glasses trained on the horizon to the north.

'Well, we'll just keep pressing on at reduced speed, I guess. So far as the world out there is concerned we're just another old rust bucket going about our lawful business. No reason anyone should bother with us. We'll press on – if that fleet turns out to be hostile we'll just fire the Tomahawks anyway. They're being brought to a ready-to-fire state right now, so it only needs someone to press the button. Whatever happens, nothing can stop us now.'

'But I thought you said we wouldn't be in range until later tonight.'

Whichelow shrugged.

'It's close, but the technical people reckon we've got a better than fifty-fifty chance of hitting them from here. Every sea mile we cover increases that chance.'

'New contact bearing zero four zero. Range five thousand metres.' The watch keeper, his face a ghoulish green as he peered down into the radar display, was calm as he reported this latest development. 'Wasn't there before, sir. Can only be a submarine – must have just surfaced.' At exactly that moment a terse message from the radio shack came over the tannoy.

'Bridge, we have a signal from USS Decatur demanding we heave to. Any reply?'

All eyes went to Whichelow, who chomped on his cigar ruminatively.

'No reply. Maintain radio silence and ask the launch team how long before we can fire.'

There was a brief silence.

'Launch team advise all missiles ready to fire now, sir.'

Whichelow turned to encompass all assembled on the darkened bridge. He was smiling.

'Gentlemen. It seems we will begin our enterprise rather earlier than originally planned. However, I have no doubt we shall succeed ...'

'The submarine is calling again, sir.'

Whichelow ignored the radio shack.

'Fire all missiles and initiate Exodus.'

To Hawkhurst's amazement a whoop of joy went up from the crew manning the bridge. Some clapped, some punched the air, others exchanged handshakes. Taken aback and horrified at the inexorable turn of events, he stepped forward to stare down the length of the ship's dimly lit deck.

'Launch control reports firing sequence initiated, sir.'

First there was a dim glow up at the distant bow, a vague ellipse of light, as the hatch above the launch tube was slid back. Then another and then another.

God. Tom thought. They're going to fire all three missiles.

'Submarine calling again, sir. Respond to my signal immediately or I will open fire.'

There was a flash and puff of white smoke as the white, pencil slim fuselage of the first Tomahawk slid slowly and menacingly from its launcher, the deep throated roar of its engine vibrating the glass of the wheelhouse windows. Above the bows of the ship the missile arced slowly, almost gracefully, into its pre-planned flight path and then soared away. As the stubby wings deployed Tom caught a glimpse of the hated red sword insignia. Then it was gone, a flickering acetylene flare scant metres above the black sea that diminished and finally disappeared in the night. Long before it had vanished over the horizon, however, the next missile was already aloft and outward bound. Within a matter of minutes all three were out of sight. It had begun.

'I think the submarine has launched a missile at us, sir.' The watch keeper's eyes flicked nervously from the radar screen to the darkness outside. A pinpoint of light was weaving its way across the black sea between the invisible submarine and the Nagasaki Maru. Tom checked his watch; it was time to get out. But first, he slid the knife from his pocket and turned to where, seconds before, Whichelow had stood. That space was now empty, only the crew remaining at their stations and, fearing Whichelow had designs on the lifeboat, Hawkhurst quit the bridge and headed aft at the double, cursing as he went.

To his relief only Potgeiter lurked there in the shadows, Angahrad already having climbed into the boat.

'Get aboard, Piet. The bloody balloon's gone up. There's an incoming missile on its way.'

The South African needed little encouragement and within seconds they had joined Angahrad in the steel cocoon of the lifeboat. Slamming the hatch shut behind him Tom took in his surroundings. The inside of the boat was bathed in dull yellow emergency lighting. Angahrad, wearing a lifejacket now smiled weakly as he climbed inside and blew him a kiss. He grinned back – at least they were all still alive. As Potgeiter hammered at the stubborn retaining pins that kept the lifeboat in place, from forward there came a deep throated rumble and the Nagasaki Maru shook from stem to stern as the missiles struck home. Normally the first missile would have been fired across the bows of the tanker as a warning to heave to but today it seemed the US Navy wasn't too concerned with nautical etiquette.

As the last pin came free the lifeboat began to descend on its steel cable falling towards the sea. It dropped slowly at first but gathered momentum all the time and Tom braced himself against the impact, a steadying arm about Angahrad's shoulders. With a sickening jar they smacked into the sea and all three were thrown sprawling into the scuppers of the life boat which was shortly being tossed about on the churning wake of the tanker like a leaf in a maelstrom. Eventually, as they drifted away into the night, the motion eased and they climbed unsteadily to their feet.

The life boat was a totally enclosed construction, a fat cigar of solid steel, the only openings being a few port holes and the steel hatch in its port side. Its design incorporated massive inbuilt buoyancy chambers that would make it virtually unsinkable. Once they were clear of the wash from the Nagasaki Maru, Potgeiter pulled the hatch door open and they stared up at the towering mass of the vessel. She was still underway but moving much slower now. Despite the threat to the shaft bearing it looked as though they had decided to risk a manoeuvre astern after all, perhaps trying to evade further missiles. Tom wasn't too worried by this. They had plenty to keep them occupied. He turned to the others, his face grave.

'They launched the missiles,' he said simply. 'I couldn't stop them.'

'Fuck,' Potgeiter's curse was almost inaudible. He shrugged: 'So what happens next?'

'There's an American submarine lying off somewhere to the north of us. There are other vessels heading this way too. I guess there's nothing more we can do but sit and watch.'

They returned to the open hatchway. Across the intervening waters now came the sound of aircraft engines being revved up and the hydraulic groan of the flight deck lifts. They were evacuating the Nagasaki Maru. It could only be that for, if Whichelow was to be believed, they were still too far from their target to launch any ground attack. However, it seemed doubtful if many would succeed for Tom now saw another light come swerving across the sea towards the stricken tanker and knew the submarine had fired again. Having observed the Tomahawks being launched the Captain wouldn't want to give Whichelow the opportunity to fire any more that might be on board. They were closing in for the kill. Fascinated, Tom pointed, and all three of them followed its path, recoiling at the impact as it slammed into the Nagasaki Maru, hitting the tanker's port side amidships. There was a brief silence then all hell broke loose. A ball of yellow flame billowed skyward, the heat of the explosion singeing the flesh on their faces and arms even at that distance. Instinctively they all turned away from the searing fireball, crouching in terror behind the boat's steel canopy. Potgeiter slammed the hatch shut.

'Must have hit the aviation fuel stowage. We've got to get as far away from here as possible. She's packed with ammunition – if the magazines go up and she goes down fast she'll suck us under with her. He moved quickly aft removing a varnished housing that concealed a small diesel engine and tossing it aside. He studied the engine briefly then, taking the tiller, switched on the batteries and pressed the start button. The start motor whirled and the engine coughed briefly then died. Potgeiter cursed, adjusted the throttle and pressed again.

'Come on you bitch,' he grated. This time the engine coughed again, faded, hung on, then finally caught and roared into life. He smiled broadly, turning the lifeboat's stern to the tanker and taking them into the safety of the night.

Tom returned to the porthole, staring back in disbelief at the horror they had so narrowly escaped. The Nagasaki Maru was burning fiercely along the whole length of her flight deck now, flames of electric blue like huge blow torches, roaring up from below through the open lifts. So far as he could see no helicopter had succeeded in escaping but small pathetic figures, some with their clothes and hair on fire, were now hurling themselves from the flight deck into the sea. It was the equivalent of a leap from a five storey building. He doubted any would survive the impact and tried to imagine the awful inferno below decks that drove them to such a pitch of desperation. Nearly three thousand men packed in cheek by jowl like animals, were trapped inside a steel crematorium. The thought made his stomach churn but he recognised there was nothing he could do. He turned his thoughts to more important matters – to survival.

'I think we'll keep well out of the way till morning,' he said softly. 'No point in blundering about trying to find any friendly vessels. If we come sailing out of the night they might mistake us for the Church's people and open fire. These boats are fitted with automatic emergency signal systems so someone will find us eventually.'

Angharad was by his side watching in mute horror. The shouts of desperate, dying men swimming in the blazing water, perhaps five hundred metres away, came to them clearly. Her voice was small, frightened.

'Will we go back to pick up survivors?' she asked.

Hawkhurst looked at her. The boat was designed to carry up to fifty survivors according to the instructions stencilled on the bulkhead, twice that number at a pinch. There were emergency medical kits, food and water available on board as well.

'No.' He said shortly, turning his face away from her. 'They weren't the kind of people to show any mercy. Let 'em swim.'

From astern came a low rumble and he returned to the hatch. Clearly there had been further explosions aboard, probably in the magazines low down inside the hull below the waterline and ammunition, bombs, shells, grenades were 'cooking off'. The Nagasaki Maru, rapidly breaking up, was now well down by the bows, her single screw, still slowly turning, almost clear of the water. Another thunderous rumble rolled across the water to them and the huge vessel settled lower in the water. Then before their eyes, like a sleeping man, she rolled easily over onto her starboard side, the full length of her keel rearing above the sea, cascading black water, as she went into her death plunge. In a matter of seconds she was lost to sight and gone forever. Tom breathed out his tension.

'She's gone, Piet. That last explosion must have ripped her bottom out. We'd better come round. She'll have pushed up a hell of a swell – we'll be better heading in to it rather than let it take us by the stern.'

Potgeiter nodded grimly and brought the helm over.

'I can't see anything from here,' he said. 'Open the hatch and stick your head out, Tom. Let me know when we're about to hit it. Make sure you shut it before we do.'

Hawkhurst peered ahead into the darkness. As the blazing ship had gone down she had taken the light with her and now he stared with slitted eyes into the blackness, trying to discern sky from sea. As the seconds ticked away he could see nothing and began to wonder if their fears had been unfounded. Perhaps the Nagasaki Maru had gone gently into her final voyage to the bottom. Then he gasped, gritting his teeth to master the fear that dried his mouth like parchment. The wave was almost on them roaring out of the night, its jagged peak rearing thirty feet above the tiny lifeboat. It seemed at that moment like some Jurassic sea monster hell bent on their destruction. He slammed the hatch shut and swung the securing clips home.

'Now, Piet. The bloody thing's on us!'

As he spoke the bow of the boat jerked skywards and he was thrown backwards between the seats. For what seemed like hours but was probably less than ten seconds it felt as if they were vertical, the boat standing on its stern as it climbed the leading edge of the wave. Any minute it seemed she would be turned beam on to the relentless surge, roll over, and be carried under. Only Potgeiter's strength saved them. Both massive hands on the tiller he wrestled to keep her head on to the onslaught, his teeth clenched in effort and concentration. Then, as swiftly as it had struck, the behemoth was gone, its great black shoulder rolling away into the darkness to be followed by a series of other, still frightening but decreasingly threatening, waves. It was about half an hour before the motion had finally subsided. In the time since the first wave had struck no one had uttered a word. It was Potgeiter who broke the silence.

'I make it three thirty five so we've got about three hours before daylight. We'll switch the engine off now and drift till then. We'll keep watches. Tom, you take the first watch. I'm gonna grab some shuteye, call me at six.'

Constructing a makeshift yet comfortable mattress from lifejackets, of which there was a plentiful supply aboard, he settled himself into the bottom of the lifeboat and in minutes was asleep. Tom stared out into the darkness. Out there men, thousands of men, had died in the space of less than an hour. What few survivors had managed to scramble from that man-made hell were now probably suffering a similar, more lingering, fate. He could feel no sorrow for the dead, destruction was what they craved and destruction they got. But everything was overshadowed by the awful, empty feeling that the missiles had flown and would soon, if they had not already, kill millions. He doubted Whichelow would worry overmuch about that, he had done his duty to God as he saw it and that was all that would matter. By dawn the final battle, the battle to determine which deity should inherit the Third Millennium, would begin and the world would never be the same again. Angahrad, catching his mood came to his side, curling an arm about his shoulders.

'It's not your fault, Tom. You did everything you could to stop it. Perhaps that madman Whichelow was right. Perhaps it is God's will.'

'Then God is evil,' he said bitterly.

'Perhaps,' she said, looking away.

CHAPTER TWENTY SIX

At first light Hawkhurst shook Potgeiter and Angahrad. Yawning he handed them each a bar of high protein chocolate and a mug of water from the emergency rations. It was chilly and condensation dripped from the steel canopy of the lifeboat.

'Breakfast,' he said. 'Bit spartan, I'm afraid, but with any luck we shouldn't be here too long.' He hesitated, looking now directly at Angahrad and jerking his head towards the open hatch. 'Better be prepared for a bit of a shock when you look out, darling.'

She frowned, brushing her tangled hair out of her eyes and hoisting herself up on one elbow to stare outside. It was misty, a clammy uniform greyness that obscured the horizon with a low hazy halo of pearl light, behind it that was the sun. The sea was flat calm and oily with the smell of diesel and carbon pervading everything.

'What's that?' she asked sleepily, pointing to something black that floated inertly about twenty metres from the lifeboat.

'A body,' he grunted. 'They've been floating past all night. I've been fending them off with the boat hook. You really don't want a close up, some of them are pretty badly burned.'

She saw others now, perhaps a dozen or so within the limited circle of visibility. They all lay face down in the water, arms encumbered by bulky lifejackets outstretched in front of them as though, too late, they were raising their arms in surrender. Beneath their lifejackets some wore full combat gear, others pyjamas while some were naked. Between the floating bodies drifted other wreckage from the tanker, a pathetic collection of empty life jackets, plastic bottles, clothing and magazines. When the second missile from the submarine had ripped the side of the Nagasaki Maru wide open these men would have been below, marshalling the ingrained discipline needed to meet an emergency that had fallen upon them without warning. As the huge vessel had capsized and settled on the bottom they had floated to the surface through the shattered hull. When, in the early hours, Tom had seen the first dead man coming bobbing towards him across the oily waters he had hooked it with the boathook and pulled it alongside. His anger had subsided now and he would have been prepared to take survivors aboard had there been any. It had been horrific: a lipless grin and eyeless sockets in flesh burned to blackened meat by the exploding aviation fuel. After that he had not bothered, content to push any that came close away into the cloaking darkness of the night.

'Once this mist lifts I reckon we'll be picked up pretty quickly,' he said. 'I've heard the sound of engines a couple of times but these conditions must be making things difficult for them.'

Thus far none of them had seen fit to mention the black dread that hung foremost in their thoughts. A few hours ago three nuclear weapons, the first to be fired in anger since Hiroshima and Nagasaki more than fifty years ago, had been launched toward the east. By now they would have struck home and the inevitable political and military repercussions would be in train. Drifting silently there among the dead, the only sound the gentle hollow slapping of waves against the hull, such a thought seemed totally inconceivable, yet it had happened. With his own eyes Hawkhurst had watched the missiles fly and they had all witnessed the first victims of the war, the Nagasaki Maru and her crew, go to their death. What other horrors were now being enacted elsewhere they could only surmise. To him it almost seemed as if to stay where they were, isolated and at the mercy of the elements but with food and shelter enough to sustain them for months, might be preferable to finding out. Potgeiter, still reclining in the bottom of the boat munching appreciatively on his chocolate bar, had no such doubts. He raked his fingers through his cropped hair as if gathering his sleep scattered thoughts.

'No point hanging around. We might as well go and look for them. Any idea where the sound came from?'

Tom pointed.

'To the east, but it could have been boats or choppers. I couldn't really tell. They were a long way off.'

Potgeiter got to his feet and went to the engine, bringing it coughing to life.

They nosed cautiously through the greyness, Potgeiter at the helm, Angahrad and Tom sitting at the hatchway, easing through the sea of bodies, nudging them unprotestingly aside as they went. A book floated past, blue bound, its open pages spread like wings on the water. Angahrad leant over the side and scooped it up. It was a Bible. Inside, written on the flysheet in water-smeared biro was a dedication. *To Michael, Hoping you will fight the good fight. Love Mum and Dad, Twin falls,*

August 23rd, 1995.' She looked at it sadly for a moment then tossed it back into the water.

After half-an-hour the scatter of bodies and wreckage on the water began to thin out but, although they heard the sound of aircraft flying over on several occasions, the mist remained stubbornly in place. Not until well after ten o'clock did it begin to disperse and the sun's rays filtered through to play weakly upon the sea. For the first time rescue hung over the boat like a tangible weight. Aboard the Nagasaki Maru, Hawkhurst had been subjected to a continual stream of information about what was going on in the outside world, much of it so horrible he had at times wished he could have been spared it. Now there was nothing, just the limits of imagination which were infinite. He returned inside to relieve Potgeiter at the helm. The South African, his foot steadying the tiller, had opened a can of corned beef and was spooning the dry meat into his mouth. He was deep in thought.

'What do you figure on doing after all this is over, Tom?' he asked, passing the tiller to the Englishmen. Hawkhurst shrugged.

'Get back to the mountains and stay there. I had everything I needed there. I was a forgotten man so far as my career was concerned and I was up to my neck in hock to the bank. But I could just about handle that.' He nodded towards the hatchway which framed Angie's bare feet hanging from the deck above. 'I had, still have, a good woman and the chance of a future. Whichelow's plans would have gone ahead regardless of whether we'd unearthed the Grail or not but at least Angahrad and I are observers of whatever history is going to throw up. With luck we'll come through this safely, Piet, and then you won't see me for dust. I'm all for the quiet life from now on. I want to be as far away from the action as possible and I want to be damn sure Angie isn't in the firing line again.' He remembered the thirty thousand dollars the Church had paid him and took heart. Then his gaze went to the South African. He couldn't imagine the quiet life suiting Potgeiter. 'What about you?'

'Depends. If that cheque hasn't bounced,' he laughed harshly. 'I guess Whichelow's not in a position to cancel cheques anymore, I'll buy another plane and carry on. Wars are always good for my line of business.'

Sitting there, the low steady putter of the engine between them and the gentle tug of the tiller in his hand, Tom thought for the first time about Laura. He was not surprised to find he was saddened by her death, recalling the days when they had been so close, yet he was well aware that she had not hesitated to use him without compunction and, even if she hadn't been fully aware of the lunatic scope of Whichelow's plans, the part she had played in aiding them had been decisive. Mary Lou, McNaughton and Whichelow were in a different league, they were evil people and his only regret was that their deaths had come too late to prevent the coming misery and pain. To his mind Laura was a somewhat different case: she was vain and arrogant yet he considered her foolish rather than wicked.

'I think I can see something.' Angahrad's voice came distantly from outside and Hawkhurst killed the engine. Quickly all three of them were standing on the narrow strip of deck that ran around the lifeboat, straining their eyes. The mist had nearly gone by now and there, lying dead in the water on the horizon to the north, was the faintest hint of darkness that they knew was the hull of another vessel. Going below Tom returned with a couple of parachute flares from the emergency pack. Aiming the first into such little wind as there was he pulled the lanyard down sharply and fired it, sending the red glowing projectile hissing skywards. As the first flare reached its apogee and, with its parachute deploying, began its slow descent, he fired the second.

'They've seen us, they're turning this way.' Angahrad waved her hands over her head and they watched as the distant vessel came towards them picking up speed as she approached and circling wide around them before decelerating, finally coming to a neatly judged halt alongside the clumsy lifeboat, bobbing slightly in the water, her engines growling. A battered visage thrust out of the wheelhouse of the newcomer.

'Dr Hawkhurst, I presume.'
Tom smiled. It was Harry Brennan.

*****

Once they had transferred to the Lucia Silvio, the possibility of salvage money in mind and determined to make the most of the situation, took the lifeboat in tow. This done, they headed north-west for the Italian port of Brindisi. Hawkhurst, Potgeiter and Angie stood outside in the strengthening sunshine eager for news.

'Well it's bad,' Brennan told them. 'But not as bad as it might have been. Luckily, thanks to Silvio's report, we were able to find you. Using satellite surveillance we scanned the Nagasaki Maru and detected nuclear weapons aboard. Of course, that started alarms going off in Washington and then – better late than never – we got all the co-operation we needed at last. The navy deployed ships in an anti-aircraft screen across the eastern Mediterranean and we put the Patriot missile batteries in Israel on alert. Two of the Tomahawks were shot down over the sea but the third, God knows where it was intended for, maybe Baghdad, came down in Jordan. Luckily it fell in a very remote area. That, plus the fact it was a comparatively small tactical warhead of around one megaton, means we should count our blessings. The official line being put out by the US government is that it was a tragic accident and that the missile came from a US warship as the result of an accidental firing during exercises. It's pretty galling for the navy having to take responsibility for that kind of crap but better than letting the truth get out.'

'Thank God casualties were light but of course the militants have made the most of it and there's a hell of a row going on. There's a full scale uprising on the West Bank and Syria has moved tanks up close to the Golan. Saddam has displayed at least ten Scuds which were supposed to have been destroyed during the Gulf War. He says they are chemically armed and aimed at Israel. It's a nice touch, using chemical weapons. Even if we can hit them in the air it only serves to disperse the chemical agents over a wider area. The US has protested of course and threatened reprisals against anyone who launches any attack on Israel but, after an accidental nuclear strike on a nominally friendly power, we're hardly in a position to claim the moral high ground.'

'What about the new peace initiative?' Even as he asked Tom realised how naïve the question sounded. Brennan shrugged.

'Forget it. Even the Saudis have been well and truly pissed off by this episode. If they weren't so fucking greedy they might just cut off the West's oil. Everything's on hold. The only hope is that no one acts too hastily. But that's not all, Tom. It's even more complicated than that. What time did the Nagasaki Maru go down last night do you reckon?'

Tom blinked, amazed to realise that only fourteen or so hours ago he had been seated at dinner with Whichelow and his crew.

'Around nine thirty I guess, maybe a little later.' He smiled. 'I didn't consult my watch, Harry, things were a little hectic on board.'

Brennan nodded.

'That more or less fits in with what the Captain of the Decatur said.' He looked at Hawkhurst closely. 'And you say the last you saw of Whichelow was about half an hour before that?'

'Yes. Once the submarine opened fire he and McNaughton disappeared.'

'Did they manage to launch any choppers so far as you can tell?'

'Not that I saw. Why?'

'At three o'clock Central European time this morning the Reverend James J. Whichelow, or someone purporting to be him, was on the phone to the President of the United States deploring the current situation and offering the Church of Christ the Warrior's good offices in any peace initiatives. He has, within the last hour, also made a personal appeal for Firdasi to end his retreat so that the pair of them can unite in prayers for peace and discuss what can be done to produce their own peace plans.'

Tom stared.

'What?'

'Not only that, supposedly at the insistence of his friends in the French Government, Cardinal Martinette has conveniently elected to end his retreat at some remote Spanish monastery in order to speak on French television this evening. Of course, until you told us about his being on the Nagasaki Maru, we didn't have anything on His Eminence. Now it begins to make sense, they must have had a fall back plan, just in case things didn't work out.'

Tom recalled the last frantic moments on the bridge of the doomed vessel. Initiate operation Exodus, Whichelow had said. It began to add up. That would have been why they hadn't bothered with the lifeboat. They must have had at least one helicopter on standby – just in case.

'You mean to say they're still out there, after everything they've done?'

'It looks that way. It wouldn't be too difficult for Martinette to get to northern Spain from here but I don't see how Whichelow could have got back to Gethsemane in time. Maybe he wasn't calling from

Gethsemane or maybe it wasn't him at all but it means that we're going to have a hell of a job tying him in with the Nagasaki Maru.

The agency's doing its best to get some firm action against the Church but the President's got plenty on his mind at the moment and Whichelow doesn't come very high on his priorities. All it means is the son of a bitch has gotten himself an alibi.'

They were entering the outer harbour of Brindisi now and Silvio, aware of the need for speed, threaded his way through the crowded car ferries that hooted angrily at his impertinence. The port was busy. As elsewhere, with war looming, prudent Muslims who could afford the inflated fares were getting out of Italy and European Christians were coming home. There was a strong security presence all around the harbour with police and soldiers at every corner. Even on the fishing quay armed police patrolled, mainly searching for fleeing Albanians who might seek to enter the country illegally. Minorities everywhere lived in the perpetual fear of atrocity and counter atrocity. As the Lucia tied up alongside the harbour wall, a black-windowed limousine pulled up at the head of the seaweed slimed stone steps that led up. Having thanked Silvio for his efforts on their behalf they made their way carefully up to the waiting car that Brennan had organised.

*****

Brennan had booked them into a modest three star hotel built into a hillside just outside the town. It was adequate but hardly picturesque, giving as it did a broad panorama of cranes and petro-chemical installations that stretched away down the Adriatic coast. Once they had settled in and showered they assembled in the American's room. He handed them all a drink and then sat down.

'I'm sorry about this, guys, but I have to give you some sort of de-briefing. I've still got to get after Whichelow and his cronies. But it's not going to be easy. Unless I can tie him in with the task force and that nuclear strike he'll walk away from this scot free. I need hard evidence and I need it quickly. We've got divers down on the Nagasaki Maru now and from what I can see the only survivors were yourselves and Whichelow's group. It's very messy, and politically embarrassing. Right now bodies in US uniforms are being washed up all along the Libyan and Egyptian coasts and, naturally, people are drawing their own conclusions. Gadaffi and others have already made the connection with the nuclear strike in Jordan. Tehran, Tripoli, Baghdad are all calling it evidence of an abortive invasion attempt – another Bay of Pigs – and claim the US is behind it. Given the amount of US equipment stored aboard the Nagasaki Maru it's hard to argue with them.'

Potgeiter sipped his drink thoughtfully.

'But surely if Tom, Angie and I gave evidence about what we've seen it would be enough to put Whichelow and the rest of them away for good.'

Brennan shook his head and smiled ruefully.

'It might not be enough. We flooded agents into Gethsemane a couple of hours after his phone call to the White House. There he was, large as life, and Mary Lou with him, carrying on as though nothing had happened. We've got people going over Reachwood with a fine tooth comb but they've come up with nothing exciting. The place has been sanitised – converted into an adventure camp for boy scouts would you believe? As we know, Martinette hasn't been missed at all so there's nothing we can touch him for. There're no reports on McNaughton but, according to our London office, Laura Woods turned up for work at the museum this morning.'

Tom blinked, so Laura was alive too. He was glad, although he couldn't say why.

'Then you think they're going to get away with it. Is that what you're saying, Harry?'

Brennan sighed.

'Unless we can get some hard evidence they might. In the end it could come down to your word against theirs. Think of it. The word of a man of God, a man who is on first name terms with the President, against that of a grave robber and a mercenary. A good attorney would have a field day. Of course, we'll have them all on file from now on, Tom, so they won't be able to put another operation like this together in a hurry. But then again, maybe they won't need to. Seems to me they've more or less achieved their aims already. It's better than evens Iran will sanction anti-US actions. Trouble is, we can't pre-empt anything now, not after we've taken the blame for Whichelow's strike. We can only wait and react to events.'

Brennan leaned forward and switched on the TV. Tom's Italian was not good enough to enable him to understand the finer detail of the commentary but the pictures of white clad men in respirators standing in the desert looking down into a huge, blackened abyss were eloquent enough. Brennan grunted.

'We've put monitoring teams in and relief operations are under way. So far as we can see casualties are confined to a small village that was just on the fringe of the detonation. Four hundred was the last count, mainly dead; just what the final body count will be is anyone's guess. We've no idea how far or in which direction the nuclear fallout will drift.' He rubbed his face in his hands. He hadn't slept for two days. 'God, what an almighty fuck up.' He brightened up.

'One other thing. Since they've decided to play the innocent we don't want them to know that you three have survived. Not for the moment anyway. It's reasonable to think they will assume you went down with the ship and are no longer any threat. Let's encourage that line of thinking. What I'd like you all to do is to go home and carry on as if nothing had happened – for the time being at any rate. If they think they're safe they may get careless. Also, if they think you're still alive, they may decide to have you eliminated. As you know they are not nice people. I suggest you and Angahrad go back to the farm, Tom, it's pretty remote and the locals know nothing about your involvement with the Nagasaki Maru. I suggest you, Piet, take a trip back to the Republic – spend some of Whichelow's money on a new plane.' He smiled. 'The agency have checked your account and the money went in on schedule. I'll give you a number where you can contact me if anything occurs to you or if you feel you need protection. For the time being we'll just have to wait and see. I'm going to be busy over the next few days but I'll make contact within a week. Until then just go home and pray.'

CHAPTER TWENTY SEVEN

Back at the farm it took some time before anything like a normal routine was achieved. Thanks to Llew's attentions none of the animals had suffered during Angahrad's absence and despite her sorrow at the loss of her dogs she was soon training a pair of replacements of which great things were expected. Determined to keep close to her in case of danger, Hawkhurst had transferred his few belongings from the cottage to Sarnafon and now passed the days helping out around the farm while continuing to monitor events in the outside world through TV and radio. Brennan had emphasised the importance of keeping a low profile for the time being and accordingly Angahrad kept her visits to the village to a minimum. This was probably unnecessary for no one there was likely to connect them with the apocalyptic events unfolding in the Middle East. They did not, however, want to invite prying from Powell and his cronies for Hawkhurst's suspicious disappearance along with the Grail had been widely reported. Brennan remained elusive and it was well over a month now since they had last seen the American, although he had phoned on two occasions to ensure all was well with them and to give them such information he had about Whichelow.

This was considerable since, unlike them, the Reverend had made a point of placing himself firmly in the public eye during the period since the abortive crusade, positively courting attention with his statesmanlike homilies and Christian exhortations for moderation in the West's relations with Islam. On repeated occasions he had appealed for Firdasi to come out of his solitude to talk peace but The Master had remained elusive. Whichelow had also been seen several times at the White House and clearly continued to enjoy the President's confidence. Also, he had toured extensively across the States preaching brotherly love and forgiveness while at the same time subtly emphasising the full evil of what he was proposing his audience should forgive. Even the thick-as-pigshit red necks who formed a large part of his burgeoning congregation got the message: Love thy neighbour but don't take any crap from him. This did nothing to actually diminish the chance of war which was still very real indeed. Military forces remained at a high state of alert everywhere and the internal ethnic conflict continued to fester. In Northern Ireland Protestants and Catholics were now standing aside from their traditional mutual hatred to burn Pakistani corner shops and Indian restaurants, indifferent to the religion of the owners. As a quid pro quo Christians in many Muslim countries daily went in fear of the bomb and the gun and the tourist industry in these areas had virtually collapsed. The economic effects of declining trade on those Islamic countries not blessed with oil were severe and another cause of simmering resentment.

The Americans, badly wrong footed by Whichelow's botched nuclear strike, remained very much on the defensive, restricted to making low-key diplomatic or even lower key military intervention and so stepped back. The State of Israel had not been deserted by its allies but it was no longer enjoying the same level of backing it was accustomed to in the UN. Even friendly powers were becoming increasingly critical of its current vigorous, some would say brutal, response to Palestinian rioting on the West Bank and Gaza.

It was inevitably difficult for Tom and Angahrad to slip easily back into a routine that had been so savagely disrupted by the interlude with Whichelow and the Church of Christ the Warrior. The matter of Suzie, his infidelity with the girl and her subsequent death, still weighed heavily on Hawkhurst's conscience as, to a lesser extent, did his easy but essential seduction of Laura in the museum vault. He had not opened up with Angahrad about either incident and knew now that he probably never would. She on the other hand still had nightmares about her captivity and humiliation at the hands of the Church's man. Each night she woke whimpering, half expecting to see him rearing above her, choking on the thick, hot fluid in her throat. Then she would sigh in relief and turning over would burrow her face into the solid, reassuring bulk of Tom's back, wondering if she should tell him the sordid details of her imprisonment. She did not. They were still as loving as ever but both noticed that there were silences between them now which had not been there before as each mentally re-lived the traumatic events of the immediate past. In the evenings Tom would be totally absorbed by news of the world situation, switching from channel to channel, transferring his attentions between radio and TV. Angahrad on the other hand, wished for nothing better than to forget everything: if only she could block out the awful dreams of that sordid room.

And eventually she did just that. The spring turned to summer and the past, for Angahrad at least, slowly began to recede. The dreams became less frequent, the rhythm of life on the farm absorbed her again and she threw herself into the work with a vengeance. Tom, on the other hand, became ever more obsessed with events elsewhere, sitting morosely in front of the TV far into the night. Then, one evening as they sat outside the farm drinking red wine and watching the sun go down behind Cwmdower, he suddenly broke the silence.

'I'm thinking of going down to London,' he said.

Angahrad looked at him questioningly.

'Harry Brennan asked us to keep out of the way. It might make things difficult if you were spotted down there. If the Church thinks we are dead it means we are at least safe up here.'

'We can't hide forever,' he said shortly. 'It's been nearly seven weeks now since we got back and we've only heard from Brennan twice in that time.'

'What will you do down there?'

He shook his head.

'I'm not sure. Maybe I'll see what Laura is up to. If she's still in touch with Mary Lou she may have some idea about what the Church is planning next. I'm sure that bastard Whichelow hasn't given up his mad schemes. He'll know that things are very finely balanced now and that he must act quickly to maintain the momentum. There's the faintest glimmer of a new peace initiative being launched within a month or two. If that does happen it could mean all his plans will come to nothing and he'll want to avoid that at all costs. It's simply that we don't know what he has up his sleeve. The task force failed, just, but it caused enough trouble to keep things on the boil.'

'But if they know you're alive, they'll try to kill you, Tom. What good will that do?' She asked, a little desperately, for she knew there was little chance of dissuading him now.

'I don't think Laura will want that to happen. I think she was pretty shaken when she found out that the Church of Christ the Warrior wasn't the altruistic organisation she first thought. She was never really religious, anyway. I'm fairly certain her commitment to Whichelow was entirely bound up with her college friend McNally. I think a lot of Whichelow's supporters thought they were supporting a humane cause. There's another reason why talking to her now would be a good thing. For the last couple of weeks previews for the Age of

Arthur Exhibition have been appearing in the papers. I have no doubt, thinking we ended up at the bottom of the Mediterranean with the rest of those poor misguided devils, she will have doctored my report, the Penda penny will have been removed from the coin collection, and all her thoughts will be on making a success of the exhibition. The report, along with the miraculous recovery of the Holy Grail, means no one will be likely to carry out another scientific analysis of the finds for many years. She's home and dry. If I know Laura, having come so close to disaster once, she'll be concentrating on getting on with her career. When I turn up she'll be so surprised I don't think she'll make any waves. I intend to make it clear that if she helps us I won't spoil her chances of a seat on the museum board. If she won't I shall make her life much more complicated. She'll understand the situation perfectly.'

Angahrad slipped her arm around his neck and kissed him. She had often sensed there was something more, something that ran deeper in his desire to pursue the thing that would not let him rest. Twice in his sleep he had cried out a girl's name. Suzie! She had not mentioned it to him nor did she feel any threat from the unknown girl. She felt secure in his love and recognised that it was something only he could come to terms with, as she had to come to terms with her own personal nightmare.

'Whatever you think is right. Just be careful, that's all I ask.'

He pulled her close, nuzzling his face in the fragrance of her hair, his hand sliding to the warmth of her breast. Then the phone rang and he gave a grunt of disgust. It was Brennan. The American had little new information to offer beyond what Tom had already gleaned from other sources and he listened attentively as Hawkhurst told him of his plans to sound Laura out. Tom had half expected he would be opposed to any such move but in fact Brennan, perhaps having exhausted all other avenues and out of options, proved cautiously agreeable.

'It could be dangerous, Tom,' he said. 'But, so long as you don't put Potgeiter and Angahrad at risk it might be worthwhile, I guess. Once they know you're alive things could really take a lively turn. It will hopefully make them nervous enough to show their hand. Tell you what, I'm going to be in London the day after tomorrow, I'll be around to provide back up if they get muscular. The agency have already told the British police that you are back in the country and not to be apprehended. The museum has got the Grail back and has agreed to drop any charges relating to the theft, so I don't think that will pose a problem.'

Tom considered Brennan's proposal to act together and had to admit it made sense. They would liaise before he revealed himself to Laura. He gave Brennan the name of the hotel where he had stayed with Angie on the day of the press conference and they agreed they would meet for lunch at Smollensky's on the Friday. Before Brennan rang off, Tom put in one final request.

'Can you get me a gun, Harry? Something not too big but powerful enough to stop a man in his tracks. Mine went down with the Nagasaki Maru.'

'Consider it done, old buddy.'

*****

The restaurant was deserted when Hawkhurst entered, a little after midday, so he went to the bar and ordered a beer. He hadn't been in London for two months and after the peace and quiet of Sarnafon its pace and bustle grated on his nerve-ends. It wasn't just the usual hustle and bustle, there was war fever in the air. The news stall placards announced rioting in Israel but they had probably not been changed in days, continuing to reflect the situation in the country. He bought an early edition *Evening Standard* and flicked through the litany of violence from around the world. While all eyes were on the Middle East, however, the slow working poison was seeping through societies everywhere. As his train had pulled through the suburbs he had seen a row of eight terraced houses, burnt out and their roofs fallen in. He had read about the incident in the nationals a week before. Seventeen people had died in the fire which had clearly been started deliberately. The dead had all been young Hindus. Every wall that faced onto the railway line had been defaced with graffiti – racist, religious, war-mongering. Wogs out! Niggers out! Crusade now! Take up the sword! And, occasionally, a defiant Allah Akbar! He was surprised to see that along with this depressingly mindless litany of hatred had appeared a rash of fly posters showing a stern-faced Whichelow. Beneath the unsmiling features in large white capitals was a single word – Prepare! Prepare for what, he wondered?

'Terrible isn't it.' It was the barmaid who spoke, nodding at the paper that lay before him on the bar. She was young and plump with a friendly rounded face that for him was only slightly marred by the row of gold studs around the arch of each ear. She wore a too tight white sweater and a short black skirt that revealed sturdy rather than shapely legs. Yet it wasn't her physical appearance that gained his undivided attention but the small enamelled pin brooch that she wore upon her ample left breast. There could be no mistaking the flaming red sword emblem and Hawkhurst felt a frisson shiver through him. He stayed calm. Surely they would never be so obvious as to send a spy who advertised.

'Dreadful.'

'I reckon there's going to be a war.' Her accent was south London. 'My boyfriend says it'll be a good thing too. Get it over with. There'll never be any lasting peace until we've sorted them Arabs out.' She cast a wary glance about her to see who might be listening. 'And the ones over here too – the way they stole that Holy Grail.'

He nodded in a vaguely agreeing fashion then pointed to the brooch.

'That's attractive.'

She giggled suggestively.

'My boyfriend got it for me – he's a fan of that Reverend Whichelow.' She screwed her nose up. 'Church of the Warriors or something? All his mates are wearing them. We're going to see his show when he comes over next month.'

This was news to Hawkhurst and he was keen to learn more. Unfortunately the arrival of more customers, this time a pair of German tourists, took her to the other end of the bar and it was several minutes before she returned.

'This Reverend Whichelow. Who is he?' he asked innocently.

'Oh, he's some kind of preacher,' clearly her interest in the man himself was limited, 'he reckons the Americans and us should take charge in the Middle East.'

'Us?'

'You know, Christian countries. He reckons we should put the Arabs in their place, stop them attacking Israel all the time. My boyfriend reckons he's right. Sort 'em out once and for all.'

Hawkhurst could imagine the boyfriend.

'And you say this Reverend Whichelow is coming over here?'

'S'right. He's doing a European tour, he's at Wembley next month.'

'Prepare!' Now he understood.

He ordered another beer and took it to a window seat to await Brennan's arrival. Outside in the Strand the lunch hour crowds were just beginning to leave their offices. It was a warm day and few wore coats. After five minutes he had counted nearly twenty of the red sword brooches parading past. Clearly Whichelow's malign influence was growing. Hawkhurst guessed it had been boosted by the backlash against the highly vocal outrage of the Arabs who had so nearly been blasted to kingdom-come by nuclear missiles. The last he had heard, Whichelow was preaching peace and reconciliation. Now it seemed he was coming out of the closet. It was a clever ploy, to tailor his message to what his audience flocked to hear. Give them what they wanted. As attitudes hardened in the West so the Reverend began to ratchet up his war-mongering. As he considered these developments Brennan arrived. He, too, had been shaken by the rash of red swords on the streets.

'I don't believe it. I'm sitting on a plane from Rome and the stewardess is wearing one – almost put me off my bourbon. When I get to Heathrow the bastard things are everywhere. I don't like it, Tom. We're just about keeping things under control in the Middle East and if we can get the peace initiative moving we might, with patience and a lot of luck, prevent war, maybe even get some sort of a lasting settlement. But if The Reverend is allowed to go around whipping up hysteria against the Islamic League it'll force them closer together and strengthen the influence of the hawks in Tehran and Tripoli. So far the United States has spent over fifty million dollars cleaning up the mess after the Tomahawk strike. We've managed to minimise the radiation risk although there's an area of a hundred square miles that'll be uninhabitable for the foreseeable future. By the time we've paid out compensation to the victims – just about everyone within a thousand miles seems to have lost his camel – we'll be looking at two billion dollars. And all the time we're trying to kiss it better we're getting nothing but abuse from all around the world. This is making a lot of people back home wonder if it wouldn't be better to walk away from it.'

'Walk away from it. How do you mean?'

'Accept that war is inevitable and act accordingly.' He lowered his voice. 'I've heard rumours that in the event of the peace initiative not getting off the ground, the Pentagon has already drawn up plans to put a large ground force into Israel and to seize oil producing facilities in Kuwait and Saudi.'

'And they think that will make for a lasting peace?' Hawkhurst was incredulous.

'Frankly, Tom, they don't give a flying fuck at the moment. They know we've got the technology and money to impose some kind of solution. The two overriding strategic aims are to ensure the survival of Israel and maintain oil supplies. They also know that the chances of anything nasty falling on them back home are very remote. So to a lesser extent do people in Europe. Basically they are fed up to the back teeth with the Middle East and they're increasingly calling for drastic action to settle things once and for all.'

'You know Whichelow's preaching over here soon?'

Brennan looked out of the window. A group of young men in shirt sleeves meandered past, each wearing the hated red sword.

'Yeah, I heard. Looks like he'll be preaching to the converted.'

Ordering lunch they continued to discuss developments. Brennan and his agency were still committed to bringing Whichelow and the Church to book and, more importantly, to giving the peace initiative every chance of success. However, he did not hide the fact that they were becoming something of a voice in the wilderness. In Washington the hawks, mainly Republicans, were now being listened to with increasing attentiveness and there was a growing consensus of opinion between the major industrialised powers that, while the prospect of war was horrible, it might in extremis be an acceptable alternative to the current endless impasse. The situation brought about by the cruise missiles of the Nagasaki Maru, despite its limited success, had engineered a situation very close to Whichelow's wildest dreams. Now it only needed one more push and the Third Millennium would belong to the Church of Christ the Warrior.

'If I can get any information out of Laura, I'll pass it straight on, Harry, but I'm pretty sure she was only peripheral to his grand scheme. She'll be scared, of course, but I don't see her being able to help us much. Let's hope she can get a message to Whichelow. Once he knows I'm still alive it may make him show his hand.' He eyeballed the American. 'Of course, there's one way to make all this academic –

can't your agency arrange an assassination, Harry? I know it's unethical but surely these circumstances call for desperate measures.'

Brennan shook his head firmly.

'It's too late for that. We considered it, of course, but we can't afford to make a martyr of him. He's building up such a following now that anything that happened to him would be blamed on Muslim terrorists. Things are bad enough for minorities these days – we can't risk a massacre.'

CHAPTER TWENTY EIGHT

Laura, hands on hips, stood back with her head slightly to one side and gave the poster a final critical scrutiny. The design team had done a good job; had got the emphasis exactly right, she decided. The tenor of the coming Age of Arthur exhibition was dramatically evoked by the figure of a mounted warrior, sword held high above his head, a round shield slung across his shoulder. Burning mystically in the background the Grail hung in the sky beyond. It was not a picture of the actual bowl they had excavated but close enough to stimulate the most stolid of imaginations. The whole poster glowed with subtle, subdued colour and was strikingly effective in conjuring the spirit, if not the reality, of the Dark Ages. More importantly, there at the bottom, foremost among the list of credits was her name: Exhibition Director, Laura Woods, BA BSc.

The past weeks had been a time of unremitting labour as the opening of the exhibition drew nearer. Every day had been a continuous round of meetings, consultations and marketing conferences. She had been glad of the distraction, it had served to keep the horrors of her brief sojourn aboard the Nagasaki Maru at bay. Even now she could not believe what had happened, even less that she had briefly stepped in and out of that nightmare scenario and escaped unscathed. She still worried every time the phone rang, fearing the Church might call on her services again, for, given the option, she wanted nothing more to do with them. In the first place, her only purpose had been to lend her influence and funds to an attempt to release an old friend from captivity, she told herself. She had supported the idea of a commando raid: nothing had been said about missiles.

None of it was her fault she told herself. Yet somehow she could not quite square her conscience with Hawkhurst's death. It had been her who involved him in the first place, thinking his part would be only functional and carrying no personal risk. Now he, along with thousands of others, was dead. She blamed Mary Lou Berkowitz for that, for it had been the American woman's obsession with the Grail that had led Hawkhurst, lured on by the siren song of fame and fortune, into his fatal involvement. Yet she also knew that it was only due to Mary Lou that she was alive today. When the second missile had struck home it had been she who insisted Laura be taken off the stricken tanker in the helicopter that was standing by to evacuate Whichelow and Martinette. Laura had seen the look in Whichelow's eyes and had known instinctively that he would have had no compunction about leaving her. It was only because, sensing the power she wielded within the Church, she had permitted Mary Lou to court her in the past and allowed her to take some limited liberties in the privacy of her cabin that she had survived. By no means a lesbian, nevertheless Laura had not been in the least put out by the older woman's advances, so long as they gave her some personal leverage. It had been this practical approach that had saved her life the night the Nagasaki Maru went down.

The thought of sex, even Mary Lou's clumsy fumbling, brought her back to life. Thankfully, the pressure of work had meant she had not seen very much of Dixey over the past few weeks. She was glad to be relieved of his attentions and suspected he might be equally happy to be free of the increasingly burdensome responsibility of pleasuring her. Whenever they met in passing he was still friendly enough but she sensed he was distancing himself from her, perhaps unsettled by the mysterious events surrounding the Grail and Hawkhurst's ominous disappearance. Laura didn't care anymore. Her place on the board was already guaranteed and, once the exhibition was opened, she would make her first moves towards ousting Dixey as Curator-General. It was a long term strategy, she knew, and one which would require some careful manoeuvring in the corridors of power, but nothing she couldn't handle. The first priority was to forge an alliance with Dixey's enemies. Luckily these were legion among the museum board and staff and she had already caught the eye of Martindale, the head of the manuscript department. The man's wife was a notorious lush with a wicked tongue and he would be easy to distract. He was also still comparatively young, no more than forty, and that would help to ensure the attraction was mutual. Once the exhibition was up and running she would invite him out for a drink. Putting these delicious musings aside, Laura got back to business. There was lots to do. Satisfied with the quality of the display material she phoned the agency to give them the go-ahead to print. Next week they would begin to appear all over London.

She glanced at her watch. It was nearly three pm and she hadn't had a chance to grab a bite to eat since that morning. In the outside office, Jan, her secretary, was painting her nails.

'I'm popping out for half an hour, Jan. I need some fresh air and a sandwich.' She was at the door before the girl responded.

'There was a call for you, Laura. A man. He wouldn't give a name. Just said he was an old friend and left a number for you to ring.' She wrinkled her nose. 'Said to say 'Armenia' and you would know.'

*****

By the time she entered the restaurant Laura's head was spinning. Her gaze swept around the crowded room, finally settling on the two men in the window. Hawkhurst, seeing her standing there, waved a cheery hand and beckoned her over. They had drawn up a chair ready for her and she sat down heavily, her eyes wide. She had already rehearsed her reaction to this bolt out of the blue.

'God, Tom, this is wonderful – I mean, I thought you were dead.'

Hawkhurst and Brennan, both comfortably replete after a meal and several drinks smiled at her consternation benignly.

'Dead? Good lord, no. May I introduce my friend Mr Smith.'

Laura recognised the scarred features as belonging to the man in the car outside her flat and smelled trouble here. She smiled politely but said nothing. In those few seconds she could see all her plans crumbling to dust.

'I thought you went down with the ship. Who else got away?' Her tone was one of pure compassion and concerned humanity but Hawkhurst was sufficiently on guard to avoid the trap.

'Only me. Everyone else is gone.'

She lay a comforting hand on his arm.

'Oh, Tom. I'm so sorry. Poor Angahrad.' She reached into her clasp bag and produced a handkerchief, dabbing moist eyes. 'And it's all my fault. If I hadn't taken her aboard ...'

He was at pains to reassure her that he bore her no malice. It was not entirely true but it would serve their purposes better if she were given plenty of rope.

'It wasn't your fault, Laura. A lot of people, myself included, were taken in by Whichelow and his lies. He's the one we're out to get and it has to be quickly if we're to avoid a war. Are you still in contact with the Church?'

She shook her head.

'No. They dropped me and Martinette off somewhere in southern Italy. That was the last I saw of them. We all went our separate ways after that. I hope I never have anything to do with them again.'

'You didn't think of going to the police and telling them what had happened aboard the Nagasaki Maru?'

She shook her head.

'No. To begin with I was too scared. Who would have believed me anyway? Then I guess I just wanted to get on with my life, try and put the whole thing behind me. I thought everyone else was dead so it wouldn't make any difference.' She laid her hand on his. 'It wouldn't bring you back.'

Hawkhurst smiled. Same old Laura: she could rationalise everything. In that sense she wasn't unlike Whichelow. For him God made everything OK, for her it was her career. The fact that the world teetered on the brink of disaster didn't enter into her calculations for a minute.

'How's the exhibition coming on?' He enquired casually.

His words brought a nervous tightening of her mouth.

'Fine, we open in two weeks' time. Why do you ask?'

'Just wondered what became of my report on the coins, that's all.'

'We managed to get Karelian to edit it for us.'

He raised a questioning eyebrow.

'Edit? It was finished. It didn't need editing.' His tone remained light, he wasn't intending to get heavy. Just let her sweat a little, he thought. 'You mean you removed the Penda mark and all reference to it and then asked him to give the coins the once over. Is that it, Laura?'

'Something like that.' Her tone was sullen. 'But it doesn't mean anything. You know damn well it didn't come from the tomb. You only put it there to blackmail me.'

Hawkhurst considered her words, taking his time, allowing the fragility of her position to sink in. He looked to Brennan.

'Do you think we should have another drink, Harry? I don't know about you but all this thinking gives me a terrific thirst.'

Brennan picked up his mood.

'It would be rude not to, Thomas, my boy.' He looked to Laura. 'What can I get you, Miss Woods?'

Laura hesitated, at that moment she wanted nothing more than to be as far away from that place as possible. However, she knew these men had the power to destroy her and her career forever, and the last thing she wanted was an ugly scene. If only the place wasn't so damn public. She produced a pair of Ray-Bans from her clasp bag and slipped them on.

'I'll have a gin and tonic, please. Just the one, then I really must be off. There's so much to do at the museum. Perhaps we can get together later.'

'Relax Laura. We've got a lot to talk about.' Hawkhurst raised his hand to bring the waiter to the table. He ordered the drinks and then returned his attentions to Laura. 'The coin doesn't matter one way or the other anymore. What we've got on you and your dealings with the Church is enough to put you away for years. I know you were taken in by them but that doesn't mean you wouldn't go down for aiding and abetting, not to mention kidnapping. I reckon you'd be looking at ten years minimum.'

'But I didn't know what they intended,' she wailed, shaking her head at the unfairness of it all. 'I was just trying to help an old friend.'

Their drinks came and the conversation died until the waiter had departed.

'You and Mary Lou Berkowitz seemed to be hitting it off aboard the Nagasaki Maru.' Hawkhurst took a testing sip of his drink. 'Very cosy.'

She shrugged indifferently.

'You know me better than that, Tom. What you saw was just for show. If it hadn't been for her I'd be dead. She had the hots for me and I didn't do anything to discourage her. But for her I'd have gone down with the rest.'

'Did you know she was in London at the moment?' Brennan asked.

Laura shook her head, it seemed she wasn't to be allowed to simply walk away from the Church of Christ the Warrior.

'Yeah, that's right, she's over here setting up the Reverend's next big production. She's staying at the Savoy. It was in yesterday's papers. She's got a whole team of advisers, McNaughton included, tagging along. We want you to help us. We'd like you to make contact with her.'

Laura stared at them, her gaze going from one man to the other.

'No. I don't want anything more to do with those maniacs. You've seen what they're capable of for God's sake.'

She was close to panic now and made to get up but Tom seized her wrist, forcing her back down into her seat. His face was stony, implacable.

'You'd do better to consider what I'm capable of, Laura.'

*****

If Mary Lou had been in the least suspicious to receive Laura's phone call, she certainly didn't show it. In the tasteful surroundings of the Savoy she had greeted her like a long lost friend with a bear-like hug and lingering kiss. They took a table and coffee was brought. Within seconds they were deep in conversation exchanging details of their respective projects, the exhibition and Whichelow's coming presentation at the Wembley Stadium. It was as though the whole affair of the Nagasaki Maru and the missiles had never occurred, as if it had all been a bad dream. Laura knew that what she was supposed to do, spy on the Church of Christ the Warrior, would be dangerous and hesitated. Hawkhurst had instructed her to get a full schedule of Whichelow's movements from the moment his plane landed at Heathrow to the time he flew out. She was to get timings, hotel bookings and travel arrangements. If she failed to do this he would go straight to the press and declare that the tomb, far from being the last resting place of Arthur, was most likely an elaborate hoax. He had retained a copy of his original report and the discrepancy of the missing Penda mark would reveal how Karelian had been deliberately duped.

'I'll enjoy that, Laura,' he said. 'Think of the scandal. It'll make Armenia look like a tea party. It'll finish you, and Dixey, forever.'

Laura knew he wouldn't hesitate for one moment to do exactly that. With Angahrad dead he must absolutely loathe her and the chance to bring Dixey down along with her would be seen as a bonus. If she was to retain any sort of control over her life it seemed she had no choice but to do as he ordered. Yet, as she considered her predicament more closely, it slowly dawned on her that there was one other option remaining open to her. She could come clean with Mary Lou and let the Church of Christ the Warrior deal with things. A few hours ago she had hoped with all her heart that she would never have to deal with them again. Now she wasn't so sure. She had seen their methods at close quarters, and there seemed little doubt they would have the organisation to remove Hawkhurst and his mysterious friend once and for all. Eliminating them would solve all her problems. Mary Lou was chattering on about how support for the Church was growing at a fantastic rate. Laura barely heard a word of it: she had made up her mind. She leant forward, lightly running her fingers over the back of the older woman's beefy hand.

'It's really good to see you again, Mary Lou.' She breathed. 'We never had the chance to get properly acquainted on the ship, I hope we'll get some time alone while you're here in London. I'd like to show you around.'

The American woman smiled knowingly and took Laura's petite hands in hers.

'I want us to get to know each other real well, my dear.' She said, standing up. 'You look tired. I guess we've both been working too hard lately. Why don't we go up to my suite and lay down?'

*****

That afternoon in Mary Lou's penthouse suite passed slowly. Having been granted free access to Laura's body was an opportunity that the other woman was determined to take full advantage of. She was incredibly strong, more powerful than many men Laura had known, and threw herself into the lovemaking with a practised roughness that bordered on the brutal. Laura understood. Men or women, they were all different in bed. If this was what Mary Lou liked it was up to her to play the submissive role in convincing style. All that mattered was that in the end the woman was convinced it was love that had brought them both to that luxurious bedroom. Obediently, she had let the American undress her and then bathe her in the sunken bath, anointing her lithe body with fragrant oils. As she was washed Mary Lou's heavy breasts brushed across her cheek and, growing bold, she took the hardening nipple in her mouth, sucking gently. A hand caressed the nape of her neck and Mary Lou, clearly becoming aroused, stooped to lift her dripping from the water in one easy movement that made her gasp.

Now she was standing over Laura, hands wandering across the curve of her slick wet shoulders, huge wet tongue sliding into the wide welcoming mouth.

'My God, you're beautiful, honey,' she said softly, taking Laura's hand and placing it in the coarse hair that sprouted between her thick thighs. 'Let's hit the sack.'

After an hour of Mary Lou's lovemaking Laura felt increasingly reassured that, if she opened up to her about Hawkhurst's survival and his interest in the Church's activities, the woman would protect her. Certainly she couldn't imagine Mary Lou would stand by and allow anything to harm her. Not after this. The American woman was standing at the cocktail cabinet, fixing them a drink. Like Laura she was naked, the muscles of her broad shoulders highlighted by the slanting shaft of sunlight that fell between the half closed curtains. Sprawled languorously across the bed, the fingers of one hand idly caressing an erect pink nipple, Laura eyed the heavy buttocks, solid legs and broad feet. From here she could have been a man. Mary Lou turned and seeing Laura's eyes on her, smiled tenderly.

'You OK, honey? I wasn't too rough?'

Laura looked at the obscene rubber phallus that now lay tangled in its strapping on the floor by the bed. She had hated the thing and Mary Lou's over-physical style had left her sore. No matter. She smiled coyly.

'Oh no, it was wonderful. I want some more before I go.' She took the offered drink, her mood becoming thoughtful. 'It's all been so fabulous, meeting up with you like this again. I don't want anything to spoil what we have here, Mary Lou.'

The American sat down beside Laura, pulling her face roughly into the warm moist valley of her breasts.

'What could spoil it, honey?'

Laura hesitated, she didn't want to be too obvious.

'Oh, I don't know. It's just that Tom Hawkhurst has turned up out of the blue. He's alive and he hates me for what happened to his woman. He's threatening to stir up all sorts of trouble for me.' She expected this revelation to produce some reaction from Mary Lou but it was received in total silence. This was worrying. Perhaps the Church wasn't that bothered about Hawkhurst being on the loose after all, she wondered. Maybe they reckoned that they had covered their tracks sufficiently well to ignore him. If so, it was bad news for her. She was thinking fast now – there was just one chance left. She reached down, her hand searching for the veined and ridged shaft of the dildo. She lay it on the bed beside Mary Lou. 'He's such a swine. He's says he'll ruin everything I've worked for unless I ...' She choked her words off, shaking her head.

Mary Lou grasped her shoulders, holding her at arm's length, fingers like talons biting into the soft flesh.

'Unless you what?'

Laura hung her head, the dildo still clasped to her breast. There were tears of desperation glistening in her eyes as she raised them to meet the other's gaze.

'Unless I go to bed with him.'

Mary Lou took the rubber shaft from her and laid it aside. Standing over her she roughly pulled Laura's face into the sweat scented triangle of her vagina, groaning as the soft tongue darted, finding and caressing her mollusc-like clitoris. For minutes she stood there, eyes closed, lips parted, her hand clamping Laura's face to her. Then she shuddered and the black eyes opened.

'Hawkhurst,' she asked quietly. 'Do you know where he's staying?'

CHAPTER TWENTY NINE

Marko Bubka rested his back against a convenient rock and assessed his situation. They had taught him that in the army: always take time to think out your next move. He was glad of the rest,: it had been a steep climb. He was a stockily built man somewhere in his mid-twenties, with unruly blonde hair and a ready smile that had made him many friends among the opposite sex. He wore a drab green cagoule and waterproof trousers. By his side lay a bulky canvas rucksack of similar colour. Taking time to allow his breathing to return to normal he looked around him, taking in the detail of his surroundings. About five hundred metres away and slightly above him the ragged black line of the crest was etched against the dying evening. In an hour it would be dark enough for him to move.

He drew the map out of the side pocket of the pack and unfolded it. He had marked the position of the cottage with a neatly inked circle. It was not really necessary since this was the second time he had been there. However, on the first occasion he had openly driven up the unmade road in the scarlet Ferrari Testarossa that was his pride and joy. This time he had left the car in the village below and made his way here by paths that skirted around to the rear of the cottage. He hoped it would be safe, he knew how the trappings of success bred envy in others. Of all the many material acquisitions he had accumulated since leaving Mother Russia it was the car that gave him greatest pleasure. He dreamed of one day returning to his native village, just outside Kiev, to show it off to his school friends. Like many of his generation Marko had been drafted into the Russian army. Once the ogre of Europe, it was an army that was demoralised and disintegrating, an army had nothing for him to do, no inclination to train him properly and, far worse from his point of view, no money to pay him. However, he was an adaptable youth and determined to make the best of things.

After the most superficial induction and training he was posted to an armoured unit in the grim Kolya barracks, just twenty minutes from the centre of Moscow and all its salacious delights. Here, eighteen years old and very much on the make, he cultivated a circle of friends who could only be described as dubious. Prostitutes and their pimps, small time thugs, drug dealers and, eventually, what could best be described as middle management in the Moscow Mafia. From there on in he made a steady living smuggling weapons and ammunition out of the barracks, not difficult in the general chaos and muddle that was the legacy of the departed Soviet Empire, and selling them on to his friends outside.

It had not been easy nor had he grown rich quickly for there were always people to pay off and sweeteners to be found for the heavies who moved through this demi-monde like sharks. Trust in these circles was not easily given: it had to be earned. Once, to prove his credibility, he had been taken by a Mafia Godfather to a deserted factory about fifty miles out of town. Here, to test his nerve, he had been left alone with a gun and two trussed up drug dealers who had incurred the wrath of the underworld. He had not enquired about their offences nor hesitated in his grisly task, to have done so would have been to share the fate of his victims and a bullet in the back of the head.

On the drive back to Moscow, rejoicing in a job well done, the Godfather and his heavies had got hopelessly drunk on vodka, slapping his shoulder and telling him what a fine fellow he was. Marko had drunk just enough to be sociable and thought of the eyes of the men he had killed. He was surprised to find he had felt nothing. No pity in the moments before the act, no remorse afterwards. He was a natural killer. Anyway, apart from the moral considerations there were the financial factors to be taken into account. He had been paid a hundred US dollars for the demonstration – hard currency – and began to wonder if he would not be wise to contemplate a change of career.

From then on he divided his time between selling arms and whatever else he could steal from the army and carrying out beatings or killings at the request of the Mafia. Within a short period he had five dead men to his credit and was very much an up and coming figure in the Russian underground. He was especially valued by his masters because while he remained in the army he had access to those of his comrades who had fallen foul of the outside world. These had usually fallen from grace by way of unpaid gambling debts or drug bills and now skulked fearfully within the grim barrack walls. This gave him power inside and soon he was supplementing his income by collecting protection money from other soldiers' pitiful wages.

But despite his success Bubka always yearned for something more, he wanted the good life which for him meant fast cars, big houses, sophisticated women. It meant getting out of Russia and the army. After six months he had accumulated enough money for a false Polish passport and, having driven across the border to that country via unguarded back roads, flew from Warsaw to Paris to begin his real life. There he set himself up in a modest flat on the Rue de Crimee overlooking the Parc des Buttes Chaumont and set to work. Alone in a strange city making contacts was his first priority and to this end he began to frequent the less salubrious bars. It did not take long, for he was a personable young man and when he met Sharone, the Senegalese bar girl who within weeks shared his bed and his flat, he was on his way. Through her he met the kind of lowlife he had known so well in Moscow, people with whom he could relate easily and who, he knew, he could ultimately control.

His relationship with the Church of Christ the Warrior had come about in unlikely fashion. The daughter of a French politician had fallen hopelessly in love with a fellow student at the Sorbonne. The student, a perfectly amiable young man, intelligent and hardworking, suffered from one devastating weakness – he was poor. To mitigate this failing he worked as a waiter, three evenings a week, at a small bistro just off Boulevard Haussman to where, naturally, the girl would regularly repair. Her father, wealthy, right wing and a devout Catholic had, through long-standing contacts with Cardinal Martinette, arranged for the boy to be discouraged.

It had been Bubka's first real job in Paris. Until then he had lived on his savings and Sharone's earnings from the bar. The task of discouraging the boy, the Church had regarded it as pretty low key stuff, had been given to Marcel, an overweight ex-boxer who worked at the same bar. Wanting to be on the safe side Marcel had invited Bubka, young and solidly built, along as back-up and they had gone together to the bistro shortly before midnight when things were quiet and the place about to close.

The girl had sat waiting inside, smiling through the glass at her young lover as, fully as eager as her to be home and in bed, he hurriedly folded away the tables and chairs and carried them inside. Perhaps he had been expecting something for, as Marcel had approached him with Bubka following a few paces behind, the boy had turned to face them. He was tall and slim, with short dark hair and although he was scared his fear hadn't unmanned him. Marcel grunted, moving in close, intent on breaking ribs with short jabbing blows but the boy was too quick for him. Pivoting on the ball of his left foot he hooked out a perfectly timed right heel to make jolting contact with the Frenchman's chin, sending him staggering backwards. Alarmed at these developments Bubka stepped back into the darkness: the boy was a skilled kick boxer and would need careful handling. He watched as Marcel came bullocking clumsily forward again, only to receive the same treatment, this time the kick supplemented by two sharp chops to the throat which dropped him to his knees, clutching his windpipe and gasping desperately for air. He was finished as a fighting unit.

'M'sieu,' Bubka called softly, 'It is OK, the flics are on the way. I saw what this man tried to do. I was a witness to everything.'

The boy, breathing heavily and shaking with reaction now, turned towards him, relieved to hear a supportive voice. He smiled shyly then turned to wave to the girl who had watched the whole incident from behind the glass, intent on letting her know that all was well and he was unharmed. It was in the instant he turned away that Bubka had jabbed the stiletto home just below the right ear, feeling the steel split through muscle and the hot blood surge up his arm before, with a savage twist of the blade he withdrew it. The boy was dead before he hit the ground and Bubka, seizing the gagging Marcel by his collar, dragged him to his feet and away down the street into the night.

After that things had taken off for Marko Bubka. On the night he had no idea who was employing him. Marcel would pay him five hundred francs and that was all he needed to know. But afterwards the Frenchman had been grateful enough to introduce his name into circles where it counted. Work for the Church of Christ the Warrior had initially been very mundane, normally involving flying from Paris to the United States with a briefcase that he would hand over to a contact there and returning the following day. He guessed, rightly, that they would be testing him during this period. They would be checking him out, seeing whether he was subject to weaknesses – sex, drugs, alcohol or greed. In fact he was vulnerable to all of these failings but sufficiently controlled to conceal the fact – something he couldn't say about his New York contact who always stank of bourbon. Having served his probationary period six months later he was moved on to escort duties, accompanying sick and disturbed people who were heading for a spell in the Church's rehabilitation centres. On one of these trips he had been alarmed to recognise his ward as the girl who had watched him kill her lover outside the bistro. Yet his fears were unfounded for the mad staring eyes did not look into faces anymore, saw nothing now apart from the recurring horrors that had filled her mind since that night.

It had been an unnerving incident but Bubka had swiftly rationalised it and put it behind him, continuing with his chosen career until now he was at the top of his profession. His elimination of the hapless Mathews at the airstrip had brought him a big bonus. That had been easy; the man had been no more than a terrified rabbit, this time he would need to be more careful for Hawkhurst, he had been told, had a reputation for doing the unexpected.

Bubka shivered, it was cold up here on the mountain. He looked at his watch, it was nearly ten and dark enough to risk breaking the skyline as he crossed the crest. Carrying the heavy backpack in one hand he covered the intervening ground, the dim forms of grazing sheep moved aside as he passed. At the crest he lay flat on his belly his light intensifying night scope trained on the dark block of the cottage. A wisp of wood smoke rose from the chimney and a solitary light burned in the window. Good. Someone was home, this time he would not have a wasted journey. He recalled the last time he had been at the cottage: sent on a fruitless search for a collection of coins. He had not liked the place, it was cold and with few comforts. It reminded him of his mother's place, the clapboard shack she kept with Yuri, his sad alcoholic elder brother who had lost both legs to a landmine outside Kabul. As he had come up in the world Bubka had moved to a luxurious apartment at Fontainebleu and Sharone had been replaced by Martine, a small time actress who was dynamite between the sheets but came with expensive tastes. The Ferrari had been the cherry on the top of the cake. Anything humble, like the cottage, anything that spoke of frugality was distasteful to him now and it made him doubly dangerous. To ensure he would never have to live like that again he was prepared to do anything and to do it supremely well. Having carefully checked out the area surrounding the cottage through the night scope he lay silently, listening for any indication of dogs in the vicinity. He didn't mind their barking, it would cover the noise of his approach, and up here in this isolated area there was no likelihood of any outside intervention. Most importantly he wanted to be as prepared mentally as humanly possible. He didn't intend to be surprised like Marcel had been.

Satisfied, he reached into the backpack, took out the Uzi and laid it on the damp grass beside him. It was a good weapon, light and reliable. He also had an old wartime Luger in his pocket and a stiletto strapped to the inside of his left forearm. He lay the backpack aside, he would pick it up on the way back, then rolled the last few yards to the crest and down the gently clattering scree of the reverse slope. Once below the skyline he rose to his feet and began to move slowly towards the dull yellow gleam of the window.

*****

Hawkhurst sipped his Scotch and stared into the dying embers of the fire. Had it been a good move to have returned to the cottage, he wondered. Having put the pressure on Laura he had left London and come here, thinking it safer than his hotel. He had hoped she would have phoned by now with some news of Whichelow's plans although, were he honest with himself, he seriously doubted she would be able to get anything useful out of Mary Lou. Somewhere on the hillside outside a fox yelped, making him start and raising the hairs on his neck. He was getting jumpy. He would have liked to phone Angahrad, listen to the soft lilt of her voice for comfort, but knew that to do so would be to compromise her safety. He reached for the Scotch, slopping a healthy measure into his glass, then reached out and switched on the television. TV had become a soporific for him these days.

The main news was, as usual, the tense situation in the Middle East although nothing had really changed there. The details of the Saudi peace initiative had been made public now although, with typical toughness, the Israelis had flatly rejected them in their present form and the hard line Arab countries had described them as totally unacceptable. It may just have been posturing for home consumption but it did not bode well. There had been more trouble in Egypt too with six German tourists injured in a machine gun attack. Following the international news came a brief report on Whichelow's coming European tour. It was a sound bite from Mary Lou, red sword gracing the lapel of her jacket.

'Do you think that in the current situation such tours are wise?' she was asked. 'Are they not perhaps likely to inflame the situation?'

She shook her head firmly.

'That is certainly not the intention. What the Reverend Whichelow hopes to achieve in his time over here is to encourage the Christian Churches in Europe to reach a consensus with their co-religionists in the USA that will allow them to negotiate with our Muslim counterparts from a position of strength. The very positive response we are getting in Europe suggests many Christians here see benefits in uniting at this time. This is in no way threatening. The Church of Christ the Warrior accepts the right to freedom of worship for all creeds, so long as they extend the same courtesy to Christians.' She smiled condescendingly. 'You know I sometimes think we may have placed too much emphasis on 'blessed are the meek'. There is a fine line between being liberal in our attitudes and being submissive. The Muslims say Allah the merciful, Allah the compassionate yet we have all seen terrible events on our television screens recently, events perpetrated by these very same people. We believe these have occurred because of a perceived ambivalence within the Christian world – an unwillingness to stand up and be counted. We want to eliminate that ambivalence and speak with one voice for Christians everywhere, especially where they are suffering oppression. Only by taking a non-aggressive yet firm stance on interfaith relations can we ensure freedom of worship. It isn't just a religious question either – it goes further than that, of course, it affects the wider basic freedoms such as democratic elections, civil rights and women's rights. The Church's approach to all these matters emphasises the need to integrate Christian theology into the formation of strategic political, economic and philosophical policies in the Western world.'

'Would you describe your campaign as a crusade?'

Mary Lou smiled as she considered the question.

'Yes,' she said. 'Yes, I believe I would.'

Hawkhurst switched off and stared at the blank screen. The more he saw how things were working out the more he felt that, even if open warfare could be avoided in the immediate future, the polarisation of attitudes would inevitably be an increasingly important factor in politics in the year to come. Yet he wondered if things would work out as Whichelow foresaw, the establishment of the Kingdom of God on Earth and the ascendancy of Western capitalism. Would not the new aggressive economies of the east, China, Japan, Korea see the conflict as a perfect opportunity to exploit? The sheer weight of population numbers and economic clout of the east would put them in a perfect position to intervene. The nations who did not allow religion to overly influence their policies but kept their eye on the main chance would certainly be well positioned to intervene, hopefully economically but possibly militarily. He shook his head. This sort of thinking was getting him nowhere. What he needed was some sort of blinding inspiration that would present a chance of eliminating Whichelow and his kind forever. Getting to his feet he turned and found it. There standing at the open window was Marko Bubka, the Uzi aimed directly at his heart. He raised his hands.

'Stay very still, Mr Hawkhurst, and do nothing foolish.'

Tom stared as the man stepped over the low windowsill into the room, the muzzle of the machine pistol unwavering. Bubka came directly towards him, smiling. The pale blue eyes bored into Tom's face, wanting to make sure he had the right man. Satisfied he nodded towards the chair from which he had just risen. 'Please, sit down Mr Hawkhurst and finish your drink.' His eyes flicked around the room: he had been instructed to make this look like an accident and now he was looking for the appropriate means. It was not going to be easy; there was no gas or oil heating supply to the cottage to fuel a fire, only electricity. But Bubka was an adaptable man. The smile widened, 'I think you need a bath, Mr Hawkhurst. Bring the bottle with you.' He nodded towards the bathroom and with a jab of the machine pistol indicated that was where they were bound. Tom shaking his head as though confused but knowing full well what was intended moved towards the door. He swayed slightly as he went, as if the few inches of Scotch he had drunk had taken hold. Bubka relaxed a little. 'Fill up the bath, please, Doctor.'

Hawkhurst turned, appalled.

'But the water's cold,' he protested, 'The heating goes off at ten.'

Bubka laughed at his lack of grasp of the situation.

'Don't worry, Doctor, just do as I say. You won't even notice the temperature, I promise.'

Tom ran the peaty water into the bath. When it was about half full Bubka called a halt. When Tom faced him the man was holding the small portable radio. It was plugged into the mains.

'Now take a good long drink and get undressed, Doctor Hawkhurst. We want this to look convincing, don't we?'

He frowned. Why, he wondered, despite his perilous situation was Hawkhurst so strangely unconcerned, smiling over his shoulder. The Russian felt the first stirring of doubt. It came too late.

'I think that's enough, don't you Harry?'

A supernova flared in the cortex of Bubka's skull and his next cogent impression was that his right arm was being torn from its socket. In a second the Russian was disarmed and lying face down on the bathroom floor, Brennan's .38 at his head pressing painfully down behind his right ear. First administering a sharp salutary slap with the side of his gun that made his ears ring, the American rolled the Russian onto his back and thrust his face into Bubka's; familiar bourbon fumes wafting over the prostrate man. As his senses stabilized, recognition dawned in the frightened eyes.

Brennan smiled, shaking his head sadly.

'Oh boy, Marko baby. Have you ever fucked up – big time.'

CHAPTER THIRTY

The queue outside the museum, three deep, stretched for over eight hundred metres. From beneath the Doric columned façade the shuffling serpent of humanity extended down the steps of the museum, across the forecourt, through the ornate wrought iron gates and then down the street and around the corner. As its head disappeared into the museum's dark maw its tail was constantly replenished by new arrivals. All this despite a cold drizzling rain that had fallen all afternoon. The Age of Arthur exhibition had caught the public imagination like nothing before.

'Business is certainly brisk,' noted Hawkhurst as with undisguised glee he parked neatly in the space marked 'Curator-General only'. He turned to Brennan at his side, his tone becoming serious. 'Of course the decent thing in the circumstances would be to make a discreet entrance. Low key. Avoid fuss and all that. Don't want an unseemly scene in front of all those people.'

The American gave the matter serious consideration.

'You mean try not to embarrass the museum authorities too much? Be sensitive to the finer points of etiquette? Apply a little circumspection to our entrance, perhaps? You could be right.' He craned his neck to look at the man in the back through the driving mirror. 'What do you reckon Piet? I always understood you Afrikaners were the epitome of social delicacy and refinement.'

Potgeiter smiled, joining in the general mood of restrained hilarity.

'Well, goes against the grain but, once the police get here, I reckon we should kick the fucking front door in and then proceed to generate as much high profile arse ache as we can. Let's enjoy ourselves a little.'

With two police cars drawing up alongside, they got out into the thin rain, running lightly up the steps with the police bringing up the rear, their impudence at seemingly trying to jump the queue drawing angry remarks. At the main entrance the security men made an abortive effort to halt their progress but a hefty shove from Potgeiter and the arrival of the police soon took them inside. A panicked phone call from the desk brought Dixey and Laura hurrying from their offices. As ever, Dixey was pumped up with indignant outrage at this intrusion; she white faced. Her hand went to her mouth when she saw a smiling Hawkhurst standing there. It had been three weeks since she had listened to Mary Lou arrange his murder. The fact that neither he nor Brennan had subsequently made contact had lulled her into a false security. On her subsequent liaisons, increasingly brutal and bizarre, with Mary Lou not a solitary word had been spoken about Hawkhurst. She had willingly submitted to perversion and degradation in the fond belief he was dead and that she was safe. As they descended the broad staircase that led down from the administrative floor towards the knot of silent police and the hushed crowd behind them, the inspector stepped forward.

'Laura Anne Woods, I am arresting you for conspiracy to murder. I am also charging you with deception and fraud concerning the authenticity of certain items in this exhibition.' He turned to Dixey. 'Paul Charles Dixey, I am arresting you on charges of deception and fraud concerning the authenticity of certain items in this exhibition. You have the right to remain silent but anything you do say may be used in evidence at a later date.'

'This is your doing, Hawkhurst,' Dixey snarled, 'But you won't get away with it. Believe me, when the museum's lawyers are finished with you, you'll wish you'd never been born.'

Laura uttered not a word as they were escorted away past the dumbstruck crowd and down the steps towards the waiting police vehicles. As he was led past, Tom winked broadly at Dixey.

'It's fun isn't it. Destroying people's careers!' He turned his gaze on to the woman. 'It's not all bad Laura, we're doing our best to arrange for you to share a cell with Mary Lou Berkowitz.'

When they were gone and the stunned crowd of visitors resumed its relentless onward press. Tom looked to Brennan and Potgeiter.

'Well,' he said, 'while we're here I suppose we might as well take in the exhibition – it may not be open much longer. Come on boys, I'll give you a guided tour.'

In the crowded galleries they drifted down a range of fascinating Dark Age exhibits, artefacts assembled from museums and private collections all over the world. Among them were a few he had excavated himself in the old days. It was a tour-de-force of presentation and in other circumstances Tom could have spent hours pondering over the wonders gathered there. However, aware that Dixey and Laura were only bit players in the grand scheme of things and Whichelow's forthcoming extravaganza might prove critical, he kept up a lively pace. Eventually they found themselves approaching the focal point of the whole exhibition, the artefacts that, four short months ago, he and Laura had taken from the ground.

The gallery containing these was darkened and each exhibit in its case was expertly lit to highlight its unique individual features. Softly over the sound system came background music, the words of Beowulf recited to the plangent accompaniment of lute music. Some might have dubbed it Dark Age muzak but it had all been very well done: it had Laura's mark on it. As he looked at them: the sword, the cap and mail shirt, the chalice, he reflected on how much they had changed his life. What had been undertaken as a routine job, a welcome chance to make some badly needed money, had evolved into a nightmare of death and destruction that was still not properly resolved. Tomorrow Whichelow began his European tour. Despite Bubka's evidence of the Church's involvement and Mary Lou's subsequent arrest, nothing had been found that could implicate The Reverend. Indeed, the moment he had heard of her arrest and the serious charges levelled against her he had been at pains to denounce her publicly on several occasions. She was, he said, an abomination in the eyes of God. To the public it was of little import, a jealous woman had tried to eliminate a rival for her lesbian lover's affection. Big deal. The ubiquitous Mallinson, the Church's man in Britain had taken over the organisation of the coming tour and sales at the box office said the Wembley meeting was going to be a sell-out. As these thoughts ran through his mind he cast a last look at the chalice. From the moment it had been lifted from the grave it had brought nothing but death and misery and the promise of worse. He moved off.

'Harry,' he said softly, 'let's get out of here. I need a drink.'

Ten minutes later in the quiet saloon bar of the Woodman, the three of them sat around a small circular table discussing their next move. Until Whichelow showed his hand the following evening – showed his hand in front of a hundred thousand highly charged acolytes – there was little to be done. Brennan spelt it out.

'Unless we can get the Berkowitz woman to go public on Whichelow we can't make a move. To be honest I don't see her doing that. She's a pretty tough cookie. I reckon pressurising the Woods woman may offer a better chance of getting information. She's only had a peripheral part in the big picture but she's smart enough to know she's in deep shit and sinking lower all the time. By the time she's spoken to her attorney maybe she'll be aware her best bet is to come clean on Whichelow. But that's going to take time.'

Potgeiter sipped his beer thoughtfully.

'But, given the current situation, why doesn't the British government simply ban the meeting tomorrow? They must be able to see what's likely to happen afterwards. It's a matter of maintaining public order. Even if half of those who turn up tomorrow are only looking for spiritual guidance we know damn well the Reverend will have his agent provocateurs in the crowd. Even if nothing happens in the stadium you can be damn sure the locals, especially the local Muslims, are gonna be in for a rough night afterwards.'

'My office tells me that the American government asked the Prime Minister to do just that three weeks ago. Best legal advice was that it would amount to interference with religious freedom and as such unconstitutional. Anyway it's too late now. The mob will turn up tomorrow whatever happens and if they get frustrated early on God only knows what might follow.'

Tom, who had listened in silence until to this point, stretched out his legs. He was frowning, puzzled.

'There's something else. I don't know how it's happened but somehow it looks as if either Whichelow has still got the real chalice or it went down with the Nagasaki Maru. That one back there in the museum is the dummy we palmed off on them. Laura must have switched them when she came aboard.'

*****

At Paddington Police Station Hawkhurst was kept waiting for two hours before he was allowed to see Laura. As he sat in the dreary pastel painted interview room, a succession of police officers and her solicitor, having been given precedence over him, came and went. He didn't complain, he knew he was only being allowed to see her at all thanks to Brennan's influence with the powers that be. At seven in the morning, she was finally led in by a stony faced policewoman. She looked tired and drawn and despite everything he could not deny a pang of pity. He realised that, even in the face of everything she had done, he still felt the urge to comfort her. Twelve hours earlier she had been a national celebrity with the kind of fame and fortune that few could ever aspire to. Now she was ruined. Laura, however, despite her situation was unrepentant.

'Don't waste your pity on me, Tom,' she said flatly. 'I shall be out of here within the hour. They are preparing the papers right now. I have already instructed my solicitors to issue a statement to the effect that I intend to bring charges of wrongful arrest against the police and of falsification of evidence against you. I intend to prove that the reference to the Penda mark in your original report was a malicious act intended to ruin my reputation. I think I'll look good in the witness box don't you? I shall wear something sober and respectable.'

A little taken aback to learn she was to be released so quickly, the more so that she was also attempting to take the offensive, Tom shrugged.

'There's just the small matter of conspiracy to murder as well.'

She tossed her head carelessly.

'Whatever that crazy bitch Mary Lou may or may not have done has nothing to do with me. There's no way anyone can tie me in with it. All I have to do is prove how, out of professional, possibly sexual jealousy, you tried to ruin my career. She, besotted with me, tried to stop you. Sounds a pretty reasonable defence to me.'

'The matter of the coin is immaterial now. I took a stroll round the exhibition yesterday afternoon. Where's the real Grail, Laura?'

Her mouth tightened. She hadn't expected this.

'I don't know what you're talking about.'

'I think you do. I think you passed it to Whichelow on the Nagasaki Maru and brought the copy back with you. Once the phoney Grail was placed in its case at the museum nobody was going to get the opportunity to examine it closely until the exhibition closed in November. It was just unfortunate, unfortunate for you, that is, that I decided to take a look around yesterday, I'm probably the only person in the world who would have known the difference. Once I saw it things began to fall into place. The more I thought about it, your turning up on the Nagasaki Maru, right out of the blue like that, was just too good to be true. The way I see it, you got cold feet about cheating on the Church and decided to curry favour by coming clean. If you presented them with the real Grail they might let you off the hook. You didn't care that once Whichelow knew that the Grail I had already delivered was a phoney he would probably have me murdered. But for the fact that he had already contacted his friends in the Pentagon and had any surveillance called off, your decision to hand it over would mean I could well be fish food by now. I guess he was looking forward to showing me how clever he was – he never could resist displaying his superiority over mere mortals. When Angahrad turned up at your flat it would have been a nuisance, I guess, but then you reckoned she might make another useful bargaining tool. You wouldn't have known they had held her once already. You must be pretty scared of them to take all those risks, Laura. Why, what have they got on you?'

She did not answer and for Hawkhurst the mist began to lift a little more. Somewhere back in her past must be some dark secret that the Church had used to blackmail her. For some reason, possibly even before her discovery of the grave, she would have been in their power. Only when the Grail was discovered and they considered she had a role to play did they move in to put pressure on her. Early on, from the first time he had checked her flat over, Brennan had voiced suspicions that there was some contact between her and the Church of Christ the Warrior, although he had found nothing concrete to establish any link. Tom reached across the table and gripped her wrist tightly.

'What's Whichelow planning?' He growled.

She tried to pull away but his grasp was unrelenting.

'You're hurting me,' she grated.

'Listen you silly little bitch,' he hissed. 'Whatever your motives might have been you are in deep shit. Your only chance now is to help us.'

From his pocket he drew a folded copy of the early edition of *The Time* tossing it onto the table. Blazoned across the front page was the headline. 'Is Arthur's grave a hoax?' Beneath, in only slightly smaller type, was: 'Top archaeologists held on deception charges.' There were pictures of her and Dixey. Even the Middle East was temporarily taking second place to these revelations.

Her head dropped and he released his hold.

'They're saying that on the basis of the coin. What do you think they'll say when they find out the Grail is a cheap imitation, knocked out overnight.'

'I got into trouble at college.' She said softly. 'Drugs. Patrick McNally was a big time dealer up at Cambridge before he got religion and within a few weeks of meeting him I was hooked – hooked on him and speed. I didn't have much money in those days so for a few months, and it was only a few, I was paying McNally and his friends with sex. It was pretty disgusting and in the end I kicked the habit and dumped McNally. That was when I started working really hard. It was a brief episode in my life that I regretted bitterly. All I wanted was to forget the whole sordid business and get on with my life. McNally was busted by the Cambridge police shortly afterwards and moved back to the States. I thought that was the end of it.'

Hawkhurst looked at her, she was crying, big warm tears running down her cheeks: falling onto the green baize table in dark little blossoms. It was the first time he could recall seeing her display real emotion. He handed her a tissue.

'But it wasn't.'

'No,' she sniffed, 'last year Michael and I took a vacation and spent a couple of months touring the States. Our relationship was on the rocks but we were trying to make a new start for the umpteenth time. He'd known Whichelow for years apparently, had acted as a consultant when the Church was setting up its own TV network, and since we were driving through Wyoming he suggested we stop off at Gethsemane. It was there I met Mary Lou. I'm sure I don't have to tell you that she was very attentive from the first. I was flattered. She'd seen me on television, read all my books and took great pleasure in showing me the Church's collection. She was very kind but there was no question of any sexual advances at that stage, although I pretty soon came to the conclusion she was a lesbian. Anyway, we got on well and kept in contact when I returned to Britain – she was always very interested in any work the museum was doing on religious sites. In one of her letters she mentioned the hostages, Patrick McNally among them, and, naturally enough, I asked her if it was the same Patrick McNally who had been up at All Saints in 1990. It was of course – apparently the Church had helped him kick the habit – and I asked if there was anything I could do to help obtain his release. I was already something of a celebrity by that time and would have been happy to put my name to any appeal or even provide cash. She thanked me for the offer but said at the time negotiations were stalled and there was little that could be done. I forgot all about it.'

She had recovered her composure now and once again, despite everything she had done, Tom could not help feeling a pang of sympathy. They had blackmailed her as mercilessly as they had tried to blackmail him.

'Then we found the grave and the Grail and they decided they wanted it for their own purposes?'

'That's right. A letter arrived at the flat the night after the press conference. It had one picture with it.'

'You and McNally?'

She flushed crimson.

'Me, McNally and three of his friends.'

He avoided her eyes: he knew from personal experience exactly how she must feel.

'And they said you had to deliver the Grail or they would send the rest to the press?'

'That's right. Despite the interest Mary Lou showed in the Grail at the press conference I didn't connect the letter with her or the Church at first. I thought it was from someone I'd known up at Cambridge trying to make a quick score but later that evening she phoned me at home and then everything became clear. She knew the time and place it was taken and the name of every student in the picture. How she got hold of them I don't know but apparently McNally had taken a whole reel of film that night. I couldn't even say what occasion it was – that sort of thing happened more than once – I just knew I was in trouble. I said I'd do anything she wanted but then she told me not to worry. She had thought of a better way. She had heard about your Armenian adventure by this time and asked me if I thought, properly motivated, you'd be prepared to play ball. I told her you were pretty hard up and might be bought. I didn't really think you would but it was what she wanted to hear and it got me off the hook. I was to forget the whole unpleasantness, she said. I didn't understand her motives at the time but I guess even then she was thinking of getting me into bed, making me grateful.'

Hawkhurst nodded. It made sense and it had the feel of the Church about it. They had tried to buy him and when that failed they had blackmailed him.

'No wonder you didn't side with Dixey when he went apeshit over the TV appearances. Once I had agreed to go to Gethsemane, you thought I'd taken the bait and you were home and dry.'

'Not really, I knew I was still in their power: once you had taken the Grail I just kept doing whatever I could to keep in favour with them. I was scared, Tom. One minute I was on top of the world, the next I stood in danger of being branded a drug crazed pervert – just because of a mistake I made when I was nineteen.'

Tom shook his head as if to clear his mind of this additional mental clutter. He wasn't here to moralise.

'Where's the real Grail?'

'I don't know. I handed it over to Mary Lou just before dinner on that last night. She hasn't mentioned it since – it may have gone down with the ship.'

He smiled.

'It's not going to be easy explaining away CIA microchips in the base of the one in the museum.' She looked at him blankly and he let it drop. 'Did Mary Lou give any indication of what Whichelow is planning tonight? Anything, anything at all? Think hard Laura, a lot depends on this.'

She smiled bitterly.

'Her mind wasn't really on business matters last time I saw her. She just said the arrangements were going well and that it should be spectacular. The only thing I can remember that was slightly odd is that when she was sleeping, two or three times she said: "red x-ray fifty three ".'

Tom blinked.

'Just that? "Red x-ray fifty three"?'

'Yes. Like I say, she didn't talk about the Church at all. It was only when I told her you were alive that she ...'

'Made the necessary arrangements for my removal?' He smiled. 'It was a big mistake, Laura. Brennan had the phone in Mary Lou's suite tapped before we met you in the restaurant. We knew exactly what was going on all the time. You should have played it straight, Laura. You'd still be in there with a chance if you had.' He nodded at the paper. 'Forget the exhibition. Right now, in your shoes I'd be worrying about what the Church will do next. They'll assume you were to some extent responsible for Mary Lou's arrest and whatever their public stance may be they are not forgiving people. I wouldn't be at all surprised if a selection of McNally's artistic snapshots didn't turn up on some picture editor's desk any time now.'

He stood up. Looking down at the slumped, defeated form of the woman, he didn't feel any sense of triumph, quite the reverse. He felt very, very sorry for her.

'Red x-ray fifty three.' He said softly. 'If it helps us I'll put a good word in for you with the judge.'

CHAPTER THIRTY ONE

The sun had gone now although what light remained was still sufficient to etch the twin domed towers of Wembley Stadium ink black on the pink sky. Down the Empire Way the crowd continued to pour in, a broad river of humanity trudging determinedly forward towards the stadium just as it had for three hours already. A sell-out had been predicted and a sell-out it was. The audience for The Reverend James J Whichelow's opening meeting comprised a strange mixture of humanity. An uneasy amalgam of the sacred and the secular, the pure and the profane. There were religious groups of all persuasions. Young, happy clappy, born agains mingled freely with nuns, monks and priests of ancient orders and widely differing traditions. T-shirts, habits and cowls were acceptable garb as Anglicans, Methodists, Baptists and Catholics all pushed forward, shoulder to shoulder, in a solid phalanx. Lutherans, Presbyterians and Salvationists, all had put aside sectarian differences for the occasion. There were black bible groups from the inner cities and Welsh chapel choirs. There were Plymouth Brethren and Scottish Covenanters. All down the broad avenue leading to the stadium, spaced at intervals among the hamburger stands, preachers of even more esoteric persuasions, wild of eye, had set up dais. From these vantage points they were haranguing the passing crowds. The promise of hellfire and damnation was heavy in the air yet in the main they were treated with good humoured indifference by the subjects of their pious wrath.

Not all of those assembling were British for many thousand had come from all across Northern Europe and Scandinavia and many of these groups carried their national flags. As they went it looked like nothing less than a medieval army on the march. It had been part of Whichelow's plan to obtain the widest audience for his message and to ensure maximum impact it had been arranged that Cardinal Martinette would celebrate mass in Notre Dame at precisely the same time as he was appearing in London. Afterwards His Eminence would preach on the subject of religious freedom and the threat posed by militant Islam both at home and abroad. A week later they would appear together in Berlin for a culminating meeting that would embody the symbolic union of the many Christian denominations and its commitment to defending the faith. At that meeting an ecumenical ceremony symbolising the unification of the Christian world would be held. It would be during that that they would produce the Holy Grail like a rabbit out of a hat. The Germans, always suckers for mystical symbols and cult religions, would go for it in a big way. The Church of Christ the Warrior already had a strong following in the GDR especially among the Osteners, former East Germans, keen to be rid of the Muslim guest workers who had helped build a miracle economy that was now looking rather frail.

And still the crowds came. Since early evening they had flocked towards the stadium: they came by car, coach and railway. Some, for it was well known that a number of leading politicians, sensitive to the current climate, had judged it politically correct to show their faces, even flew in by helicopter, roaring in and out of an area of car park set aside for that purpose. Although, for security reasons, it had not been publicly announced, it was widely rumoured that several members of the royal family would be present, as would the American Ambassador. The symbols of power, sacred and secular, were drawing together.

Despite the hour, it was nine thirty, the night was warm and humid and as the great bowl of the arena slowly filled with circling humanity, an air of excitement, a tangible electric charge, was building relentlessly. On the floor of the stadium some groups were holding meetings of their own, their piping voices fighting a losing battle with the excited growl of the swelling crowd as it thrust into the arena. Over the loudspeaker system gospel music thumped out, adding to the galvanic atmosphere.

Yet this was not an exclusively religious gathering, for all those among the eager throng of a religious bent there were many groups, quite large groups, of bare chested, shaven headed youths for whom the death's head spectre of nationalism was resurgent. Tattoos of the Union Jack were very popular with these groups although, from what Tom saw, the red sword emblem enjoyed a wide following too, with many a sweaty forearm and bicep now sporting such. They were generally truculent and their belligerence was fuelled by a regular infusion of lager as they swaggered along, chanting football slogans or bellowing obscene songs. Coaches of black Christians, dignified old men and women in suits and large hats, were sometimes racially abused as they nosed through the sweating press of bodies. There was a large police presence, both uniformed and plain clothes, and thus far there had been little trouble. It was rowdy and intimidating, especially for the children in the crowd, but they had kept their studied unpleasantness sufficiently damped down to avoid open confrontation. Along with them swept a highly charged circus of civil rights activists, feminists, gays, lesbians, fascists, anarchists, flat earthers and the downright deranged.

At the centre of this jostling, sweating sea of humanity three men; two large, one short and stocky, moved grimly forward. Brennan took a gulp from his hip flask and passed it to Potgeiter.

'I gotta feeling tonight's gonna turn out to be real interesting,' he grunted, shoving a swaying skinhead aside with little ceremony.

The skinhead, his arms covered in a web of tattoos, turned and cursed colourfully but, seeing the cold steel in the American's eyes and the menacing bulk of Potgeiter and Hawkhurst, satisfied himself with that. Ignoring the thug they pushed on through the ticket barriers and into the stadium which by now was almost packed to capacity. Beneath the stands, apart from the usual hot dog stalls and bars, many obscure Christian groups had set out their stalls and with prayer and music doing their best to gather as many converts as they could. Ever hopeful, a band of shaven, saffron robed Hare Krishnas chimed, chanted and swirled, adding to the general air of unreality. The bars were doing good business too and here and there occasional, alcohol induced and rather unchristian flare ups were marring the generally good natured, if expectant, atmosphere. A number of arrests had been made for minor drug offences but no more than were to be expected given the generally youthful audience. Ticket touts were another problem. From the day Whichelow arrived in the country there had been tales of tickets changing hands at extortionate prices and of widespread counterfeiting. It was an eventuality that had been catered for and large screens had been erected outside in the vast car parks to allow the proceedings inside to be shown to latecomers and others. As they took their seats the yellow sodium lighting dimmed and slowly the excited buzz of the crowd stilled to a hush.

Hawkhurst trained his eyes on the stage, half expecting Whichelow to open the proceedings in person. He was to be disappointed for when the slim pencil of white light shafted down to the stage it revealed the figure of a minor TV and stage celebrity, well known, indeed knighted, for his Christian views but definitely a lightweight in evangelical circles. He was greeted with cheers and stayed just long enough to introduce the opening act of the evening – an American Gospel Group from the Deep South. Tom fidgeted in his seat, it was not to his musical taste, and he turned his gaze down the bank of seats fifty metres to his left. Despite the capacity crowd, seat red x-ray fifty three remained obstinately unoccupied. He sighed and returned his attention to the stage where the group, highly professional were quick in building up an infectious hand clapping, foot stamping beat that was soon taken up by the crowd, continued its performance. They were on stage for about twenty minutes and as the performance went on Tom became slowly aware that something else was going on around him. From all round the oval of the vast arena lights, red lights, began to pulse out, flaring and dying in time with the music, dimly at first but slowly increasing in intensity and crystallising into a recognisable form. Swords, red swords of light, were playing across the floor of the stadium and up the crowded banks of seats. Eyes everywhere followed the flickering, hypnotic flight of the swords as they swept about the huge bowl, dancing like hands of children. The choir stopped singing and a hushed silence settled across the packed stands. For several minutes the phantom swords continued their magical ballet until one by one they were extinguished and the darkened stadium grew deathly quiet.

'Ladies and gentlemen,' the invisible voice was portentous to a degree that suggested that Moses might just about be ready to display the tablets. 'THE REVEREND JAMES J WHICHELOW!'

All hell broke loose. To wild cheering the curtains parted and there, centre stage, stood the huge bulk of Whichelow, hands raised in acknowledgement of the pandemonium his appearance had created. He was dressed quite soberly in a dark suit and dog collar, the silver sword glinting against the dark cerise of his silk shirt. His usually unkempt hair had been carefully disciplined and the grizzled beard neatly trimmed for the occasion. As he waited patiently for the thunder to subside he looked out across the sea of humanity and smiled benevolently, nodding humbly in recognition of his tumultuous welcome. As the noise slowly died he stepped forward.

'Good people of Britain: my fellow Christians,' he roared. 'It is an honour to be amongst you.' The smile died. 'Let us pray.' The crowd rose to its feet as one man and Whichelow, his hands clasped before him, rolled his eyes heavenward. 'O Lord. We give thanks for your bounty and for the occasion. Grant this night that we may gather in peace to celebrate our Christian fellowship and to give thanks for your many mercies. We know Lord that evil is at large in the world and in these dark days we ask for your strength and guidance as we prepare to face Satan in all his many forms. Make us all soldiers in the good fight and fill us with your holy spirit as we go forward into battle.'

It was pretty low key stuff, Hawkhurst thought, although these were early days. Perhaps he would get into rabble rousing as he went on. After an hour it had become clear that was exactly his plan. After the platitudes came the poison. By way of explaining the evangelical and humanitarian work of the Church of Christ the Warrior around the world, he was able to introduce the subject of the hostages. Grantly, Edberg and McNally were martyrs, he said, pointing to their photographs projected, ten metres high, onto the screen behind him. These fine young men, going about God's work, had been held in captivity for years by Muslim gunmen and now no one was sure if they were even alive. It was, he confided, almost certain that they had been brutally murdered by their Muslim captors.

Tom looked at the smiling, fresh faced image of McNally. Perhaps he was a martyr but, whatever the Church may have made of him, he had at one time been a drug dealer and, judging from what Laura had said, a sexual deviant. As, deep in thought, he stared down at the stage Potgeiter elbowed him sharply in the ribs, bringing him out of his reverie. Shuffling along the line of occupied seats, excusing herself as she stepped, a trifle unsteadily, over feet, a woman was making her way to seat red x-ray fifty three. So far as Hawkhurst could discern she was oldish, well into her sixties, wearing a none too clean scarf over her head and a bulky padded body warmer that seemed excessive for such a humid night. The three of them watched her intently as she made her way along the line. There was nothing for them to do since police marksmen positioned at strategic points around the stadium had a clear line of fire on red x-ray fifty three and were doubtless already zeroing their telescopic sights. Anything in the least unusual and they could and would, in the blink of an eye, drop her dead where she sat. To Hawkhurst however she seemed too ordinary to constitute any real threat: maybe Laura had misheard Mary Lou's slumbering mutterings or perhaps red x-ray fifty three meant something else. He returned his attention to the stage upon which the impressive power and devious direction of Whichelow's oratory were beginning to reveal themselves.

'Are we,' bellowed Whichelow, 'are we going to allow the sons of Satan to terrorise and bomb their way to power?'

The question brought a low growl from sections of the crowd.

'Are we going to stand by, time and time again, and let innocent women and children be massacred as we saw in that awful outrage on the Nile? Do you truly believe God wants us to stand by and watch?' The sinking of the Rameses the Third had occurred over six weeks ago yet the memory was still fresh, the wounds still open. A whole class of British school children had been aboard and many had died.

The responding growl swelled. 'No.'

'Good people, ask yourselves this. Does God want us to stand meekly by while the sons of Satan spread their infidel heresy around the world with the bomb and the Kalashnikov?'

'No!' Many of the skinhead groups were on their feet now. They were very drunk and although Whichelow could keep them under control by the strength of his personality and his seductive message they were determined to express their solidarity. Some were giving Nazi salutes, others punching the air in rhythmic time to their chanting. 'No. No. No.'

The Reverend held up his hand for silence. When, after several minutes, it was achieved he continued in a less combative tone.

'People of Britain. Violence is an abomination to the Lord. Blessed are the meek, He said. Yet did He not also say that He came not to bring peace but a sword? Love they neighbour, we are told, and that is a mighty fine sentiment, one we should embrace throughout our lives. Yet when that neighbour works day and night to undermine your faith, to insinuate his own faithless creed into the countries that declared for Christ hundreds of years ago, is that man truly a neighbour?'

'No! No!'

The first signs of hysteria were beginning to show now and some of the more pacific groups were heading for the exits, many shaking their heads in disgust at what they were hearing. But they were few in number and the vast majority were obviously very much in tune with the Reverend's preaching. Where departures were noticed it drew abuse and the occasional blow.

'You know, good people, you see that the enemy is among us already. We have welcomed them with open arms into the nations of God – into your country and into mine, to share those freedoms we all hold so dear. And how do they repay us? They plot by night and day to destroy those freedoms and to impose the tyranny of Islam. A tyranny where women are treated as second class citizens and the victims of mutilation, a tyranny where slavery is still openly practised. A bloody dictatorship where the rule of law is administered by the executioner's sword and the lash. Do we need neighbours like that?'

'No!' The roar went up again and again. 'No! No! No!'

In the arena the crowd was slowly but surely working itself into a frenzy, whole groups leaping to their feet to affirm the truth of what they were hearing. The whole stadium was in restless motion, rippling and jostling like the surface of a choppy sea. Sensing trouble, files of uniformed police were sidling into position at the exit points. On paper they had seemed a formidable force but now, faced with this kind of mob, half of it driven by religious fervour, half by racist hatred, it seemed a very fragile shield indeed. Whichelow's performance was approaching its climax now and even Hawkhurst, hating the man and everything he stood for, could not deny the dark attraction of his message. He was expressing the inner thoughts of people throughout the western world. The dark, secret, xenophobic thoughts that common decency, education and civilisation would normally keep in check, or at least in proportion. They weren't thoughts unique to this crowd. Far from it. They were present in just about everybody, regardless of race, religion or nationality. All Whichelow was doing was drawing them forth, bringing them to the surface, releasing their awful, poisonous potential for destruction. At his side Brennan produced a hip flask and, taking a long pull, passed it along in silence as Whichelow continued his remorseless tirade. He was serious now, choosing his words with care, knowing he held that entire gathering in the palm of his hand.

'You know, good people. When I hear the ayatollahs, the imams and all the rest of those tyrants and potentates tell me: 'There is no God but Allah,' I ask myself just what kind of God is it that allows, no, actively sanctions, such behaviour? What kind of God is it that encourages bombings and killings, that encourages the suppression of the basic freedoms, that encourages the enslavement of women and ethnic minorities? I tell you, good people. No God at all. No God but Satan himself. Only the evil one would encourage such things.'

The arena was still now, hypnotised, held in total thrall by the man's magnetic personality, his eyes glowed as he seemed to speak directly to every person present in that packed auditorium.

'I tell you. I am here among you to spread a message. And it is a simple message.' He drew himself up impressively to his full height his head slowly turning to take in every upturned face. 'SATAN IS HERE. HE IS HERE TODAY. HE IS HERE NOW. HE MOVES AMONGST US IN MANY GUISES. IT IS FOR US TO CAST HIM OUT. IN LITTLE MORE THAN A YEAR FROM NOW WE SHALL ENTER THE THIRD MILLENNIUM. THE BATTLE FOR THE NEXT THOUSAND YEARS IS UPON US. LET US TAKE UP ARMS TOGETHER AGAINST EVIL. LET US GO FORWARD TOGETHER TO THE FINAL VICTORY.' As he spoke the pictures of the hostages behind him faded away and in their place crystallised the image of a huge red sword. 'TAKE UP THE SWORD.'

The crowd roared, a deep throated roar that seemed to shake the whole stadium, reverberating beneath the roofing, sending roosting starlings swirling skywards in a black snow storm of squealing terror. Then it happened.

Standing to allow him to keep his eye on the Reverend over the crowd, Hawkhurst heard the faintest staccato patter and saw his huge figure reel backwards, his arms spread out crucifix-like. Like a huge tree he staggered a few steps before collapsing on the stage. At first there was a stunned uncomprehending silence. Then reality dawned.

'Jesus Christ,' Potgeiter gasped. 'Someone's shot the bastard.'

Brennan was up and running in seconds with Tom and Piet in close pursuit.

'Come on,' he said. 'Let's get down there. All hell's going to break loose.'

It was at the precise moment they reached the exit that the woman in red x-ray fifty three exploded.

CHAPTER THIRTY TWO

'Ladies and gentlemen please remain in your seats.' The voice booming over the stadium sound system was calm and reassuring. 'Remain in your seats. There is no need to panic.'

But no one was listening just now; certainly not in this section of the crowd: everybody wanted out of there in a big way. The three of them turned in their tracks and, with Brennan leading, barged their way back through the howling, panicking mob towards the smoking charnel house that surrounded the remains of red x-ray fifty three. At first it was like fighting against an irresistible river of flailing arms and legs; a nightmare succession of bloody, wild-eyed faces thrusting past, open mouthed, trampling the groaning injured underfoot. Less determined men would have been carried back by the sheer weight of numbers and it took savage kicks and punches to clear a path through, although as they got closer to the epicentre of destruction the fleeing melee thinned out and progress became easier.

'Stay where you are.' The voice over the sound system was desperately trying to maintain control. 'Stay in your seats.'

In some areas of the stadium, those furthest from the explosion, there was little panic but right here it was the halls of bedlam as screaming, clawing people fought to reach the exits. As the crowd fled and the vacant space around them grew Hawkhurst looked down in horror and gritted his teeth to stop himself vomiting. All that remained of the seat and its occupant, as well as a dozen of those immediately surrounding it, were a few inches of twisted metal and a contorted heap of mangled flesh and bone. Around their feet, dismembered limbs; arms, legs and hands lay scattered about, a litter of smashed bone, ripped clothing and lacerated flesh. Blood ran down below the terraced seating in long scarlet fingers. Tom estimated at least thirty people were either dead or would shortly be so. It was a while before any of them could speak.

'A goddamn kamikaze,' Brennan grunted. He alone had experienced this sort of thing before. There were flecks of blood and brains on his face and the blast had blown his thin ginger hair awry as he knelt to take a closer look at the horror.

Hawkhurst looked at the carnage about him and moved to help a dazed teenager to his feet. The youth, hyperventilating, his face blackened, seemed otherwise unhurt but in deep shock and Tom gently eased him into an undamaged seat.

'Take it easy,' he said softly. 'You're OK. You're OK.'

The boy looked at him blankly for a moment then his eyes rolled up and the heaving chest stilled. Tom stared then realised he was gone.

Potgeiter was down on his knees vainly attempting to calm a badly injured woman: both legs gone below the knee. He had removed his belt and with bloody fingers was attempting to fix tourniquets but her agonised thrashing was making the task near impossible. Within minutes the police and emergency services were on the scene and the three of them gratefully stood back. Tom's hands were shaking.

A full scale evacuation of the stadium was under way now. It was in the main an orderly affair although there was a certain amount of shoving as the possibility of other bombs dawned on the stunned audience. Going up to the senior officer at the scene, a silver haired sergeant, Brennan produced his ID and pointed down at the stage where the prostrate figure of Whichelow, surrounded by medical orderlies and police, was being lifted onto a stretcher.

'We need to get down there – fast.'

The policeman hesitated, he was as shocked by the carnage as anyone else there, but then produced his radio. On the stage below the spare figure of Inspector Bullivant turned his eye up to where they stood. The sergeant, half expecting an official roasting for even suggesting such a thing in these circumstances, listened blank faced to the responding crackle of his radio then shrugged.

'OK.' He said simply, 'He says it's all right, down you go. I'll send a man along to see no one tries to stop you.'

As they descended the steps towards the stadium floor the distant sounds of sirens came to them as word of the outrage spread to the world beyond the stadium. From all around the rapidly emptying arena the wailing of police cars, ambulances and other emergency services rose to the skies. Accompanied by a young special constable they strode towards the raised podium, wading through a shallow sea of crumpled programmes, empty lager cans, popcorn packets and other abandoned detritus. Ascending the steps leading up to the stage they stood in silence as Whichelow's unconscious form was carried past.

There was blood over his heart, seeping darkly through the red blanket that had been tucked around his grossness, and a medic was holding a drip that had been inserted in his arm. The face was ashen under the stage make-up and the silver sword about his neck dangled down at the side of the stretcher. Brennan went up to stand by Bullivant who, hands thrust deep in his pockets, was staring out over the deserted stadium where a sprinkling of police, heads down, were already sifting through the garbage in search of evidence.

'What happened? We were up by the explosion when the shooting started.'

The inspector turned to face him. In normal circumstances the last thing he would have wanted was the involvement of civilians or foreigners – even if they were American secret agents. Nevertheless, they had delivered up Bubka on a plate and the Mathew's killing had been a case where he had not expected to get a result. He owed Brennan and Hawkhurst. It had been Tom who had alerted him to the machinations of the Church of Christ the Warrior in the first place and at least Scotland Yard were now keeping a watching brief: the only reason he had been at the stadium that night.

'Three shots, all in the chest, close to the heart. Luckily the Church's own doctor was in the wings. They've got a surgical team standing by at the Cromwell Hospital right now but personally I wouldn't give much for his chances of even reaching surgery.'

'Who did it?'

Bullivant pointed down to the stadium floor where from beneath a silver thermal blanket an ankle and one worn training shoe protruded. Lying there among the discarded rubbish it had just seemed like so much more of the same.

'It's early days but my bet is that he did it – there was a handgun under the body. We're gathering up all the security camera videos right now and we've located a couple of eye witnesses.'

Brennan looked at the pathetic bundle.

'What happened to him?'

Bullivant shrugged.

'Not sure yet. Probably suicide. No immediate sign of any wounds on the body – could have been poison.' He jerked his head up the banked seating to where the bloody survivors of the bomb were being tended and the dead removed. 'Let's get back to the station and have a look at the security videos. I'll need statements from you.'

*****

Before breakfast at the hotel the following morning Hawkhurst went to the foyer for a newspaper. It made grim reading. On the front page, under the headline 'Assassins', the attack on Whichelow and the bomb in the stands were documented in great detail. Whichelow, who was still undergoing surgery when the paper had gone to bed, was described as being in a critical condition and the doctors tending him had rated his chances of survival as poor. Eight people had been killed in the explosion and another twenty injured. This in itself would have been bad enough yet even more worrying was the terminology being used in a supposedly responsible broadsheet. Whichelow was described as a 'champion of religious freedom and civil rights' and a 'crusading priest' while the attackers were variously 'fanatics', 'terrorists', 'Muslim fundamentalists' or 'ideological zealots'. In the current climate these terms were clearly considered interchangeable. Editorial comment in all the papers, the frivolous and the deadly serious alike, demanded firm action against 'the enemy within'.

This was very much what people wanted to hear – that part of the population that was listening at all – but what they wanted most of all was revenge. After the events of the previous night large sections of the fleeing crowd had run amok across west and central London, smashing shop windows and setting fire to cars. These mobs had largely, though not exclusively, targeted black and Asian property and for several hours the police had been unable to gain control of the situation. Around Gerrard Street, a number of Chinese restaurants had been petrol bombed causing diners to flee in terror. In some of the target areas the inhabitants had barricaded off streets to protect themselves. Shots had certainly been fired in some Asian ghettos, although by who and at whom was unclear. Ominously, within the few short hours since Whichelow had been shot, messages of solidarity for the beleaguered minorities had been received from Tehran and Tripoli, drawing warnings from Washington, London and Paris of the dangers of interfering in internal affairs. The stance that Washington had adopted in the wake of the shooting was increasingly aggressive. Embarrassed by the Nagasaki Maru incident, the attempt on Whichelow's life was an eagerly seized opportunity to regain the moral high ground.

From his hotel room window Tom had looked out across the rooftops at the columns of black smoke that rose lazily from smouldering vehicles and properties into the bright morning sky. Even here in the centre of the capital the ever present wail of sirens was a constant reminder of a city on the edge of anarchy. And as the news spread around the world the anger and violence went with it. In Paris Martinette's performance at Notre Dame had been hailed as a landmark in the history of the Catholic Church. It had been a masterpiece of stage management, widely reported, in which His Eminence had sternly declared that the outrage in London only served to underline the warning he had delivered. He had also accused certain Islamic leaders, naming them so there could be no doubt as to whom he referred, of having declared war on the Christian world and calling on the western democracies for strong action. Despite the attack on Whichelow the Cardinal emphasised his intention to proceed with the Berlin meeting the following week. He prayed that The Reverend would recover sufficiently to attend in person but, failing that, made it clear his followers would maintain the faith and carry forward the flame of freedom their leader had lit. In this struggle all Christians were as one.

Tom, depressed by the turn of events, had phoned Angie, wishing he could have her there with him but knowing she was safer where she was. She, for her part, had been eager to come down, if only for a few hours, but reluctantly he had told her not to. As he went in to breakfast he realised he felt weary and recalled it had been three that morning before they had got back to the hotel. Brennan, coffee before him, looked up.

'Any news?' he asked, knowing the American's contacts in London and New York would be monitoring events. Brennan shook his head.

'Whichelow's out of surgery but remains in a critical condition according to the hospital. He hasn't recovered consciousness and they've got him on a life support system. But that's the least of our problems. The Arabs are all saying that the rioting last night was orchestrated by western governments. Coming after the Nagasaki Maru incident they say it's clear evidence of our warlike intentions. As a result the price of oil has gone sky high and, word is, there's going to be some tough action from the West within twenty-four hours.'

Tom shook his head.

'But that's giving Whichelow just what he wants. Even if it doesn't amount to out and out war it'll mean an end to the peace initiative.'

Brennan shrugged.

'I know, but there's no alternative. If the industrialised world lets the oil producing states hold them to ransom by pushing up the price of oil it'll mean recession and economic ruin on a global scale. Remember 1973? The West can't let that happen again.'

Potgeiter appeared, a sheaf of newspapers under his arm. He dumped these on the table with a thud.

'It's like Beirut out there,' he grunted, reaching for the coffee. 'Between here and Oxford Circus I counted twenty burnt out cars and half-a-dozen wrecked buses – they're using bulldozers to clear a way through – and there's hardly a shop front with glass left. The looters must have had a field day, there are armed police on every corner.'

Breakfast was late arriving, many of the staff were having trouble getting to work, the manager explained, and the Muslim kitchen workers were unlikely to venture far from the comparative safety of their homes for the time being. They ate in silence, the weight of events hanging over the table. Tom was appalled, he had been born in this town. It was rough and tough in some areas and had seen riots before but nothing on this scale. He pushed his plate away half finished. He wanted to look around for himself.

'I'll see you guys at lunch,' he said tersely.

*****

It was as Potgeiter had described it. Within a few yards of the hotel a car was still smouldering at the kerbside, the acrid stench of burnt rubber hanging on the air. The blackened paintwork was blistered and peeling and jewel-like shards of shattered windscreen lay strewn about. He walked on, the crunch of broken glass underfoot. Along Tottenham Court Road police were winching other wrecked vehicles onto transporters in an attempt to get traffic flowing again. Shop owners were busy among the shattered remnants of their stock collecting up what little the looters had not taken, burnt or spoiled. Piles of clothing, larger electrical goods, fridges and freezers, together with cases of tinned foods lay about on the pavements. Anything attractive or portable had disappeared with the mob. The faces of commuters making their way to work reflected stunned disbelief as they took in the panorama of destruction that now stood where yesterday they had left the ordinary and familiar sights of the working day. Stony faced patrols of armed police were everywhere and the wail of sirens unceasing.

Surprisingly, the Underground was still operating and he took the Northern Line down to the Embankment, intent on seeing how widespread the rioting had been. Here there were fewer signs of the disturbances: the proximity to Buckingham Palace, Westminster and Whitehall would have meant prompt police action. He stood at the riverside, taking in the broad sweep of sunlit skyline that stretched from the Chelsea Harbour to Canary Wharf. Smoke rose from a dozen points and along the river a convoy of fire engines were making their wailing way over Westminster Bridge. He walked towards Westminster, the familiar sight of the Houses of Parliament and Big Ben no longer so solidly reassuring somehow. Here road blocks, manned by red bereted members of the Parachute Regiment, had been set up. Ostensibly they were checking cars for looted goods but with the country in its current near hysterical condition the possibility of terrorist activity, Islamic or Irish, could not be discounted.

Moving on, he made his way towards Victoria Station. There were no signs of damage here although the police presence was just as heavy as elsewhere. Across the forecourt of the station, groups of Asians, Arabs and other easterners stood amid their baggage. Mainly women and children, Tom assumed they were heading for Gatwick and an early flight out. The adults looked nervous, the mothers scolding noisy children in hushed tones, afraid of attracting too much attention. Not that anyone paid them much attention but it made Tom angry to see what dark avenues Whichelow's evil obsession had dragged, what had been, by and large, a tolerant and inclusive society.

He glanced at his watch: it was a little after eleven. There was to be a broadcast by the Prime Minister at eleven-thirty and he spent the next ten minutes locating a Thameside pub with a television. Taking his beer he settled himself into a corner seat. The bartender, a lugubrious Australian with a lisp, who was not that interested in the outside world, totally preoccupied as he was with zapping flies with a rubber band. However, at Tom's request he turned up the sound. It was brief and to the point. The PM was his usual toothy, sincere and concerned self, deploring the racist statements and activities and calling for calm and understanding within the community. However, when he had got through the expected platitudes a certain steeliness of tone entered his voice. The hike in prices announced by the oil producing states of the Middle East was, he said, totally unjustified and tantamount to economic blackmail. Any such unilateral move was unacceptable under international law. Therefore measures, both diplomatic and military, were in hand to ensure the West's supplies were guaranteed at an acceptable price. There would be further bulletins when these measures had been finalised.

    A price acceptable to whom, Tom wondered, well aware that it would be the Americans who were dictating policy here. For its part the UK, with its sizeable reserves in the North Sea and Atlantic, could be virtually self-sufficient in oil if she chose. But, of course, that was only part of the story. If second division nations like the British and French wanted to be taken seriously on the world stage they had to flex what little muscle they retained every so often. The Americans would want as many allies as they could muster in the coming fighting, not necessarily for the military input they could make, but for the respectability they would, by association, lend to any act of aggression. He wondered what form the 'measures' would take. Brennan had spoken of seizing oil wells and there was still a large multi-national naval force on station in the Gulf of Hormuz. It included several vessels that had amphibious capability and several thousand American and British marines. No doubt once they had established a beachhead they could be reinforced by substantial land forces in very short order. The devastating efficiency of these forces had been graphically demonstrated in the past, however, unlike the Gulf War of 1991, here there could be no possible moral justification for such action, no Saddam to hate, no invasion of neutral Kuwait. Here was only naked commercial self-interest supported by overwhelming military power. It would be imperialism on a scale unmatched since the nineteenth century. On the brink of the Third Millennium the world appeared to be heading back to whence it had come.

    Stepping out into the sunlight he looked around for a cab, intent on returning to the hotel. The cabbie was Jewish, with relatives in Israel, and took a deep, extremely loquacious, interest in the way things were developing. Tom could have done without the commentary and contented himself with the odd 'yes' or 'no' in response. Because of the disruption in the West End, blocked roads and police diversions meant the route back was a circuitous one and everywhere he looked there was evidence of the night's violence; telephone booths smashed, windows shattered. It was all very depressing. As they drove along Holborn Tom broke into the cabbie's monologue.

'Stop here, please, I want to get a paper.' He pointed at a news vendor and the taxi slid to a halt. He stared at the billboard. 'Jesus,' he whispered. 'Nothing can stop it now.' He took the paper and sat back in his seat while the driver made to pull out into the traffic.

There across the front page was printed: 'The Reverend Whichelow close to death.'

CHAPTER THIRTY THREE

The rioting went on for three days, spreading to all the major British cities; spilling across the channel to Europe and beyond. The assassination attempt on The Reverend Whichelow sparked a wave of killings, beatings, burning and looting, largely, but not exclusively, directed at Muslims, and there were major disturbances around the world, especially in the United States. Here the trouble was heightened by inter-factional fighting notably within the ghettos of Washington and Los Angeles where black Christian fought savagely with black Muslim, a situation exploited to the full by the criminal element who for a while burned and looted at their leisure. Only the National Guard was able to bring a halt to the disturbances and that at a high cost in lives and property.

Throughout the period of unrest two factors, two sides of the same coin, dominated the political arena: the hike in oil prices imposed by the oil producers of the Middle East and the relentless build-up of western forces. The original 'pre-planned' exercises in the Gulf of Hormuz had been extended, indefinitely it seemed, and the participating fleets had been reinforced by three aircraft carriers and a flotilla of support vessels that had sailed from the US seaboard at short notice. Air power was also being bulked up at strategic locations in the eastern Mediterranean and the same fleets of ancient yet brutally effective B52s that had pounded Ho Chi Minh's armies a quarter of a century before and more recently brought Saddam Hussein's hopes to nought were again being mustered at bases in the Indian Ocean. The code name for these exercises, Ocean Wind was, some said, ominously, suggestive of their true purpose for had not Desert Wind preceded Desert Storm in 1991. Then, the West had acted decisively to remove a perceived threat to its oil supplies, although on that occasion there was at least the pretence of a moral justification. Here there was none.

As the tension grew the American President appeared at an emergency session of the United Nations to explain the reason for the invasion. It was, he said, essential to ensure that the world economy was not held to ransom by the threat of excessive and an unjustifiable increases in the price of crude oil – economic warfare he called it. The allies would not stand by and watch while the world order was destabilised by supporters of international terrorism. Despite his assurances that the military build-up was a purely precautionary move and designed to protect the interests of third world countries as well as the industrial nations, the sabre rattling was roundly condemned by the majority of unaligned representatives. There was no chance of the moves receiving UN approval. His offer of talks to establish a mutually acceptable level for oil prices was also rejected out of hand by all the oil producing countries. There could be no question of negotiations while America held a gun to their heads.

Despite the outcry, the President remained unrepentant, beyond the economic considerations there were other factors, moral factors, involved, he said. The recent outrage in London, in which an eminent US citizen and man of God had been savagely attacked by Islamic terrorists, demonstrated all too clearly the hatred and hostility that some heads of state bore towards the West. He himself had little doubt that the attack on Whichelow had been sanctioned by Tehran. Faced with such a threat the allied forces would not hesitate to defend democracy and civil liberties against those medieval tyrants who had hoped to undermine these fundamental rights of man by a sinister mixture of economic warfare and international terrorism. After the collapse of communism another evil empire, fuelled by religious fanaticism, was attempting to spread its influence around the world. It too would be opposed by the democratic nations of the world.

Once the world turned its attention to the international posturing, the domestic situation eased. This was expected, intended indeed by the allies who had seen the threat of all-out war as a welcome diversion from the deteriorating home front. In London ringleaders were arrested, the streets were cleared of the wreckage and life returned to normal as boarded up shop fronts were slowly reglazed. The government, faced with the imminent breakdown of law and order, had acted decisively and the police made the most of new, hastily introduced, emergency powers to crack down with a vengeance. With war clouds gathering, the silent majority recognised the need for national unity and strong government and the public now looked on approvingly as measures that would have been condemned as dictatorial a month before became the norm. Baton charges and rubber bullets, live rounds on some occasions, had been widely used and the presence of army patrols in the street was now hardly remarked upon. Apart from curfews in the ghettos, both words with a singularly un-British ring, within a week things were almost back to normal.

Following the assassination attempt on Whichelow a book of 'condolence and prayer' had been temporarily placed on view in the hospital chapel. The chapel was a small, brick built edifice in the leafy gardens below the window of the private ward where he now lay in a deep coma. A statement by the Church elders said this had been done at public request to allow the Reverend's many followers in Britain to register their support in a simple and dignified manner. To Hawkhurst it was just another ploy to keep the poison working, yet, for reasons he could not quite explain, he had taken a taxi down to the Cromwell Road and joined the motley queue outside the drab little church. It was quite an impressive turn out, perhaps a couple of hundred standing in line at any one time, and comprised a melange of skinheads, ordinary working people, casual gawpers, over pious God botherers and a highly vocal sprinkling of weeping hysterics. Nearly all wore the red sword in their lapel. Taking his place at the rear Tom shuffled forward.

Inside the little chapel it was cool with a damp, musty smell about it. The queue shuffled up the left hand aisle to the transept where a thick leather bound tome lay open on a well waxed lectern borne on the outstretched wings of St John's eagle. There were, he noted, three other similar books, presumably full, resting on a shelf beneath the lectern. A couple of bulky heavies loitered in the background just in case of any spontaneous hysteria. As he approached the lectern Tom watched those ahead of him as they made their contributions. The thug element usually just stared for a few seconds at the words they had written then moved along, although a couple of the thicker sort could not resist the opportunity to present Nazi style salutes. Others contented themselves with a brief nod of acknowledgement while others, distraught, cried out aloud in distress.

As he came abreast of the lectern Tom ran his eyes down the list of entries. Some were banal: 'In God we trust'. Others simple: 'You are in our prayers'. Some were downright frightening. 'One people, one God, one religion.' As he looked, Tom considered the irony of recent events. Despite their best efforts Whichelow was on the verge of succeeding in everything he had planned, plotted and connived at for over twenty years even if he did not live to see it come to fruition. Even if, as seemed likely, he died he was assured a shabby sort of immortality and to future generations he would most likely be seen as a latter day Archduke Franz Ferdinand, the catalyst for the war to end all wars. To some he was already a saint and martyr. Moving on, Tom headed towards the side door and out into the sunlit gardens. Beneath the window of Whichelow's first floor room lay hundreds of wreaths and other floral tributes, many of them already wilting. Each bore a well-wisher's card or note. Not since the tragic death of Diana, Princess of Wales the previous year had there been such a spontaneous outburst of public grief. Suddenly Hawkhurst wanted to be away from there, to be free of the heavy, cloying atmosphere of death that clung to everything that had been touched by The Reverend James Whichelow.

  He walked for a while, considering his next move. Although there was little that could be done to affect the march towards war now, he had agreed to accompany Brennan and Potgeiter to the meeting in Berlin in three days' time. Despite a certain level of opposition from more moderate political and religious groups Martinette had insisted that it should go ahead out of respect for Whichelow and as a demonstration of Christian solidarity for the benefit of the Church's enemies abroad. With Whichelow *hors-de-combat* Martinette had quickly become the focal point for the campaign and had not been slow to use his position to condemn what he called the economic terrorism of Islam. The German government, fearful of causing a public outcry if it moved to ban the meeting, limply allowed it to proceed although at the same time drawing up plans to impose the highest level of security. Just how inadequate these were to prove only became evident later.

  Yet there were things that still worried Hawkhurst about the assassination attempt. Despite the sweeping statements issued by the American President, all the evidence suggested that the supposed assassin had no known Islamic connections. Donald McLeish had been an unemployed building worker, twenty four years old, with no previous criminal record and, although his fingerprints were on the gun, the post mortem showed he had himself been killed by a fatal injection of strychnine administered to the kidney area. Suicide was extremely unlikely. It was true that the bomber, Leyla Malik, had been born a Muslim, but she had been a sixty year old alcoholic, a sad old bag lady with a long history of mental illness who had been cast out by her family years ago. From questioning her down-and-out companions it appeared that some benefactor had given her the smart new body warmer, half a bottle of Booth's Gin and a ticket to the fatal meeting – red x-ray fifty three – about half-an-hour before the explosion. The jacket had been lined with explosives and, from the forensic evidence of recovered fragments, was probably detonated by radio control, possibly from within the stadium itself. It seemed more likely to Hawkhurst that she had been set up to provide a diversion for the assassin but in her gin induced fuddle had arrived late. He reflected that it had been fortunate for the three of them that they had been at the exit and heading for the stage when the explosion occurred. A few moments later and they would have caught the full blast.

Of course, Whichelow had enemies, not least the cast aside Mary Lou, now banged up in Holloway. Mary Lou must have known about the plan, why else would she have mentioned the seat? But somehow that did not ring entirely true – the ultimate success of the Church of Christ the Warrior's conspiracy had turned on that meeting. Up until the moment she had ordered Bubka to eliminate Hawkhurst she had been a loyal supporter of the Reverend and, apart from her lawyer and US embassy officials, she had no contact with the outside world since her arrest. Of course she might well have seen it as a neat way of achieving conflicting ends, killing the treacherous Whichelow would serve to strengthen the Church's claim to the moral high ground and precipitate war.

It was a strangely unsatisfying state of affairs so far as Tom was concerned. Whichelow was as good as dead but the evil he had set in train wound on and on. In one way he wanted nothing more than to get back to Sarnafon and Angahrad yet the need to see the thing through to its culmination in Berlin was equally strong. There was a perverse fascination in the whole unfolding process. Powerful allied forces were prowling the coasts of large parts of the Middle East and were obviously at a high state of readiness although, with further reinforcements still being assembled in America and Europe, it seemed unlikely that they would attack within the next few days. If talks on oil prices could be started they might not even be needed – always assuming there were no aggressive military moves by the oil producers. Given the overwhelming numerical and technical superiority of the allies this was not regarded as a real possibility.

The West's policy, if undeclared, seemed transparent enough: unless the oil producing states were prepared to give long term guarantees on prices, oil rich territories would be occupied. It was obvious this would be unacceptable to the Arabs, amounting as it did to negotiating under duress. The situation was made worse by the suggestion already being made by some western governments that the high cost of maintaining any occupying forces should be met by selling oil from installations that fell under allied control on the open market. Not satisfied with stealing the oil, they would use the loot to pay for the theft. If such a policy was introduced Tom knew it would be a humiliation that no Arab could accept and the Jihad would be inevitable.

*****

As the meeting in Berlin drew nearer so its significance in global terms increased. All the major industrial countries would be sending representatives and a round of high level talks about the international situation would be held in the German capital during the week following Martinette's meeting. As yet the allied forces in the Middle East had made no overtly aggressive move, content for the vast Armada to cruise, just outside territorial waters, up and down the Persian Gulf. The problem now was with dwindling reserves of oil it could only be a matter of time before action was inevitable. Behind the scenes talks were going on between the various parties and a negotiated peace remained a real, although tenuous possibility.

During this period Martinette, upon whom the mantle of leader of the Christian camp had now fallen, maintained a subtle yet effective public relations assault from his extensive family estate in the Loire valley. Each evening he would appear outside the gated entrance to his chateau and regale the gathered news organisations with his personal interpretation of that day's developments. In the main this consisted of a pious rejection of violence followed by a half regretful demand for strong action to ensure the control and pacification of aggressive Islamic fundamentalism within the West. In fact it went deeper than that. What His Eminence really wanted was the wholesale repatriation of Muslim immigrants from France – from Europe if possible. He also wanted to outlaw Muslims from gathering in any group larger than twenty individuals and to implement the sequestration of Muslim assets. Along with all this went the closing down of all Mosques – those hotbeds of religious heresy and political sedition. He never quite said as much to the press, of course, but to effectively achieve his long term aims such things would be a natural progression. Apart from the Nazi era, Europe had not seen religious intolerance like this since the sixteenth century. But his words were well heeded in political circles and it was noticeable that very little came from the Vatican to refute his vision these days. The Pope was ill, dying some said, and Martinette, once anathema to the Catholic Church but now very much a contender for the highest role in Christendom, was gathering support in the cloisters of power. At each of his evening camera calls one question invariably came up: how was the Reverend Whichelow?

The Reverend remained in a deep coma he told them. He was in daily contact with the hospital and prayed constantly for the recovery of his brother in Christ. However, the omens were not good and the saintly Whichelow was reported to be sinking into a vegetative state. Best medical advice was that he was unlikely to regain consciousness. Eventually a decision might have to be taken to switch off his life support system. It was his intention, His Eminence told them, to visit the hospital on his way to Berlin. He commended them all to pray for a full recovery for the man who had so eloquently preached for a crusade – a crusade that would claim the world for Christ. Each evening he would bless the media mob and, ignoring the hurled questions and flashing cameras, return through the wrought iron gates to the sanctuary of his country home.

*****

At Heathrow the Air France Airbus came to a halt some distance from the terminal. It was a planned ploy. The hundred metres or so of red carpet down which His Eminence would shortly walk allowed the gathered crowds the optimum opportunity to view the Cardinal. Thousands had gathered to see the man who in a few short months had become one of the most powerful Churchmen in the world and heir to Whichelow's mantle and the throne of St Peter's.

Potgeiter, sprawled out on the floor of the hotel room, can of lager in one hand, stared at the television screen as a low-loader manoeuvred the steps down which His Eminence would shortly descend into position. Hawkhurst and Brennan sat slumped side by side on the settee, each with a glass of whisky to hand. The days leading up to tomorrow's Berlin meeting had dragged. Perhaps because their role in the relentless decent into destruction was now marginalised they had simply to eat, sleep and listen to the radio and watch television. They were undoubtedly demoralised, yet Hawkhurst couldn't quite accept that this thing had run its full course. If the Church of Christ the Warrior and its allies wanted a final solution to the Islamic problem they would know well enough that they had to exert even more pressure on world leaders. The meeting in Berlin, when it came, must surely be the Church's last throw and he felt it would inevitably have to be something special, something so spectacular that it would negate all the patient negotiations that might yet bring peace and sanity to the world. Yet what could they do now? Whichelow was as good as dead and despite the very real possibility of an invasion there was no real fighting in the Middle East.

  The television cameras played across the crowds at the airport. Many carried banners: 'One God, One Religion', 'The Lord is a Man of War', 'Cast Satan Out.' The suitably robust brass band played Jerusalem. It was hardly an appropriate theme for a French Catholic priest yet somehow fitted the occasion exactly. Then the door on the aircraft opened and after a final adjustment of the steps the diminutive figure of Martinette stood framed there. He wore his full regalia, scarlet robes and wide brimmed hat as he carefully began to descend the steps, acknowledging the cheers of the crowd with a raised hand that made the sign of the cross at regular intervals. At the base of the stairs he was welcomed by the Foreign Minister, half the Cabinet and an impressive selection of British religious leaders including the Archbishops of Canterbury and York and the Chief Rabbi. As Martinette was escorted down the strip of scarlet carpet towards the terminal buildings and the waiting cavalcade of limousines he stopped and spoke to the accompanying politicians. The group about him had halted and was now milling around in a somewhat haphazard manner. There was, it seemed, some confusion in the ranks and Tom stared closely. Martinette was now looking back to the aircraft from whence appeared a robed figure who ran quickly down the steps towards where they stood. In his hand he bore a wooden box. As he came up to Martinette he dropped to his knees and removing the lid offered the case to His Eminence.

  Hawkhurst whistled softly.
  'So that's where it went.'
  It was the Grail. Martinette lifted the chalice towards the crowd who, initially uncertain as to what was happening, quickly

realised what it was the little priest now held aloft. Second only to the Middle East in column inches, the papers had all given a great deal of coverage to the ongoing subject of the bogus Grail at the museum, and the arrest and subsequent bailing of Laura Woods and Dixey. Pictures of the fake chalice had appeared in every paper and there could be scarcely a person in the country who wasn't aware of what it looked like. Now this Catholic priest, this crusading Christian, had presented them with what could only be the genuine article.

'I don't like the look of this,' Brennan grunted as, after several minutes of wild cheering, the Cardinal and his entourage disappeared inside the terminal building. 'What the hell is he trying to do?'

Tom shrugged.

'Beats me, although I guess it will certainly serve to keep people's interest in the Berlin meeting at a high level. Can you imagine what it'll do to a meeting like that? Presenting the Holy Grail will send them wild. It'll make the old Nazi rallies look like a scout camp.'

They watched in silence as Martinette appeared outside the terminal and climbed into the stretch limousine. Making off, accompanied by outriders and a convoy of other official vehicles, the whole journey from the airport to the hospital, where the inert body of Whichelow lay, was covered from the air by a helicopter-mounted camera. Towards central London the crowds lined the streets three deep. Word about the Grail had spread like wildfire, swelling the throng as people came onto the streets, and to maintain the interest Martinette now travelled with the chalice balanced on his knees in full view. In twenty minutes, amid strict security the convoy of official cars had drawn up outside the hospital where Martinette was welcomed by the physician heading up the medical team caring for Whichelow. Officially the hospital was honoured to receive so prestigious a visitor although the administration was less than happy about the situation for half its revenue came from rich Arabs who could afford the exorbitant prices charged. Most of these had now left the country and those remaining in the hospital had made it clear they did not greatly relish mixing with militant Christians, even those in a deep coma. Nevertheless, Martinette was greeted warmly enough.

No cameras were permitted inside the hospital although a step-by-step description of the Cardinal's movements was transmitted by a suitably obsequious newscaster. His Eminence was now proceeding directly to the room where The Reverend Whichelow lays unconscious, the commentator said in appropriately awestruck tones. He is now entering the room. Surrounded by doctors, his own staff, politicians and security men, Martinette stood for a moment at the bedside, staring down into the blank, sunken features. Then he dropped to his knees, eyes clamped shut, hands knotted in prayer. His staff did likewise while those others present stood round, slightly embarrassed and not sure what to do next. After several minutes in prayer Martinette got to his feet. He turned to his secretary, a pimply faced youth who was holding the Grail, and took the vessel from him. Raising it on high he then lowered it onto Whichelow's chest.

'In Nomine Patri, Fili et Spiritus Sancti,' he sang shrilly, genuflecting expansively.

At eleven thirty eight precisely, at the exact moment the Holy Grail was placed upon his inert form, The Reverend Whichelow's eyes snapped open.

CHAPTER THIRTY FOUR

'Back From The Dead', 'A Modern Miracle', 'Resurrection', the headlines screamed. It was pure hysteria yet, no matter if more rational minds pointed out that Whichelow had not been dead in the first place, the mania had developed an unstoppable momentum all of its own now. Evidence of divine intervention, of the supernatural powers of the Grail, was what people were thirsting for and the media was determined to see they got it. The reappearance of the Grail and how it came to be in the possession of Martinette drew surprisingly little comment. Following the discrediting of the copy in the museum people weren't that bothered about how the original had now come into the hands of the Church. They were more interested in its miraculous, life giving powers, in speculating about its divine nature. Martinette, after holding a short thanksgiving service at Whichelow's bedside, had departed for Berlin, taking the Grail with him. News of events in London had preceded him and his arrival at Templehof had drawn huge crowds. Once again, surrounded by secret service men and outriders, he had carried the chalice before him down crowded streets on his drive to the hotel. Tomorrow, he promised, he would present the Holy Grail to them at the meeting.

It was impossible now to deny the Grail's powers for Whichelow had indeed regained consciousness at its touch and, although still very weak, was within hours communicating lucidly with his doctors. Twelve hours later he was taken off the life support system and capable of movement. A full recovery was confidently predicted. Despite protests from his medical advisers he made it clear early on that he wished to make a public statement at the first opportunity. Since his physical condition was still far from robust it was agreed only a single TV camera belonging to TVCW would be allowed into the hospital. However, thanks to a neat and doubtless profitable arrangement brokered by the Church of Christ the Warrior, the Reverend's words would be put out worldwide over as many channels as were prepared to pay the asking price. Few refused the offer and an estimated three million dollars swelled the Church's coffers. Afterwards, as they sat in the airport bar, sipping coffee and waiting for their flight to be announced, Tom, Brennan and Potgeiter reviewed the situation.

Hawkhurst was increasingly inclined to suspect that the whole thing was a put-up job; that Whichelow hadn't really been shot at all. When the assassination attempt occurred, the Church's men, including a doctor, had been conveniently on hand to hustle the supposedly dying man away. A medivac helicopter had fortuitously been on standby, engines running, to fly him to the hospital where a private suite was conveniently available. The hospital's surgeons, off duty at that time of the evening had been summoned from their homes to attend him but found themselves quickly brushed aside by the Church's own team who were already on hand within minutes. Having supposedly removed the bullets and handed them over to the police for forensic examination, they had kept him incommunicado ever since. The bullets were confirmed as having been fired from the gun found on the supposed assassin but, so far as Hawkhurst was concerned, that might well have happened long before the meeting.

As he recovered his strength the police had interviewed The Reverend but he could tell them very little. Little, that was, about the actual attempt on his life. What he could tell them, and did so to the point of tedium, was that, it seemed to him, he had been away on a long journey to a far country. He could recall little of the far country other than that it was a place more beautiful than words could describe and that he had not willingly returned to this vale of tears. It was a theme he was to return to for the benefit of the TV camera.

'I believe it was only the divine power of the Grail that brought me back,' he said. 'That it was God's will that I should live a little longer in order to prepare the way for the Second Coming. I had no choice but to submit myself to His will.' Lying there, propped up with pillows in the hospital bed, he looked positively saintly. His grizzled hair and beard had been neatly trimmed and his pink cheeks glowed with returning health. Three bullets close to the heart and here, within days, he was proclaiming the imminent return of Christ to earth. 'We were told it would be a time of wonders and miracles,' he said, 'and that time is here and that time is now. The attack on me means the Anti-Christ has at last shown his black hand, for he knows now that he and his acolytes will surely be swept away on that glorious day when the Son of God walks amongst us once again.'

Hearing this Brennan had been less than respectful.

'What we need here is a Doubting Thomas to see the wounds. Still, I guess we should be grateful the bastard's only trying to emulate Lazarus. If he decided to play Jesus Christ I think I'd have to throw up.'

Whichelow's TV appearance, necessarily brief to husband his strength, was relayed to the Berlin stadium where Martinette was presiding over the final meeting. The contrast to the London fiasco, at least to begin with, couldn't have been more marked for here discipline was extremely tight. The audience, for audience it was and as such, in sharp contrast to the London mob, had been limited to forty thousand and these carefully vetted. Security was extremely high profile with painstaking bag and body searches at the ticket office with sniffer dogs everywhere. Over ten thousand police had been drafted into the German capital from out of town, although many of these had from the outset been kept fully occupied by the gangs of skinheads and punks who roamed the prosperous Berlin avenues. Loose, dangerous looking squadrons of leather jacketed bikers prowled through the streets and it took only the least suspicion of an insult to erupt into violence. After London the mob had given itself a new name – they were all Red Swords now. Although great efforts had been made to exclude the violent element from the meeting itself, the Red Swords had flooded into the city from all across Europe and were making their presence felt in no uncertain manner. Many shops were shuttered against the chanting gangs that circled menacingly outside the stadium. Later it was estimated that over a million people had entered Berlin simply to be there when the Holy Grail was revealed by Martinette. For the police it was like dealing with fifty football crowds.

Sensing trouble brewing, the exodus of Muslims workers had gained pace and few remained in the city, the majority of those who did seeking safety in numbers behind the walls of the large Mosque on Nietzsche Strasse. From first light the elegant building, its gilded, crescent surmounted dome and minaret gleaming golden in the morning sun, was surrounded by police cars and water cannon. It was a wise move for if, within the stadium, Martinette was ostensibly officiating at the solemn ceremony, outside the hysteria was building by the second. Whichelow's TV appearance had been watched in many bars and the word resurrection was on everyone's lips. Whether or not people truly believed the second coming was imminent or that the Grail really had life giving powers, they did know that war was coming and the primal urge to participate in such momentous events was winding up the mob to new heights. If, as some were saying, the coming months would shape the next Millennium they would shape the coming months.

No one knew exactly how the trouble started although some said afterwards that it was an overzealous policeman retaliating to an insult and striking out at a Red Sword. Whatever the cause, violence flared first in the east of the city among the shabby tower blocks of what had been the old Russian Zone of occupation, and when it did, it was unstoppable. For the first few hours the police struggled to maintain control, trying to keep the violence confined to the side streets and away from the stadium which was expected to be the natural focus of the thugs' attentions. The Red Swords were at first held, having only such improvised weapons as they could make from ripped up fencing and garden railings. With protective clothing, shields and batons the police could force the demonstrators back almost at will but as the violence spread further afield the sheer weight of numbers arrayed against them began to turn the tide and the first cracks in the wall appeared. Other weapons were being used now, stocks of petrol bombs materialised and it became clear that some of the biker gangs were carrying firearms. Soon police casualties, including several dead, were mounting and what had been isolated pockets of unrest, were linking up into a broader front, outflanking the over-stretched police line and pushing them back. In an attempt to ease the pressure on their colleagues on the ground police helicopters dropped tear gas canisters. For a while it worked but soon gunfire from the ground had brought at least one helicopter plunging to earth in flames and the other moved off with shattered windows and bullet-stitched fuselage. The scream of sirens was everywhere as the forces of law and order struggled to regroup.

Although initially there had been no specific target for the violence, as it spread and gained in intensity the press of bodies slowly began to acquire an unstoppable momentum and as it did, to move in a specific direction. Who first thought of the Mosque is impossible to say but slowly the mob began to take on a new sense of purpose and to swing westward across the city towards Nietzsche Street, smashing windows and upending cars as they went. By the time they had reached the Mosque most of the police guard had been withdrawn to deal with problems elsewhere and only a single water cannon and a handful of officers remained. The police now steeled themselves to meet the storm.

With a feral roar the mob of Red Swords charged the fragile line of shields, the leaders throwing themselves at the shield wall with berserker fury. Some were sent skidding by the pressure of the water jets but others were quick to close with the police line knowing that once they were at close quarters the cannon would be of little use. The water cannon itself was soon the target for a dozen petrol bombs. With its paintwork dripping flame and tyres melting under the attack it was forced to slowly withdraw its support for the buckling police line. A few pursuing hotheads, their faces masked, had climbed onto the roof of the wagon, blindly battering at the nozzle aiming mechanism with whatever weapons they had to hand. Screaming like fiends they eventually succeeded in jamming the levers so the water now sprayed impotently skywards. And all the time the police were falling back towards the Mosque. Within a few minutes the outer wall of the building was within range of petrol bombs and the last of the police, many with their clothes and shields smouldering, slipped thankfully within the protection of its ornate doors.

For a few minutes the mob stood silently, thwarted by the solid doors, some kicked at the ornate panels in frustration while others daubed the plain whitewashed walls with the red sword emblem and anti-Islamic obscenities. Then, scaling the iron railings that marked out the perimeter, they spilled around the sides of the Mosque and out into the neatly kept gardens behind the building. Here were tall, curtained windows, soon smashed by bricks and other hastily gathered up missiles. Then came a cheer and a flicker of light as the first petrol bomb arced over the heads of the crowd, exploding with a dull thud. Within seconds yellow flames were licking hungrily up the exposed damask curtains. More bombs followed and soon the entire rear façade of the Mosque was ablaze. Driven choking, back from the flaming curtains, those Muslims, some fifty in all, who had sought sanctuary within now joined the trapped police huddling behind the main doors as the flames rapidly gained control and moved ever closer. Desperate telephone calls to police HQ for reinforcements received the response that there were no reserves left and the defenders of the Mosque would have to fend for themselves. For those trapped it was clear that soon they would have no choice; it would be a matter of facing the murderous mob beyond those doors, a mob that they could hear clearly baying for blood or dying of asphyxiation where they stood.

As the rich furnishings of the Mosque, centuries old carpets and ornately carved screens, were consumed in the crackling inferno the heat became unbearable. In alcoves around the main auditorium thousands of copies of the Koran smouldered, their leaves curling into brown ash as they were devoured by the blue flame, crisp shreds of charred paper floating on the updraft. Soon it became too much to bear and, fearfully, they threw back the great bolts and stumbled, coughing and smoke-blinded out into the blessed coolness of the night and whatever fate had in store for them. Some, their faces blackened and clothes smouldering, fell forward gasping for air while others stared uneasily around them, preparing for the worst. What they saw made them stare in disbelief.

Down the whole length of Nietzsche Street the mob was down on its knees, silent, seemingly oblivious of them. All eyes were on the tiny figure who stood in their midst, the silver bowl, reflecting fire from the Mosque, raised in his left hand. Unsmiling he stepped towards the shocked, smoke-stained survivors stopping before each individual. Dipping his forefinger into the water contained in the chalice, he beckoned them forward and sensing salvation from the mob's fury they meekly submitted as he then traced a moist cross on the forehead of each Muslim and police officer. When he had so anointed all there, he led them away in single file through the kneeling ranks of Red Swords, every thug and hooligan stunned to silence by what they had just witnessed. As they followed his progress, their eyes locked on the chalice in his hand, from the blazing Mosque came a low rumble as the great dome collapsed. To those present it was symbolic. Martinette's action had saved their lives and, in his mind at least, converted them to the true religion. It had also, once again, revealed the power of the Grail.

*****

Five thousand miles away the sun rose like a brazen eye over the light-splintered waters of the Gulf of Oman. Firdasi, seemingly unaware of the small group who stood behind him, stared out at the azure sea. It was empty, not a ship to be seen, although he knew that just below the horizon the allied fleet, growing in strength daily as reinforcements steamed in to join them, was only waiting for the word to launch its attack and invasion. He also knew that when it came it would be irresistible. The Muslim countries of the region, Arab and non-Arab alike, would fight bravely he knew, but they were as divided as ever. Divided by festering feuds, some as old as Islam itself, others stemming from more recent years of conflict. Even had they not been so divided Firdasi recognised they could never hope to prevail against the might of America and her allies with their vast resources, unlimited manpower and technological superiority. Saddam Hussein's mad, yet not uncourageous, stand had shown that in 1991 and the forces being brought against Islam today were infinitely more powerful than the allied forces that had been ranged against Iraq.

'What is to be done, Master?'

It was Heydar. Brave, young, dark-eyed Heydar who would accept a martyr's death without a moment's hesitation should he, Firdasi, demand that sacrifice of him. He smiled at the boy and sat down in the warm sand, wrapping his white djellaba around his knees. The others, perhaps a dozen men, all similarly garbed, a few carrying Kalashnikovs but most unarmed, did likewise.

'What is the cause of all our troubles, Heydar?' Firdasi asked softly.

Heydar frowned.

'The Great Satan, Master. The United States of America.'

Firdasi nodded.

'The Americans are indeed a great trial. An offence in the nostrils of Allah the Prophet, peace be on him. But they are not the root of the problem. The root of our troubles is the oil that lies beneath our lands. Oil is the lifeblood of their world and starved of it their world will die.' He waved a hand around him to indicate the sea at his back. 'Do you think those people out there would bother with us if we had no oil? Of course they would not. We have vast supplies of their lifeblood and so they will never leave us in peace until the last drop is sucked from the ground. Without it their factories will grind to a halt, their cars will not run, their aircraft cannot fly and their ships cannot sail. If that happens they cannot make money and without money they are nothing. They are vampires and we are their victims. But it is the oil that draws them and if we will not sell it to them they will take it by force.'

'What is to be done, Master?' Heydar repeated his first question.

Firdasi brushed away a sand fly.

'Remove the oil and, inshallah, the Great Satan must go elsewhere for his lifeblood. He must go elsewhere or wither and die.'

Heydar frowned but it was Ali, an older man, a Marsh Arab who had lost a hand in the endless ebb and flow of fighting along the Shat Al Arab during the Iran-Iraq war, who spoke. He had a face lined by the sun and by years of suffering in an Iraqi prison camp, when he opened his mouth to speak the teeth were black stumps worn down to the gums.

'I believe I know what you are saying, Master, but can it be done and at what cost to ourselves and our cause?'

Firdasi's jaw clenched: it would not do now to reveal his own doubts.

'It can be done if we do not allow ourselves to be weakened by pity or doubt. The cost will be immense but, believe me, it will strike the death blow to the vampire – the stake through the bloodsucker's heart.'

Heydar was still puzzled. The older followers had been with Firdasi longer and naturally were closer to The Master. Clearly they had discussed the possibilities open to them but – to remove the oil?'

'How can we remove the oil, Master? It is there and there it remains until they suck the victim dry.'

Still smiling but not answering the boy's question Firdasi got to his feet, dusting the folds of his white robe clean of sand. The others followed his example and together, a small knot of serious, stern faced men, they strode down towards the deserted golden sweep of the shoreline, the hollowed slopes of the wind carved dunes at their back, their shadows sweeping before them. Small wading birds fed at the water's edge, darting to and fro in time with the rush and retreat of the small lapping waves. As the men approached they rose in a gauzy cloud of white wings, piping in alarm. Firdasi placed an arm about Heydar's slim shoulders as they walked.

'How old were you when Saddam Hussein went into Kuwait?' he asked. 'Nine? Ten?'

'I was seven, Master, but I remember it clearly.'

Heydar was an Iranian Arab, a Sunni, and although he knew the Iraqi dictator was his country's sworn enemy he also knew that many

Iranians had wished him well in his defiance of the western invaders and the greedy, self-seeking politicians in Jeddah, Cairo and Damascus who had welcomed the infidel armies into the heart of Islam. But Saddam had been defeated and humiliated and the Middle East remained as securely bound to the West as ever. It had been a godless, despised nation but one which had for so long provided at least the semblance of a superpower counter threat to the Great Satan.

'Saddam is an evil man and one who will never stand before the gates of Paradise. But he understands power – how to achieve it and how to hold it. He understands that to succeed you must be totally ruthless in pursuing your aims, that you must set no limits upon what you are prepared to do to achieve your aims or the risks you are prepared to take. In that, if nothing else, we should take him as our example.'

'But the oil, Master. How can we remove it?'

Firdasi looked down at him.

'Do you not remember the great burning?'

Heydar's eyes grew wide. Of course he remembered the great burning, the acrid, rolling black columns of smoke that rose from the burning well heads of Kuwait were visible for hundreds of miles. Saddam, looking defeat in the face, had spat defiance at his enemies and set fire to over seven hundred Kuwaiti wells. What he could not have he would destroy. For months, long after the war was over, the sun had been obscured by the stinking brown cloud of vaporised oil that befouled everything for a thousand miles downwind with a viscous coating of tar. It had taken thousands of men and billions of pounds to extinguish the fires and Kuwait oil production had been crippled for years afterwards. Not content with that the Iraqi dictator had deliberately leaked three million barrels of oil into the Persian Gulf, turning its beaches and teeming, crystal waters to a foul, stinking, life destroying sludge. He looked at the azure ocean beside which they now strolled. Saddam had defiled earth, sky and sea, surely The Master, the ever gentle Firdasi would never contemplate such an obscenity?

'Master, I do not understand. How could such a thing help our cause?'

Firdasi looked sad.

'You are right to question such a terrible course of action, Heydar. I myself have questioned if for over eight years now, ever since Saddam showed us what a terrible thing it is. I have questioned and I have prayed for Allah's guidance yet here I stand, convinced that if we are to mortally wound our enemies we must use the most devastating weapons we have. And we must do it now for, so long as there is oil for the taking, the greedy capitalists will not spend money developing alternative technologies. They estimate there are another fifty years of reserves waiting to be extracted, the vast majority of it right here in the Middle East. If we can eliminate the greater part of those reserves at a stroke their economies will be on the verge of collapse within months. They will be so busy squabbling among themselves over the paltry remainder they will, I promise you, have little time to concern themselves with us. The wells will burn for years and, remember, we are able to torch twenty times as many well heads as Saddam, and can cripple every loading and refining facility from here to Turkey. It will be awful and there will be a terrible price to pay but we must steel ourselves to the horror of it and not be deterred, for what we are about to do will turn great parts of the world into a hell on earth.'

He stopped and turned to face the group about him. Their faces, like his were serious, thoughtful. It was a terrible option and one they had agonised over ever since he had first gathered his band about him. He knew and shared their fears and made no attempt to gloss over the ramifications.

'Heydar, is right. We will be vilified and persecuted for our actions, doubtless some of us, perhaps all of us, will pay with our lives. But that is a small price to gain the gates of Paradise. We have agreed that the only hope for Islam lies in breaking the insufferable chain that binds it to the West and all that it stands for. Is it not written: Allah changes not what is in people until they change what is in themselves? If we are to break that chain, once and for all we must break it now. Unless anyone has any last thoughts or any misgivings, I suggest you all return to your own countries and wait for the signal from me. My informants in Jeddah tell me the allied invasion is still at least a week off – they take no chances, an Anglo-French airborne division is being moved to Cyprus and two more carrier groups have sailed from Pearl Harbour – so you will have time to warn your men that the day of destiny is approaching. Tell them that soon, very soon, they will avenge their fellow Muslims and that the flames and the insults offered to our fellow Muslims at the Mosque in Berlin last night will pale into insignificance when the great burning begins.'

Firdasi smiled at the circle of dark, worried faces about him and for the first time Heydar saw a new light in his eyes. It was not cruelty or hate he saw there but love, a love so all-consuming and implacable that it would plunge the world into the pit of hell before it would give up the beloved nation. The Master raised the book in his hand.

'Tell them to look to the Koran. It is written in the Surahs that when Allah instructed his messenger Abraham He foresaw the coming days, for did He not say: Thou wilt see the guilty shackled by chains upon that day. Their raiment will be of pitch and the fire shall cloak their faces.'

CHAPTER THIRTY FIVE

The long awaited sign for Firdasi's followers to begin the holocaust that was later to become known as the Great Burning was given three days later. When it came it was dramatic and an ominous portent of what was to follow. From the western mountains of Iraq, fired from a mobile missile launcher that had lain hidden since the defeat of Saddam, a solitary Scud soared high into the thin mountain air and arced lazily to the south west towards Israel. Despite its leader's theatrical posturing Iraq had been considered effectively neutered by United Nations' sanctions and all eyes had been on the build-up in the Persian Gulf. As a result the attack came as a complete surprise and allowed little chance of interception. It fell into a fashionable suburb of Tel Aviv. Twenty three people died and twice that number were injured, mainly middle class Israelis; bankers and businessmen who dwelt in the smart Bauhaus flats and houses around Dizengoff Square. Indeed, so unexpected was the attack that initial reports said it had been caused by a gas main exploding, then the possibility of a terrorist bomb was mooted. It was only several hours later, as the wreckage of the Scud was dragged from the rubble, that a rocket attack was confirmed. The Israeli security forces, for once caught off guard, immediately enforced an information blackout and declared a state of emergency while the world held its breath as it waited for whatever response the Likkud would consider appropriate. Nuclear retaliation seemed a distinct possibility but where would it fall? Baghdad appeared a likely target and within hours the population of that ancient city was fleeing into the surrounding countryside.

    The fact was the Israelis were at something of a loss. Although radar had indicated the Scud had come from somewhere close to the Iraqi-Syrian border both of those countries were involved in multi-lateral talks to normalise the tense international situation and the launching of a single missile, uncoordinated with other military moves, amounted to nothing less than a masochistic request for swift and painful punishment from the Israelis. It was sufficiently bizarre to make the Likkud hesitate from taking any over-hasty reaction.

    The trouble was, during the seventies and eighties the then Soviet Union had sold several hundred, no one knew exactly how many, Scuds to various Middle East countries. While the technology, reliability and accuracy of the missiles were of poor standard, possession of such weapons gave neighbouring Arab counties at least the pretence of parity with Israel. Soviet arms salesmen were sufficiently adroit to see them deployed in sufficient numbers to pose a viable threat. Saddam Hussein had used them in anger against Iran in the savage Battle of the Cities and against both Israel and Saudi Arabia in 1991 but with only mediocre results. But even if they were now regarded as yesterday's weapons, it had proved hard for MOSSAD to keep track of all the Scuds. Some had been destroyed, others decommissioned, and yet others sold off to arms dealers who could move them on at a profit. According to British sources at least three were known to have been shipped to Argentina for research purposes. But this was only part of the problem for even had it been possible to accurately estimate numbers held in the various hostile armouries, pinpoint location of the launchers was an intelligence nightmare. Transported on carriers that were nothing more sophisticated than heavy duty trucks and which with a little imagination could be easily disguised as commercial vehicles, the missiles could move openly along roads and cross borders undetected.

But while the world watched and wondered other disturbing reports began to filter through; reports of puzzling incidents from all along the Persian Gulf. There was a major fire raging at an oil loading installation at Abu Dhabi then another at an offshore well. Hour by hour, throughout that fateful day, the reports multiplied and grew grimmer and the fires burned fiercer. There were explosions at refineries, massive leakages from storage facilities and fires the length and breadth of the Gulf as Firdasi's followers lit the first flames in a campaign of destruction that would sweep like wildfire around the world. Within 48 hours there had been nearly a thousand incidents, mainly along the western coast of the Gulf. These installations would almost certainly have been the prime targets of the allied invasion force for they were highly productive, vulnerable to attack and easy to supply from the sea once they had been securely occupied. Now many of the prizes so coveted by the Americans and their allies lay in ruins, belching black oil vapour high into the darkening sky and spewing tons of crude into the slowly coagulating sea.

Having lost the initiative the West now had to decide what its response should be. This was easier said than done for the governments of Saudi Arabia and Kuwait, whose installations were among the first to be hit, were as shocked at events as the allies and now began to suspect Iranian backed terrorism on an unprecedented scale. Now they called on the United Nations for strong measures to punish such outrages and as an inducement announced that oil prices would be pegged back to their pre-crisis level. When the Iranian loading installations at Abu Musa were similarly fired upon it brought counter accusations and the threat of military action. The chaos spread and intensified by the hour and any approximation to a unified front presented by the Islamic nations thus far was to prove as fragile as ever. Yet all the while the allied fleet streamed aimlessly to and fro just outside the waters of the Gulf and did nothing. While they delayed, the glittering bonanza of unlimited oil was turning to ashes.

*****

After the Berlin meeting Hawkhurst had been glad to return to Sarnafon, all the more so as news of the burning began to filter through. There was nothing he could do to affect events. What he needed, he decided, was to get back into some sort of a routine that would, given time, allow him to return to something like normality. For the time being at least he had no money worries for, in addition to the payments he had received from the Church of Christ the Warrior, Harry Brennan had managed to wring a substantial payment out of his agency in recognition of the risks Tom had run in infiltrating the task force and boarding the Nagasaki Maru. Now Brennan was back in the Middle East somewhere, no doubt acting as the eyes and ears of his masters in the States. Potgeiter had returned to South Africa, intent on acquiring another aircraft and picking up his somewhat dubious career where he had left off. Although glad to be back in the real world, Tom missed them both.

'We'll keep in touch,' Brennan had said. 'You've got my New York number and Sinead will always take a message,' he smiled, recalling an earlier encounter. 'I've told her you're OK by the way, so she most probably won't bust your head if you do ever meet again.'

Potgeiter had also promised to maintain contact although somehow they all knew they probably wouldn't meet again. For a few brief months they had been at the centre of world shaping events and during that time they had become close friends. Now, if still friends, they were just redundant bit part players. The madness, the task force and now the Great Burning, had erupted and events had swept on, leaving them without a useful role to play. The day before the burning had begun the three of them had held a farewell dinner in a smart Berlin restaurant just off Unter Den Linden.

'Whichelow's back in Gethsemane,' Brennan told them as they rather sadly sat around the table. 'I guess we'll never know whether he was really shot or not. Anyway, he's up and running again – screaming for immediate military action against the Islamic League. I guess he knows it's gonna happen anyway. The force that's building up out there's not for looking at. Within a couple of days they'll go ashore and seize some pretty impressive real estate and declare that the West's oil supplies are secure forever and a day. Then, if I'm any judge, the allies will start squabbling over who gets what.' He smiled shyly as if uneasy to reveal a thoughtful aspect of himself. 'I've done some reading about the Crusades. Seems the Christians could never agree amongst themselves and because of that could never hold on to what they took. I can see that happening here. Oh, it'll be fine for the first few months but then I suspect they'll stop being satisfied with a guaranteed supply of oil and start manoeuvring for influence over the Arabs. Whichelow's dream is impossible. His dream is of a unified Christian empire that will dominate the world in the next Millennium, yet already Martinette is saying the discovery of the Holy Grail shows how the Catholic tradition is proving to be the truth. What he means is, he's got the Grail, he knows how to tap into its powers and, ergo, should be the next Pope.'

This mention of the Grail made Tom think of the last time the world had seen it, borne away in triumph by the Cardinal along with his terrified, smoke stained 'converts' down a street lined with thuggery, perverted religion and racist malevolence. Following its reappearance and the discrediting of the copy in the museum, there had been a discreet request from the British Government that the Grail be returned and this request had been acknowledged by Martinette personally although, so far as anyone knew, not complied with and the chalice still remained safely locked away in the Vatican treasure house. At the museum a discreet notice now lay by the phoney Grail. It read: 'Facsimile. Original removed for research purposes.' It made little difference to the crowds who continued to flood in.

'Any news on Mary Lou?' Potgeiter asked, draining their third bottle of Chateauneuf du Pape and holding it aloft to signify another would be appreciated.

'Released on bail and back in the States.' Brennan grunted. 'Whatever he may have said for the benefit of his public it seems like Whichelow hasn't abandoned her. He's hired the best criminal lawyers in the UK. The case won't come to court for months yet and from what I hear the defence intends to prove there's no evidence of any link between Bubka and Mary Lou. We've only got her taped phone calls, which weren't strictly legal in the first place, to prove otherwise and they may not be considered as permissible evidence in a British court of law. According to the agency's legal advisers she's got a better than fifty-fifty chance of getting off scot free.'

'And Laura along with her?' Even as he spoke Tom was aware he hoped it would be so.

'Could be. She's still facing deception charges over the Grail, of course, but the authorities are so shit scared of the whole can of worms they may be prepared to accept that placing the copy on view wasn't necessarily a deliberate case of deception. The museum, especially your old pal Dixey, are saying it was simply a way of allowing the Vatican's experts time to give the final seal of approval as to its provenance as, indeed we have seen, they have been more than happy to do. Given the so called miracles that have occurred since – the resurrection of Whichelow and the cockamamie conversion at the Mosque – there will be little doubt in the general public's mind now. It's a clever twist if you think about it – it neatly answers all questions without anybody having to take any responsibility. I reckon the lovely Ms Woods will be even more of a star when the dust settles.' He stared morosely down at the glass in his hand. 'Anyway, with war likely to break out any minute, who's gonna give a shit now?'

But this had been before the burning had begun.

*****

The new tractor arrived, just as he had planned, while Angahrad had been up high on the crags, bringing down those few elusive sheep that had escaped the last dipping. When she had safely penned these last recalcitrant beasts in the stone-walled paddock to the rear of the farm she came into the kitchen where Hawkhurst stood pouring a welcoming glass of wine. Kissing him warmly, she took it gratefully, running her fingers through wind tousled hair.

'Thanks. I can really use a drink. I'm knackered – I think the little buggers get smarter and faster each year. How's your day been?'

He grunted non-committedly, suddenly pre-occupied with the ragout he was preparing for supper.

'Nothing special. Oh, the postman called – I think there's something out front for you.'

Puzzled, she walked to the window that gave out onto the yard then she turned, smiling, her eyes brimming with tears. 'Thomas! You did it.'

Blank faced, he feigned ignorance, though the unalloyed joy on her face made his heart sing.

'Did what?'

'You put the deposit on the tractor – oh you darling.'

He wandered to the window and stood by her side, slipping an arm about her slender waist.

'Good Lord,' he said. 'How did that get there?'

Later that night, after they had made love and lay, arms about each other, listening in the darkness to the eerie wail of a tawny owl that had taken up residence in the loft of the old outhouse, Angahrad spoke about Whichelow. For days, weeks now, they had avoided all mention of the man's baleful influence.

'He got away with it after all, didn't he?' she said. 'He'll get the war he wanted and when it's over he'll probably go on to become one of the most influential men of the decade. All of this; the burning and the slide into war, is his doing yet no one will ever know about the evil, scheming and wickedness of it all.'

'Maybe, but Harry thinks there will be a falling out with Martinette once His Eminence is firmly ensconced on the Papal throne. It makes sense. Whichelow was pretty indiscriminate in picking his allies – he was only interested in the influence and resources they could bring to the thing – but Martinette is a Catholic with a capital C and he's in the driving seat for the time being. He's the one who's doing the talking and making policy, while Whichelow's back in Gethsemane, supposedly recovering from his brush with the Grim Reaper, and well away from the action.' He rolled over and kissed her gently on the cheek. 'To hell with the lot of them. Let's just be grateful we will never have to deal with any of them again.'

But she could not relax and as he slipped hopefully towards sleep she spoke again.

'But the war, Thomas, it is coming isn't it?'

'It is, I'm afraid, nothing to stop it now. But it will be a long way from here and although it will be bad I don't think it will last very long. Just be thankful we live where we do in this peaceful valley, far from the fighting, and that we have each other.'

'Oh, I am Thomas, I truly am. It's just that ….'

He blinked awake, suddenly aware that she was crying and that there was something more she was trying to say, something more important than all the wars and religions that man had contrived since time began.

'What is it? What's wrong?'

In the dark she smiled through the tears that fell warm on his shoulder and clung to him.

'Nothing is wrong. It's just that I'm pregnant. That's all.'

*****

The following morning, firmly rejecting his insistence that, as a mother to be, she should contemplate spending the next eight months in bed or at least sitting down, Angahrad departed the farm and resumed her search for any remaining sheep that had escaped her eye. Hawkhurst watched her go, dogs at her heels, turning to wave to where he stood in the doorway. He still had difficulty taking in the fact that he was to become a father and the prospect of parenthood both fascinated and frightened him. On balance he thought he was pleased. Returning inside, he switched on the television, it was an almost Pavlovian reaction these days. The news was bad and likely to get worse.

A week after Firdasi had launched his campaign of destruction it was estimated that over 8,000 wells, spread throughout Saudi Arabia, Kuwait, Iran and Libya, had been fired now. At least fifty refineries, vast, sophisticated feats of engineering that had been years in the building, had been sabotaged and more than a hundred fully laden tankers, delayed from sailing because of the war of words over prices, were now either burning or seeping their cargoes into the sea. Over the greater part of the Middle East a cloud of smoke and noxious, toxic gases, a thousand feet thick at its epicentre, totally obscured the sun and was now drifting eastwards towards Afghanistan and the former southern Soviet Republics. An estimated 150 million barrels of crude, the equivalent of a dozen Exxon Valdez catastrophes, had poured into the sea forming an oil slick that was now two hundred miles long and fifty wide. This was being slowly blown down the Gulf by the Shamal, the relentless southerly wind pushing and spreading its black fingers out towards the allied fleet. It was, according to experts, an environmental disaster of such a scale that its ultimate effects could not even be guessed at. The possible impact on global warming, erosion of the ozone layer, atmospheric pollution and the greenhouse effect, all added up to a doomsday scenario.

From the sheer scale of the destruction it was evident that Firdasi had been as diligent and unrelenting in his planning as Whichelow and still the burning continued. During the years spent travelling between the capital cities of Islam, years when ostensibly he had preached peace and reconciliation, he had been recruiting and planning. The Master had revealed himself every bit as ruthless as Whichelow and infinitely more effective. In those areas first put to the torch vigorous attempts were made to extinguish the fires, initially with some success. But for each well head fire that was put out two would erupt elsewhere and the exhausted fire fighters were soon overwhelmed by the task. A state of emergency had been proclaimed throughout the region and security forces, the threat of invasion a minor consideration now, were ordered to turn their guns on Firdasi's followers in an attempt to stop the burning. Many died yet, no matter how many went down beneath the bullets, others took their place.

Ironically, when the belated invasion eventually took place it came not as an act of aggression but a mission of mercy, undertaken at the urgent request of the Saudis and other previously pro-western Arab states whose facilities had been hit first. Unable to cope with the scale of the disaster and seeing the region sliding inexorably into anarchy they were forced to accept that only western forces could enforce a military solution and only western money and technology could hope, inshallah, to deal with the chaos. As the Sheikhs watched their most valuable asset disappear in smoke before their eyes, the future price of oil was no longer even a factor. The American, Europeans and Japanese could name their own price if only they would stop the creeping horror of fire and foulness. Only Iran and Libya, sustained by their implacable hatred, still refused all offers of outside assistance and those countries were slowly drowning or suffocating in their own ordure.

Yet as the great grey warships began to move northward towards the burning, the effects of the catastrophe were to hinder their progress. The oil slick, several feet thick in places, fouled the thrusting bows and hulls as the black slime parted and coiled malevolently along their length. For the larger vessels, the carriers, cruisers and big support ships, progress was unhindered by the sea of filth but the smaller classes, the destroyers and frigates and especially the flotilla of minesweepers that made the seas safe for their more glamorous comrades, life was more difficult. Shallow draft meant that emulsified oil was often sucked into engine cooling systems, clogging heat exchangers and rapidly bringing on overheating that required the engines to be stopped and cooling systems cleaned before they could go on. The further north they struggled the thicker the oil became and delays more frequent. Unwilling to proceed into areas that had certainly been mined in expectation of invasion without his screen of minesweepers, Admiral Theroux, USN, overall commander of the huge allied armada, could only proceed at a snail's pace as ship after ship was brought to a halt by the black tide.

As they watched from the decks of their vessels, beneath a shadowed sky that rained a fine drizzle of oily soot, sailors stared down in silent disbelief at the black morass that surrounded them, stretching away to the horizon. On its surface floated hundreds of birds, as black as the oil that swamped them; near dead and in the last stages of exhaustion as they made pitiful attempts to swim or fly through the heavy choking sludge and every so often the fin of a dying dolphin would thrust through the oil as it tried to suck at the polluted air.

Winding up, the TV newscaster said that some assistance was being flown in but poor flying conditions were limiting these operations and most of the heavy equipment remained aboard the ships. Until that arrived there was little that could be done to ameliorate a deteriorating situation.

Suddenly depressed, Tom switched off. Until that moment he had known little about Firdasi or his fanatics apart from what he had read in the newspapers. To him, compared with Whichelow the man had seemed positively benign, a final hope for peace and common sense. Now he had unleashed something so terrible it made the Church of Christ the Warrior seem like naughty school children. Tom knew his depression and this sudden rush of hatred for the Sufi stemmed from the fact he had, or would soon have, responsibilities. From the moment Angahrad had told him of the child, things had stopped being black and white. If Angie would, as he had heard others say, be eating for two, he would from now on be worrying, and hating, for three.

Lost in thought he went to the window, staring up at the cloudless sky where a pair of ravens tumbled and twisted in playful flight. It was still early and the sun below the hilltops as yet, but its rays were already touching the surrounding peaks, picking out the russet patches of heather that presage the advance of autumn. Pray God that foul cloud of corruption never comes here, he thought. So deep was he in these melancholy musings it took several bursts of the telephone to shake him from his dark reverie. To his surprise it was Laura.

'Tom,' she said, her voice shaky. 'I'm in trouble, I need help.'

He was unmoved by her plea: assuming she was hoping to persuade him to get the charges against her dropped.

He was not impressed.

'Don't worry, Laura. I'm not the least bit interested in persecuting you or your girlfriend. It's the police you need to convince.'

'It's not that. Dixey's dead – the police say it was a heart attack but I think he was murdered. I'm scared, Tom.' Her voice was small, childlike in its terror. 'I need help. Can I lay low with you for a bit? I've nowhere else to go.'

Hawkhurst, needing time to absorb this latest news stared into space. Would he never be free of this mire of intrigue?

'No,' he said roughly. 'Not here. I don't want Angahrad placed at risk again.' He racked his brain for a suitable rendezvous. 'Go to that hotel we ate at the day we opened the grave. What was it called? The Ashleigh? Book in under an assumed name and wait for me. I'll try to get to you sometime this evening. You know where I mean?'

There was a brief silence then, seemingly reassured, she spoke.

'Yes, I remember the place. I think I can find it again. Please don't let me down, Tom. I'm sure it's the Church's people. I think they killed Dixey to keep him quiet and I think they mean to kill me next.'

CHAPTER THIRTY SIX

As he drove up to the hotel Hawkhurst wondered what the hell he was doing there. He owed Laura Woods absolutely nothing. From the very outset she had used him, deceived him and, through Mary Lou Berkowitz, she had set him up for murder. Why was he putting himself at risk again when his place was back at the farm taking care of Angie? Yet here he was, getting involved again. Perhaps it was just the generally unsatisfactory way things had panned out that drew him in. Great areas of the world were being slowly poisoned, the evil Martinette stood poised to assume the Papal robes, the most powerful religious office in the world and, if Laura was to be believed, the Church of Christ the Warrior was still active, eliminating anyone who might expose their schemes. It was mainly this last development that had brought him here. If what she said was true both he and Angie would fall into this category it would be judicious to find out as much as he could.

He parked the car at the rear of the hotel and went in search of Laura. He found her in the deserted bar sitting in a shadowy booth, a large gin and tonic before her. There were black circles under her eyes and her hair was an untended tangle. She smiled weakly.

'Thanks for coming, Tom. I didn't know what to do.'

'What happened to Dixey?'

She threw back the remains of her drink in one, her gaze immediately searching for a waiter to bring more.

'He died at his flat yesterday evening, I found him lying on the kitchen floor. I called an ambulance but I knew he was already dead. There will have to be an inquest, of course, but the doctor said it was probably a massive heart attack.'

Tom considered the facts dispassionately.

'Could be, he's been under a lot of pressure recently. What makes you suspect murder?'

She had finally got the waiter's attention and indicated that two large gin and tonics were required. When these were delivered to the table she swallowed eagerly, as if it might help the situation.

'He was wearing a red sword on his lapel. You knew him, Tom, he'd never do anything as tacky as that. Anyway, apart from the jiggery pokery surrounding your supposed theft of the Grail he knew next to nothing about Whichelow and his mad schemes – certainly nothing that could have incriminated the Church. I think the sword was the Church's way of letting me know they are after all of us.'

Tom had to admit it made sense. The ultra conservative Dixey would never in a thousand years be associated with anything as tainted with hysteria as the Church of Christ the Warrior, far less advertise the fact by wearing its tasteless emblem. But, as Laura had already pointed out, even though he would have known next to nothing of their lunatic plans, if her suspicions were correct they had not hesitated to kill him. It boded ill for the rest of them.

'I don't suppose anybody has contacted you recently?' He asked, smiling cruelly. 'No word from Mary Lou?'

She reddened and shook her head.

'She's back in Gethsemane as far as I know. My solicitors advised me to keep well away from her until after the trial. I guess Mary Lou's attorney has said much the same to her. I hope I never have to see her again.'

'What's happening about the Grail?'

'It's coming back to the museum next week. Martinette is bringing it back personally. He's made a big deal about how the Vatican had been asked, by Dixey, to check its authenticity and now, having proved its miraculous powers and given it the seal of approval, is handing it back. It's a pretty flimsy story but with Dixey dead no one's going to argue. I think the museum board may have struck a secret deal to let the Vatican hold it in perpetuity after the exhibition is finished.' She shrugged, her next words spoken with evident bitterness. 'I don't know for sure. No one there confides in me anymore.'

Tom considered this turn of events. With things as they were he wondered how Whichelow would feel about it. When they were aboard the Nagasaki Maru Martinette had definitely been the junior partner in the unholy alliance but now, apart from being on the verge of taking ultimate power, he had succeeded in acquiring for Rome the most potent symbol of Christendom, a prize Whichelow had lied, connived, stolen and murdered to possess. At the same time it raised questions about precisely who had ordered Dixey's elimination. Both Whichelow and Martinette had their reasons but, to Tom, the

Cardinal's seemed more pressing. Laura was less concerned with such matters than with her own personal safety.

'What can we do?' She whispered. 'We need somewhere to hide.'

He smiled. It was 'we' now – they were all pals together.

'You'll have to decide for yourself what you intend doing, Laura, but I reckon trying to hide will just prolong the agony. We need to get organised and then take the fight to them. At the moment they think they hold all the aces. I guess they think they can take their time and pick us off one by one. Like I say, we need to get organised.' A few guests were drifting into the bar from the restaurant. It was time to be moving. 'You didn't tell anyone you were here I take it.' She shook her head, unhappy that he was obviously not contemplating running. He looked at his watch, it was nearly ten. 'All the same, no point in taking risks. You go and get your stuff from your room,' he ordered curtly. 'We'll find somewhere else to stay – just in case you were followed. Leave me your mobile – I need to make a few phone calls.'

When she had departed he rang the farm. Before he left he had phoned Brennan's agency and within three hours a black saloon had arrived at the farm bringing a team of four heavies. They were all British and Tom guessed they would be ex-SAS or similar, freelancers who provided the agency's muscle in the UK. Whatever, they certainly inspired confidence. Now, wherever she went Angahrad had an armed escort. Knowing her commitment to the farm and her routinely covering many miles of rugged country every day, he didn't envy them the task. As they spoke he knew one of the escorts would be listening in to their conversation.

She was naturally concerned for him, but there was a happiness in her voice that had been missing for many months and he knew it was the coming baby that had exorcised the ghosts of the past. He also knew that he had his own demons to be purged, demons that still lingered and that could only be done by finishing Whichelow once and for all. When he and Angahrad had finished speaking he rang Pretoria.

*****

Exactly seven days after he had initiated the campaign of burning and polluting, Firdasi was captured by Israeli commandos. With the faithful Heydar he had sought sanctuary in the Old City of Jerusalem, deep underground in the vaults of the Al Aqsa Mosque. As his followers had embarked on their mission of destruction he had retired to his prayers, thinking in such a sacred place he would be safe. Had not Allah instructed the Prophet Mohammad to shelter here after his night journey from Medina? However, some of his followers, men who had supported him wholeheartedly when the theory of torching the oil was first mooted, had been appalled by the reality of what they had unleashed. Now, terrified by the repercussions, they sought to save their own skins by betraying him. Only Heydar had been with him when the Israelis burst into the vault and the boy, faithful to the end, had been cut bloodily down when he attempted to protect his Master.

Normally, heavily armed Jewish soldiers bursting into a Mosque, certainly one as revered as the Al Aqsa, would have meant the Intifada flaring up in savage confrontation within hours. But now, as Firdasi was led away, a bruise over his left eye and his hands cuffed behind him, the Arab crowd hurled abuse not at the Israelis but at The Master. His robe was spattered with his acolyte's blood but he was calm and totally composed, even the suggestion of a smile on his lips as he was thrust into the back of an army Land Cruiser and driven away. He had reason to be pleased, even if the havoc his followers had wreaked was losing some of its impetus now, with those sites not already blasted or blazing placed under guard. Even to those who still had stomach for more carnage, the permanent half-light that now reigned from Jordan to the foothills of the Himalayas seemed like a judgement and made them hesitate. But it mattered little that they baulked at this time for by now the damage was done and would take years, decades probably, to put right. The cloud was still being fed by the burning wells and likely would continue to be so for many months. Already respiratory diseases were killing the old, the infirm and the very young in their thousands as the prevailing westerly winds slowly drew the foul garland of sulphur around the northern hemisphere like a shroud. In those countries directly under its baleful shadow suicides became an everyday occurrence as men looked on and despaired.

The oily gloom of the burning wells also concealed other offences against God and man as international leaders moved to make political gains out of the chaos. The nations of the West were very much in the ascendancy now with America, the greatest polluter of all time, taking an admirably responsible and statesmanlike stance. Billions of dollars were quickly allocated by Congress to deal with the problem and the armies that had, a few weeks earlier, been ready to unleash bloody war now turned to the less glorious task of cleaning up the morass and salvaging what they could of the oil. Currently a series of huge floating booms was being constructed across the mouth of the Persian Gulf in the hope of confining the defilement as it spread and drifted southwards towards the open waters of the Indian Ocean. Earliest estimates suggested it would be at least a year before all the burning wells could be extinguished. It might be as long as three years before regular supplies could achieve a level approaching fifty per cent of world demand. Such shortages would inevitably mean an economic slump of unprecedented proportions in the industrialised countries and famine and death in the third world. All the industrialised nations had imposed fuel rationing and companies like Honda, Nissan and Ford were already laying off workers in their thousands.

A few oil producing nations could hope to prosper from the disaster, among them Britain which had always preferred to leave as much as possible of its own reserves in the ground and use cheap imported oil, but these sources could never hope to satisfy the world's insatiable appetite for any length of time. Priority was being given to opening the new sources of oil and along with this went a return to older fuels such as coal and wood. It was a policy that spelt disaster for the atmosphere and the forests of the world. Also, the demand for oil revived old territorial disputes. As an extra precaution the British garrison in the Falkland Islands, in whose surrounding seas were rumoured to lie massive reserves of high grade oil, was beefed up with the addition of three infantry battalions and two squadrons of Harriers. Many other nations were taking similar precautions to protect their interests. If oil had been important before, it was now the elixir of economic life.

America, as the only superpower and undisputed leader of the industrialised world, also took a tough line on the question of dealing out justice to Firdasi and those five hundred or so of his followers who had been apprehended thus far. It was announced that there was to be a series of public trials of The Master and his minions. They were to be held in New York at the United Nations Building where a special court was already being assembled. There was some argument as to which legal system would be appropriate and a great deal of thought and pedantry was being applied to the problem. Firdasi had already announced he would recognise no law but the Sharia. What no one doubted was that the death penalty was the only appropriate punishment for a crime so horrible it even had a new name: Eco terrorism. Among the most vocal supporters of the trials were Cardinal Martinette and The Reverend James J Whichelow, indeed, it was widely rumoured that the whole idea of a show trial had emanated from Gethsemane.

Both men had been much in the news, especially after the phoney resurrection, and in the weeks following the Great Burning they used their new found fame to project an image of wisdom, restraint and forgiveness on behalf of their respective versions of the faith. The horrors of the Great Burning, an offence against God if ever there was one, had deeply affected people around the world and in its wake came a hunger for spiritual guidance. Islam, the thinking went, had in Firdasi revealed its true colours and many were quitting its ranks. Converts flocked to Rome and to Gethsemane, coming in such numbers that both found it necessary to hastily ordain thousands of missionaries to spread the good word among the benighted. Especially busy was the Church of Christ the Warrior's London branch.

*****

The shabby, red brick building was but a pale shadow of its mother temple in Gethsemane. It stood in a South London back street, surrounded by a sea of mean terraced houses that fell only just short of deserving the title of slums. It was a run down, working class area, multi-racial and with a big drug problem on the streets. Outside the church a poster, black on fluorescent yellow, carried the exhortation to 'Fight the Good Fight'.

Within its walls business was brisk when Tom stepped inside that bright October morning. It had the same musty smell of all churches but inside, thanks to some imaginative décor, it was a surprisingly cheery place. In one corner a small group of younger children, mainly black, were sat about a fresh faced white American girl who was recounting the story of Noah and the flood. In another, an ancient crone was picking her way through a box of second hand clothing. On the wall was a chart showing monthly donations to the 'Fight the Fires Fund' the Church's own charity which had already subscribed tens of thousands of dollars to the clean-up operation, although with little visible effect. Hawkhurst found himself confronted by a young woman wearing a long print dress, sandals, gold rimmed granny glasses and a pleasant toothy smile.

'Can I help you, sir?' The look of sly pleasure on her face suggested she smelt a potential convert in the offing. He was quick to disabuse her.

'I'd like to speak to Mr Mallinson please. Simon Mallinson.'

The smile slipped a little.

'Mr Mallinson is in conference with The Reverend Whichelow at present, I'm afraid. He can't be disturbed.'

Tom stared.

'Is Whichelow here?'

The girl laughed at such gullibility, a hand going to her mouth to hide the uneven teeth.

'Oh no, sir. It's a tele-conference. We have satellite facilities that allow us direct visual access to Gethsemane.'

Tom considered the situation. He'd come here to make Mallinson an offer the Church couldn't refuse but, he asked himself, why bother with the monkey when the organ grinder was available. Gently putting the girl aside he made for the only door he could see, ignoring her little yelps of protest at his heels. He pushed the door open. Mallinson was stretched out, hands clasped behind his head, feet up on the cheap laminate desk. On the desk was the screen which allowed him face-to-face access with Whichelow ten thousand miles away. Hawkhurst's appearance surprised him and there was no doubt recognition was instant but it brought no undue reaction. He simply raised his eyebrows and waved Hawkhurst into a chair across from him. The Reverend, unaware of Tom's presence, was still talking, his deep rumblings echoing tinnily as it came over the land line.

'We need to keep a grip on things, Simon. Martinette's getting too powerful. We need to clip his wings a little. The Church hasn't come all this way to see the Whore of Rome lead us into The Millennium. I want you to come up with an idea of discrediting him. I don't want him destroyed, we may still need him, but I'd like to see him out of the race for the Papacy. If you have any thoughts let me know.'

Mallinson looked thoughtful, his hand going to the volume control to allow Tom to participate in the conversation.

'Reverend. I have a visitor – Dr Hawkhurst is here.'

There was silence as Whichelow took in this information.

'What?'

Like Mallinson he had expected that following Bubka's murder attempt Tom would have remained in hiding. Indeed, until Laura's pillow talk with Mary Lou they had believed him dead. Now they wanted him and any other survivors from the Nagasaki Maru silenced. Mallinson kept his eyes locked on Tom as he explained the situation to Whichelow, his manner urbane, his words slightly mocking. Hawkhurst suspected he had himself solved one of Mallinson's problems by offering himself up like this: a lamb for the slaughter.

'Dr Thomas Hawkhurst, the bold grave robber, has just entered my office. His presence here is totally uninvited and unwelcome so I imagine he must have something important to tell us. Do you want to speak to him before I have him thrown out?'

'Put him on.'

Tom, apparently concentrating on his words but actually watching Mallinson's hand slide imperceptibly towards the half opened right hand drawer of his desk, kept his manner irritatingly breezy.

'Morning, Reverend. Nice to hear your voice again. You really had us worried with that stunt at Wembley. Still no harm done – you're back in the land of the living.'

'What do you want Hawkhurst? Make it quick. I'm a busy man.'

'I think I can help solve your problem with His Eminence.'

There was a pause.

'Now why should you want to do a thing like that, Doctor Tom?'

'Let's just say I don't want to end up like Professor Dixey and nor do my friends.'

'Go on.'

Tom, his hands thrust deep into the pockets of his jacket, saw Mallinson's hand hovering over the open drawer. He smiled easily.

'If you move another inch Mallinson, I'll blow your head off.' He jerked his hand in his pocket. 'It's a .38 Smith & Wesson. At this range it'll go right through your skull and out the back.'

Mallinson's hand drew swiftly back to the centre of the desk, his eyes wide. Whichelow, unaware of the unfolding drama was getting irritable at the delay.

'Well? I'm listening.'

'The Grail is coming back to London in a day or two. I'm still in a position to get it for you and I'm one of the few people who can say, hand on heart which is the original and which is the phoney. If I can switch them, and I think I can, you could have the real Grail and maybe a little later, shock horror, you can expose Martinette as a fraudster and a thief. That would do his chances of becoming Pope no good at all.'

'How do I know I can trust you, Hawkhurst? Why shouldn't I just let Mr Mallinson and his men take care of you?'

Tom smiled across the desk. He knew Whichelow would be calculating all the angles, weighing the prize against the pitfalls.

'Well, it's up to you, Rev. But I have to tell you at this precise moment Mr Mallinson has got his head jammed nine miles up his arse. If he's the best you've got I'd suggest you consider doing a deal.' He smiled sweetly across the desk as pure malice burned in Mallinson's eyes.

Whichelow's tone grew brisk.

'When will you have the Grail?'

'By Friday. I'll need to take care getting it out of the country but I'll deal with that. I want St Michael One or something similar waiting for me at La Guardia. I intend to fly straight in and out of Gethsemane. Oh, there's one other thing. I want a million dollars in used notes waiting for me. Can you do that?'

He pictured Whichelow at the other end, tempted but suspicious, eager but nervous.

'You seem to have acquired expensive tastes since we last met, Doctor Tom. I'm disappointed. I had come to regard you to be that rarest of birds – a man of principle. Now I find you're no better than the rest of us.'

Tom thought it would be no bad thing to reaffirm his fall from grace.

'Have you seen what's happening in the world? It's falling apart, exactly as you predicted it would. I just want to make sure I've got enough money to keep me cushioned from the unpleasantness. When you consider the mystique that's built up round the Grail, especially since your miraculous recovery, it's a very reasonable price. I reckon that if you want to be in the driving seat when the dust settles you'll need it to fix Martinette.'

'Seems to me you're very trusting Tom. You say you are prepared to fly into Gethsemane all alone, deliver the Grail and then trust us to let you fly out again. Suppose, just suppose, we turned out to be less than honourable. What's to stop us taking the Grail and then arranging an accident? Accidents do happen you know – especially at Gethsemane Field.'

The old anger rose in Hawkhurst, he had not forgotten Suzie, but his voice remained even.

'Let's just say I will have taken certain precautions, Whichelow. The Grail will be in a sealed box and it will be packed in phosphorous explosive. Once locked it can only be opened by two keys, one of which I will retain until you've delivered the money and I've flown out. There will be a timing mechanism fitted to the locks. If anything happens to me the damn thing will be melted down into nothing more exciting than a lump of silver.'

'How will I know what's in the box? You might be pulling a fast one, Hawkhurst.'

Tom knew Whichelow was still suspicious but knowing the man guessed that the more devious the plan the more he would be prepared to accept it. He had to convince him that here was a chance of obtaining the Holy Grail and, by so doing, of eliminating or at least reducing the threat posed by Martinette. Tom gave him a little encouragement.

'Send Mary Lou over here. She can watch me pack it into the case and accompany me on the way to Gethsemane so there's no chance of me tampering with it.'

There was another silence as Whichelow pondered, still wondering if there was any threat here.

'OK Hawkhurst. You've got a deal. Mary Lou will be with you in two days' time.'

His eyes still on Mallinson, Tom leant forward and switched the conference facility off.

'Well, Mallinson. Looks like you won't have to bother with me after all.' He stood up, taking his hands out of his pockets to reveal nothing more dangerous than a ball point pen. He gave a humourless grin. 'Unless you'd like to teach me a lesson in manners, that is.'

Mallinson snarled like a mad dog, lunging wildly across the desk at Tom who swayed easily out of range. Seizing the man's arm in a grip of steel he took a handful of hair and, grunting with the effort, slammed the man's face down onto the desk top, blood from the shattered nose spattering across a pristine blotter. Three times he rammed Mallinson's head downwards with a sickening thud until finally he hung limp. This was the man who had organised Mathews' murder and Angahrad's abduction. This was Bubka's paymaster. Releasing his hold Tom watched dispassionately as the inert form slid to the floor. After a second or so the eyes, dazed and distant, fluttered open. Tom took a last look at the groaning figure at his feet then, teeth gritted, drove his foot hard into the unprotected crutch, bringing an agonised squeal of pain from the writhing figure.

'That,' he said softly and to no one in particular, 'is just for starters.'

CHAPTER THIRTY SEVEN

Mary Lou had simply oozed malevolence from the moment she stepped off the aircraft at Heathrow. The fact that she had put a contract out on him no more than a month previously seemed to be a minor consideration, at least so far as she was concerned. It was patently obvious that her only regret was that Bubka had failed.

'Well, have you got it?' She demanded as they drove away from the airport. Hawkhurst chose not to answer immediately, preferring to concentrate on the traffic about him and to take a spiteful pleasure in luxuriating in her frustration. Once on the M4 and heading towards London he suddenly deigned to acknowledge her presence.

'Sorry. Did you say something?'

'I said have you got the goddamn Grail?' She snapped.

Smiling at such blasphemy from one so pious he took a cautious glance in the rear mirror. The Black Honda 4x4 that had pulled away behind him at Heathrow was two cars back. There were four men in it, four very large men. He couldn't be certain but he fancied the driver of the shadowing vehicle sported some kind of dressing on his nose. He smiled to himself and accelerated sharply pulling out into the fast lane. The Honda mirrored his move.

'Oh, the Grail? Yes, I've got it. Martinette returned it two days ago and I switched it with the phoney last night. Since Laura fell from grace at the museum I've taken over a lot of her work – they've grown very trusting. I more or less come and go as I like these days. What I'd thought we'd do is go to the museum first so you can see the fake in its case, then I'll take you to where the real Grail is so you can see we are people who keep our word.'

'We?' Mary Lou was instantly suspicious. 'Who's in this with you, Hawkhurst?'

'Just those people who feel themselves at risk from the Church. Laura and me – especially me. The only reason we're doing this is to save our skins, I thought you understood that. None of us want to end up like Dixey. You get the Grail, we get to live – and a million bucks for me, of course.'

She looked out of the window sourly and he wondered if his mention of Laura had set her thoughts running in the direction he intended. It had.

'Where is Laura?' She asked.

'Safe,' he said, adding spitefully, 'Definitely doesn't want to see you, I'm afraid.' He paused but was unable to resist a final barb. 'She's great in bed isn't she?'

As Mary Lou settled into a sullen silence Hawkhurst took another glance in the mirror and eased over, indicating as if intending to quit the motorway at the next turn off. The Honda did likewise and, satisfied, he switched off his indicator and continued to follow the signs for central London.

At the museum he used his official pass to jump the still burgeoning queue and led her into the gallery where they had first met all those months ago. It was crowded. As Brennan had predicted the added spice of vanishing Grails, resurrections, conversions and, allegedly, murder plots and lesbian sex, had boosted the public interest. Mary Lou had little interest in anything other than the Grail, elbowing her way through the crush until her nose was inches from the cabinet glass. She stared hard at the chalice for several minutes before Tom was certain, as he had long suspected, that she didn't exactly know what she was looking for. This was all to the good for he had no intention whatsoever of placing the power of the true Grail into Whichelow's hands and it was this they were looking at. He made as if to lighten her darkness.

'You see the seams there, that fine raised ridge running around the rim of the bowl and the one that goes down into the base? That shows it was produced as a casting and not beaten out by a silversmith.' He smiled sweetly. 'I was surprised you didn't notice that aboard the Nagasaki Maru. Stands out a mile to anyone who knows what they're doing.'

She ignored his needling.

'OK. So you've made the switch. Where's the genuine article?'

'All in good time. We're going there next, Mary Lou.' He stood for several minutes more, staring contemplatively at the Grail as if seeking inspiration but actually gaining badly needed time to allow Brennan's men to deal with Mallinson and his heavies.

At Laura's flat Mary Lou's gaze wandered about her, no doubt recalling many pleasant hours spent there in her company. Hawkhurst took the Grail from the wall safe and held it out for Mary Lou to inspect. Taking it from him she walked to the window, holding it up to the light, some of the old reverence returning to her manner.

'At last,' she breathed softly, greatly relieved to have it in her hand.

He noticed her gaze stray to the street below and he couldn't resist a smile.

'If you're looking for Mallinson I'm afraid you'll find he's been unexpectedly delayed,' he said. 'I spotted him the moment he turned up at the airport. Don't worry, he's in no personal danger, my friends will just keep him and his pals entertained until we're safe out of the country and on our way to Gethsemane.' He shook his head sadly. 'You know, if I was of a suspicious turn of mind I'd be tempted to think you were thinking of double crossing me, Mary Lou.'

The black eyes slitted in pure hate. It had been a long shot but she had hoped an opportunity to seize the Grail might present itself. If it did Mallinson had orders to remove Hawkhurst once and for all.

'Cut the crap Hawkhurst. What happens next?'

'Next we pack the Grail in its crate.' He pointed to the small but stoutly constructed wooden box that lay on the floor. 'You do the packing. That way you'll know exactly what the deal is.'

Handing the Grail back to him she took up the crate and placed it at the centre of the table, peering inside suspiciously. There was a lining of polystyrene packing and a recessed circle in the bottom to take the Grail's base. Tom produced four small, grey plastic-wrapped packages which he placed at the corners of the box, pressing them snugly home.

'Semtex,' he explained simply. 'Only a few hundred grams but enough to blow anyone foolish enough to tamper with the locks and the Grail into a thousand pieces.' He raised one package to his nose and sniffed appreciatively. 'Nice nose – you can always tell the good quality stuff.'

She stared, horrified at what she was hearing.

'No one said anything about explosives to me. I thought you were using phosphor.'

He smiled knowingly and tossed another couple of packages, both orange , onto the table.

'Don't worry. I'm using that too. The crate will have two locks – Semtex wired up to one lock, phosphor to the other. You'll have a key to one lock and I'll have a key to the other. The electronics are a bit complicated but the principle is simple. Only by inserting both keys at the same time will the fuses be bypassed. Any attempt to tamper with the locks will mean instant destruction of both tamperer and Grail. When we get to Gethsemane and St Michael One has taken on enough fuel to get me where I want to go, you will take the crate and your key to Whichelow – I want Whichelow there when the hand over takes place – just so I can keep an eye on him. Once the plane is ready for take-off you will bring me my one million dollars and I will give you the second key. Then we go our separate ways. Understood?'

She nodded sulkily.

'But I'm not touching that stuff, Hawkhurst. I'm no explosives expert.'

'Suit yourself, but I suggest you watch me wire the explosives very closely. That way you will be well aware of what I'm doing and what any trickery will bring.' He grew grimly silent as with infinite care he inserted a pair of wires, one brown, one blue, deep into the first package, connecting the other ends to a small solenoid. 'Have to be careful not to shake the box too much when you're carrying it,' he said absently. 'Very unstable stuff phosphor. Not really certain if it did ignite whether it would trigger the Semtex or not.' He looked up from his work and grinned at her. 'I guess it's academic really. We won't be around to worry about it anyway.'

Mary Lou stared as he continued to wire up the other explosives packages, finally connecting them to terminals in the two solid brass locks set into the lid of the crate. His hands were deft and sure in their movements. Taking the Grail he then lowered it into the crate to nestle snugly between the charges. He looked up, pleased to see there was a film of sweat glistening on her forehead.

'Right,' he said, lowering the wired lid into place. 'Here's the key. Once we've locked it the solenoids are primed and only both keys can safely unlock the crate. You got that?'

She sure as hell had and as a result was one deeply unhappy lady.

'You sure you know what you're doing, Hawkhurst? How come you know so much about explosives? We could all get killed here.'

Tom slipped his key into one lock and waited for her to do likewise. He shrugged off her doubts.

'Who said I know what I'm doing? Maybe the whole thing'll go sky high when you stick your key in that lock.' She hesitated, her eyes fixed on the crate, and he snorted impatiently. 'Oh, for heaven's sake, Mary Lou, give it here.' Taking the key from her hand he slid it home. 'Right, here we go. One, two, three.' He smiled to himself as, teeth clenched, eyes closed, she twisted her face away and he turned both keys sharply, locking the crate shut. 'There,' he said soothingly. 'No harm done.'

*****

Sandy, at least, was delighted to see him when they boarded St Michael One at La Guardia. Even Mary Lou's glowering presence could not diminish the warmth of her welcome.

'Good to see you again, Dr Hawkhurst. Are you staying over long at Gethsemane?'

'No, just straight in and out,' he smiled. 'How's Bob?'

Her face dropped a little.

'Oh, Bob's out in Saudi at the moment. Flying in equipment to fight the fires. Isn't it just terrible what's happening out there, Doctor? Captain Kruger is at the controls today. He's not one of our regular pilots, he's Dutch I think, doesn't talk much but I guess he's OK or the Church wouldn't have hired him. The mention of Bob, now far away on a mission of mercy, drew her on to the events in the Middle East. Despite all the efforts being made, progress in stemming the pollution was heartbreakingly slow. The cloud of poisonous fumes had now spread as far as Siberia and thousands of wells were still ablaze, feeding the creeping putrescence. She shook her head sadly.

'Who would think people could be so wicked?'

Hawkhurst glanced at Mary Lou, who looked sharply away.

'Who indeed?' He sat down in a window seat across the aisle from Mary Lou, leaving the seat beside him empty. He smiled up at Sandy. 'Have you had Mr Brennan on board since my last trip?'

She giggled wickedly.

'No, I think he must be abroad again – you two sure did get on well as I recall.' It was a recollection that made her recall her duties. 'Can I get you anything – bourbon maybe?'

He smiled.

'That would be just fine.'

As she went, Mary Lou broke into his thoughts.

'We had to fire Brennan. He was getting unreliable, always disappearing on benders. You should watch your drinking, Hawkhurst, or you could end up like him. You make too many mistakes when you're drunk.'

He shrugged and patted the crate at his feet.

'So long as I've got my key to this baby I don't think I'm likely to make any mistakes.'

She fell silent and he considered how professionally Harry and his agency had infiltrated the Church and then slipped out of its clutches. His cover, Hawkhurst was never quite sure if it was a cover or not, of being a complete and utter lush meant he would, initially, have looked like a typical world battered recruit, an emotional cripple who would be welcomed into the fold with open arms. It also gave him a convenient excuse for falling short of their standards and disappearing on a bender when the agency needed his talents elsewhere. Sandy had returned, handing him the bottle with a glee that was, he knew, purely to spite Mary Lou. He patted the seat by his side. 'Take a seat and tell me all your news, Sandy.'

She did so readily, again, he was sure, to rile the other woman. She lowered her voice to exclude her from the conversation but Tom could sense her excitement.

'Oh, this is my last trip, Doctor. I'm quitting the Church. There was a time I needed them but I reckon I'm over my bad times so I'm going back to teaching. I guess we'll be flying back to New York together which will be nice.' She hesitated. 'Matter of fact, you had a lot to do with my decision to quit.'

He looked at her blankly.

'Me?'

'Yes, the television programmes you did on your first visit here back in the spring made a big impression on me. You were honest. You wouldn't say what they wanted you to say. You stuck to what you believed to be true. It made a lot of us think about what we were doing with our lives. The Reverend thought he was so clever pulling all those Biblical quotations out of the air but it didn't make any difference to what you believed and stood up for. Most of us have just got used to taking orders and learning religion parrot fashion. I'd stopped thinking for myself. Sometimes that's not such a bad way to be, not when you've been right down on the floor for a while, but you can't do it forever.' Her eyes sparkled. 'So, I'm going back to Fareham, Connecticut to teach math – just like my Mom always wanted.'

He smiled.

'That sounds really nice, Sandy.'

'Any chance of some food?' Whether or not she knew of Sandy's defection from the Church, Mary Lou was getting irritated by their friendly intimacy. 'I thought that was why you were here.'

'Sour old bitch,' Sandy whispered in his ear, though her smile never faltered. Getting to her feet she turned to face Mary Lou, hands clasped primly in front of her. 'Certainly Mrs Berkowitz. What can I get you?'

As she went Tom once again ran the details of the approaching hand-over in his mind. He had spelt out his requirements to Mary Lou who had, in turn, advised Gethsemane as to the procedures to be followed. They had taken off early in the morning from La Guardia so it would be mid-afternoon when they arrived. St Michael One would remain on the runway for refuelling: at least five hundred metres from the control tower. Captain Kruger, who was to be told as little as possible about what was going on, would supervise the refuelling and then return to the flight deck and prepare to take off. Once clearance to take off had been received Mary Lou would take the crate containing the Grail across to where Whichelow would be waiting with the money. When she returned with it and Hawkhurst had counted it he would hand over the second key. He had kept it simple, perhaps too simple. Mary Lou was terrified of the crate exploding in mid-air so was unlikely to act rashly and Sandy was unlikely to pose any threat to the plan. But it would only need the pilot, Captain Kruger, to be in Whichelow's confidence to pose a whole range of problems. He sighed, and wondered about the man at the controls.

With Gethsemane still an hour ahead, and two large bourbons inside him Tom felt distinctly sleepy. Outside the sun shone on the torn grey cloud below and on the pristine wings of the plane. He put the bottle aside and tried to concentrate on the task ahead. He somehow doubted that he would be allowed to get away with things so simply. They wanted the Grail and were prepared to pay handsomely for it. The fact that it would have to be kept hidden away in Mary Lou's treasure house, perhaps for years, did not seem to bother them. Possession of the Grail and its supposed powers was all that mattered to them and he was counting on this all-consuming passion to bring them down. He might be a million dollars the richer afterwards but that was not at all important, it was window dressing. He was here for revenge.

Sandy returned and, ignoring Mary Lou's disapproval, sat down beside him again. She was in a distinctly rebellious mood today and it lifted his spirits to see. Hawkhurst thought, if things went to plan, he might just give her some of the money.

'Do you think I might try a little of that Jim Beam, Doctor?' she said, blithely defiant as she fastened her lap belt. 'I know it's strictly against the rules but since, officially, I ended my association with the Church at mid-day,' she consulted the gold watch on her slim wrist, 'and it's now twelve o' five, I guess it won't hurt none.'

He poured her out a good measure and smaller one for himself, raising his glass.

'Cheers, Sandy, good luck with the teaching.'

She threw back the bourbon in one, replenishing her glass. Then she looked out at the towering banks of slate grey cumulus that were building up to the west.

'Looks like some turbulence coming up ahead,' she said. 'I hope Captain Kruger's got enough sense to go above it. He sure is a surly son of a bitch – haven't had a civil word out of him since we took off.'

As if the captain had sensed her concern the plane lifted and began to gain altitude.

*****

The remainder of the flight passed smoothly enough, although below the storms raged, and while they side slipped into their final approach run, the rain ricocheted viciously off the hull and wings as they dropped down through the cloud. The aircraft shuddered and bounced as the turbulence seized it and Hawkhurst found his hands were distinctly sweaty. Mary Lou, all too conscious of the crate and its highly volatile contents, gripped the arm rests of her seat and offered up a silent prayer, her lips mouthing the words. Only Sandy, slightly drunk and well used to this sort of thing retained her high spirits.

'Yippee,' she yelled, 'ride him cowboy.'

Finally they broke through the cloud base and the turbulence eased. Below them Tom could make out the unmistakable tower of the Temple of Christ the Warrior thrusting up towards them from the neatly laid out streets of Gethsemane. Soon they were taxiing along the runway, the rumbling undercarriage throwing up sheets of spray as they hissed through broad puddles of rainwater before coming to a halt, precisely as Tom had insisted, five hundred metres from the control room. Helping Sandy release the pressure doors and lower the steps, Tom stared bleakly across the windswept tarmac through the drizzle to where he could just make out a huddle of figures sheltering in the lee of the control tower. A bright red tractor towing a fuel bowser had detached itself from the line of emergency service vehicles parked on the apron and was now, blue light flashing, approaching St Michael One. Stepping aside, Tom caught his first glimpse of the pilot: a tall burly figure, his gold peaked cap pulled low and the collar of his white, ankle length rain coat turned up against the rain outside. Without a word he descended from the plane and waved to beckon the bowser into position.

Tom looked at Mary Lou, now somewhat recovered from the ordeal of landing. He smiled.

'Not long now.'

She ignored his words but gingerly lifted the crate and made towards the open door in preparation for her first departure.

CHAPTER THIRTY EIGHT

Tom, careful not to make himself an easy target for any possible snipers, kept well inside the aircraft as Mary Lou gingerly descended the steps to begin her long trek across the airstrip towards the control tower. She carried the crate, held out as far away as possible from her body, by two rope handles. She walked very slowly and with infinite care, as well she might. It took her a good five minutes to reach the apron and he watched as, surrounded by the huddle of figures that included Whichelow's unmistakable bulk, she was ushered inside. On the tarmac the tall figure of the pilot had quit the fuel bowser and was returning towards the plane, running lightly up the steps. Presumably the fuelling was completed. As he reached the door and stepped inside he removed the long waterproof coat and tossed the peaked cap aside, running his fingers through the tawny hair. He grinned widely at Hawkhurst.

'So far, so good.'

Sandy looked confused.

'Do you two know each other?'

The pilot bowed deeply as Hawkhurst made the necessary introductions.

'Sandy, may I present Mr Piet Potgeiter, flyer extraordinaire, Piet, this is Sandy who is the provider of good things of an alcoholic nature.' He poured them all a very small bourbon and grew serious. 'How's the fuel situation, Piet?'

'All tanks full. We're ready to go. But do you still think they'll let us fly out of here that easily?'

Hawkhurst shrugged his shoulders.

'Who knows? Anyway you obviously had no trouble dealing with the real Captain Kruger at La Guardia.'

Potgeiter examined his right hand, the knuckles of which bore signs of bruising.

'Not a lot.'

Tom smiled then went to one of the small perspex windows and stared towards the tower. The waiting was making him edgy.

'Where the hell has that bitch Mary Lou got to?' he said softly. 'She should be on the way back now with the money.' He turned to

Sandy who had fallen silent, aware there was something brewing here that might spell trouble, possibly even danger. 'Don't worry, Sandy,' he reassured her, 'As soon as the money is delivered you can choose to stay here or come with us. We won't involve you in anything.'

Her chin jutted, she was a feisty kid.

'Whatever it is you're up to, Doctor, if it pisses off that old dyke Mary Lou, count me in,' she said eagerly.

Potgeiter shook his head and looked to Tom questioningly.

'I don't know, Tom. This could still get very nasty and I wouldn't want this young lady to get hurt. We both know from past experience the kind of bastards we're dealing with. I think we should put her off right here and now.'

Tom nodded, sharing the South African's fears. Outside the rain had passed and the warm autumn sun was raising a miasma of steam from the puddled silvered tarmac, a tarmac that remained worryingly devoid of any sign of activity. The delay made him fear treachery and he tried to put himself in Whichelow's shoes. So far as Mary Lou and Whichelow were concerned they could not safely unlock the crate containing the Grail without the second key. To obtain that they had to deliver the money on board the plane. What they didn't know was that the crate, from the moment he had set the solenoids back at Laura's flat, was primed to explode at any interference with the locks, regardless of whether one key, two keys or a locksmith's pick was used. He didn't believe anyone would be so foolish as to tamper with the crate, certainly not so long as Mary Lou was in the immediate vicinity. He had expected that the money would be delivered post haste and that in their eagerness to lay eyes on the Grail they would insert both keys and blow themselves and the Grail to pieces. He had hoped it would explode precisely as St Michael One lifted off for New York.

When he devised the plan he had recognised that besides Whichelow and Mary Lou, others would almost certainly die, yet had felt no compunction about that. Whichelow was undoubtedly the most evil man he had ever met and his close followers were little better. The Grail, even a forgery, had showed itself to be an instrument of enormous potential power and one that, in the wrong hands, could generate superstition and hysteria enough to shake whole continents. If the leadership of the Church of Christ the Warrior could be purged in one flash of searing flame then, to his mind at least, the world would sleep the safer. However, there was still no sign of Mary Lou and each passing minute increased his doubts.

Potgeiter, who had gone forward into the cockpit to check the fuel gauges, now returned. He looked grim.

'I think we've got problems. Whichelow's on the R/T. He wants to speak to you.'

Tom followed Piet into the cockpit and placed the radio headset around his neck, drawing a deep breath before he spoke.

'Yes?'

When Whichelow spoke the now familiar and hated rumble had the air of a man who thought he had triumphed totally.

'Hi there, Tom. Just thought you'd like to know we won't be needing your key now. We've managed to open the crate without it. Just as well too. Seems like the locks were in quite a dangerous condition. Good thing we took the precaution of x-raying it first. Anyway, luckily we have people on hand who know about such things.'

There was silence and Piet and Tom stared at each other as they waited to learn the worst. Tom could imagine The Reverend looking down on them from the control tower, lighting one of his fat cigars, taking his time over the ritual, playing with them as he had so often before.

'Anyway, like I say, we've got the Grail – we're planning on holding a service of thanksgiving for its deliverance this evening – all we have to decide now is what to do with you. Tell me, Doctor Tom, do you intend to come out quietly or are we going to have to come in and get you?'

Tom was thinking fast.

'If I see anyone within three hundred metres of this plane, Whichelow, I'll shoot the pilot and the stewardess.' Potgeiter smiled at Sandy to reassure her although when he responded Whichelow did not sound overly bothered with their ultimate fates anyway.

'Suit yourself, Doctor Tom. We're in no rush and you ain't going anywhere. If you take a look down the runway you'll see that, while we've been talking, my men have run out chain spikes. Got them on loan from our friends in the Wyoming Highway Patrol. They'll rip your tyres to shreds long before you can get any speed up so there's no way you can take off. Well, I'm a busy man, got a thanksgiving meeting to get on the road – perhaps you'd care to join us – Temple doors open at eight. Goodnight, Doctor Tom, sleep well. Perhaps we'll talk again tomorrow. One of my men will be standing by on the radio here – just in case you change your mind and decide to join us at the meeting. Night.'

They returned to the saloon to consider their options. Piet suggested they might try to slip away under cover of darkness but Tom, recalling his first landing at Gethsemane, told him how the field was lit up like a huge cross at night and Whichelow would most probably have his men posted all round the perimeter.

'How about taking off? Is it completely out of the question?' he asked.

Potgeiter shook his head.

Not a chance. Once the undercart hits those spikes our speed will drop to next to nothing. We might try to bust our way out through the perimeter wire. It all depends if the ground will support the plane's weight once we're off the tarmac. If it's sucked up too much rain we could end up with mud up to our ears and going nowhere. Still, it might be worth a try, as we landed I saw a few cars and emergency vehicles parked beyond the control tower. If we did succeed in getting through the fence we might be able to hot wire one of them and get clear but it'll be bloody risky. This baby's loaded up with high octane, if a fractured wing tank and one spark get together we'll all be roasted alive in seconds.' He looked at Sandy who sat listening. 'I think you should get off while you can, honey. You've done nothing wrong. Once off here you might even get a chance to get in touch with the authorities outside and bring the cops. So long as you're on board you can't do anything to help.'

She was not enamoured of the idea of leaving them but the possibility of summoning assistance helped sway her decision.

'OK. Tell then I'm coming out.'

Tom returned to the cockpit and switched his headset on. He called up the control tower.

'Listen, I'm prepared to let the girl go. She's only another mouth to feed and there's no reason she should get hurt. But make no mistake one false move and the pilot gets it right between the eyes.'

There was a pause as the operator consulted his superiors.

'OK, send her out.'

They all stood up and Sandy took down her flight bag from an overhead locker. She stared at them, still unsure. She felt like a rat deserting a sinking ship.

'I'll phone the FBI first chance I get,' she whispered. Then reaching up she kissed them both on the cheek. In the doorway she turned and winked. 'Take care, you guys.'

They watched as she strode briskly away from the plane, her shadow dancing before her over the fast drying tarmac. As she neared the control tower she turned and gave them an encouraging wave.

'Nice kid,' Potgeiter grunted. 'Hope she's going to be OK.'

His hopes were to be shattered even as he spoke. The single crack of a high velocity carbine, fired at extreme range, echoed across the strip a full second after they saw Sandy thrown backwards like a rag doll, tumbling over and over to finally lay in an untidy heap. The report rang in their ears as they stared out at her distant body that lay relaxing into eternity, arms outstretched, the trickle of blood oozing from the gaping hole of her left eye socket forming a sticky pool on the bitumen. Like Suzie she had unwittingly become involved in the Church's plans and like Suzie they had removed her without pity. There would be no teaching math at Fareham High now.

There were tears in Hawkhurst's eyes as he returned to the radio.

'You bastards,' he roared. 'You bloody murdering bastards.' He tore the headset from its socket and hurled it in impotent fury across the cabin. The distant voice that came over Potgeiter's still connected head set was unmoved.

'One down, two to go. Oh, and by the way, you can go ahead and kill the pilot anytime you like. It'll save us a job. I don't know who you've got there with you but the real Captain Kruger was supposed to make his getaway on the fuel bowser.'

Brushing his eyes, Tom returned to the saloon where Piet was still staring out at the butchered girl. He had evidently heard the operator's last words. Whatever his feelings his voice was hard, matter of fact almost.

'Right. So they know you won't kill me. Why the hell don't they just walk in and take us?'

Tom shrugged.

'Why bother? Why risk taking casualties and damaging a perfectly good aircraft when we'll be dying of thirst within a few days. What's the chance of getting a Mayday off over the radio? Surely someone will pick it up? It might just attract someone's attention.'

Potgeiter nodded.

'Why didn't I think of that? It's certainly worth a try.'

He returned to the cabin and Tom watched as he switched the radio to the emergency frequency.

'Mayday, Mayday, Mayday. This is St Michael One. Call sign November Charlie Charlie Whisky One. Am immobilised on Gethsemane Airfield and under terrorist attack. Repeat: Am under terrorist attack. Mayday, Mayday, Mayday. This is St Michael One, Call sign November Cha…' As he made to repeat the distress call a harsh rasping growl came from the radio and he put the headset aside with a shake of his head.

'Bastards in the control room are jamming us. I got something away but it's unlikely anybody would pick it up. Even if they did, unless they know where Gethsemane Field is, I doubt they could locate us because I guess they'll be jamming our satellite transmissions too.'

'I guess that only leaves us with the break out option.' Tom said, tersely. 'Let's get ready. We're only going to get one shot at this.'

*****

By six that night the sun was already lost behind the distant hills, the evening sky a ragged jumble of smoky grey cloud and russet sunlight. Tom took a glance out of the saloon window. If he looked to one side he could just make out the towering edifice of the Temple, perhaps two miles distant, its steel swathed, sworded pinnacle glancing fire in the last dying rays. There, tonight, Whichelow would hold his triumphal meeting. He would present the Grail, present it as the true Grail that had held the blood of Christ and which would bring a proud Cardinal down, to his faithful followers. Great areas of the Islamic world were defiled, the West had achieved hegemony over what remained of its oil supplies and Whichelow, a truly holy man brought back by the grace of God from the brink of death, would claim the world for Christ. The thought made Tom's anger burn the deeper. Sometime during the afternoon they had removed Sandy's body. Her limp form had been lifted into an ambulance and the area hosed down, although even at this distance he could still see the dark stain where she had lain. There had been no further contact with the control tower and the jammer was still rendering the radio useless.

They had hardly exchanged a word since the shooting, Potgeiter, withdrawn and thoughtful, checking his instruments and rehearsing the procedures he would go through that evening. They had both come to Gethsemane to kill Whichelow, each with his own good reasons for so doing. Now they were the ones likely to die. Yet, if they were afraid, the desire for revenge had not been blanked by that fear. For both men, the callous killing of Sandy had forged and honed their hatred into a steely, blood lusting resolve. First they must escape, then she could be avenged.

The plan was simple. At seven o'clock exactly Potgeiter would run up the engines as if contemplating a desperate attempt to take off. Why they had chosen seven o'clock was not clear to either of them other than it would be dark by then and, always assuming the control tower did not switch on the landing lights, they might profit from the cover of darkness. Once moving they would roll down the airstrip for about fifty metres gathering speed all the time as they approached the savage sharks' teeth of the chain-rings. At the last possible moment Potgeiter would swing St Michael One off the tarmac and, hopefully still accelerating, across the hundred metres or so of rough esparto grass that lay between the strip and the perimeter fence. Provided they could maintain sufficient thrust they calculated it should be possible to break through, or at least pull down, the high perimeter wire at a point about two hundred metres from the control tower. Hopefully, they would then be carried by their own momentum on into the car park beyond. How far they would run on was not clear but Potgeiter warned that once they became entangled in the wire it was unlikely to be more than twenty metres or so and that, once through, he intended to kill the engines to prevent the hundreds of litres of fuel they now carried from exploding. From there they would have to fight their way out of the car park. Obviously this course of action brought its own problems: there would doubtless be armed men on duty. However, they had weighed this up objectively and agreed it made better sense to break out where vehicles were to be had and close to the road. The alternative, smash through at a distant point and attempt an escape on foot, was rejected on the grounds that there were obviously snipers all round the field and once clear of the plane and in the open they could easily be picked off. The car park, being comparatively close, held the advantages of surprise, at least some cover, plus the possibility of creating confusion among the vehicles. The door would be on the side of the fuselage away from the control tower allowing them to exit the plane out of sight of any snipers. The plan was indeed simple.

Whether it would be effective remained to be seen. Over all of these considerations hung the fact that what they proposed was to be undertaken in a fully fuelled aircraft – nothing less than a flying bomb.

While Potgeiter busied himself in the darkened cockpit, all lights had been doused to avoid prying eyes, Hawkhurst remained in the saloon, surrounded by bottles taken from Sandy's stock. The whisky and brandy he simply uncorked and, pouring a little out of each re-stoppered it with a twist of rag torn from dish cloths in the gallery. Others, more exotic drinks whose combustibility might have been suspect, he poured away entirely and refilled with aviation spirit siphoned from the emergency tank dipstick beneath the saloon floor. By the time he was finished he had two dozen petrol bombs primed and ready to go. On the seat beside him lay the Smith & Wesson .38 that Harry Brennan had procured for him. He would have preferred his old Webley for its greater stopping power but that was at the bottom of the Mediterranean and at least the .38 was lighter. Potgeiter had replaced his old Berretta with a Czech made .45 automatic that looked as if it would drop an elephant at fifty metres.

His work complete and his head spinning from the pungent fumes Hawkhurst got to his feet a little unsteadily and went gratefully forward to the air-conditioned atmosphere of the darkened cockpit. He proffered Potgeiter a half empty bottle of Scotch. The South African, his sidearm already strapped at his belt, took it and swallowed hard.

'How's it going?'

'Well, we're all ready to go. It's nearly dark and as luck would have it they still haven't switched on the lights. Could be a good omen.'

Tom frowned.

'I was wondering about that. If I was in their shoes I'd want all the light on the subject I could get. Maybe they're thinking of making an attempt to take us.'

Potgeiter nodded decisively.

'Could be. Well, let's beat them to the punch.' He reached forward and threw a switch, bringing the control panels to glowing life. 'You all set back there, Tom?'

Tom nodded. Neither man was under any illusions about the risks they were about to run or their chances of success. He held out his hand.

'Good luck, Piet – it's been a privilege.'

CHAPTER THIRTY NINE

Within ten seconds of bringing the two Pratt & Whitneys to screaming life Potgeiter had released the brakes, eased the throttles forward, and they were rolling. Whatever their plans, Whichelow's men had left it too late to attempt an assault on the airstrip. From the saloon Hawkhurst watched the yellow lights of the control tower slowly slide out of view as the plane rumbled down the airstrip. Around his feet the improvised petrol bombs rattled like milk bottles in a crate. He knew Potgeiter would keep to the tarmac until the last possible moment, building up as much momentum as possible before swerving off to the left and steering directly for the perimeter fence. When the manoeuvre came, the nose wheel no more than ten metres short of the savage, linked teeth of the chain-spikes, it almost threw him to the floor and he hung on grimly to the pressure door release lever. Desperately trying to stay on his feet as St Michael One bounced wildly across the uneven tussocks of grass towards the fence and the car park beyond he prepared himself for the impact. About his feet the deadly bottles tumbled drunkenly, skittering away in all directions and slopping their contents on the expensive carpet. Tom, totally occupied with staying upright knew it was too late now to worry about the finer details. All he could do was hope.

Everything depended on Potgeiter hitting the wire at a point equidistant between the stout reinforced concrete posts that supported it every thirty metres or so – no easy task in the darkness. Hit one of those and it would smash wings and fuel tanks like matchwood, almost certainly starting a fire that would turn St Michael One into a fiery coffin in seconds. He estimated the aircraft had a wingspan of just over twenty metres and both men knew there would be very little room to spare between the posts. Hawkhurst gritted his teeth and waited.

The big pilot got it just right, the nose cone of St Michael One pushing the linked wire back before the irresistible twenty thousand pound thrust of the banshee howling engines. Even so, for a heart stopping second or so the wire held, the links distorting and stretching to absorb the pressure. Then the post to their left snapped like a twig and the whole section of the fence sagged forward. They were through. The flattened wire ran easily enough under the port wing but to starboard, the fence still held half upright by the further post, snagged along the leading edge of the wing, ripping off the airspeed indicator head and smashing the green perspex of the navigation light. Its hampering pull slewed the aircraft round for second and Tom held his breath. If they became trapped here, still fifty metres from the nearest cover, they would be picked off like flies. Then, with a dry crack, the second post gave way, toppled forward, lifting the solid base from the ground, and they were free, heading now for the first group of vehicles. Wrenching the securing lever to one side he kicked the pressure door open, the cool evening air a balm on his sweating face. Once he had breached the perimeter fence Potgeiter cut the engines and although the plane continued to trundle forward under its own momentum the whine of the engines was already dropping to a moan. Hawkhurst, his fingers clumsy with the tension, reached down for the first petrol bomb. Potgeiter had quit the controls now and was at his side, the ugly automatic in his hand.

'I've opened the cocks. We're dumping fuel right now so don't hang around. She could blow at any minute.'

With that he was gone, jumping down into the darkness, landing cat-like on his feet and sprinting for cover towards a shadowy phalanx of vehicles fifty metres away to their right. Hawkhurst took one last look around him and lit the first fuse, lobbing it in a gentle arc towards the rear of the fuselage. It didn't break, the thick carpet absorbing the shock, but still blazed, dribbling a small lake of fire across the carpet towards him. Cursing, he picked up another bottle, this time hurling it with all his force towards the first without bothering to light the fuse. Both shattered into a mosaic of green shards and a blazing gout of flame flared to the ceiling with a dull thud, blistering the white plastic to a brown bubbling goo that in an instant wreathed black toxic smoke towards the open door. The heat was ferocious and Hawkhurst, a protecting arm across his face, coughed violently as the first choking fumes reached him. He knew he had to get out fast and prayed the fire had taken hold. As he stood in the open door the plane lurched violently as it struck a parked car, coming to a sudden screeching halt, tail up, as its nose wheel collapsed and suddenly Hawkhurst was aware of gunfire outside. Leaping down, he stumbled, twisting his ankle painfully, then he was rolling away from the crippled aircraft. Next he was on his feet and running head down in the direction he had last seen Potgeiter heading. Ahead were half a dozen

Nissan pickup trucks, parked in a neat line and forming a comfortingly solid looking shield. He threw himself behind these, gasping for breath, his heart pounding. When he had regained his composure he cautiously raised his head above a tailboard and looked back towards the plane.

A writhing vortex of flame and black smoke was billowing from the open door and carried low by the wind back across the airstrip. From beneath the wings he could see fuel gushing onto the car park, forming a broad puddle that reflected the dancing flames. Tom knew it could only be a matter of seconds before the whole thing went sky high. From the control tower came the wail of sirens and the occasional crack of rifle fire, although he thought they were firing wildly, probably at the plane, and at nothing more specific. He suspected that the Church's men had been deployed all around the perimeter as a prelude to an assault on the aircraft and now found themselves mostly in the wrong place. It was encouraging to know what they had at least succeeded in creating was confusion among the enemy. The next thing was to get away from there. Reaching inside his jacket he slid the .38 from its holster and, keeping low, went in search of Potgeiter.

He found the South African lying, pistol in hand, beneath the fuel tanker they had picked out as a rendezvous from the airstrip that afternoon. He smiled as Tom slid beside him.

'You cut that fine, Tom.'

Hawkhurst, rummaged in his pocket and produced a half bottle of Scotch.

'Couldn't leave that behind, could I?' He said, passing the bottle to Potgeiter who, despite the awkward position, managed to swallow down a good mouthful and handed it back. 'What happens next?'

Potgeiter tapped the chassis of the bowser over their heads with the barrel of his gun.

'I reckon we wait for the plane to blow then we take this baby and head for Gethsemane.'

Tom twisted his head to look into the South African's eyes.

'We're definitely going for it then?'

Potgeiter returned his gaze steadily.

'I think we owe Sandy that much, don't you?'

Tom nodded.

'OK, let's get on with it.'

Despite their eagerness to pursue their vendetta to its conclusion, they were forced to remain where they lay for now as there were other figures in the car park. Sinister shadows were carefully feeling their way forward by the eerie light of the burning aircraft which, although fuel continued to cascade from the plane's tanks, stubbornly refused to ignite. Occasionally a shot would ring out and angry voices would be raised. For the time being it seemed the Church's men were shooting at shadows but, if the fuel didn't take fire soon and create a diversion it was going to be difficult to get the tanker started without being spotted. Suddenly, Tom was aware of footsteps approaching the bowser and a pair of battered Nike trainers and plaid golfing socks appeared to his left. There was a plangent liquid splashing and Tom frowned before realising that the man was urinating against the wheel.

'See anthin' Charlie?' The voice came from far off.

'Nope.' They watched as the trainers shuffled round the bonnet of the bowser. 'Ah'll jest check unner these wagons heyer. But ah reckon the damn fools are still in thuh plane.'

Tom curled his trigger finger a fraction tighter. If the luckless Charlie's face appeared below the bowser he would shoot him dead. He drew a deep breath and waited. But the man moved off without checking and they both sighed, beginning to despair of the fuel ever igniting. Tom took another mouthful of whisky, eased himself into a more comfortable position and waited.

When St Michael One did finally blow, it was cataclysmic. Even beneath the bowser, well clear and shielded by ranks of parked vehicles, they felt the searing heat on their faces as a fireball erupted a hundred metres skywards, the updraft lifting the dead weight of the plane a good metre into the air before it sagged to the ground, collapsing in a barely recognisable heap of broken, twisted, melting metal. In a trice Potgeiter and Hawkhurst had rolled out from beneath the tanker and into the next phase of the routine they had evolved during the long hours of waiting on the airstrip. Two shots into the lock, inaudible over the roar of flame, from Potgeiter and the door of the tanker swung open. Once inside Hawkhurst ran his fingers under the dash until he had located the ignition wiring. It was an old skill, honed to perfection at an early stage of his career when junior field officers were forbidden access to official museum transport. A quick twist of the contacts, a brief spark, and the engine purred smoothly to life.

As Potgeiter pulled the idly swinging door shut they sat in the darkened cab looking towards the blazing aircraft, the heat coming to them through the toughened glass of the windscreen. Every so often there came further explosions as the flames found the petrol tanks of the surrounding vehicles and superheated truck tyres burst. Around the fringes of the inferno, black figures were silhouetted against the flames, some, from their wild gesticulations, attempting to take charge of the situation. It suited their purposes perfectly. They had fully expected to have to shoot their way out of the airfield car park. Now it seemed they might be able to slip away quietly. Tom, vehicle lights off, engaged gear and moved the tanker at low speed towards the highway that ran eastwards to Gethsemane. Behind them St Michael One billowed black smoke like a funeral pyre to the heavens.

Once on the road and after Potgeiter had pointed out that Americans drove on the right; something which would improve their chances significantly were Hawkhurst to follow suit, they switched on the headlights and the flashing red warning light on the roof of the cabin. Thus far fortune had smiled upon them but when they saw similar lights approaching from the opposite direction, a convoy of police cars and fire engines, sirens blaring, lights flashing, both men feared the worst - had they been spotted leaving the airstrip? However, the cavalcade swept past unheeding, all heading for the inferno at the airstrip.

'If they don't miss the tanker till the morning we may just have them believing we're both dead, at least for the time being.' Potgeiter mused. 'It gives us a little time to think out our next move. Any suggestions?'

Tom looked grim.

'How much fuel do you think is left in this tanker?'

'Hard to say, the gauges are reading empty but I guess there'll be a few litres left in the bottom. Why?'

Hawkhurst pointed to the soaring height of the Temple of Christ the Warrior. They were on the outskirts of Gethsemane now and about two kilometres away from the tower. Illuminated by powerful floodlights it stood white against the night sky.

'The price of petrol these days it would be a shame to waste it.'

*****

The ceremony had been under way for the best part of an hour when Tom slipped inside the Temple doors. The auditorium was packed, each silent, awestruck face turned towards the altar, at the centre of which, under the steely gaze of Christ the Warrior, rested the Grail. Every seat had been occupied hours beforehand and the crowd had still pressed in, now standing three deep at the rear and down the side aisles. Whichelow, wearing the long black gown of a Doctor of Divinity, fingered the silver sword about his neck as he ran his challenging eyes over the silent, enraptured congregation.

'Tell me, brothers and sisters, are we not entering a time of wonders and miracles?' His deep eyes burned in their sockets as he waited for the response. It was a little ragged but it came. 'Alleluia.'

'And tell me, do you believe that Jesus is coming, coming back to us soon?'

The audience were fidgeting, restless, as they answered. 'Alleluia.'

'Yes. Oh yes, brothers and sisters, I tell you, sweet Jesus is coming soon.'

Whichelow smiled, feeling the audience's fervour building in the old sweet way and the power in him rising. His next words came low, confidential.

'That is right, brothers and sisters, that is right. The time is coming, coming soon, when He shall come in glory to walk the earth amongst men once again. The signs are there, we have seen them clear as beacons in the night. Have we not seen His enemies smitten hip and thigh? Have we not seen the infidel brought low by his own evil?'

'Yes, yes, yes. Alleluia'

Now the responses were coming together, combining, swelling. Standing at the back of the auditorium, Tom shivered, feeling the brute emotion building around him, seeing the way in which Whichelow could, with a few platitudes, turn people who, if a little disturbed were basically gentle souls, into an unthinking rabid mob. The Reverend drew himself to his full impressive height.

'Brothers and sisters. You have seen the signs with your own eyes. Indeed, the unbeliever has been laid low by his own treachery. The east is burning. We were told to prepare the way. I tell you the way has been well prepared.'

'Yes. Alleluia.'

Whichelow turned to the altar behind him and reverently lifted the Grail in both hands holding it out towards the assembly.

'What more certain sign of God's blessing could we of the Church of Christ the Warrior ask than to be made custodians of the sacred chalice, the vessel that Christ used to initiate the Apostles into his divine mysteries? The Holy Grail has lain hidden in the bowels of the earth for countless centuries, so why do you think it has been revealed to us now?' He suddenly looked to the rear of the hushed auditorium and for one heart-stopping moment Tom thought he had been recognised. But the gaze lingered for no more than a second and swept on. 'I'll tell you why. Because, brothers and sisters, because the second coming is at hand. Soon, perhaps tomorrow, perhaps next week, perhaps next month, but soon, very soon, the Son of God will walk amongst us once again. The Kingdom of God is upon us – the Third Millennium is His.'

The audience exploded, on its feet now, clapping, cheering, swooning, crying. For several minutes pandemonium reigned then Whichelow, laying the Grail back on the altar, raised his hands for silence and the hubbub subsided. He grew grave.

'But now, because the way is prepared, we must all look into our hearts and decide what we do next. You fine young people will go forth from Gethsemane and continue the good fight around the world. You will build on the strong foundation we have laid here. You will spread the word. You will succour the weak, you will cure the sick and ... you will smite the unbeliever.' He paused. 'But I must go away.'

A buzz, a worried murmur, ran round the auditorium. Puzzled looks were exchanged and Tom stared down at the figure on the stage, diminished by distance, and wondered what was coming next.

Whichelow nodded.

'Yes. My work here at Gethsemane is done and now I must go away.'

'No!' A solitary voice rang out, Hawkhurst fancied it might have been McNaughton's, its message taken up by others in quick succession, until the whole congregation was chanting. 'No. No. No. Stay.'

The simple announcement had produced consternation, at the moment of triumph their leader, their surrogate father, was to be taken from them. In that instant Hawkhurst saw the full power of the man and the frailty of his followers. But Whichelow did not respond to their pleadings simply taking up the Grail and with great dignity walking from the stage. As he went the great head came up and his eyes went to where Tom stood. He smiled, the old arrogant smile, and gave a brief nod of the head. It was the acknowledgement of a game, but inevitably futile, attempt to thwart the will of God.

In the auditorium chaos reigned all about and Hawkhurst, sensing trouble pushed his way back to the main doors which had been left open to allow easy access to the Reverend's impromptu farewell. Down the street he could see the tanker with Potgeiter behind the wheel. The South African gave him the thumbs up sign that said the last dregs of fuel had been pumped down into the air conditioning outlets at the rear of the Temple. The intention had been for Hawkhurst to get as close as possible to Whichelow, shoot him and then make his escape under the confusion of the fire. Now Whichelow had disappeared and the Grail with him. That it was still the phoney Grail was small consolation. It seemed that at every turn the man was always one step ahead. No matter what they did to foil his plans, he always managed to produce a surprise that left them wrong footed. As Tom stood amongst the milling crowd outside the Temple from within came the first cries of fire and the audience began to pour out onto the street.

The Temple was a well designed building and thanks to the stringent fire precautions the auditorium was quickly evacuated with no more human damage than a few cuts and bruises suffered in the crush. Knowing the limited amount of fuel Potgeiter had at his disposal and that the fire would probably not spread, once the exodus had slowed down Hawkhurst went back inside, standing just inside the door. A layer of black smoke had formed in the dome above his head and the sprinkler system had come into action. The jets of water hissed down in a fine mist, clouding the air and drenching every inch of the auditorium. Behind the altar the great painting of Christ the Warrior was beginning to disintegrate under the deluge, soot and the black pigmentation surrounding the eyes clouding the fierce blue of the irises and running like muddy tears down the cheeks and into the blurring beard. The gold of the Grail dripped in gilded rivulets onto the altar cloth and the steel blue of the sword of retribution was melting into a soft blur. Behind him, came the wail of distant sirens as fire engines, hastily recalled from the airstrip, came hurrying to deal with this latest calamity. Brushing the wetness from his clothes he stepped outside pushing his way through the gawking crowd towards the waiting tanker.

Once on board Potgeiter drove away in silence, heading out towards the next town. Once there they would ditch the tanker and hire a car, heading eastward all the time. It was not until they were well clear of Gethsemane and heading down the empty highway through rolling cattle country, the stars diamond sharp above, that Potgeiter spoke.

'No luck?'

Tom shook his head, galled to admit failure after everything they had been through. In the rear mirror he could see the diminishing tower of the Temple, a finger of whiteness against the night sky.

'The bastard walked. Just like that, Piet. I didn't even get a shot off.'

The South African was philosophical.

'Well. We're still alive, that's the main thing. He'll turn up sooner or later, we may get another chance.'

Tom wasn't sure.

'I don't know. Somehow, the way he spoke, I think he was intending to disappear for good. Told them he was going away. Almost as though he was going on a spiritual journey – death perhaps.'

Potgeiter snorted.

'Perhaps he's going to try the old resurrection trick again. He thinks he's got the Grail now.'

It took two hours to reach the next town, Marysville, and at near to midnight the place was almost shut down. Only Vasco's bar, a dull, half-lit dive occupied by a dozen stetsoned cowboys, offered any sign of life. Parking the tanker round the back to avoid attracting the attention of the Highway Patrol, they went inside. Heads along the bar turned as they went in but no one spoke. The juke box was playing some mournful country and western dirge and most of the customers listened in an alcoholic trance, staring into space. It was a sad place, inhabited by sad, lonely men – good ole boys with cowboy boots and nowhere to go. The barman, a lean, grey haired old timer with thick pebble glasses, was friendly without being nosy.

'What kin I get you boys?'

'Bourbon on the rocks twice.'

At the back of the bar a television flickered, the sound turned down so as not to impair the juke box. The bar tender jerked his head towards the screen.

'Sounds like quite a night over at Gethsemane.' Gethsemane was a hundred miles distant yet to him it was a neighbouring township.

'That so?' Tom didn't want to sound too interested.

'Yup. Plane crash and a fire at the Temple.'

'Anyone hurt?'

'Don't rightly know. State police say they think there were three people aboard the plane when it crashed. Only recovered one body so far though.'

Potgeiter looked at Tom, his eyes hard. They both knew in that instant that to destroy all evidence of the murder the people at the airstrip had casually thrown Sandy's body into the fire.

'What about the Temple?'

'Well, it's a bit of a mystery. Not much damage to the Temple but seems like the Reverend Whichelow has disappeared.'

Tom threw back his drink and indicated another was needed.

'Do you have a phone here?'

CHAPTER FORTY

It took another four days before Hawkhurst and Potgeiter finally got back to Sarnafon. From Maryville they had hired a Hertz Cadillac and driven the thousand or so miles to Chicago to rendezvous with Brennan. Another day had been spent debriefing the American on events at Gethsemane. The fire and supposed plane crash had been seized on by the FBI and other agencies as an opportunity to flood their people into Gethsemane in general and the Temple in particular but they had come up with nothing that threw any light on Whichelow's disappearance or the Church's intrigues in the Middle East. For his part Tom was glad to be back in the real world. He felt totally drained and for the next few weeks both men moped about the farm awaiting news from Brennan.

The period of inaction affected the Englishman least for he was content to fuss about Angahrad who had now received confirmation that she was indeed pregnant. It was November now and the days were growing short. High on the dark hills a light dusting of snow lay in the gullies and the sheep had already been brought down onto the lower pastures in preparation for the coming lambing. As he grew accustomed to the idea of fatherhood – it would be a May baby Angahrad predicted - Hawkhurst felt the tension of the past months begin to seep away and somehow the question of Whichelow seemed to lose importance. In preparation for the birth he had moved his meagre belongings into the farm and the cottage was up for sale, although he doubted there would be a mad rush to purchase such an isolated and run down place. Despite his own ability to relax he could, however, sense the frustration building in Piet. The time hung heavily for the South African and when they finally heard the horn of the big black limo heading up the drive towards the farm, the dogs, tongues lolling, loping easily alongside, Potgeiter tossed his paper aside and almost ran to the door.

Brennan looked sun tanned and fit, sitting there across the table, an appreciative hand curled round a large drink. He had spent the last month in the Middle East trying to pick up the pieces of a world order that had been shattered forever.

'They've finally got a grip of the well head fires,' he told them. 'Another two months and that should be the last of them.'

'Will the pollution come here?' Angahrad enquired anxiously. It was an abiding fear that the creeping filth would pollute her beloved valley.

Brennan shook his head.

'I don't know. It's unlikely but no one knows for sure.'

Traces of the cloud had been detected in Alaska, and on the west coast of Canada as well as the north-west United States. The pollution levels were only very low as yet but it was predicted they would grow worse as the winds continued to push the clouds eastwards. But if in these areas the effects were as yet minimal and the cloud slowly dispersing, in those parts of the Middle East, Asia Minor, and further east, directly in the path of the cloud the effects had been nothing short of disastrous and were set to worsen. Apart from the direct effect on human health a new twist had appeared in the form of what the experts termed oleaginous rain – oily rain.

At first it had been hoped that the late Autumn rains would help to clear the atmosphere and to some extent this had happened, but the rain that fell was to spread a slimy, poisonous patina across whole nations. It covered fields and forests, cities and villages. Everywhere the crops wilted and died as did both the domestic and wild creatures that browsed upon them. Endless steppe lands that had once been the breadbasket of half the world now withered under the brown drizzle. Every lake and river bore a greasy film and a silver scattering of dead fish and flocks of migrating birds fell stone dead from the sky once within the deadly cloud. The poison also seeped into the ground where it was drawn up into the root systems of many kinds of grasses and quickly passed up the food chain. Soon stinking carcasses of cattle lay strewn unburied amid their sick and dying fellows in the fields. Eventually the world would turn its attention and resources to these secondary effects but for now every effort was being targeted on the fires and stopping the pollution at source. Elsewhere, for the time being, it was for every man to fend for himself as best he could.

Two thirds of the Persian Gulf had been affected by leakages but at least the boom across its mouth had held, preventing any wider spread, and now giant skimming vessels were slowly recovering the black sludge. These, like great steel hogs at the trough, sucked up the oil and separated it from the sea water via huge centrifuges, pumping their treasure into accompanying tenders to be refined and eventually shipped abroad. Japanese industry had provided much of the money and technology for this fleet of outlandish vessels and their reward was to keep every litre of crude they recovered. According to even the most optimistic estimates it would take at least six months to clear the sea up to the mouth of the Euphrates and even then, waters that had once teemed with life would be effectively sterile for many years, perhaps forever. Potgeiter had heard all this before: he was more interested in what he saw as the basic cause. It was the capacity for evil, perpetrated in the name of supposedly benign deities, of people like Whichelow and Firdasi, that fascinated and appalled.

'Any word on Whichelow?'

'Not a thing. It's as if he vanished from the face of the earth. Which, of course, is just what he wants the world to believe.'

Although it had been overshadowed by the cataclysmic international events, the Whichelow mystery, as it was widely known, still held the public's attention. As he had doubtless intended, the idea of divine intervention and his apotheosis was widely accepted by many. The possibility of his having died in the fire at the Temple was universally rejected and on good grounds. It had been a small conflagration and quickly brought under control. On top of this there was always the matter of a body – or rather the lack of it. No. The whole world was reminded incessantly that The Reverend James J Whichelow had not completed his God given task. He had given his followers an assurance that he would return at the appropriate time. In less reverent circles alien abduction was also mooted. Along with Lord Lucan and Elvis Presley, sightings were reported from Peru to Peking. Yet such levity was misplaced for whatever had happened to him, in absentia, Whichelow now enjoyed a cult following that grew by the day.

There had been one redeeming aspect to his disappearance. The Grail he had so proudly presented to his followers at that last meeting at Gethsemane had been no more than a clever forgery. This hadn't stopped a furore over who actually held the original. The Church's people, Mary Lou and Colonel McNaughton, most vocal among them, had claimed Whichelow had taken the true Grail with him on his mystic journey and it would return with him. Hawkhurst had already countered this by insisting that written affidavits be taken from a panel of experts and these, suitably framed, were exhibited in the cabinet along with the Grail itself. One, a suitably ornate document with a huge red seal that bore the cross keys of St Peter, was initialled by the Vatican's leading authority on antiquities. The Martinette camp was as keen as anyone to avoid any confusion. As Hawkhurst had told Potgeiter: 'No bastard is going to argue with that.'

Cardinal Martinette, had played a masterly hand, and now with Whichelow off the scene found himself acknowledged as the leader of the Christian religion worldwide – a religion that was very much on the offensive. He had happily confirmed that so far as the Vatican was concerned the real Grail now resided in the museum and there could be no doubt about its provenance. It was a masterly move. At a stroke he had raised a question mark about the credibility of claims made by the Church of Christ the Warrior, safely distanced himself from his erstwhile allies and now had only to wait for the demise of an ailing Pope to assume the Pontiff's white robes. In the meantime he had lost none of his zeal and was encouraging missionary work among the peoples whose lives had been rent apart by the great burning; drawing converts from the Crescent to the Cross. However, for every convert dozens of others wallowed in an agnostic despair and ever more bizarre cults and sects were springing up to offer consolation.

'What about Firdasi?'

'The trial won't begin until the mess is cleared up. The US government says it would colour opinion too much and they couldn't guarantee a fair trial. It's a pile of horseshit. You could leave it fifty years and no one's ever likely to forget what Firdasi and his friends have done.' He shook his head. 'Even now I can't figure out what made the guy do it. He was everyone's best hope for peace and then he goes and burns the wells. What the hell did he hope to gain by it?'

Hawkhurst pursed his lips.

'I wonder if he thought it was the only way to prevent a war – at least the kind of war that Whichelow was so intent on starting. We all knew it would have been a war the Islamic countries could never win. Perhaps he thought that if you removed the oil there would be nothing to fight over. In a sense that's what's happened. If Whichelow is still alive and planning to stage the Second Coming, with him in the starring role, maybe Firdasi's manoeuvering to be in a position where he can be sure of getting major coverage when he gives it the lie. I believe there was a greater degree of contact between the Church and Firdasi than we realise. In a way they mirror the relationship between the Templars and the Assassins during the crusades – mortal enemies but symbiotic. Without the other, neither had a purpose.

On trial at the UN he'll have the whole world press concentrating on him and him alone. Think about it. We're just over a year away from the Millennium. If Whichelow intends to return from the dead and claim the next thousand years for the Christian Church, what's to stop him? Look around you, there's near hysteria everywhere. Not surprising when you see what's happened but to many people the burning isn't just an ecological disaster it's a sign from God. The Kingdom of God is at hand. That's what they're all saying. People are flocking to the churches again and every vicar and priest is encouraging the illusion. There are fire cults springing up everywhere. In Africa whole tribes are worshipping Christ as the bringer of fire, making human sacrifices in his honour – burning themselves alive. And, believe it or not, there are cults in San Francisco and Tokyo doing very much the same thing. I've got a nasty feeling it's going to be a long time before sanity returns. The only way we can hope to help is to show people like Whichelow and Firdasi for what they are – maniacs.'

His train of thought was suddenly broken by the sharp ringing of the cooker alarm from the kitchen and Angahrad rose to her feet.

'Sounds like dinner is ready.' She smiled weakly. 'If I burned that, I think I'd scream.' They all laughed, but it was a hollow joke.

At midnight, as they sat round the fire replete and comfortably drunk, stockinged feet stretched towards the comfort of its gentle crackling, Potgeiter asked Brennan if there was anything else they could do to bring Whichelow to account. To wait for him to reveal himself and stoke the flames of mania even higher, all in his own good time, seemed unthinkable. But Brennan could offer no comfort.

'The bastard has disappeared. We've searched every inch of Gethsemane and his picture is on the notice board in every precinct in the US. We're liaising with all the other police forces and intelligence agencies but I don't think we're going to see or hear from the Reverend Whichelow again until he's good and ready.'

Potgeiter shrugged.

'Well, if that's the case, I suppose I might as well get back to work.' Tom knew the South African was disappointed. The killing of Sandy had given his lust for revenge a boost. He looked to Hawkhurst.

'What about you, Tom? Now you're about to become a father I guess you'll need to start looking around for work?'

Tom smiled at this mention of the coming child, fumbling in his back pocket to produce a crumpled sheet of note paper. He smoothed it out with the palm of his hand and they saw the embossed letterhead bore an impressive coat of arms.

'Well, I had this letter from the museum yesterday. With Dixey dead and Whitford retired, it seems they may have a position for me – maybe, given time, even a place on the board. Nothing concrete yet but it seems as if Laura has lost a lot of her friends in high places and will be keeping a pretty low profile for the time being. Despite the fact that no charges are to be brought against them, the scandal of her relationship with Mary Lou Berkowitz hasn't helped her any. Of course, the museum has made it clear that a lot hangs on my willingness not to kick up a fuss about Karelian's report and not to make any reference about the Penda mark in future. I haven't made up my mind whether I'll accept yet.'

Angahrad reached across and kissed him on the cheek.

'Of course you will accept, Thomas. It's no more than you deserve. You know you're only delaying your decision to make them squirm.'

Brennan was on his feet in a trice.

'A baby on the way and a new job. If that doesn't call for a celebration my name ain't Harry Brennan,' he said, heading for the ice bucket and the champagne they had saved for this, their final night to be spent together. He returned bearing four sparkling glasses on a tray and handed them round. The American was clearly delighted. 'First, let me congratulate you both on the forthcoming happy event – for the child's sake let's hope it looks like its mother.' He raised his glass. 'To the future!'

They raised their glasses and sipped carefully, drinking in the convivial atmosphere. Recalling the momentous events that had drawn them together brought a thoughtful silence that was only broken by the soft crackle of the dying fire and the low moan of the wind outside. Suddenly Hawkhurst broke the spell.

'Shit!' He was staring into space, his eyes a thousand miles away.

Angahrad, suddenly frightened, reached out and touched his cheek.

'What is it, Thomas? What's the matter?'

He looked down at the letter from the museum in his hand and screwed it up into a ball, tossing it into the flames. It smouldered then charred on the grey ashes, finally igniting in a yellow flower that blossomed briefly then guttered and died, uncurling black petals that crumbled to nothing.

Softly he said, 'I know where Whichelow is.'

CPSIA information can be obtained at www.ICGtesting.com
Printed in the USA
BVOW06s0233150616

452129BV00018B/85/P